𝒯USCANY
for
𝓑EGINNERS

Tuscany for Beginners

A NOVEL

Imogen Edwards-Jones

BALLANTINE BOOKS NEW YORK

2005 Ballantine Books Trade Paperback

Published in the United States by Ballantine Books, an imprint of The Random House Publishing Group, a division of Random House, Inc., New York.

Ballantine and colophon are registered trademarks of Random House, Inc.

Originally published in Great Britain by Hodder and Stoughton, a division of Hodder Headline, London, in 2004.

Library of Congress Cataloging-in-Publication Data can be obtained from the publisher upon request.

ISBN 0-345-47880-0

Printed in the United States of America

Ballantine Books website address: www.ballantinebooks.com

9 8 7 6 5 4 3 2 1

Text design by Laurie Jewell

To Scazza and the Colonel

With Love

"Poggibonsi, fatti in la,
che Monteriano si fa città!"
Poggibonsi was revealed to her as
they sang—a joyless struggling place,
full of people who pretend.

—*Where Angels Fear to Tread,*
E. M. FORSTER

ACKNOWLEDGMENTS

I'd like to thank my husband, Kenton Allen, for his help, his humor and his love while writing this. I'd like to thank my sister, Leonie, my brother, Marcus, and my father for their support and well-feigned interest. I would also particularly like to thank my mother and stepfather, Colin Campbell, for all their help, their ideas, their comments, their corrections and their contributions—I hope they know how grateful I am.

I am also totally indebted to my old friend Ben Faccini for the hours he spent eating "prawn gunk" discussing this idea and for his brilliant, novel-saving suggestions. I'd also like to thank Daisy Waugh for her life-enhancing phone calls, Candace Bushnell for her advice and acerbic wit, Claudia Winkleman, Kris Thykier, Sebastian Scott, and Peter Mikic for their delightfulness, Ciara Parkes for her vodka, Antonia Camilleri for her cigarettes, Katya Galitzine for being Russian, Jessica Adams for her spiritual guidance, Caroline Coogan, Gay Longworth, Xander Armstrong, Tom Hollander, Jamie Theakston, Alek Keshishan, Beatie Edney, Laurie Taylor, Cathie Mahoney, and Sarah Vine for their conversations, their cocktails and their invaluable friendship. And lastly I'd like to thank the voyaging Sean Langan for never being here, so I could actually get on and do some work.

And on the work front, I would like to thank James Herring and Sam Mortner at Taylor Herring for all their genius help with my last novel, *The Wendy House*. You were amazing. I would also like to thank Philippa Pride, sadly leaving Hodder, for her fine editing and publishing skills. And finally, I would like to give thanks for special agent Stephanie Cabot, a living goddess if ever there was one. Thank you all.

Belinda Smith moved to Tuscany five years ago, after she found her husband in bed with another woman. Returning home early one afternoon, she was halfway up the stairs when she heard the unfamiliar sound of sex. She squeezed off her slip-on heels, tiptoed toward the door and poked her head around it, to be greeted by the sight that changed her life.

The image of her husband's pink, dimpled, crinkled behind pounding up and down was shocking. But the sight of Marjorie's spread thighs and raised hooked knees as she panted away like a begging dog was enough to give the poor woman nightmares. Which indeed she'd had. For two whole weeks. Until her friend Fiona introduced her to the joys of Valium, and the candy-coated musings of *Under the Tuscan Sun* by Frances Mayes.

In the months that followed Belinda's divorce, and the unequal division of the marital assets, her destiny became clear. She would leave behind the dull dormitory town of Tilling, where nothing ever happened. She would start her life again. On her own. In Tuscany. She would run a B&B and keep a diary. She would jot down her thoughts, share her ideas and *aperçus.* She would pass on her delicious recipes to the next generation. She might even one day have them read by the general public. But, most important of all, Casa Mia would be her business, run by her rules, and she would never ever be humiliated again. . . .

Giovedì ❖ Thursday

Clima ❖ *fa caldo* (Hot! Hot! Hot!)

This is the beginning of my fifth season in *questo bellissimo* valley—Val di Santa Caterina, Toscana—and although I have been here for quite a while, it is only now that I'm feeling quite *pronto* to write a diary and share my thoughts, and my ideas, and the little life lessons that I have gleaned from my very own corner of *Paradiso*.

And what a corner of *Paradiso* it is! Val di Santa Caterina is one of those terribly beautiful unspoiled valleys in Toscana where the locals still farm, the land is still worked, and the Italians continue to live a simple peasant existence like they have done for hundreds of years. It is just too, too divine!

We are also lucky enough to have a small, yet vibrant, expat community in the area, which—thankfully—consists mainly of us English, although there are a few Australians, some Belgians (who keep very much to themselves), and the odd German (whom everyone tries to avoid at all costs!). But the social life is mainly made up of us Brits, who are nearly all writers and painters or just artists in general.

My little spot, Casa Mia, is a very large, converted gentleman's country villa and has to be one of the most *fortunato* finds of one's lifetime! Perched on top of the hill, handily near the road, it has been sensitively restored by an English developer, who has been living near Florence for seven years and very much knew what he was doing. With new terraces and a new sun-soaked terra-cotta roof, Casa Mia has vistas galore and none of the drawbacks of any of those very old properties. Also, because I used a developer, I was lucky enough to avoid all that well-known Italian inefficiency when it comes to doing up a house. I mean, why put oneself through the terrible hell of carpenters not arriving, plumbers overcharging, and all that, when you can get a place, move in more or less immediately, and set about putting in those little touches that make a villa a home?

And so, for the past few years I have enjoyed welcoming guests into my lovely *casa*. It gives me great joy to share my little corner of *Paradiso* with visitors from all over the world. I enjoy being generous with my views, my villa, my little bit of heaven on earth where the birds sing and the sunflowers grow.

As I said, this is my fifth season, and I must confess that I feel ever so much at home here. It is lovely, really, how much the people have taken me to their hearts. I am very much part of the *comunità*. Some would say an essential part of it! At the risk of blowing my own trumpet (which would be very unattractive), I can safely say that nothing really happens here without me or my highly motivational involvement! Quite what everyone did before I arrived, I shall never know!

Only last night at supper at Giovanna's (our local *ristorante*), Derek took my hand and announced to the table that from now on everyone should call me "La Contessa of the Valley." It was terribly sweet of him, but after the way I ran last year's panto, I did rather reluctantly have to agree. In fact, the more we discussed my achievements in the valley, the more we all agreed that it was such a terribly good name. So "La Contessa di Val di Santa Caterina" it is, then! What a mouthful! I wonder if it will ever catch on?

But there are more pressing matters at hand. My daughter is arriving this afternoon. There is much to do. Casa Mia is in need of a good spring cleaning before my summer visitors arrive. I am so used to all of this now—being a hostess is more or less second nature to me. Making the beds, scrubbing the floors, clearing the terraces, and tidying the drive are all taken care of by my local help—which, of course, frees me to make things look authentically Italian, placing a bowl of lemons here, a bunch of wild flowers gleaned from the roadside there. *Perfecto!* Quite frankly, I'm so settled here I find it quite hard to think of my life before I left the U.K. behind, and made the heavenly move to Toscana. Home of olives, sunflowers, and tobacco. Plus, let's not forget, *buonissimo* cooking!

BRUSCHETTE DI CASA MIA

I like to call these my little slices of toasted sunshine. I picked up this little gem of an idea from Victor, who runs the divine café at the railway station, and who charmed me with his perfect English and splendid coffee when I first arrived here all those years ago.

* bread
* garlic
* extra-virgin olive oil
* tomato paste

Take four hearty slices of fabulously **rustico** Italian bread—handmade by your local baker. For those of you unfortunate enough not to live in Italy, and who do not have a local baker anymore due to Tesco and Sainsbury taking over everywhere, Marks & Spencer bread will do. But do try and source your **pane** from somewhere a little bit special as—take it from me—you really will notice the difference.

Lightly toast the slices. Then rub with fresh garlic (from your own garden would, of course, be preferable). Drizzle on the extra-virgin olive oil. Cover in tube of tomato paste. Grill until ready.

Serve on a sun-blushed terrace in a **simpatico** atmosphere.

✤ ✤ ✤

CHAPTER ONE

Belinda Smith is sweating profusely. Her face is contorted with the strain of pretending to understand Italian. She is enunciating slowly, and loudly, down the telephone, while her short fingers tear frantically through the mini-Italian dictionary. *"La grippa?"* she repeats. "You have *la grippa?*" she says again. Tucking the receiver under her chin, she licks the tips of her fingers and flicks through the tissue-thin pages, trying to understand exactly what has so incapacitated Giulia.

"Oh," she says suddenly, straightening up. "You've got the flu, you say." A gentle feverish moan comes back down the receiver. "What a shame—*che pecorino!*" she exclaims. *"Che pecorino!"* she nods, vigorously, yet unconsciously complimenting Giulia on the excellence of her sheep's cheese. "Well . . . you . . . stay where you are, then. No *vieni* Casa Mia, I'll see you when you *tutto va bene*," she shouts, smiling at her own generosity. "Um . . . *ciao,*" she adds, her head cocked to one side as she slams down the phone.

"Well, that's just bloody *perfecto,*" she mutters. Sighing, she runs a hand over her brow, wiping off the efforts of communication. "The flu, the flu, the bloody flu. I can't understand why the stupid woman can't work with the flu. Starve a cold, feed a fever, work the flu. It's famous," she says, her small blue eyes shooting heavenward. "Everyone knows that . . . everyone . . ."

Exhausted, Belinda flops into her ex-husband's favorite armchair and, stretching out her plump forearms, starts to knead the upholstery with her pink painted nails.

Although certainly rounder since the day she discovered her other half at it like a terrier with her dear friend-and-next-door-neighbor, Belinda looks quite a lot younger than she used to. Gone is the demi-wave in favor of a more Bohemian brown, ear-length bob, which only tends toward the Einstein on washdays. Gone also are the stiff skirts and high-buttoned shirts that used to frot with efficiency around Safeway on Friday afternoons. They have been replaced by more Italia-friendly floaty skirts and floral-print frocks. Gone also are the navy slip-ons: Belinda's collection of jazzy flip-flops, fun sandals, and jaunty town heels just keeps on growing. In fact, if you didn't know any better, Belinda Smith looks like she's been going to art galleries and eating garlic all her life, instead of just the last five years.

Hitching up her navy, red, and white flowered skirt, Belinda points her dry shins toward the open terrace door and warms them in the sun. Eyes half closed, a furious frown on her not un-attractive face, she runs through the Rolodex of chores that Giulia should be doing, if she weren't so Italian and unreliable. The sweeping, the scrubbing, the dusting, the eviction of spiders from their winter homes, the clearing up of dead scorpions, the ushering outside of the occasional disoriented lizard, all are jobs that are seasonally assigned to Giulia. But this year, with a brace of Belgians arriving at the weekend, these tasks have obviously fallen to Belinda's remit. Yet Belinda is not overly fond of wild-life. In fact, she can't stand any of the beasts or bugs that populate her house. However, she is not one to let standards slip. With little choice than to don a pair of industrial-strength rubber gloves, she slaps the arm of the chair and stands up, resolved in the spirit of stiff upper lips to get on with it. Walking toward the kitchen, her steely determination is, rather fortunately, interrupted by the telephone. Its foreign sound—one long ring, plus a short intermission—always takes her by surprise.

"Pronto," she says, after a suitably relaxed six rings. *"Pronto?"* she repeats, pursing her lips, placing her head to one side, assuming the pose of an elegant hostess. "Casa Mia?" she says, her voice rising optimistically at the end of the sentence.

"Mum?" comes a muffled and distant reply, as though through a decade of dust down a receiver in Florence railway station.

"Pronto?" says Belinda again, frowning with practiced confusion.

"Mum? It's me—Mary. Can you hear me? I'm at Florence station," shouts Mary, above the noise of a departing diesel.

"Oh, Maria, darling," says Belinda eventually, after a tricky pause. "Darling," she says again. "I'm so sorry I almost didn't understand you." She laughs. "You're speaking English!"

"Oh, right, sorry."

"Yes, well," says Belinda, allowing a sliver of irritation to slip into her voice. "When will you be arriving? What time is your train?"

"Umm," says Mary, accompanied by the distant crackle of paper.

"Because I do hope it's at a convenient time. We have a huge . . . *come si dice* . . . crisis going on here. Giulia has grappa and I have no one to clean the house."

"What? She's been drinking?" asks Mary, sounding confused.

"No. What are you talking about?" says Belinda, frowning with annoyance. "Don't be ridiculous, she's terribly ill, so you must come here as soon as you can. There are beds to be made and rooms to clean."

"I won't go shopping, then," suggests Mary, "and I'll take the earlier train."

"Oh, *grazie,* Maria darling, would you?" says Belinda, smiling tightly down the telephone.

"It'll mean waiting an hour at the station as a train has just gone."

"Oh, would it? Well . . ." Belinda pauses. "See you at just after two P.M. *Arrivadeary!*"

"Arrivadeary?" repeats Mary, quite slowly.

"Arrivederci, arrivadeary," giggles Belinda. "It's our new little joke."

"Oh," says Mary.

"Arrivadeary!" replies her mother with a little laugh, and replaces the telephone.

There is a renewed spring in Belinda's stride as she wanders toward the kettle next to the dusty Gaggia coffee machine. The arrival of her daughter, her only child, could not have happened at a more opportune moment. Belinda allows herself a special satisfied smile as she flicks the switch, her face assuming the expression usually reserved for minor victories over Derek's wife, Barbara. For not only does this mean that Mary will be able to assist in the catering right from the start of the season, which she has not managed before due to pressure of work, but she will be able to fill in for Giulia while the woman is unwell. Thus Mary's arrival has saved Belinda the unpleasantness of making beds, cleaning floors, and tidying spiders. It's perfect. She decides to treat herself to a cup of Nescafé on the terrace and a *po' di* her favorite Russell "The Voice" Watson CD to celebrate.

While Watson's soaring renditions of "Bridge over Troubled Water" and "Nessun Dorma!" roll down the valley, pouring through the open windows of Giovanna's trattoria, Belinda relaxes over a thirteen-month-old British *Vogue* left by one of her previous guests and a cup of coffee with Hermesetas. This is her idea of a perfectly perfect morning: sitting on her terrace, surrounded by her large terra-cotta pots of candy-pink geraniums and urns of turquoise hydrangeas, browning herself in the mid-morning sun and—with the help of her trusty binoculars—spying on or, as she would put it, keeping herself acquainted with, exactly what is going on in the valley.

As Tuscan valleys go, the Val di Santa Caterina is relatively small. About five miles long and a mile wide, it descends gently toward a small, often dry stream at its floor. The single white dirt road that winds past Belinda's house and through the valley is lined, in part, by cypress trees that stand to attention like bright green feathers. The poor rocky land on the crest of the surrounding hills supports only the occasional bush or tree, but it gives way to fertile pasture below, green and lush in the soft light of early summer. Neatly terraced with stone walls, the intensely cultivated lowlands of Val di Santa Caterina certainly sing for their supper. Fields of sunflowers, maize, wheat, tobacco, vines, and olive trees jostle for hillside space, like some sort of fecund patchwork quilt. The overall impression is of an authentic, fully functioning agricultural valley that, although most definitely beguiling, would not, by Tuscan standards, win any beauty competition. This, coupled with its proximity to the singularly unattractive, war-damaged town of Poggibonsi, makes the houses in the valley slightly more affordable than others in the glamorous Chianti area.

Directly opposite Belinda, and on the east side of the valley, live Derek and Barbara, one of the first expat couples to grace the valley. They have been doing up their not insubstantial to-bacco farmhouse for the past ten years. Brash and flash with his cash, Derek made a lot of money in ladies' underwear in the early nineties. Having started out in "large nylon panties with a breathable gusset" in the eighties, he was one of the first Man-chester clothing manufacturers to make the move into under-wired bras and thongs. So having made enough money from lifting and separating the nation, he and Barbara took early re-tirement and moved into what had been their holiday home on a permanent basis. And they have been doing it up ever since: expanding it, altering it, refurbishing it, adding a pool to it, ex-tending the drive, replanting the olive groves, laying out rows of new cypress trees, seeding the lawn. Derek is one of those men who finds it difficult to sit still and, since his arrival in Val di Santa Caterina, he has been instrumental in both the setting up and running of the local Christmas panto, as well as increas-ing the Brit involvement in the *Festa di Formaggio.* Belinda's arrival relieved him of both these responsibilities. So now he spends his time thinking up other plans and diversions.

Farther along the valley, and still on the lower east side, is the local farmer's large villa, with its collection of outhouses, cot-tages and barns, which house not only Signor and Signora Bi-anchi, but also his mother, their three sons, two of whom have wives and another three small children. One son, Gianfranco Bianchi—more informally known as Franco—is the handsome handyman who helps the ladies of the valley with their tricky maintenance and DIY problems. A source of great comfort to them in their time of need, he seems to do rather well in the bargain, particularly around Christmas and his birthday, when he is showered with expensive trinkets from all corners of the valley.

Almost directly opposite the Bianchis and down the valley from Casa Mia is La Trattoria di Giovanna. The hub of all action, the scene of all gossip, the epicenter of all that goes on in the Val di Santa Caterina, it is open all day, every day, except Sunday nights and Thursdays, and sells, among other things, *panini,* rolls with slivers of prosciutto and shots of kidney-killer coffee for lunch, then yards of shiny homemade pasta and cartwheels of stringy cheese pizza for dinner, plus an amazing assortment of home-cured hams and seasonal dishes like stuffed zucchini flowers. Its long bar is piled high with bottles of Montepulciano, Orvieto, locally produced Chianti, and packets of cigarettes; it is the second home of Howard, the alcohol-fueled author, who lives farther along the hill from Belinda. As thin as a stick, with a Brillo pad of blond hair and a face as red as the wine he drinks, Howard Oxford is forty-four and had a literary hit called *The Sun Shone on Her Face,* back in the eighties. A romantic love story set in turn-of-the-century mid-Wales, it was made into a two-hour special by the BBC. Howard became famous. He drank and fucked most of London, and went on to develop chlamydia and writer's block. Although now fortunately fertile, he is still unfortunately blocked—so blocked, in fact, that the only thing he has written since his arrival in the valley three years ago is a PR piece for the *Spectator* about the Gordon's gin juniper-berry harvest, plus a version of *Puss in Boots* for the Christmas panto.

Back on the other side of the valley, past the empty Casa Padronale with a chapel, which Belinda has her small blue eye on for future development, is the Monastero di Santa Caterina. A stunning piece of real estate, in a sublime location, with prime views and an old Etruscan road leading right up to it, it was sold to a lesbian cooperative from Sydney two years ago. The sale caused something of a sensation: the idea that the valley would be overrun by leagues of hirsute lesbians going about their Sapphic business made everyone hot under the collar—well, hot, certainly.

However, when it actually came to any girl action, the lesbians moved in quietly and quickly and seem now to spend little time in the Northern Hemisphere. When they do grace the valley with their presence, they tend to keep themselves very much to themselves. They have only ever appeared once en masse in the trattoria, after a volleyball competition against another lesbian group from within the *comune*. But that one sighting was enough to keep the valley going for weeks. Truth be known, Belinda is not *au fait* enough with the comings and goings at Monastero di Santa Caterina. For when she claims she can see the whole valley from the lounger on her terrace, it is, like many of Belinda's claims, not entirely true. Even when she is out standing on the edge of her land, raised high on the balls of her feet, she can see only the front steps of the building through her trained lenses and, rather annoyingly, none of the expansive garden over the monastery wall.

Now, lounging back on the green-and-white-striped sunbed, sipping her coffee and gently conducting Russell "The Voice" Watson with her right hand, Belinda busies herself by keeping her eyes and her binoculars pointed on the Bianchi farm below. Three Bianchi grandchildren are running around in the garden, chasing what could either be a piglet or a puppy. Belinda can't follow it quickly enough to find out which. At the far end of the kitchen garden, Franco has his shirt off and is chopping wood. The yellow sun plays on his bronzed back, and the sweaty shine of honest labor gleams across his shoulders. Belinda soon loses interest in the children and follows his every manly swing, the tip of her tongue protruding through her dehydrated lips.

It is only when the strains of Russell Watson's glorious rendition of the Ultravox hit "Vienna" die down that Belinda hears the sound of a car. Such is the isolation of the valley and, indeed, its shape that the sound of a motor car reverberates with every gear change, demanding attention. Normally, due to Casa Mia's proximity to the only road, there is not an arriving or departing vehicle that Belinda Smith does not notice or remark upon. She can also, if she concentrates, tell apart everyone's mode of transport. Derek and Barbara's BMW's shooting brake purrs like a pussycat as it comes up the hill. The lesbian cooperative's people mover rattles like a prescription-pill junkie as it negotiates the white pot-holed road. And while Howard's jaded Renault almost never leaves his drive, all of the Bianchis' Apes, Cinquecentos, tractors, and Pandas cough and break wind like incontinent old men as they come past the corner of the house.

But this engine sound is different. It is glamorous, chic, expensive, environmentally conscious, and rather well maintained. Belinda searches the curves of the white road to find it. Somehow it eludes her. She follows the twists and turns from just outside her own house and down the hillside across the stream at the valley floor toward Derek and Barbara's and . . . nothing. Just as she is about to give up, she spots it coming down the drive of the empty Casa Padronale. Belinda pulls the binoculars into focus, her fat hands turn at speed, but the flare of the sun prevents her seeing through the windscreen.

"Damn it," she mutters, turning on her lounger as she follows the smart blue four-wheel-drive Jeep down the far side of the hill and up toward her. Twisted onto her side, one thigh over the other, Belinda continues to squint but is unable to pry through the smoked-glass windscreen. "Urgh!" she moans, throwing down the binoculars in disgust. "That's just inconsiderate." She heaves herself up and makes her way briskly into the house and to the telephone. She dials a short number with a few clicks of her pink index fingernail, and waits.

"Hello?" A breathless, northern male voice as if in the first stages of emphysema answers.

"*Pronto,*" says Belinda, rolling the *r* and popping her *p* in her very best Italian. "It's the Contessa here."

"The who?" The sound of head scratching comes down the line.

"The Contessa," repeats Belinda, smiling at her Uffizi souvenir calendar hanging on the wall. There's an unpleasantly long pause. "Honestly," she sighs, her head falling to one side, "Derek, you were the one who christened me."

"Oh, Belinda! My Contessa." He chuckles. "Of course. I beg your pardon. . . . How are you this fine morning?"

"Oh . . . *fa caldo,*" she says, fanning herself with her free hand. "*Fa molto caldo.*"

"It's always bloody hot here, dear," says Derek, clearing his throat of thick phlegm. "Barb's already out there getting her cancer. Flat on her back with a thong up her crack, getting an all-over tan for some reason." He hoots, and his loud, throaty laugh dissolves into a hacking cough, followed by a long, loud theatrical blow into his handkerchief.

"Yes, well, whatever you say," says Belinda, holding the receiver away from her ear. "But all I know is that when you have skin as fine as mine, it's not advisable to put it in the sun. Barbara, on the other hand, is such a lucky woman," continues Belinda, her voice cracking with contentment. "I mean, she's been out here so long she's almost turned native." She laughs. "She's so brown you can hardly tell her apart from the laborers in the fields."

"Well, she's got to be kept busy somehow," says Derek, and clears his throat again. "Anyway, what can I do for you, Contessa dear?"

"Just a little *questione,* Derek," says Belinda. "The blue car? At the Casa Padronale? Whose is it? And what is it doing here?"

"What blue car's that, then?"

"What do you mean 'what blue car?' The blue car that's driving up my half of the valley as we speak," she says, her small eyes narrowing as she checks its progress out of the kitchen window.

"Oh . . . the blue Jeep," says Derek.

"There is no need to be pedantic, Derek," Belinda replies brusquely.

"I'm sorry."

"Car, Jeep, car, Jeep, what is that blue vehicle doing in my valley?"

"I'm not *totally* sure," says Derek, "but—"

"I don't need totally sure, Derek," interrupts Belinda, who likes to be abreast of things, "just tell me what you've heard."

"Well," says Derek, sounding jolly, "the Casa Padronale is up for sale, that much I do know—"

"For sale? For sale?" Belinda starts to pace. "What do you mean, for sale?"

"Well, it's on the market, dear."

"I know what 'for sale' means, Derek," snaps Belinda. "I just don't know why you know and I don't. Why didn't anyone tell me? For sale . . . Honestly. How long have you known it's for sale, Derek? How long?"

"What? Well . . ." falters Derek. "Um, a couple of weeks?"

"A couple of weeks?" Belinda stops in her tracks. "You mean you've known that the Casa Padronale has been on the market for a couple of weeks and you haven't told me?" she asks very slowly indeed.

"Er—"

"Who told you?"

"Giovanna."

"Giovanna?"

"Yes, Giovanna."

"Oh," says Belinda, staring at the Uffizi calendar, one hand on her plump hip. "Oh, God, silly me." She announces suddenly, flapping her free hand in front of her now pleasantly smiling face, her small blue eyes pointing heavenward. "Of course!" She laughs. "Do you know what? She told me that as well. . . . Now, that you mention it, I can hear Giovanna's voice telling me . . . and as I'm so busy these days, I quite clean forgot!"

"She did?" Derek's sigh of relief down the telephone is both palpable and audible. "I was sure you knew, dear," he says. "That's why I never bothered to tell you." He laughs.

"Yes, quite," says Belinda. "In fact," she pauses. "I think I knew first."

"Yes, exactly. I was absolutely sure you would."

"Y-e-es," she agrees.

"Anyway," continues Derek, sounding increasingly confident and garrulous, now that the first hurdle has been successfully scaled, "apparently someone's interested in buying it—"

"Oh, I know!" exclaims Belinda.

"An American."

"An American?"

"Yes, an American," laughs Derek. "How . . . brilliant?"

"Ghastly!"

"Terrible," adds Derek, at speed.

"An American moving into this valley!" proclaims Belinda, her short nose wrinkling. "That is almost as bad as having a whole dictatorship of Germans. In fact," she adds, "I think it's probably worse."

"Well, he may not actually buy the place," suggests Derek. "All I heard was that an American was interested. That doesn't mean to say—"

"Yes, yes, 'only interested.'" Belinda nods. "I've heard that as well."

"So," says Derek, after a stiff pause, "do you think that the blue Jeep was his?"

"Well, most certainly," asserts Belinda, flicking through the calendar with increasing distraction. "Jeeps are very American cars."

"I knew you'd know, Contessa," says Derek. "I knew you'd be the person to talk to about all of this. How lucky you phoned."

"Yes, I know," agrees Belinda. "Isn't it?" She lets go a long and languid sigh. "Anyway, I can't stand around chatting all day. Things to do."

"Right you are, then," says Derek. "Mustn't hold you up. Busy woman like you."

"Yes, absolutely. *Arrivadeary!*" trills Belinda.

"Right you are. Speak to you later. *Arrivadeary!*"

Belinda puts down the receiver and stands stock-still, deep in thought. Her legs hip-width apart, she squeezes together the fleshy corners of her mouth with her right hand. The unpredictable twists and turns of her morning are making her feel out of sorts. It's just one thing after another. Unreliable staff and a demanding daughter would normally be enough to blacken her mood, but couple that with her ignorance of a possible new arrival in the valley and she is really and truly put out.

"An American," she mutters. "An American," she repeats, as a small shudder travels down her spine. "How frightful!"

Fortunately for Belinda, she has little time to dwell on the wretched possibility of a new arrival in the valley as she has an arrival of her own to collect from the station. She straightens her navy blue short-sleeved shirt in the full-length mirror in the hall, runs a comb through her short brown hair, places a pair of gold-rimmed sunglasses on the top of her head, and efficiently locks up the house before she walks out into the sunshine. She removes the various yellowed pages of the *Mail on Sunday* from the windscreen of her ex-husband's six-year-old silver Renault Mégane, and opens the doors to let out the thick, hot air.

"Phew!" she pronounces, as she collapses into the black velveteen upholstery. *"Fa molto, molto caldo . . ."*

She reverses slowly out of the drive, careful not to take out the terra-cotta pot of purple pansies and the wooden pergola to the left of the house, which sports one of her many dead vines. She turns right and heads down the valley.

She drives slowly past Giovanna's and, straining her neck to the left, poised to wave, checks under the Campari-branded umbrellas on the terrace to see if Howard, or any of her *conoscenti,* is having lunch. Flanked by fat green vines loaded with pubescent grapes, only one of the four tables is occupied—by a couple of wide-thighed tourists sweating in their shorts—and neither Howard nor indeed Giovanna is anywhere to be seen. Belinda continues down across the stream, past the small church, the village green where they hold the *Festa di Formaggio,* and on toward Derek and Barbara's imposing new row of cypress trees and the Bianchis' farm. She slows down as she reaches the gate. Hoping for a glimpse of Franco's firm flesh, she is instead greeted by a collection of barking hounds and one waving grandchild.

Up the hill toward the monastery, Belinda notices that the single metal pole barrier that blocks the drive to the Casa Padronale is open and pointing toward the sky. This distracts her to such an extent that she forgets to check for any signs of life at the monastery. She doesn't remember until she hits the open road and it is too late.

Half an hour later, she swings into the car park of Sant'Anna station, with Russell Watson at *grande voce* on her car stereo. She spots her twenty-year-old daughter perched on her suitcase, her fellow passengers having long since been meeted, greeted, and conducted away from the provincial station.

Neat and petite, Mary is strikingly more beautiful than she was last year. Having recently shed almost ten kilos, her features are decidedly sharper and more defined. Her nose is small and straight, her cheekbones are high, her hair is long and dark, and her lashes are so thick that they appear to knot at the corners of her eyes. She sits serenely on the pavement and doesn't seem to hear the chorusing crescendo of her mother's operatic arrival. She remains motionless. Her face is raised, her eyes are closed as she soaks up the unfamiliar sun, toasting her transparent white skin in its warming rays. A mild ecstasy curls her pretty lips.

Belinda grinds to a halt, silences Russell, gets out of the car, slams the door, and marches up toward her daughter, blocking out the sun. Mary opens her eyes.

"Hello, Mum," she says, standing up and smoothing down her denim skirt, a searching smile on her face, apparently trying to gauge her mother's humor.

"Buongiorno, buongiorno, buongiorno!" exclaims Belinda with suitable dramatis. Lips pursed, arms out like Jesus, she is waiting to be embraced. "Maria, welcome, darling! Welcome back to Toscana!"

"Hi," says Mary, leaning forward and kissing her mother on one cheek.

"Come va?" asks her mother, her eyes closed as she waits for her daughter to kiss the other. *"Come va?"*

"Oh, well, you know, fine," says Mary, with a shrug of her shoulders. "Been a bit depressed since I was fired but—"

"Yes, well," says Belinda, opening her eyes, "we'll have no mention of that while you're here." With a flick of her short brown hair, she turns to walk back to the car. "Hurry up, now. Put your suitcase in the boot, we've got lots to do."

"Absolutely, of course," says Mary, as she trots along behind her mother, her body arching under the weight of her suitcase. "But what exactly is the problem?"

"Well, Giulia has grappa and is very ill," explains Belinda, hands on hips, as she watches her daughter heave her suitcase toward the car.

"Grappa?" grunts Mary. "Don't you mean *grippa*? *La grippa?* Flu. Giulia has the flu?" She turns to her mother. "It's an easy mistake to make."

"Have you put on weight?" asks Belinda, covering her mouth with her index finger, as she looks her daughter up and down.

"No," says Mary, with a final thrust, pushing her case into the boot. "I've lost over eight kilos since you last saw me."

"Really?" says Belinda, raising her plucked eyebrows. "How odd. Maybe it's just because I always forget how short you are." She smiles. "Just like your father."

The two women get into the car in silence. Belinda starts the engine. Russell breaks back into song. Mary rests her chin in her hand and stares out of the window at the boxes of scarlet geraniums lining the car park. "So, how is everything else?" she asks eventually, as her mother turns left at the baker's and down the hill toward the main road and the Santa Caterina valley.

"Busy, darling, busy, it's very, very busy."

"Well, that's good."

"Yes," says Belinda, concentrating very hard on driving. "Yes, I suppose it is."

They continue in silence, driving through the gently rolling Chianti countryside, past pointed cypress trees bending in the breeze, past fields of green sunflowers waiting to turn gold, past rows of plump young vines and the occasional black prostitute standing, half naked, in a lay-by waiting to ply her trade.

"I see the girls are still here," says Mary, staring out of the window.

"Mmm," replies Belinda, with a disinterested glance. "The Orvieto–Todi road is much worse, I counted seventeen prostitutes last time I drove that way."

"Right," says Mary. "I always wonder how they get there."

"Some man in a van," says Belinda.

"Right," says Mary again, shifting in her seat.

"I've still never seen a single Italian use them," observes Belinda. "You would have thought that in all my travels I would have seen at least one man doing up his fly, or a van in the throes of passion, but no. Nothing. Not a single liaison."

"Mmm," says Mary. "So what's the gossip?"

"Far too much to go into now," says Belinda. "But Derek and Barbara are thinking about adding a new terrace below their rose lawn."

"Oh."

"I know, I think it's too much as well, but Derek has got to spend his money somehow, I suppose. Howard, on the other hand, is so impoverished that I don't think he can even afford to go to Giovanna's for lunch anymore. He wasn't there when I drove past this morning."

"Oh dear."

"Can't say I'm shocked," says Belinda. "He had his old editor out here a while back and all they did was drink bottles and bottles of red wine and they ended up having some row about something. He left on Ryanair the very next day."

"Oh dear."

"Yes, well . . . Franco has a new girlfriend, I think."

"Really?"

"See? I knew you'd be interested in that!"

"Mu-u-m, don't be insane. I'm not old enough or rich enough for Franco."

"Well, I've heard he's been doing some work for that sculpture woman in the valley on the way to Serrana."

"That doesn't necessarily—"

"I know . . . but he's looking unreasonably cheerful these days."

"Oh."

"And we haven't had any lesbians out here for ages."

"Really? That's a shame."

"Isn't it? I really thought they'd be here much more. Particularly after they spent so much money on the house."

"Did they?"

"Oh, yes." Belinda nods. "Franco told me they had marble sent from Carrara, you know, where Michelangelo got his from."

"Right."

"Although I can't see where it all went."

"Right."

"Oh, and apparently there's some American sniffing around

the Casa Padronale," says Belinda, as she pauses at the junction in the road.

"Really?" says Mary.

"Mmm," says her mother, as she looks left, then right.

"That should spice things up a bit."

"D'you think so?"

"Oh, yes," replies Mary, with a smile.

"Really?" says Belinda sounding surprised. "I wouldn't have thought it would make any difference at all."

Venerdi ❖ Friday

Clima ❖ *fa caldo* (Hot! Hot! Hot!)

Tuscan life is always full of the most glorious surprises. The way the sunflowers slowly turn during the heat of the day to keep their faces pointing toward the sun. The way the simplest of bread and olive-oil dishes can taste like heaven on earth. The way even the smallest and ugliest peasant farmers break into a beautiful smile when I greet them.

But there are also plenty of little shocks. The way lizards shoot out of crevices in the walls. The way scorpions hide under stones. Yesterday, for example, I found out that an American has been looking around the Casa Padronale, the house on the distinctly less sunny side of the valley from Casa Mia!

It's not the interest in the Casa Padronale that is the surprise (despite its run-down state, rather poor size, and terribly poor modern frescos in the small side chapel)—there are always plenty of comings and goings in my corner of *Paradiso*—but that it is an American who is looking around! You see, we fortunately don't get many Americans in Toscana. I don't want to be rude, but I think they must find it too difficult. Far from the comfort and convenience of McDonald's, there are probably too many hills and green vegetables for them. Instead, they tend to herd together in the cities, like Florence. So it's a little bit of a shock to hear that one has ventured so far from the town! Derek was astonished when I rang to tell him. But I was pleased to inform him that the American was merely looking and that I shouldn't think he'd hang around for long once he realizes the amount of hard work and effort it takes to do up a house to the standard of something like mine. He'll be straight back to New York, or wherever he came from!

Anyway, on a lighter note, my daughter has finally arrived from England. She has managed to take a break from her busy work schedule and her career in communications to come and help me here for the summer, or even, perhaps, a little longer. She is looking well, if a little white! I suppose I am so used to looking at healthy people all the time, not pasty city dwellers from London, so it is hardly surprising! But it's always a joy to see someone from the mother country, so to speak. Such fun to hear the gossip and catch up on important news.

Maria tells me it has been the wettest April on record! What a shame. There have been terrible floods and all sorts. We, on the other hand, have had nothing but bright sunshine here for the last month. In fact, I can't remember the last time it rained, and I mean rained properly, as we don't do drizzle here. Italian rain is so much better than the English variety. It is so much more nourishing, so much more needed. It turns parched hillsides into rolling pastures over night. It is so natural.

Maria also tells me that people are *still* talking about the euro in the U.K. I can't believe it! What a bad case of *piccolo* Englanders! It seems so strange to me. As a European I find it extraordinary that silly little things like currency and sovereignty are still an issue. Oh, well, it is so good, sometimes, to be reminded of the reasons why one left!

But Maria's presence has been invaluable since she arrived yesterday. As Giulia, my cleaner, has had a touch of the Italians and not turned up for work (she says she's ill, but in this country one can never tell), Maria has been a great help sorting out the house before Casa Mia opens its doors at the weekend for the beginning of the season. This is her fourth year of helping out and, with her three-week course at Swindon catering college, not only is she useful around the house but she can hold her own in the kitchen, too! And following my usual large response from the discreet adverts I placed in the upmarket *Spectator, Sunday Times,* and *Sunday Telegraph,* we are almost totally booked right through until the autumn!

RISOTTO DI *CASA MIA E GIOVANNA*

I have so many herbs growing in my garden that sometimes I love to squander them in this delicious dish I chanced upon while having lunch at the wonderful upmarket Ristorante di Giovanna, a local spot frequented by expats, peasants, and tourists alike. It is a warm and comforting dish that reminds me of all that is wholesome and real about Tuscany.

* porcini mushrooms
* onions
* garlic
* risotto rice
* chicken/vegetable stock
* rosemary
* thyme
* mint

Boil a kettle or a saucepan of water and add a handful of dried porcini mushrooms. (Expensive but worth every euro!) Chop and lightly fry some onions and garlic in olive oil. Add four cups of risotto rice (this recipe serves four—but with the spontaneous, ever-expanding dinner and lunch tables that organically occur in Italy I often feel free to add more in case extra interesting people arrive). Boil it up in chicken or vegetable stock, or the water you used to hydrate your mushrooms. (Do keep stirring for quite a while.) When the rice is firm and fat, like a baby's arm, fold in the succulent mushrooms, plus generous handfuls of rustically chopped rosemary, thyme, and mint.

Serve with fecund friends and large bottles of ruby-red wine.

CHAPTER TWO

❀ ❀ ❀

Belinda is preparing for her morning trawl through her e-mails. Sitting at her computer, cup of coffee at the ready, she is steeling herself for this exhausting process, which requires all of her critical antennae to be on full alert.

The e-mail booking process, as Belinda says, is the "first filter"—the first opportunity she has to turn away people she doesn't like the look, sound, or indeed e-mail of. Hotmail accounts are automatically out, as Belinda likes people to have a proper job with a proper e-mail address. Those with what Belinda considers "low rent" or "unfortunate" names are also given a wide berth and short e-mail shrift. Then, the questions her potential guests ask come under scrutiny. Anyone who asks to smoke or bring children is immediately banned: there is nothing Belinda dislikes more than smokers or children. Other inquiries are dealt with according to her whim on that day. Vegetarians, vegans, asthmatics, arthritics, those with a single special need are normally vetoed, as is anyone who asks after the plebeian pastime of golf. In fact, anyone whom she thinks might irritate her in some way, shape, or form is rejected before they get a chance to cross her upmarket threshold.

Today there is only one inquiry, from a young Danish couple who want to bring their baby. Belinda e-mails back a simple "No, we are full." Babies are even more unattractive than children.

She then lets out a long sigh, and goes into the hall to ready herself for market.

"Maria! Maria! For God sake, Maria," she yells up the stairs. "What are you doing up there? I've got my *mercato* hat on and I'm waiting." She turns to her reflection in the mirror and straightens the wide-brimmed straw hat she keeps for languid summer lunches and trips to market. "Honestly," she adds, cupping her mouth to assist her voice up the stairs, "only tourists, and Derek and Barbara arrive at Serrana market this late in the day. What are you doing?"

"Coming," says Mary, bounding down the stone staircase with optimistic energy. Her swinging dark hair shines in the sun.

"Is that what you're wearing?" asks Belinda, looking her annoyingly attractive daughter up and down, taking in the pale blue T-shirt and the dark blue shorts. "Honestly, darling, you're just like your father. You simply don't have the knees for shorts," she adds, with a small shrug, as she turns toward the door.

Mary makes to walk back upstairs.

"And we really don't have time for you to change either," says her mother. "You'll have to come as you are."

"I could stay behind if I'm going to embarrass you that much," mutters Mary, rather quietly.

"What?" Belinda frowns, adjusting her hat once more. "Don't be so ridiculous. I haven't got time for this. We've got lots to do. I want to pop into Giovanna's for a *po' di caffè* on the way, so we really should get our skates on."

Amid a cloud of dust and a loud crunch of stone, Belinda

pulls up her car, turning it dramatically outside Giovanna's. The car park is a small rustic facility to the right of the terrace and to the left of the tobacco-drying tower, and can barely accommodate the permanent members of the valley, let alone passing tourist traffic. Belinda slams the car door and raises her jaw in the air so she can see beyond the confines of her hat, she then walks onto the vine-lined terrace, looking for her usual seat. Finding it fortunately unoccupied, she places herself in the valley-view-with-roadside-vista position and coughs loudly. Mary follows along behind, assiduously avoiding all eye contact with the brace of blond hiking blokes, who try to engage her with a smile. Belinda coughs again, and Giovanna's enormous husband, Roberto, appears to the tinkling accompaniment of the beaded curtain. Short and bald, save for a sprig of dark hair that he smooths across his otherwise naked scalp, Roberto is bloated and coated in fat. He has arms like legs, and plump hands like a fist of sausages; he looks like a man who enjoys carafes of sweet Vin Santo wine and plenty of biscotti. But despite the Lord's generousness when it came to Roberto's proportions, such is the man's charm and charisma that he is known valley-wide for his way with the ladies. And Belinda is no exception.

"Oh, Roberto," she pronounces, getting up and removing her *mercato* hat. Her shoulders shiver with delight as she puckers her lips, like a cat's rectum, and places her cheek near Roberto's left ear. "*Buongiorno. Buongiorno,* Roberto. *Come va?*" she smiles. "*Co-me va?*"

"*Bene, bene,*" he replies, with an ebullient laugh. "*Molto bene!*" He smiles, his heavy arms shooting into the air with ostentatious enthusiasm. "*E . . . la bella Maria!*" he exclaims, and wraps the grinning Mary in a duvetlike embrace.

"Ye-e-s," says Belinda, sitting down. "Mary's back."

"*Che bella!*" repeats Roberto to Belinda, his arms apart as he reintroduces her to her own daughter.

"Yes," says Belinda, with a small smile. "Very *bella*. For God sake, Mary, do sit down."

"*Che bella!*" says Roberto, again, as he pulls out the chair from under the table for Mary to sit in.

"Yes, yes." Belinda nods efficiently. "Lovely . . ." She smiles. "So, *tutta bene,* then, Roberto?"

"Oh, *tutto bene.*" He grins back.

"Good," says Belinda, with a little scratch of her neck. "Well . . . that's good . . ."

"*Sì, bene,*" says Roberto, with a wide smile.

"*Bene,*" says Belinda.

"*Sì molto bene.*" Roberto's grin continues.

"*Bene.*" Belinda nods. The left corner of her mouth begins to twitch under the strain of pleasantries. "Um . . . *Due caffè,* Roberto, when you're ready."

"*Bene,*" says Roberto, flicking his tea towel over his shoulder as he disappears behind the beaded curtain to charge up the coffee machine.

"Good," says Belinda, inhaling through her teeth. "So . . ."

"So . . ." says Mary, turning to look at the view of the valley as it unfolds below. The sun is warming the Bianchis' fields of sunflowers and maize, the wind is making the cypress trees that line the road sway back and forth like fans at a rock concert. "It's great to be back. I always forget quite how beautiful it is here," she says.

"Yes," says Belinda, with one of her more sensitive smiles. "It's certainly more attractive than the wretched little love nest your father shares with that wretched little woman near Slough."

"It's not near Slough," says Mary, leaning forward, putting her head in her hands and her elbows on the table. "It's in Surrey."

"Don't put your elbows on the table, dear," says Belinda, flaring her nostrils as she looks over her daughter's shoulder and inhales the view.

"Which house did you say the American man's buying?" asks Mary, following her mother's gaze.

"It's not definite, of course," corrects Belinda. "But the Casa Padronale, over there." She points to the terra-cotta roof just visible through the trees.

"I thought you had your eye on that," says Mary.

"I did," says Belinda, "but the position isn't that good."

"Oh? I thought it got the most sun in the valley."

"It gets some sun. It's just that Casa Mia has by far the best views. I can see the whole valley from my terrace, you know."

"I know."

"There's nothing that happens here that I don't know about."

"I know."

"And I think that's preferable to a couple of extra hours of sunshine a day, don't you?"

"Of course," says Mary.

"Anyway," she continues, nodding in the direction of the beaded curtain, "here comes Roberto with our *caffè*. Ask him what he knows about the Casa Padronale, would you, darling?"

"Don't you want to?" asks Mary.

"Not really, darling. I'm a little tired," smiles Belinda, looking down the valley with a sudden air of all-enveloping exhaustion. "And it's very good for you to practice your Italian. I get to speak it all the time out here. In fact, I rarely speak anything else. Whereas you—with your little English life—only get to speak boring old English all the time."

"Oh, okay," says Mary. "But only if you're sure."

"No, no, really." Belinda waves her pink-tipped hand. "I know what a treat it is for you . . . Oh, *grazie,* Roberto," she says, accepting a small cup of strong coffee. "Maria has a little *questione* for you, don't you, Maria?"

"*Sì,*" says Mary. "*Vorrei sapere . . .*"

And while Belinda smiles, and nods, and laughs at various appropriate, and inappropriate, intervals, her daughter learns, through a long and animated discussion with Roberto, that the Casa Padronale is indeed on the verge of being sold to an American and, as far as he knows, they will be moving in almost immediately. Or, at least, building work will be starting almost immediately, but exactly when the American will move in himself is anyone's guess.

✳ ✳ ✳

"So it's definite, then?" asks Belinda, her face furrowed under the strain of parking the car as she successfully reverses into a space at the fourth attempt.

"Well, as far as Roberto knows, and he's friends with the *geometra* who is selling the property," says Mary, opening her door.

"The *geometra?*"

"You know, like that sort of real estate man, Alfredo, you used to shout at all the time."

"I didn't shout at him all the time."

"Well . . ."

"I merely raised my voice when he didn't understand me."

"Well, like him anyway."

"Interesting," says Belinda, arranging her hat in the reflection of the car door. "That's very interesting. Now, I rather hope we aren't going to bump into Derek and Barbara, but it

is market day, and I did see their car leave in this direction earlier this morning, so they may well be here. If we do, just leave
the talking to me, all right?"

"Fine," says Mary.

"Come along, then," says Belinda, turning toward an Etruscan archway. High and narrow, it leads through the thick town
walls to the paved streets and honey-colored buildings beyond.

On market day, the medieval town of Serrana is packed. Most
of the inhabitants of the nearby villages and the surrounding
countryside empty into the main square to either buy or sell
their wares. The crowds are dense, the noise level is high, and
the air smells of hot pavements and ripe fruit. All down one
side of the square, under the shaded arches of the ancient stone
colonnade, are the vegetable sellers. Behind row upon row and
box upon box of fennel and aubergines, chicory and carrots,
rocket and radishes stand families of all generations, from weath-
ered, leathered grandparents to young, hopeful teenagers, shouting and shifting as much produce as quickly and charmingly as
possible.

Down the other side of the square and under a small Romeo
and Juliet balcony are the dairy vans. Rammed and crammed
with butter and cheese, they are parked at odd intervals and
populated by white-coated salesmen in paper hats. Nearby are
the smaller home-produce stalls, loaded with olives, fresh garlic, and paprika-covered crisps. Alongside is the young man
who sells slithers of whole roasted pig, and the salon-perfect
woman who specializes in virulent pink underwear. A pair of
her racy, lacy panties swings in the breeze, like some terribly
modern serving suggestion.

Despite the melee of locals and tourists, Belinda still manages to stand out in her broad-brimmed *mercato* hat, with a
navy head scarf knotted loosely at the back of her neck. At one

of the many vegetable stalls, she is contemplating tomatoes. "Plum or cherry, darling?" she asks Mary, keeping a small blue eye on the crowd as she looks down the length of her short nose at her daughter. "What do you think, Maria? For a little *insalata* later?"

Mary stands next to her mother and runs a hand through her long dark hair. "Um," she says, leaning in for a closer look. "I'm not really—"

"Questo! Questo! E questo!" announces Belinda suddenly, in a very loud, very Italian voice, as she points to random trays of vegetables in an assured manner. *"Perfecto, perfecto!"* She clasps her hands in delightful appreciation, before turning with a swing of her silk scarf. "Oh, Derek! Barbara!" she continues, without inhaling, "I was so busy chatting away in fluent Italian, I simply didn't see you there at all!" She gives a wide, ever so generous smile. "How are you?"

Side by side in the shining sun, Derek and Barbara make quite a pair. They are almost exactly the same height, but Derek's lack of elevation is more than made up for by his girth. While the rest of his body maintains a certain svelteness, particularly his arms and legs, his stomach is of pregnancy proportions. In a pair of light gray ankle socks and open-toed sandals, a pair of gray shorts and a gray short-sleeved, open-neck shirt that exposes a small isosceles triangle of chest hair just below the chin, Derek has the silhouette of a skittle at a bowling alley. Yet his face is relatively handsome: he has large brown enthusiastic eyes, a jovial curve to his lips, and his sandy hair is still quite luxuriant in most places. Thinning gently on top, it salt-and-peppers only around the temples.

Barbara's ample, glossy, tanned figure is entirely the result of fine living. An ex-model turned receptionist, turned managerial secretary, turned love of the boss's life, she once donned hot pants and knee boots with the best of them—but, never one to hold back when it comes to eats and treats like *pannacotta* or *tiramisù,* Barbara now maintains the sort of luxury fat that Clarins massages and weekend spa breaks were made for. As a result, she has a wardrobe of jogging pants and lounge suits for plump days; however, when she is three pounds lighter, she is wont to pour herself into scoop-neck T-shirts, pedal pushers and fanny clingers in varying degrees of luminosity. Today, having denied herself last night's mascarpone, she is in a yellow T-shirt and matching yellow knee-length skirt, teamed with a pair of golden wedge mules. Her blonde hair, having spent the early morning in curlers, is neat and tucked under on the shoulders, while her pale mouth sports a dark pink outline. Her bright blue eyes are hidden behind a large pair of Dior sunglasses.

"Contessa!" laughs Derek, his waistline joining in the hilarity. "Trust you to be out here bargaining for fruit and vegetables like a native. I don't know how you do it. Ten years we've been here, and we still get our stuff from the local supermarket, don't we, Barb?"

"Yes," agrees Barbara, her gold earrings glaring in the brilliant sun. "We find it's so much cleaner."

"But so much less Italian," smiles Belinda, allowing a slight wrinkle in her nose.

"Oh, my God," declares Derek. His loud flat vowels make a clearing in the crowd. "Is that you, Mary?" he says, taking a step back for a better view. "Bloody hell, look at you! Look at her, Barb. You're half the girl you used to be. Look, Barb, she's half the girl she used to be. You've slimmed down a heck of a lot." He nods enthusiastically.

"You certainly have." Barbara's lined lips crack into a smile.

"Has she?" says Belinda, looking down at her nails. "I can't say that I've noticed."

"Oh, you must have," insists Barbara. "She always was quite a big girl, weren't you, Mary?"

"Well . . ." says Mary, shifting from one foot to the other, looking at the ground.

"You must tell Barbara how you did it," says Derek. "She's always on a diet, desperately trying to lose the weight, aren't you, Barb?"

"Yes, do, do tell Barbara how to lose all that weight." Belinda smiles.

"It's the high-stress low-fiber diet," says Mary. "Ever since I lost—"

"Ever since she got promoted," interrupts Belinda, "it's just fallen off, hasn't it?"

"Promoted?" says Derek, rubbing his hands together. "Congratulations, dear, your mother must be very proud."

"Promoted?" inquires Barbara, looking ever so puzzled. "What are you doing out here, all summer?"

"She's been allowed a sabbatical," says Belinda. "You know, one of those time-off things."

"Oh, right." Barbara smiles. "The world of telecommunications has changed a lot since I was a receptionist."

"Yes," agrees Belinda. "But then again, that was a very long time ago."

"So," says Derek, hopping between the two women, "we're very much looking forward to having you for dinner tonight, aren't we, Barb?"

"Oh, yes," says Barbara. "We can't wait."

"Neither can we," breezes Belinda. "But we must get on. We've got guests arriving tomorrow and *tutto il mercato* to get through yet."

"Right you are, then," says Derek. "See you later. *Arrivadeary!*"

"See you later." Barbara waves. *"Arrivadeary."*

"Arrivadeary!" Belinda grabs Mary's hand, then wafts her way through the crowd.

❁ ❁ ❁

Back at Casa Mia, after an exhausting morning buying tomatoes, a cucumber, and a loaf of bread, Belinda and Mary spend the afternoon on the terrace. After Mary's sterling work yesterday, sweeping and scrubbing out the old animal-quarters *cantinas,* making the beds and laying out fresh towels, there is little left for Belinda to do, except develop a bad humor about the imminent arrival of her Belgian guests. As a misanthrope, Belinda is perhaps not ideally suited to her newfound career in the service industry. The eldest daughter of a schoolteacher, she knows exactly what stations are and has always nurtured ideas above them. Her current career in service is just another good reason to hate her unfaithful rat of an ex-husband, Terrence.

"Urrgh." Belinda sighs atop her green-and-white-striped lounger. Eyes closed, sporting a smaller and altogether jauntier *terrazzo* hat, which she saves for afternoons in the sun, she huffs and puffs and flaps her legs as if she were trying to rid herself of flies.

"Urrgh," she repeats.

Mary ignores her. The heat of the afternoon beats on her back and the hum of insects is lulling her to sleep.

"Urrgh," says Belinda.

"What?" asks Mary finally, through a squashed cheek on the ground.

"Did I make a noise?"

"You sighed."

"Did I?"

"Yes."

"Oh."

"Oh, what?"

"I was thinking."

"You were?"

"Yes, I was thinking that they just didn't sound very pleasant on the telephone," exhales Belinda, her plucked eyebrows rising above her sunglasses.

"Who?"

"The Belgians."

"What was wrong with them?" asks Mary, pulling her black bathing suit out of her white buttocks.

"Well, their voices for a start."

"What do you mean?"

"They sounded all nasal and French."

"Well, they *are* French."

"They're Belgian," corrects Belinda.

"I know, but they speak French in Belgium."

"Not all of them."

"Well, these do, apparently."

"Oh, God, I do hope they aren't going to be difficult." Belinda pours herself some lemonade from the lemon-filled glass jug. "I mean, the last time we had some Belgians here they started asking for bottled water in their bedroom."

"I thought you supplied that," says Mary, rolling on to her back.

"I do. But they wanted bottled-bottled water, you know, with the seals intact. Not the ones I'd refilled from the tap."

"Oh . . ."

"Well, I thought it was very demanding. I mean, if they want that sort of thing, they should go to some ghastly air-conditioned hotel in Poggibonsi with small soaps and a mini-bar. Honestly, these people don't want the real *rustica* Tuscan experience, like in Frances Mayes's, they want something sanitized with wheelchair access and picnicking facilities."

"Or just bottled water," suggests Mary.

"Well . . . as you seem so *au fait* with their little needs, it's lucky you'll be dealing with them, then, isn't it?" Belinda gets up from her lounger with a long, languid stretch. "I'm afraid it's far too hot for me out here," she announces with a flap of her hand, and picks up the old *Vogue,* which has curled like wood shavings in the sun. "I'm off for a sleep. We should be ready to go to Derek's about seven thirty."

❊ ❊ ❊

On the dot of seven thirty Belinda is in the hall, adding the finishing touches to her outfit. It seems that she has decided to go to Derek and Barbara's as some sort of gypsy. Dressed in a floor-length tiered black skirt with a tight black T-shirt and some old hoop earrings, she is standing in front of the mirror trying to work out what to do with her fringed red scarf. She ties it around her head like she's about to gaze into a crystal ball. She places it at a jaunty angle around her waist, as if she's about to dance a tarantella, then around her neck, which makes her look like some rather flamboyant doors-to-manual air hostess.

"Darling, what do you think?" she asks, turning to Mary, who is dressed in a pair of black trousers and a white shirt. "I've just seen something rather similar in *Vogue.*" She pulls down the T-shirt with a snaking of her hips and pops some upper-arm flesh back inside the sleeve.

"Well . . ." says Mary, foolishly letting doubt sound in her voice.

"Well, it's a hell of a lot better than going out looking like a waitress," retorts Belinda, eyeing her daughter up and down with practiced speed. "Honestly, haven't you got anything else to wear?"

"Well, after last summer, when I went out twice, I haven't packed much in the way of smart clothes."

"Oh," says Belinda, as she walks out of the door. "You'd better go and buy yourself some stuff in the market next week. I can't have you moping around in that all summer. You'll put the guests off their holiday."

A ten-minute silent drive away, Derek and Barbara's house, with its outhouses and chestnut barn, is significantly larger than Casa Mia. It is Italian on the outside, but the inside is furnished, as Belinda always enjoys pointing out, like a big Barratt home on the outskirts of Manchester, which indeed is where all of the furniture came from. The sitting room, along with a vast television of cinematic proportions and Derek's mustard yellow, La-Z-Boy armchair, contains a vulva pink leather three-piece suite, a large glass coffee table, and a bookshelf of videos. Hanging from the ceiling in the dining room is a gold-and-glass chandelier that was shipped especially from Harrods lighting department. In fact, interestingly—and Barbara is rather prone to tell this story after a couple of glasses of wine—it is actually the second chandelier that Harrods sent to the Hewitt household. The first ended up in a pile of small crystal pieces after it slipped off the back of a lorry down a valley on the Castellina in Chianti road. As a result the chandelier, due to its expense and convoluted arrival, holds great significance in the household. Dinners, rather than being held in the balmy evening heat of the terrace, are, more often than not, laid up in the confined and airless dining room. And tonight is no exception.

❀ ❀ ❀

Barbara is on her second gin and tonic and seventh olive when Belinda and Mary arrive. Dressed in a leopard-skin bat-winged top and white pedal pushers that fold into a camel's hoof at the crotch, she is clip-clopping back and forth from the kitchen to the sitting room, fixing drinks.

"Belinda, Mary, welcome, welcome," she says, touching opposite shoulders with both of them. "Go through to the lounge," she ushers them ahead, while continuing to tell Howard the chandelier story. He is right behind her, smiling as if he has never heard it before. "And then," she resumes, "we found that it had fallen off the back of a lorry—"

"Really?" says Howard. His parched lips are cracked. His stare is locked on the bottle of alcohol in Barbara's hand.

"I know . . . amazing, isn't it?" she says. "What did you say you wanted?"

"Gin," he says. "Please," he adds quickly.

"Gin and what?"

"Oh," says Howard, having obviously not thought as far as a mixer. "Whatever you have."

"Bitter lemon?"

"Bitter lemon is fine." Howard nods quickly, staring at the bottle, willing it to make contact with his glass.

"Oh, Belinda!" Barbara puts down the bottle and walks back into the sitting room. "What would you and Mary like?"

"I'd love a gin and tonic," says Belinda, "and Mary will have a spritzer as she's driving."

"Right you are, then," says Barbara, with a flick of her stiff blonde hair. "On its way."

"Hope you don't mind," says Howard, meeting his hostess in the doorway, a large glass of a pale green drink in his hand. "I helped myself."

"Don't be silly, Howie," says Barbara, giving him a gentle shove. "My *casa* is your *casa*. Make yourself at home. We don't stand on ceremony here. Do we, Derek? Derek?" she repeats, shouting through the brick archway toward the hall and an apparently locked door.

There's a loud flush. Belinda, Mary, Howard, and Barbara all stare at the white door. Nothing happens. There's another flurry of rapid attempted flushing, and eventually Derek opens the door.

"Oh," he says, his brown eyes round with surprise when confronted with his audience. "I had no idea our guests had arrived."

"Yes," says Barbara. "You've been in there a while."

"Sorry about that," says Derek, walking toward the sitting room and running his thumb along the waistband of his beige slacks. "I got caught a little short."

"As I said," continues Barbara, the maroon lines of her lips coming together, "there's no standing on ceremony in this house."

"So," says Belinda, fiddling with the fringed red scarf at her waist, as she attempts to raise the tone of the conversation, "have you succumbed to the muse yet, Howard?"

"Sorry?" says Howard, halfway down his glass of bitter-lemon-flavored gin. He looks at her with the pale, glazed eyes of someone who has yet to communicate with another human being that day. In an open-necked denim shirt, loose-fitting jeans, and leather sandals, Howard's lean, brown body and wild, unkempt blond hair are still haunted by sex appeal. "Um, no. What? Muse? No, not really," he stammers. "I've been staring at my computer, trying to get my hero out of bed all day."

"Really?" says Belinda, appearing both interested and intelligent at the same time. "He's stuck?"

"Well, I managed twenty words," says Howard, draining his glass.

"Just so long as they were good words," says Belinda with a little light laugh, as Derek passes her a gin and tonic.

"And then I deleted them all," continues Howard.

"Oh," says Belinda, taking a small sip. "Well, I find my *oeuvre* comes to me quite naturally. In fact, there are some days when I find myself so overtaken by the muse that I just can't stop. Scribble, scribble, scribble." Her pink-tipped hand scribbles in the air.

"I didn't know you were writing a novel," says Derek, sitting down on the low edge of his pink sofa, his slim legs akimbo as he accommodates his stomach.

"It's not really a novel," says Belinda, with a tweak of her suitably artistic outfit.

"Well, in my limited experience a book is either a novel or it's not," remarks Howard. With a rattle of ice in his empty glass, he gets out of his seat and makes his way back into the kitchen.

"I suppose you could call it a diary." Belinda is undeterred. "All I'm doing is passing on my *pensées* and *aperçus*."

"Who's got a pair of new shoes?" says Barbara, walking into the room with a tray of olives.

"No, my love," corrects Derek. "It's Belinda. She's sharing her *aperçus*."

"Oh, right," says Barbara, with a small unenlightened shrug. "I only ask because I'm wearing new shoes." She kicks up a golden mule, which is less gold and more mule than the pair she wore to market that morning.

"Those look lovely," says Mary, holding her spritzer, perched on the sofa.

"Thank you, love," says Barbara. "And so do you."

Mary smiles.

"She looks like a waitress," says Belinda, and swigs her drink.

"No, she doesn't," says Barbara.

"It's the black and white," continues Belinda.

"Take no notice." Derek pats the back of Mary's hand. "I think you look lovely."

"Hear, hear. Cheers," says Howard, who takes any opportunity to drain a full glass.

"Well, this is nice," says Barbara, leaning forward to pick up a turquoise and gold packet of cigarettes from the glass coffee table. "Derek and I haven't entertained in a while," she adds, then lights a St. Moritz Menthol and exhales.

"No, my love. Not since last week." Derek nods in agreement.

"Do you mind if I . . . ?" asks Howard from the doorway, waving his empty glass at the rest of the sitting room.

"No, mate," says Derek, putting three olives into his mouth at once. "You just keep helping yourself."

"So, have you got guests arriving tomorrow then, Belinda?" asks Barbara, with taps of her cigarette.

"The Contessa's house is full all summer, isn't it?" declares Derek, with a flatulent-sounding squeak of the leather sofa.

"We've got some lovely Belgians arriving tomorrow," says Belinda. "They're either surgeons, doctors, or lawyers, I can't remember which, but they're certainly professionals of some sort."

"That's nice," says Barbara.

"Ye-es," says Belinda, her head cocking to one side. "It *will* be nice to have some intelligent conversation."

"Yes," agrees Barbara. "That's always nice. . . . Well," she adds, with a small clap, "I think maybe we should move through and sit down. Steve said he might be late, so I think we'll forge on without him."

"Steve?" says Belinda, getting off a pink leather chair. "Do I know Steve?"

"You know Steve," Derek tells her. "Everyone knows Steve."

"Steve the builder," says Barbara.

"A builder?" says Belinda.

"He probably did your house," suggests Barbara helpfully.

"No, I don't think so." Belinda smiles. "Italians did my house."

"Are you sure?" says Derek, pulling his slacks out of his crotch as he stands.

"Didn't you buy your place already done up?" asks Howard, still by the door. "From that English developer?"

"Not entirely done up," says Belinda.

"Well, how can you be sure he didn't do your house then?" Howard takes another swig.

"Anyway, he's a bit of a real estate agent these days as well," says Barbara. "He's ever so nice."

In the dining room, the chandelier is dimmed to make the large white room appear bathed in candlelight. The windows are small and, despite being open, let in no draft at all. There is a silk Persian rug of varying shades of pink and peach on the flagstone floor, and on one wall a large, gold-framed family photo of Derek and Barbara with their two children, Paul and Diane. The long mahogany table is laid with silver plates. There are piles of fruit and nuts in large silver bowls along the middle, and carafes of wine to one side. The effect is so opulent and lush that you might mistake it for Christmas.

As lovers of all things fine, Derek and Barbara are generous hosts and enjoy sharing their fat pension schemes with their friends. While Derek pours his carafes of Chianti, Barbara busies herself in the kitchen, cutting up the slab of foie gras they bought in bulk on their last trip through France.

"I know you're supposed to serve this on that thin toast," says Barbara, as she sits down, "but Derek and I prefer chunks of bread. I hope you don't mind."

"No, not at all," replies Howard, his mouth already full.

"No," says Belinda, pulling out the inside of her bread with her fingernails. "What an ingenious way of doing it—but I'm afraid I just can't eat all this starch."

"Well, I think it's delicious and very generous of you," says Mary.

Derek is unable to reply. He is trying to swallow a rather large mouthful, and his eyes are watering under the strain. By the time he ensures its wine-assisted departure, Steve walks in holding a bottle of Prosecco in either hand.

"Derek! Barb! Ladies! Gents!" he says, with a nod and a smile to each and every one of those assembled. "Sorry I'm so late. What can I say? I just had to close a deal near San Jimmy, and I've driven here like my balls were on fire. . . . So what have I missed?"

"Nothing, nothing at all," says Barbara, pushing a parcel of food to one side of her mouth and talking out of the other. "Sit down, Steve, sit down."

Short and neat, with closely cropped hair, there is a touch of the terrier about Steve. His eyes are bright, his manner is sharp; he is full of energy and extremely alert. One of nature's survivors, he is the sort of bloke who can sniff a deal at forty paces.

"Do you want me to put these in the fridge, Barb?" he asks, waving the two bottles aloft.

"Don't be silly," says Barbara, pushing his shoulder with her hand. "You sit yourself down. I'll do that."

"Oh, great, pâté," he says, and pulls out the chair next to Belinda.

"It's *foie gras,*" corrects Belinda.

"Oh, right." Steve grins.

"Have you met everyone?" says Derek, and clears his throat.

"No, no, I don't believe I have," sniffs Steve, troweling foie gras onto a hunk of bread.

"This is Howard, our writer in residence," says Derek. Steve nods, chomping on his sandwich. "This is Mary, Belinda's daughter." Steve nods again. "And this," he pauses. "This is Belinda, our *new* writer in residence and the Contessa of the Valley." Derek is almost on the point of applauding. Belinda smiles.

"All right, Linda," says Steve. He swallows, clicks his tongue, and shoots her with his right index finger.

"It's Belinda."

"Sure, whatever," he says. "Anyway . . ."

As Steve inhales his food at the speed of the starving, the conversation is dominated by his day. Between and during mouthfuls, he tells them about the deal he has just closed with a couple of Brits who have paid over half a million quid on a villa, with a pool, just outside San Gimignano. "A nice place," he says. "Amazingly, it was worth half as much three years ago. You lot are sitting on gold mines here. The valley's not much to write home about, but you're so close to San Jimmy you're bloody laughing."

Everyone smiles and quietly congratulates themselves on the increased value of their own property, pleasantly aware of their fabulous foresight in getting their place in the sun ahead of the herd.

While Barbara serves her signature avocado-stuffed chicken breasts in a cream sauce, Steve enlightens the table on the price of reroofing Derek's chestnut barn with reclaimed terra-cotta tiles. Belinda sits, her elbows in, her head cocked to one side, a fixed smile on her face as she pretends to listen.

Howard has requisitioned his waterglass as a backup wine container and lost control of his facial muscles. The more Steve talks, the more Howard drinks—and the farther his cheeks slide off his skull and his body slips under the table.

Barbara punctuates Steve's stories and assertions with appreciative glances and little moans of agreement.

Derek nods away knowledgeably, while Mary eats her food quietly and counts the minutes until she can go home.

"Do you know they're tarmacking the white roads in the next-door valley?" asks Steve, his spoon pointed in the air, his pink strawberries-and-*pannacotta* pudding spinning in his open mouth, like clothes in a washing machine.

"Oh, really?" says Barbara.

"Mm," he continues. "They'll probably be doing it to yours soon."

"I shouldn't think so for a minute." Belinda smiles.

"Why?" asks Steve.

"Because we would know about it," says Belinda, with a quick sip of wine. "There is nothing that goes on in the valley that we and, certainly, *I* don't know about."

"She's right, you know," insists Derek, his eyes watering from the wine. "She knows everything that goes on in this valley. She is the Contessa, after all."

"Honestly, Derek, shush." Belinda tweaks her artistic outfit.

"Did you know an American's moving into your valley?" asks Steve, pushing his empty pudding bowl toward the middle of the table.

"I'm afraid we've all known that for a long time." Belinda gives a confident little laugh.

"We have?" asks Howard, his whole body wobbling with the effort of conversation.

"Oh, yes," asserts Belinda, her eyes narrowing.

"Oh, right." Howard looks quizzical. "I wonder what sort of American buys a near wreck of a property in central Tuscany?"

"I don't have a clue," giggles Barbara with a little shrug.

"An intriguing one," says Howard, tapping the side of his increasingly red nose.

"And a rich one," adds Steve. "Because that house hasn't got any water."

"It hasn't?" asks Barbara.

"Well, that's what I was told," says Steve, with a knowledgeable sniff.

"People are always saying that about the houses around here," Belinda puts in. "I mean, they said it about mine."

"But yours didn't," says Howard, leaning on an elbow that slips across the table.

"It did, actually, Howard, if you remember correctly," says Belinda crisply. "It just ran out when I filled my enormous swimming pool."

"Your pool isn't that big," states Howard.

"Well," says Belinda, her mouth pursed, "at least I have one."

"Shall we go and sit soft?" asks Barbara.

"Good idea, my love," says Derek, placing his palms on the table and scraping his chair along the flagstone floor as he hauls himself up.

"So, you've known about the American for a while, then?" asks Steve, pushing his chair back under the table.

"Oh, yes," says Belinda, trying to sound jaded. "Roberto and I have been talking about it for a while now. In fact, Derek and I were discussing it only the other day, weren't we, Derek?"

"Absolutely, Contessa, just the other day," confirms Derek.

"So you knew they were planning to open a hotel?" asks Steve, with a broad, pleased grin painted all over his face.

Belinda is too shocked to move. Atrophied by the surprise information, the notion of competition makes her blood run cold.

"A hotel?" says Barbara. "That's nice."

"With a bar?" asks Howard.

"Or a spa?" Barbara giggles.

"I'm not sure about the details," says Steve, walking through into the sitting room.

"Well, that *is* news to us," admits Derek. "Can I get any of you a sticky to accompany your chocolates? Barbara? My love? Anything for you?"

"Ooh, Mr. Hewitt!" She giggles, shoving her husband's shoulder.

Belinda is left alone with Mary in the dining room. "A hotel? Right here in my valley?" Belinda whispers slowly, holding the back of her chair for support. "Maria darling," she says suddenly. Mary gets out of her seat. "Maria darling," she repeats loudly, her face composed, her smile stiff, as she walks into the sitting room. "Barbara, dear, I have a feeling that the foie gras must have been off. I feel terrible, and have been struck down by a sudden and desperate desire to go home." She pauses as if draining her last reserves of energy. *"Arrivadeary!"*

"Oh, poor you, absolutely!" exclaims Barbara, rushing over. "You go home, *arrivadeary,* dear, *arrivadeary!"*

"Arrivadeary," the others reply.

Sabato ✢ Saturday

Clima ✢ *fa caldo* (Hot!)

Siamo aperto! We are open! Let my glorious hospitality commence! I know it sounds a little different, and not at all English, but I do love all the busy hard work of the beginning of the season. It is such fun! It is so invigorating.

It will probably also sound a little odd to those of you who are unfortunate enough to live in the city, but the beginning of the holiday season is just like when one of nature's seasons comes into my valley. It is like the germinating and the harvesting of the sunflowers, the changing and the falling of the leaves, the final gathering of the plump, ripe, oil-producing olives. So the beginning of the tourist season always heralds for me the start of summer.

And the long hot summers in Italy are so lovely. Blissfully warm days when the sky is azure and cloudless. There is not a breath of wind to stir the trees, and the swallows swoon to dip their wings in my lovely swimming pool. The evenings are just as wonderful. There is no greater pleasure than sitting on one's terrace, looking down into one's valley with a small drink in one's hand, watching the fireflies displaying to each other. Sometimes I am filled with such joy that all I want to do is don something floaty I bought in the market and run through the fields of poppies near the Bianchi farm.

I honestly can't believe how lucky I am. I remember the time I used to waste looking through the property sections of newspapers, watching programs on television, talking about buying places with my friends, and ever since I lost my husband I have been living the dream. Now I watch those shows from my own place in the sun. Whoever said that life begins at forty (or indeed forty-four) is entirely correct!

Anyway, my delightful Belgians arrive today. As I sit here at my desk, overlooking my valley, listening to birdsong, the Bianchis' water pump and the other comings and goings of peasant life, Maria is downstairs in the kitchen cooking up a relaxed, yet light, *italiano* storm. She is, fortunately, a professional. And, take it from me, having worked in the hostessing profession for five years now, I know it is the detail and the atmosphere that count. Detail and atmosphere are the hostess's mantra. Spaghetti Bolognese on its own is fine, but eat it at a table with a small vase of hand-picked spring flowers and it is sure to taste better. Another tip for the budding hostess is to keep the cuisine local.

Only last night my dear friend Barbara suffered a culinary disaster by serving some *franglais* dish that she had picked up somewhere— pâté and stuffed chicken are not the first choices when it comes to *italiano* food. But fortunately it didn't hold us back. We managed to have one of those flowing, relaxed, loose suppers again, like we always do.

The famous writer Howard Oxford turned up. He'd managed to tear himself away from his desk and his sure-to-be bestseller and make it across the valley. He regaled us with witty stories and sharp anecdotes about his glamorous life in London. A regular at Casa Mia,

Howard is a dinner party must-have on the social scene *di Toscana*. Derek and Barbara were their usual generous souls and had invited a well-known interior designer called Stephen. He filled us in with some great property stories and what we should be doing with our curtains this season! He also confirmed what I already knew—that an American was moving in on the other side of the valley. We all sat back and applauded their courage, myself especially, as the Casa Padronale is unfortunately renowned for not having any water. So the poor devil is going to have to put in a big pump, at great expense, and haul it up, liter by liter, drop by drop, from the valley floor. It may well end up putting him off all together! We shall see. . . .

POLLO DI CASA MIA

This is one of my very special signature dishes that I inherited from my mother and brought with me all the way from the U.K., and to which I have added a little twist to keep it local and terribly Italian. I find it works best with trestle tables, packed with long-lost friends, on one of those hot summer days that just go and on and on forever. (Although possibly not in the U.K., of course.)

Do try to make enough of it so that when the sun is setting, and the wine and conversation are still flowing, there are still some moist chunks for you to tease off the bones with your fingers. (Don't tell Mother I said that!)

- chicken
- lemon
- rosemary
- garlic
- olive oil

Take a free-range happy chicken that once roamed a farmyard with friends. (In Italy these are often rather bizarrely found with their heads, feet, and innards still attached.) Anyway, find one large enough to feed all your friends. Cut up the lemon, some garlic, and a few sprigs of rosemary, which I seem to be able to grow abundantly in my herb garden, and stuff them inside the bird. Cover the skin with olive oil and roast until done.

Serve generously with cold white wine in the heat of a baking hot Italian summer.

❈ ❈ ❈

CHAPTER THREE

Belinda has been up since the crack of dawn. Having drunk three cups of coffee with Hermesetas on the run, she is now pacing her terrace, working off the caffeine overdose her binoculars hanging around her neck. For the past ten minutes her routine has been the same. Dressed in her navy easy-on trousers, with elasticated waist, and a short-sleeved flowered shirt. Her hair styled like that of a genius on the verge of a great discovery. She marches to the end of the terrace, stands by a pot of pink geraniums, and exhales loudly. She then tugs at her bottom lip, stares at the Casa Padronale through her binoculars, spins on the bare sole of her foot, and returns to the comfort and convenience of her lounger, where she maintains an all-too-brief seated position, before repeating the whole process all over again.

"Mum?" asks Mary, arriving on the terrace, dressed only in a large T-shirt and underwear. Her slim legs are just beginning to change color in the sun. "What on earth are you doing?" she asks, rubbing her eyes, which are still puffy with sleep. Belinda doesn't appear to hear. "Mum?" she repeats. "What are you doing?"

"What?" says Belinda, finally grinding to a halt.

"What are you doing?"

"Oh?" says Belinda, her arms hanging by her sides. "Oh," she repeats. "I'm just worrying . . . I think."

"Oh," says Mary. "Whoever you're thinking about, I'm sure that spying on them isn't going to make any difference."

"I'm not spying," protests Belinda.

"What are you doing, then?"

"Looking."

"You're doing a lot more than that."

"Well, looking closely, then," admits Belinda.

"Yeah, well, it sure looks like spying to me," says Mary, turning to go back into the kitchen. "Do you want some coffee?" she asks.

"No," says Belinda, walking back to the edge of the terrace, fiddling with her binoculars. "Oh, go on, then, yes," she adds, with a flap of her hand. "I may as well die of something, and caffeine poisoning is as good a way to go as any."

"So, what have you found out?" asks Mary, over her shoulder.

"What?" says Belinda, distracted.

"What have you seen?"

"Well," says Belinda. Her eyes strain through the lenses and her short tongue sticks out of her mouth as she surveys the valley below. "Not much, not much." She stiffens as she spots something. Like a feline predator tensing before the kill, she takes a tentative step forward. "But there is definitely something going on down there," she says.

"I've seen at least three people walking around. Here's one of them now."

"Can you see the American?" Mary is back on the terrace, hands on her hips, waiting for the kettle to boil.

"Don't be stupid, I have no idea what he looks like."

"Well, you know, anyone who looks American?"

"If you mean someone in loud shorts the size of a beach ball, then no, I haven't," says Belinda, her tongue flicking in and out with concentration as she tries to follow a moving, and extremely diminutive figure below.

"Can I have a look?"

"No," says Belinda, holding on to her binoculars tightly. "You have no idea what you're looking for. Hasn't that kettle boiled yet?"

"I'll have a look," replies Mary, and wanders back into the kitchen.

The diminutive figure in jeans and a white top goes back inside the Casa Padronale and fails to rematerialize. Like a sniper with his weapon trained on enemy lines, Belinda doesn't move. She keeps her position. In fact, she moves a step closer. Elbows out, eyes unblinking, she searches the countryside for more targets. She scours the land in and around the Casa Padronale. She combs the long, unkempt grass in and around the two fig trees in front of the house, and between the nine or ten olive trees to the right. Nothing. The track that leads from the house to the white road is also empty.

"There doesn't seem to be any car," she mutters to herself. "They either walked or they were dropped off before dawn."

"Have you been here since dawn?" asks Mary, holding two mugs of coffee.

"Pretty much . . ."

"Gosh," she says, as she sits down on the steps at the edge of the terrace, sleepily staring into space, before blowing on her cup and taking a tentative sip. "Don't you think you're overreacting a bit?"

"Overreacting?" Belinda spins around. Her binoculars follow a full second later and hit her on the chest. "Overreacting? Are you accusing me of overreacting? Do you have any idea what this could mean to us? To me? To you and me? To my business? To your livelihood? To your future inheritance?" Mary's mouth hangs open. "The American could ruin us. His arrival— in my valley—could be the end of our world! Do you understand what that means? Do you?" By now Belinda is somewhat hysterical. The combination of too much wine last night, too much coffee this morning, and foie gras constipation has made her both jumpy and irritable. "Do you?" she repeats. "Because from where I'm standing it doesn't sound like it!"

"It's just a bit of healthy competition," says Mary, in her softest, most placatory voice.

"Since when has competition ever been healthy?"

"Since—"

"Since never!" screams Belinda, throwing her fat-fingered hands in the air. She marches up to her steaming coffee and takes a large, hot swig. Mary inhales. "Ouch!" Her mother exhales immediately, spitting her mouthful of coffee across the terrace. "Jesus Christ, that hurt!" she shouts, covers her mouth with one hand, and stares aggressively at the cup. "That coffee's bloody hot!"

"I've only just made it," explains Mary. Belinda cannot reply. "Anyway," she continues, compensating for her mother's burned silence, "he's not in competition with you."

"He's not?" she mumbles, Belinda's voice is uncharacteristically quiet.

"No," she explains. "He's opening a hotel, and you run a B-and-B."

"An upmarket B-and-B," corrects Belinda.

"An upmarket B-and-B, then, but it's still a different market," insists Mary. "I mean, when have you thought, Should I stay in a B-and-B, or Should I stay in a hotel? You might think, Should I stay in an expensive hotel or a cheap hotel? But not, Should I stay in a hotel or a B-and-B? It's a totally different experience." She struggles on. "One is about being made to feel part of a family, part of someone's home, the other is about being part of nothing. You pay your money, you take your room, you use the facilities, and then you leave. That's it." Mary smiles. "It's not competition. In fact, they could complement each other."

"Complement, you say," says Belinda, her hand still over her mouth.

"Absolutely." Mary nods.

"And that's good?"

"Very good."

Belinda sits down on her striped lounger. "That's okay, then."

"Mum?" asks Mary.

"Mmm?" says Belinda, licking her pink burnt lips with her equally pink and burnt tongue.

"Are you feeling okay?"

"Not really, no," she admits, putting her hot coffee slowly down on the terrace. "I didn't sleep very well. In fact, I feel a little odd."

"Why don't you go and have a lie-down?"

"Do you think?"

"Well, you have guests arriving in a couple of hours, so perhaps you should relax a bit before they turn up."

"I think you're right," says Belinda, limply running her hands through her hair. "I think I'll go."

With her mother taken to her bed, Mary is now free to wander the house, poke through its four bedrooms, and leaf through her mother's things, trying to remember if anything has changed from last year. The two downstairs guest rooms in the old animal *cantinas* are exactly the same. Simple and white, with double beds, wooden chairs, and vases of dried sunflowers, they have their own separate entrances, almost *en-suite* bathrooms, and lower-level terraces with red geraniums in plant pots at each corner. Above on the next floor are the kitchen and sitting room area with french windows onto the other raised terrace—home to Belinda's lounger, binoculars, and various other assorted potted plants.

Unlike the guests' area, this floor has undergone a myriad of little tweaks and changes. Her father's favorite armchair has been recovered in something more bronze, beautiful, and more befitting of Tuscany. The telephone has been upgraded to incorporate an answering machine, and there is a new silver-edged mirror in the hall. The computer and the sturdy computer desk are still the same, as is the large round café table on the patio to the left of the front door and right by the road, where Belinda serves all her guests' meals. The second floor appears less revamped. Belinda's quarters, a large purple bedroom with a terra-cotta-tiled floor and an expansive turquoise bathroom, have remained unchanged in the five years that she has lived at Casa Mia. In Mary's small white room, with a shower and basin in one corner, there is a new single bed with a springy mattress. Last year's complaints of backache and broken springs obviously did not fall entirely on deaf ears.

Back outside, the air is warm and the strong morning sun inviting. Barefoot, Mary pads around the terrace, looking at the pots of pink geraniums lined up on the floor. She inhales the sweet scent of the yellow climbing rose that clings to the lattice on the side of the house, and watches the green lizards run into the cracks in the walls as she approaches.

She walks down the stone steps cut into the side of the hill toward the small kidney-shaped swimming pool. Belinda put it in with only the most demanding guests in mind; she is not a great fan of swimming, and, as a result, the water is still unheated and in some serious need of maintenance. Mary dips in one foot. The water is not as cold as it looks. The heat of the sun has taken away the toe-curling chill. She sits down on the edge, her legs outstretched and her heels skimming the surface as she gazes at the valley below. The screaming sound of the Bianchis' giant saw drifts up the hill, and, if Mary half closes her eyes, she can see Franco and his older brother Marco slowly feed the trunks toward the whirling blade. Mary smiles. The curl of her mouth is mirrored at the corners of her brown eyes. Franco's naked chest is most certainly broader and more defined than his brother's. Not that it matters much because Mary hardly ever dares to speak to either of them. She has nodded and smiled at all the members of the Bianchi family, and even held the grandmother's shaking hand, but she has never engaged them in conversation. When Franco comes around to Casa Mia to help her mother out of some tight DIY spot, Mary always finds it easier to make herself scarce. Anyway, even from this distance, she finds it embarrassing to stare.

She picks herself up and makes her way back to the front of the house. With its smart thick gravel drive and rampant stone lions mounted on pillars at the entrance, Casa Mia presents an awful lot of swagger to the road. Mary walks down the short drive, picking up stones between her toes. Standing at the gate, she deadheads the wild red rose that seems determined to grow up the garden wall. As she pulls off the hips, making way for more blooms, she hears the sound of an approaching car. Before she has a chance to hide, a blue Jeep slows to make the corner by the house. The smoked windows are closed, but the strong sun reveals two silhouettes, one in a baseball cap. Mary stands and waves. "The American," she mutters, as she glimpses a hand wave back.

Mary turns and, clutching her round bosom in one hand, her shoulders hunched, her eyes concentrating on the ground, she picks her way through the stones, goes into the house and on up the stairs. She knocks on her mother's door. "Mum?"

"Mmm?" A groan travels under the crack below the door.

"Hi, Mum, it's gone ten," says Mary.

"Mmm," replies Belinda.

"I think I saw the American drive past a moment ago," says Mary, and waits for the reaction.

"Wha-a-at?" Belinda squawks, like a turkey that's just heard about Christmas. "Wha-a-at?" she repeats, and swings open the bedroom door. Dressed in a crumpled white nightdress that comes to her calves and her dark hair standing to attention; the whole look is post-election-victory Cherie Blair.

"Yep." Mary nods. "Just now. They drove past. I waved."

"You waved?"

"Yes."

"What did you do that for?"

"I was trying to be friendly."

"Friendly? Why would you want to do that?" Belinda scratches her head. "Which direction was the car headed?"

"They were off down the valley to the house."

"What do you mean 'they'?"

"There were two of them."

"Two Americans?"

"It looks like it."

"Two," says Belinda, grimacing as if she has just encountered a terribly unpleasant smell. "Two Americans . . . I think I'd better get dressed."

Five minutes later, Belinda is back on the terrace in her navy blue easy-on trousers and floral shirt, binoculars at the ready, scouring the slopes of the valley. "Well, you were right," she announces to Mary. "The blue car is there and I can see three or four more men moving around. I wonder which one he is." She is trying to focus more tightly.

"Shall we go over and say hello?" suggests Mary.

"Absolutely not," says Belinda, her small blue eyes round with horror. "Pop in? Unannounced? What do you think I am? Desperate?"

"It was only a suggestion." Mary shrugs. "We could take them something."

"Don't be so ridiculous," says Belinda. "Anyway, we've got . . ." Her voice trails off, her ears are straining. "Oh, shit . . . Did you just hear a car?"

"A car?"

"Yes," says Belinda. The dull thud of a car door shutting comes down the hillside. "Oh, Jesus bloody Christ," hisses Belinda, her small eyes narrow. "Don't bloody tell me the bloody Belgian guests are bloody early, because I will bloody— Oh, hello!" Belinda's service-industry smile shoots into place. "Hello there!" She waves at a thin man standing at the wrought-iron gate near the top of the drive. "You're early!" she informs him, with a little light laugh. "Really bloody early!" she mutters, under her breath.

"I am very much sorry," says the thin man. "There was simply no traffics from Pisa."

"Go-o-od," says Belinda. "What, no traffic at all?"

"No traffics at all." He grins.

"Well, that really is . . . excellent."

"Shall we come here?" asks the thin man, pointing toward the front door.

"Yes, yes." Belinda nods. "In through there." She smiles. He turns. She sighs, and her shoulders collapse at the remembered wrist-slitting tedium of it all. "Here goes," she says to Mary. "Happy faces until the end of the September."

"Yup." Mary nods. "Happy faces."

"For God sake, Mary," adds Belinda, glancing at her half-naked daughter, "go and put some bloody clothes on."

Belinda walks briskly off the terrace and into her sitting room, trying to head the Belgians off at the pass. Like an assertive guard dog marking out its territory, she arrives at a trot, arms cocked and, fixed smile in place, circles the room rapidly closing drawers, doors and cupboards, occasionally standing in front of the limited happy snappy family shots.

The tall, thin Belgian and his equally tall, thin, limp-limbed wife appear oblivious to Belinda's corralling as each one of their forays into the sitting room and kitchen areas is blocked by their seemingly ebullient hostess. In a fine-tuned, well-practiced, two-pronged maneuver, Mary appears (now dressed in a pair of shorts and a smaller T-shirt) and takes their luggage downstairs, while Belinda escorts her guests on their one and only sortie to her terrace.

"This is my *terrazzo*," she explains slowly and pleasantly, like she's communicating with the aurally challenged. "And down there are your *terrazzi,* those two small, currently shaded areas over there. This is my private area that you are not allowed to enter. Or you may only enter at my invitation."

"Oh, very good," says the thin Belgian woman, nodding keenly, then peering over the edge. "Very good."

"Good." Belinda smiles. "There are a few other little house rules that I will quickly run through before you go to your bedroom. The pool is open between ten and six for swimming, at your own risk, of course." The Belgians nod. "No wet towels on the lawn—there is a special line for guests. I will do laundry, but only if I have to, and, of course, no smoking and no children are allowed anywhere in Casa Mia. You may use the telephone, but only if it is prearranged with me at a time convenient to me. I will not take messages except in an emergency."

Belinda inhales. "We provide meals at certain times, which are listed on the piece of paper on your bedside table. No sanitary towels down the lavatory and, of course, use water sparingly. We are in the countryside here. But if there are any questions," she reaches for her pleasant service smile, "do feel free to ask." She pauses and claps her hand to indicate that the talk and tour are over. "So welcome to Casa Mia."

"So to check, yes to orderings supper this evening?" asks the tall Belgian man.

"Yes." Belinda sighs. The sheer exhaustion of it all is getting to her already. "You have asked already."

"This is a sympathetic valley," says the thin Belgian woman, optimistically.

"Yes," agrees Belinda. "Below is the Val di Santa Caterina, which is owned in part by the Bianchi family, whose farmhouse you can see over there." She indicates with a pink-tipped nail. "Down there to your left is our local *ristorante,* where you will find *molto* local delicacies." Her voice is beginning to take on the tone of a tour guide: facts and figures gather a nasal pitch as they roll out of her mouth. "I have been living here for five years, my daughter comes out and helps every summer, we are twenty minutes from Serrana, our local Etruscan town, but if you need something difficult, like a doctor *chi parla inglese,* then Poggibonsi isn't far away." She stops, smiles, and covers her mouth with her hand. "Oh, but you won't be needing one of those, will you?" She laughs. "Being *francesi!*"

"Yes," agrees the tall Belgian man.

"Right . . . anyway," says Belinda, placing her palms together. "I'll leave you to unpack in your room."

"Yes," says the tall Belgian man, not moving.

"Good," says Belinda, after a short pause. "So off and out . . . straightaway . . . after you've unpacked?"

"Pardon?" asks the Belgian woman.

"Out of the house? Sightseeing?" asks Belinda, nodding away as if it is a tremendously good idea. "Poggibonsi?"

"Oh, no." The Belgian woman smiles with equally tremendous enthusiasm. "We stay here."

"You're staying here?" says Belinda, making no effort to disguise the annoyance, irritation, and lack of humor in her voice in any way at all. "Oh," she says. "What? Here? All day?"

"Oh, yes," says the Belgian man, with a smile. "All day here." His bony finger points toward Belinda's *terrazza* by way of emphasis.

"Oh," says Belinda, remembering her pleasant smile. "No lunch for you two, then," she says, wagging her finger. "I'm afraid we simply never do guests lunch! Ever. At all. And there are no exceptions."

"Oh, we know." The Belgian woman smiles, indicating the plastic bag in her husband's hand. "We have a picnic."

"A picnic?"

Belinda is so bowled over by the fantastically rude concept of someone actually picnicking in her own house that she does not quite know what to say. Her teeth clench and her eyes water. She stands with her arms straight, gently tapping her frustration into the side of her legs as she watches her new guests make their particularly Belgian way down to their room. Everything—from *her* short, jaunty principal-boy haircut to *his* small leather lady bag, which he seemingly carries everywhere with him—annoys her. As they disappear in their "his and hers" polo shirts in pink and pistachio, all Belinda can do is let out a frustrated moan from the depths of her chest. "This is going to be a ba-a-d day," she says.

Standing on her terrace, she has no idea what to do, or where to put herself. The presence of the munching, crunching continentals on the floor below is deeply unsettling: not only are they using her facilities when they should be out on a nice long day trip to the medieval Manhattan, San Gimignano, or at least Poggibonsi, their presence in her house all afternoon means that Belinda is unable to get on with her usual after-noon chores.

Since their arrival she hasn't had time to telephone Barbara to thank her for last night's dinner, or even think about con-tacting Franco about his tidying away some flagstones or the remains of the drystone wall that runs alongside the terrace. The tension in the air makes her a little snappy. Couple this with the comings and goings down at the Casa Padronale, and Belinda is so overcome with nervous exhaustion that she has to take a gentle lie-down on her lounger to gather her thoughts.

But she is unable to keep still, and while Mary works away in the kitchen preparing supper, Belinda leaves her lounger at regular intervals and tiptoes to the edge of her terrace, peering over at the guests below. Performing a rather complicated and, indeed, athletic form of a yogic stretch, she leans, one leg in the air, her toes pointed, holding her breath for fear of alerting them to her voyeurism. Sadly, all she glimpses is a pair of puffy pink feet and a yellowed set of toenails that last saw the sun on a week's winter break to Marrakech in December last year.

After about half an hour Belinda's curiosity gets the better of her. She walks inside to the kitchen to find Mary, pink-cheeked and sweaty, doing battle with a hefty Polyfilla of a sauce.

"Oh, God, hi," says Mary, looking up from her bowl. Her long dark hair is separated into sweaty strands under the strain of catering. Her cheekbones glow. Her forearm beats a vicious circle. "I think this might be a little thick."

"Mmm," agrees Belinda, her mind most certainly on higher things. "Water it down," she says, with a small domestic wave. "I would help, dear, only I have an awful lot to do."

"Fine," says Mary, nodding. "Water it down, water it down," she mutters and walks toward the tap.

While Mary adds cold water to her cheese sauce, Belinda is upstairs in her room, leafing through her wardrobe for something suitable to garden in. Her purple bedroom with its terra-cotta-tiled floor is a complicated mixture of eclectic styles. The wardrobe is a large, square MFI affair, inherited from the divorce. Originally white with a carved filigree border around the double doors, it represents one of Belinda's least successful DIY moments. Streaked and smudged with swirls of blue and lilac paint, the botched, blotched, rag-rolled look is a long way from the lapis-lazuli effect she was after. The bed, however, is more successful. With long sheets of swooping pale green silk tacked to the ceiling with a combination of drawing pins and nails, Belinda has created the effect (when viewed not too closely) of a glamorous four-poster bed. The same silk covers the dressing table and its accompanying chair, giving the whole room a suitably coordinated feel.

Belinda stands on a small square of matting that declares itself to be a rug, and flicks her way through her hangers. The black gypsy look from last night, the floral dress, her drawstring trousers, her blue nylon A line, which somehow made the journey from the U.K., and a cream rayon blouse that sets her teeth on edge when she touches it. Eventually she finds what she's looking for: a pale blue cotton artist's smock that came free

with a magazine on watercolor painting that she once subscribed to. She pulls it over her head and ties it up at the sides.
She finds a red-and-white-spotted man's handkerchief in one
of her drawers and knots it under her hair. With a glance at herself in the mirror in her turquoise-tiled bathroom to ensure
total artistic effect, she wafts back past Mary, announcing something along the lines that she has urgent pruning to do.

❀ ❀ ❀

"Oh, hello there!" says Belinda, sounding surprised, as she
smiles her way through a lavender bush with a small pair of secateurs in her hand. "I wasn't expecting you to be on the terrace
sunning yourself." She snips. "Do carry on."

"Hello there, Mrs. Smith," says the thin Belgian man.

"Oh, do call me Belinda." She comes alongside the lavender
for a better view.

"Okay, Belinda, my name is Bernard and my wife is Brigitte,"
says Bernard, smiling from his deck chair.

With a luminously white body, Bernard is sitting in a pair of
diminutive beige swimming shorts gently reflecting the sun.
His body hair is sparse, and what little there is coats his arms
and legs in the shape of fun-fur rubber gloves and knee socks.
The rest of him is almost entirely bald, save for a circle that
trims each nipple like furniture fringing. His arms are thin, his
stomach concave, and his legs so wide apart that through the
right leg of his shorts sprouts the small string bag that contains
his balls.

"You have very nice view here." He opens his legs wider,
leaning forward to indicate the *bella vista* beyond.

"I know." Belinda's nostrils flare, and her eyes are uncontrollably drawn to his crotch. "We're very lucky here." She tries to
turn away, then looks straight back at the bag of balls.

"I like views very much," shares Bernard.

"Yes, yes, very good view," adds Brigitte, appearing behind him in a black industrial-strength one-piece bathing suit with low legs and large foam bra cups that funnel her breasts into hard points. Her long, skinny white legs are covered with a blue-marbled veined effect, rather like Stilton cheese.

"Oh, Brigitte," says Bernard, twisting in his chair. Belinda winces as his strained right leg operates a vicelike pincer movement on the string bag. She waits for his voice to rise an octave, but he does not seem to notice. "This is Belinda."

"Very nice, thank you." Brigitte smiles.

"Good," says Belinda, snipping more new growth off her lavender bush. "Did you have a nice lunch?" she asks, nodding toward the table that is laden with half a baguette, a couple of large tomatoes, a Camembert, and a family-size packet of crisps.

"Oh, yes, super good," replies Brigitte.

"There's nothing like fresh air to give you an appetite," says Belinda.

"Oh, yes—*bon appétit!*" says Bernard, raising a plastic tooth mug of rosé wine.

"Alcohol as well?" Belinda beheads almost the entire bush as she stumbles and falls.

"Oh, *attention!*" says Bernard, leaping out of his seat. "Are you okay?" he asks, his arms outstretched as he towers above her. Belinda is horizontal on her lawn. She looks up at Bernard. He is gazing at her with concern, but his shorts remain in the same crumpled position and down his right leg swings the small string bag.

"Bernard!" says his wife, her eyes trained urgently on his crotch.

"Oh," he says, looking swiftly between his legs. "Pardon

me," he adds, as he posts his balls back into his shorts with a deft tweak of his fingers.

"No, no, fine," says Belinda, getting to her feet and smoothing down the blue artist's smock. "Just glad you're settling in." She speedily picks up her secateurs and turns away. "We serve supper at seven thirty. No later, otherwise you won't get any."

The ball-bag incident is enough to put Belinda off spying for the rest of the afternoon. Instead, she takes herself down to the kidney-shaped swimming pool and, between little rests, busies herself watering and gently weeding the surrounding garden. On lazy afternoons she likes to invite Franco up to Casa Mia to perform such services and follows him around, admiring the rippling and flexing muscles in his back while pointing out the occasional particularly tricky weed. This afternoon, however, she is grateful for the distraction. With Mary cluttering up the kitchen, and her guests displaying their private parts, there is precious little sanctuary for her. But it is all exhausting work. By the time Belinda is ready for her presupper cocktail at five thirty, her mouth is well and truly parched.

"Honestly, what a day," she says to Mary, as she rattles around the kitchen getting herself some ice. "I've had no sleep, and I've had to deal with one trauma after another. And then to be confronted by Bernard's parts is enough to put any woman off her pruning." She takes a large sip of her large gin and exhales in a satisfied manner. "That's much better. I'm beginning to feel human again," she says. "So?" she asks. She puts her head up and takes in, for the first time, the chaos of the kitchen. There are three pans on the go, two dirty chopping boards, one greasy mixing bowl, and an odd, slightly acrid smell coming from the cooker. "Everything all right in here?" She opens the oven door to find a foaming dish of cream-colored something. "Yuk," she says, her short nose curling. "What the hell is that?"

"Macaroni and cheese," says Mary, running sprigs of moribund rocket under the tap.

"Oh."

"I watered it down like you said, and the sauce separated," she explains, her head bowed into the sink. "There was nothing I could do." She continues washing the salad, waiting for her mother's anger to march into the room.

Belinda takes another slug of her gin. "Oh, well," she says eventually. "Grate a whole load of cheese on top and I'm sure no one will notice. Anyway, from what I've seen so far, these Belgians are a couple of plebeian tourists who wouldn't know good food if it ran them over." She takes another sip of gin. "They appear to live on bread and cheese, so pasta and cheese won't make a blind bit of difference." She smiles. "So far they've been nothing but an irritating pain in the arse, and I'd be quite happy if they never came back, or recommended us to any of their ghastly friends. I'm going to suggest they eat in Poggibonsi tomorrow. It's their sort of place." She takes another sip of her gin, drains the glass, and goes to fix herself another drink. "D'you know?" she continues, unscrewing the green bottle, "you can always tell what people are going to be like from their first inquiry. I particularly remember this lot because they asked about walking. I can't stand people who walk. It's a miracle I allowed them to come and stay in the first place. Mark my words, darling, they won't notice the food at all."

❋ ❋ ❋

However, by the time Belinda serves the second spoonful of macaroni and cheese onto the surprisingly heavy plate, she realizes that even Howard Oxford's unkempt, unhappy, underfed mongrel would notice the food. So far Bernard and Brigitte have made all the right noises about sitting on the terrace under the stars. They have tucked into the chunky slices of salami and charred slivers of aubergine and red pepper that Mary had put together as an antipasto. In fact, they have been really rather polite, drinking their wine, regaling Belinda with stories of the lifesaving operations they perform on sick children in Brussels between dense, chewy mouthfuls.

"Macaroni and cheese," announces Belinda, with hopefully blinding confidence, as she places a helping in front of Bernard, moving a candle to prevent his closer inspection of the slowly separating mixture that oozes across his plate. "And salad." She puts a rather large bunch of leaves on top of the pasta.

The man feigns great interest, and, passing his long nose over his plate, he inhales.

"Mmm. Super good."

"Brigitte?" asks Belinda.

"Oh, super good," Brigitte runs a quick eye over the food, "but I am in fact on regime, so salads for me."

"Too many crisps earlier today?" Belinda smiles.

"Yes, too many crips," agrees Brigitte.

"Darling?" asks Belinda, addressing Mary.

"Um . . ." Mary hesitates.

"I think it is only fair that you share in your culinary triumph," suggests Belinda, and adds another spoonful to Mary's already full plate. "Seeing as there's so much here."

"So most interesting," says Bernard, as he chews slowly. "Why an Englishwoman lives on her own ways in Italy?"

"Oh, Bernard," smiles Belinda, taking a sip of her almost empty glass of white wine and serving herself a few leaves. "A clever, educated pediatrician like you should be able to work something like that out. . . ." She giggles and pushes her breasts together with her elbows on the table in front of her.

"No, but please to go ahead, thank you very much," he says, nodding and chewing.

"It's a very long story," says Belinda, pouring herself some more wine, "but you are right about one thing, Bernard," she adds. "It is *molto interessante. . . .*"

Belinda tells the well-practiced story of her arrival in Italy. The trials and tribulations that she went through—doing up her house, finding the right shutters and tiles. The workmen she had to deal with. The artisans she got to know on the way. And how she bought all the linen they are sleeping in from a super little stall in Serrana market.

"I washed it in warm soapsuds and left it on the lawn to dry in the natural bleach of the midday sun. Just like in *Under the Tuscan Sun*. I'm sure you must have read it?" The Belgians shake their heads. "Anyway, I now keep a diary as well," she continues. "It's full of little *aperçus.*"

"*Aperçus,*" they echo.

"Yes," she says, with an intelligent smile. "And *pensées . . .*" She hands Mary the salad bowl to clear away. "And recipes."

"Recipes." They smile, looking down at the food.

"Super good," says Brigitte.

"Yes." Belinda inhales her own geniality. "Super good."

"Mum?" asks Mary.

"*Sì, Maria,*" she replies.

"There are lights on at the Casa Padronale. Do you think they've moved in?"

"No? What? Impossible!" Belinda springs out of her seat and looks down the valley. "Oh," she says, frowning, "you're right. There is a light."

"Do you think they've moved in?" asks Mary again.

"They can't have, the place is uninhabitable."

"Well, how else do you explain that?" asks Mary, pointing down at a light between the trees. "Unless it's burglars."

"Burglars?" asks Belinda, wobbling with confusion and too much alcohol.

"Yes."

"I think we'd better go and investigate," announces Belinda, her finger pointing decisively in the air.

"What—now?" asks Mary, still holding the salad bowl.

"Well," says Belinda, turning to look at her paying guests.

"No, no," they both say. "Please to do . . ."

❀ ❀ ❀

Two minutes later, with her guests still at the dinner table tucking into shop-bought *tiramisù* that Belinda forgot to pass off as her own, mother and daughter are in the car heading off down the hill to investigate. Belinda is in her floral frock and *mercato* hat, while Mary is still in her shorts and T-shirt. They pass the trattoria, which looks quite full for this time of year, and speed on down the hill past the Bianchis' farm, and Derek and Barbara's, just making the sharp right turn under the pole.

The drive is dark and difficult, overgrown with long grass and riddled with potholes; Mary and Belinda bounce up and down as they career along.

"No one could be down here," says Belinda, holding on firmly to her bosom.

"Look! There's the light again," says Mary, peering over the steering wheel. "It's not far now, is it?"

"I don't know," exclaims Belinda, throwing her arms into the air, then immediately regretting it. "I've only been here once and that was five years ago."

"Oh," says Mary, pulling to a halt. "Here we are . . . I think."

They sit in the car. With the headlights switched off, the

driveway is pitch black and the silence is only broken by the gentle ticking of the engine as it cools.

"Are you sure about this, Mum?" asks Mary. "I mean, it could be anyone hanging around here late at night; poachers, vagrants . . ."

"I know." Belinda nods, determinedly tapping the tops of her thighs. "But it could also be the American."

"I can't see a thing," says Mary, her face pressed against the window. "Are you sure you don't want to turn around and come back tomorrow?"

"And miss out on being the first to meet him?" asks Belinda, sounding somewhat incredulous.

"Okay, here goes, then," says Mary, climbing gingerly out of the car.

"Here goes," says Belinda, straightening the brim of her hat. They slam the car doors.

"What do you think?" asks Mary. "Over there?"

"Sssh," says Belinda, finding her mouth with her finger. "I can hear something."

They pick their way through the long grass in what they think is the direction of the house. There is a loud scraping sound of stone against stone, and suddenly a door opens, bathing the two women in light.

"Hello?" comes an American voice.

"Hello?" replies Belinda, as she stares directly into the light. Head up, eyes looking down her short nose, she makes her way toward the gap in the door. "Hello," she says again, exuding neighborly confidence. But just as she reaches the steps, her fashion flip-flops slip on the grass and send her flying toward the ground. "God, damn it! Shit!" she yelps, as she lands, tits first, on the grass.

"Hello? Who's there?" comes the voice.

"Hi there," says Belinda, peering out from underneath her *mercato* hat, valiantly maintaining that the show is still on the road. Her voice sounds strangely English. "We're looking for the *americano,*" slurs Belinda, still managing to sound patronizing as she gets onto all fours. She clears her throat. "The American," she says again. "We're looking for the American."

"Well, I'm American," says the voice.

A slim, well-worked-out blonde steps out of the shadows. She is dressed in neat-fitting jeans, a white shirt, and flat shoes, her blonde hair is shoulder length, her arms brown and firm. She looks like she's in her thirties.

"Yes," says Belinda, dusting off grass and coming toward her. "Well, we're actually looking for the *americano.* You know, the man who's bought this villa." She smiles, her hand out ready to shake.

"I'm afraid *I'm* the person who owns this house. And last time I looked, I was, in fact, an *americana.*"

"Oh, good Lord," says Belinda, in an uncontrollably shrill voice. "A woman . . . how . . . Welcome to my—the valley. I'm Belinda Smith. This is my daughter Mary—or Maria . . ." Mary moves into the light.

"Hello," says the American. Her glossed mouth smiles, and her expensive hair swings.

"I'm Lauren. And my . . ." She turns toward a shadow in the background.

"Good, Lauren," interrupts Belinda rubbing her hands together. "Welcome to Toscana. Welcome to Val di Santa Caterina. Welcome to this little part of the world that I like to call home."

"Why, thank you." Lauren smiles. Her teeth are white and straight. She is most certainly attractive.

"I run the very upmarket bed-and-breakfast, higher up the

hill," says Belinda, pointing a chipped pink nail in the direction of Casa Mia. "You can't miss it."

"You do?" says Lauren. "That's good."

"So," Belinda rubs her hands together, "what are you doing here?"

"What am I doing here?" Lauren looks puzzled.

"Yes, what are you doing here?" persists Belinda, moving from one foot to the other.

"What am I doing here? What are *you* doing here? What are we all doing here?" Lauren laughs, briefly. "I'm here to make Tuscany work for me, pure and simple, just like everybody else in the place. Anyway . . ." She shrugs. Her hair swings as she turns. "If you'll excuse me, I'm right in the middle of something. You know, moving in . . ."

"Oh, yes, of course."

"So, see you around," says Lauren, in a tone that implies she won't. "Nice meeting you," she adds, with a wide, white, pleasant smile that Belinda recognizes only too well.

"Absolutely . . . right, yes, good," she says. "Um, how about—" Lauren shuts the door firmly behind her. "Oh? Right. *Arrivadeary!*" says Belinda, waving away in the dark.

Domenica ✳ Sunday

Clima ✳ *fa caldo* (Hot! Hot! Hot!)

It's another lovely summer's day in my corner of *Paradiso* and I'm just radiating joy. Sunday is a day that I particularly like to put aside for "me time." It is a day for quietness, relaxation, reflection, when I like to pamper myself and do a few little Italian things.

If I am not too exhausted from entertaining the night before, I try to get up nice and early. The mornings are so fresh, so young here, and there is simply no suggestion of the heat to come. After a light breakfast of toast and a little homemade preserves, I take myself, my easel, and my watercolors down the valley, and while away the early cool hours breathing in and soaking up nature. It is so much more pastoral here than it is in, say, England.

I love painting, I really do. It is one of my talents, and, I suppose, it was one of my many main reasons for coming to Italy in the first place. Italy is such an artistic place. It is a country just made for the watercolorists' canvas. It is a feast for the eyes! There is beauty and culture around almost every corner. Each time I go into Serrana market to buy my fresh fruit and vegetables (I eschew the cheaper supermarkets) I notice different things. The fabulous Medici carved crest on the walls of the clock tower, the arches above the windows of the Santa Croce church, the colors of the breast-feeding Madonna in one of the alcoves in the church. Only in Italy, from mere shopping trips for provisions, could you come back with an artistic memory to treasure!

After a long morning spent in observation, expressing myself, I tend to return to Casa Mia to change, and then I'm off down the hill to join my friends for lunch at Giovanna's. Well, when I say friends, I really mean my extended family—Derek and Barbara and, of course, the famous writer Howard Oxford.

Sundays at Giovanna's are packed and very Italian. People come from miles around to sample her homemade food. Sometimes the Bianchis tip up *en famille,* and occasionally the sporty girls who live in the monastery take a table. We all sit and talk about our busy lives. But it is so relaxed and comfortable. Sometimes hours can go by without the need to speak—although I shouldn't imagine that will be the case today as we have so much to gossip about! Not only do I have news of my lovely Belgian guests to share, but also that the American who has bought the really rather run-down property in the poor position opposite Casa Mia turns out to be a woman! Quite extraordinary!

We met last night. Maria and I popped over as a break from our busy entertaining schedule. She asked us in and was terribly friendly, but unfortunately we could not afford the time to stay and chat. I know she will be needing our friendship in the future. It is only a matter of a horrendous thunderstorm, or a total electricity blackout before she's on our doorstep desperate to be let in!

One can but admire her bravery in taking on such an obviously ruinous project on her own. I was in half a mind to have a little chat with her, and tell her what she's in for, if only to save her all that trouble! But I have found in life that people do have to learn by their own mistakes. She doesn't really look the part either. There's a touch of the skinny city dweller about her! Oh, well, I'm sure Giovanna's pasta will soon plump her up. Talking of which . . .

PASTA DI CASA MIA

This is a delicious, heartening, warming platter that I first tried with a Loyd Grossman sauce in the U.K. years ago, but have since perfected, tweaked, and made my own! I find it works best if you have spent a long day in the fields, or possibly working in the garden, as it needs a hearty Tuscan appetite to be properly appreciated.

* green tagliatelle pasta
* onions
* garlic
* olive oil
* tomatoes
* parsley

This dish is a showcase for the immense, round, lustrous, and rudely tasty tomatoes that I'm always sourcing in the market over here. So, take enough dried pasta (there really is no need to use fresh—the Italians don't!) for the amount of people you are feeding and cast it into a saucepan of vigorously boiling water. While the pasta is cooking, sweat some onions and garlic in your best olive oil, add to them some generously sliced, fecund tomatoes, and gently amalgamate. When it's all done, dish up and garnish with a plethora of parsley. Remember, the more generous you are, the more Tuscan it looks!

Serve at dusk with a warm laborer and plenty of wine.

✢ ✢ ✢

CHAPTER FOUR

Belinda has not slept very well at all. She comes downstairs contemplating the idea of updating her house-rules page on the computer, but decides she doesn't have the stomach for it. House rules require a rather vindictive concentration, and she is rather short of that at the moment.

Instead she paces around her kitchen and fills jam jars with water for her Sunday-morning watercoloring session. She is not sure whether it was the three glasses of steadying grappa that she had on her return from the Casa Padronale, or the Lauren encounter itself that disturbed her. Either way, she tossed and turned all night, and ended up with the sheets wrapped around her legs in some complicated yachting knot when she awoke.

Now, puffy-faced in her blue artist's smock, she slams cupboards and exhales unneccessarily as she searches for her brushes and paper. Fortunately, her Belgian surgeons are halfway to Siena, or there is no telling the lack of people skills they might have encountered.

It's Lauren's smile that replays most in her mind. Neat, tight, and barely lifting the corners of her mouth, it never showed any intention of reaching her eyes. It is a smile that Belinda employs often herself, so she understands its full, ghastly meaning only too well. It is pleasant and patronizing. It implies that the person you are talking to is stupid, and dull beyond belief. It also disguises superior mirth. It says that the other person is tiresome but her lack of grace and general witlessness has to be borne for the social cohesiveness of the rest the valley. Belinda knows that smile: she utilizes it all the time when she is with Barbara and Derek, and sometimes very occasionally the famous writer Howard Oxford. But maybe she imagined it. Maybe it's just the way the woman smiles. Maybe it's an American thing. Or, maybe, it was quite understandably directed at Mary.

"Mum, what are you muttering about?" asks Mary, as she clears away the breakfast trays from the terrace.

"What?" says Belinda, her face puckering with surprise.

"You're muttering, Mum, it sounded a bit strange."

"I was?"

"Yes," says Mary, putting down the heavy tray of condiments.

Bright and breezy, Mary appears unperturbed by her Lauren encounter. In fact, last night, while her mother downed grappa, Mary announced that she thought Lauren's arrival in the valley was a good thing, something that should be celebrated: it was always nice to have other women around. Needless to say, Belinda didn't entertain her daughter's point of view and reminded her, once again, on which side her bread was buttered.

"I don't know why you bother to do this," Mary announces, picking up a jam jar.

"Do what?" says Belinda, hands on her hips.

"You know, steaming the labels off the jars and putting handwritten ones on them." She is holding some Bonne Maman raspberry jam up to the light. "No one's fooled."

"I'm not trying to fool people," asserts Belinda. "It's just what they expect."

"They expect homemade jam."

"It's homemade," retorts Belinda, "just not in my home."

"So you're fooling them."

"No, I'm not. I can't help what people think," says Belinda, with a tight smile. "Anyway, isn't it time you went and made the beds? I've got some painting to fit in before lunch."

Belinda picks up her red box of paints from the kitchen table, with the jar of water and a pad of paper, then sets off for the farthest end of her garden and the view of the Casa Padronale.

Truth be known, of all the vistas Belinda could have painted on a Sunday morning, this is quite possibly the least attractive—too many terraced fields, too few cypresses, and rather too much white-tracked road. But then again, it probably doesn't matter much: when it comes to admiring Belinda's paintings it is often hard to tell exactly which image she has captured. Detail is not one of her strengths. Having subscribed to *Watercolourists Monthly*, ostensibly to receive the free paints and the artist's smock, she canceled her order as soon as they started to charge her for European postage and packing, which was at around the same time that the journal was moving from backgrounds to foregrounds and landscape details. An expert with her blue-sky wash and green hills, Belinda tends to become a little too creatively exhausted when it comes to putting the finishing touches to her views. Fortunately, foreground fatigue usually surfaces just before one o'clock and Sunday lunch at Giovanna's.

Buttocks clenched on a tussock, Belinda rests her pad across her knees as she sits on the side of the hill, painting. Her brush is poised, her brows concentrated, and her mind on the action below.

The blue Jeep has been back and forth all morning, swinging past Casa Mia like some teenage girl on a night out. Belinda has already grown to hate the cut of its jaunty jib as it glides up and down the hill with four-wheel-drive confidence.

Meanwhile, in the valley below, the clean white shirt of Lauren is very much in evidence, as she darts around the corners of her estate engaging with the workers and laborers who have appeared overnight. There seem to be hundreds of them, swarming like maggots over a rotting carcass. They are clearing the overgrown gardens, chopping down old trees, and piling all the loose stone into a yellow skip. Their jovial, good-natured chattering trips up the valley. Belinda swears she can hear Lauren's nasal vowels and the odd brash volley of laughter she shares with the man in the baseball cap. This is all happening rather too quickly for her liking.

She swirls her paintbrush vigorously in the jar, tapping the sides like a best man announcing a speech. She dips her thick wet brush into her paintbox, but such is her concentration on the action below that she does not check her palette too closely. As she wipes her paint-laden brush in big, broad strokes across the sky, gobs of black paint mix with the pale blue and cloud her view.

"Shit," she says, as she looks down at the impending storm she has just painted. The black paint bleeds into the blue sky, engulfing it, taking it over and destroying the green valley below. "That's all I bloody need." She tears the paper off the pad and screws it into a ball. "Surely it's time for lunch?" she mutters. She gets to her feet and throws her glass of cloudy water over the hillside. "I'll deal with her later."

* * *

Belinda and Mary are half an hour early for lunch at Giovanna's, but no one seems to mind, least of all Giovanna, who bustles up, a broad smile on her small, pink, lined face, which has spent slightly too many hours near the scorching confines of her pizza oven.

"*Ciao*, Belinda! *Ciao, la bella* Maria!" she says. Her tight black poodle curls nod in agreement as her bony hands grip each of their shoulders in turn, she greets them with a long-lost chamois-leather kiss.

The antithesis to her roly-poly husband, Giovanna is nothing but skin, bone, and facial hair. A ball of nervous energy, she cooks like a dervish, flits from table to table in the dining room, and talks nonstop in such a thick Tuscan accent that almost no one, except her husband, can understand. Together they make an extraordinary pair. Some people joke about how opposites attract. Everyone else murmurs about how he must drown her during sex—he's so big and fat and heavy. How does she manage to breathe? Some tourists in the valley even, erroneously, doubt that they have ever managed to do it at all. But Giovanna is the proud mother of six sons, whom she produced in quick succession, each spring for the first six years of their marriage. They have all since left the nest for various towns and cities all over Italy, from Milan to Florence. But when they return, the whole valley hears the song and dance.

Giovanna rushes around organizing Belinda's carafe of cold white wine and Mary's bottle of fizzy water, while they take their places at the long table in the middle of the restaurant. Laid for six with paper napkins and a pale pink linen tablecloth, Sunday lunch has a more formal feel to it than any of the other meals served in the restaurant. The Campari umbrellas have been grouped together to provide shade for the entire table. Another long table, for ten, is set up in the shade of the vine, while a couple is tucked away in the corner by the wall. Belinda settles down in the middle of the central table and starts to tear small pieces off a slice of bread from a brown plastic basket.

"Looks like the Bianchis have booked for lunch," she says, nodding toward the large table of ten under the vine. "I wonder who the two is?" she asks, chewing on a crust.

"Probably some tourists," suggests Mary, taking a sip of water. Her eyes fill up slightly as the bubbles go up the back of her nose.

"Mmm," agrees her mother. She takes a sip of wine. "Everything all right this morning? No horrors in the bedroom?"

"Not that I noticed," says Mary.

"It always amazes me who the revolting ones are." Belinda dunks her bread in some olive oil she's poured into the ashtray. "It's often the most refined general who skids the sheets."

"Mum!" says Mary, shoulders hunched in embarrassment.

"Doesn't bother me, darling." Belinda smiles. "You're the one dealing with it."

"Do we have to talk about these things?"

"I was only saying—and anyway," Belinda sniffs, "no one here speaks English."

"But that's not the point."

"Oh, do shut up." Belinda yawns, and turns to face the entrance. "Oh, *buongiorno* Howard. *Buongiorno!*" she exclaims loudly, with a coo-ee wave and a smile, getting out of her seat as she does so. "How are you? *Come va?*" she asks, her face all screwed up, waiting to be embraced.

"I'm very much the same as when you last saw me," says Howard, leaning over to place two rather wet red kisses on Belinda's cheeks. "I've been up since seven trying to get my character out of bed," he says, nodding to Mary as he sits down. "The bottle of wine I had at ten thirty made not a blind bit of difference."

"Never mind, never mind," says Belinda, pouring him a glass of white wine from the carafe. "Well, I've got some gossip that will surely get you unblocked."

"Really?" says Howard, leaning across and picking up the carafe, he fills his glass to the top. "Sounds intriguing," he says, opening his Burgundy-colored lips and pouring wine down his evidently dry throat.

"Well," says Belinda, her shoulders around her ears in her enthusiasm, "I've met the *americano* who bought the Casa Padronale and . . . she is, in fact, an *americana!*"

"Oh, right," says Howard, leaning back into his chair. "That's nice."

It's not quite the reaction Belinda was after. But before she can release her furious inner child, Derek and Barbara amble in with welcoming smiles on their inert faces.

"All right there, Contessa?" says Derek, running his thumbs around the waist of his beige slacks as he approaches.

"Yes, Derek, just fabulous." Belinda smiles, cheering up. "Brimming with gossip."

"Ooh, gossip!" enthuses Barbara, rubbing together her long, frosted-pink nails. "That sounds interesting."

"It is," says Belinda, standing up again and pouring them a glass of white wine. "The person who owns the Casa Pardonale is a woman!" she announces triumphantly, then sits down.

"A woman!" Derek repeats.

"Yes, a woman," confirms Belinda, folding her arms under her breasts to demonstrate her certainty.

"How amazing," says Barbara, her lined lips hanging open. "Who'd have guessed it?"

"Mary and I went around last night to meet her," says Belinda, her trump card gleaming in her eyes for all to see.

"You never?" says Barbara, her scoop-neck breasts spreading across the table as she leans forward.

"Yup." Belinda nods.

"You never?" says Barbara again, directing her question and her expanding chest toward Mary.

"We did," confirms Mary. "To check her out."

"To welcome her to the valley," insists Belinda.

"A bit of both." Barbara's frosted nails make a seesaw gesture.

"And?" asks Derek. His neck muscles exhausted after the conversational tennis match he has just supported.

Belinda inhales. "Well," she says. Her buttocks twist in her seat. Everyone leans in. And Belinda is off, holding forth from a unique position of knowledge, which is just how she likes it. She starts out pleasantly enough. She has learned from past experience that it doesn't do to be too negative about people right from the very beginning. If one is too unpleasant and too derogatory, it serves only to make one's audience empathize with the obvious underdog. So she starts out being positive about the amount of work Lauren appears to have got done in such a short space of time. She continues that if she had heard two people outside her house so late at night, she doubts she would have been brave enough to open the door. But once the door is open, Belinda starts to let little things slip. Lauren's amazing svelteness is directed straight at Barbara, who tends to dislike people thinner than her. The fact that Lauren probably works hard to maintain this svelteness is directed at Howard, who finds anything gym-related so vacuously banal and ghastly that he instantly drains his glass in disgust. So, with two of the three members of her audience already slightly uncomfortable at Lauren's arrival, Belinda delivers her final killer blow with the subtlest fanfare.

"The one thing she said that I did find a little odd . . . though . . ." she says, with affected hesitation.

"Yes?" says Derek.

"Well, perhaps it was a communication thing," continues Belinda, nodding at her understanding and general kindness. "Divided by a common language, you know, that sort of thing . . ."

"What did the skinny Yank say?" asks Barbara.

"Well, it was something along the lines of wanting to make Tuscany work for her." Belinda repeats, with a couple of little quotation marks drawn by her own fat hand.

"Oh, I say!" says Derek, evidently not enjoying the idea of someone else making money or possibly being richer than him. "Did she really say that?"

"Yes." Belinda's tone is a little sad.

"Really?" asks Howard, who seems to be trying to work out which is the more appalling: the fact that the woman works out or that she is planning to sell the romance of Tuscany downriver. "Really? That Tuscany should work for her?" he asks again, this time looking to Mary for affirmation.

"Yes," Mary says, "well, I'm sure it was meant—"

"Ssssh!" says Belinda suddenly, slapping Howard's arm so hard that he hits his front tooth on his glass. "There she is!" Belinda indicates with the back of her head, while gripping Derek and Howard by the forearms. "There! In the doorway! With the young man in the baseball cap!" she whispers, with all the finesse and subtlety of a stage drunk.

The whole table falls silent, and, very slowly, they turn their heads toward the door and stare. Engaged in conversation with the rotund Roberto, Lauren stands in her jeans and white shirt, flicking her blonde hair and casually laughing. She is oblivious of her audience. It is only when she turns to take her table that she notices the five pairs of gawping eyes, like a row of meerkats on lookout.

"Oh," she says, taking a quick, shocked step backward. "Oh, hello." She smiles, standing very much to attention.

"Lauren, hello there!" says Belinda, chin in the air, looking down her short retroussé nose. She gives her American neighbor a little English wave. "Come and meet the rest of my—the valley!"

"Oh, great." Lauren ignores the little English wave. "That's so nice of you . . . um, Betina, isn't it?"

"Belinda," says Belinda, with a light laugh. "It's quite complicated to remember," she confirms. "It's a very old, very English name."

"How quaint to be called something so out-of-date." Lauren smiles as she strides over on her long legs in her slim-fit jeans. The man in the baseball cap follows.

"Yes, well, some of us would regard that as culture and tradition," mutters Belinda, quickly and rather ineffectually. "Anyway," she says, gathering herself and flaring her nostrils, "everyone, this is Lauren. Lauren, this is everyone in the valley. And," she chuckles, "I really do mean *everyone in the valley*."

"Oh." Lauren feigns a little surprise. "I thought there was an Italian farming family here."

"There is," says Belinda, "but none of us . . . you know, with them . . ."

"I'm Derek," says Derek, standing up and attempting to help Belinda out of her increasingly large hole. "This is my wife, Barbara."

"Hello." Barbara's plump buttocks keep contact with her seat.

"Hi," says Lauren. "And this is my son, Kyle."

"Your son?" says Barbara. "But you look far too young—"

"No, God! I wish! I'm forty-eight." Lauren smiles.

"That's the same age as you, isn't it, Belinda?" says Howard, over the top of his glass.

"Yes, well . . ." mutters Belinda, suddenly looking for something over her shoulder.

The group looks from one to the other, and no one says anything.

"Hello, everyone," says Kyle. He takes off his baseball cap to reveal a shock of thick dark hair, and a broad, generous smile. He has tanned skin, large dark eyes, a straight nose, and a square jaw; he is very handsome. His voice is deep and male. Mary stares at the floor, and starts to shred her paper napkin.

"I'm Howard," says Howard, getting to shake hands formally.

"Howard's a famous novelist," says Belinda, like he's her own son. "He wrote *The Sun Shone on Her Face.* You may have heard of it?"

"Um . . . ?" Lauren pauses. "No."

"It wasn't published in America," admits Howard, getting back to his wine.

"It wasn't?" says Belinda. "Oh, how unfortunate for you."

"I didn't catch your name," says Kyle, looking directly at Mary with his large brown eyes.

"Oh," says Mary, with a lapful of shredded paper, "I'm Mary."

"Mary is Belinda's daughter," says Barbara helpfully.

"Oh, really?" says Lauren, looking from mother to daughter. "You don't look at all alike."

"Yes," says Belinda, with another flare of her nostrils. "It has been said before."

"What do you do, Mary?" says Lauren.

"Um . . ."

"She helps me out," says Belinda.

"And works in communications," adds Barbara.

"That, too." Belinda nods. "What does your son do?"

"He's a music major at Yale," says Lauren. "But he's helping me out, too. Aren't you, darling?"

"Sure am."

"Mary's musical," declares Barbara.

"No, I'm not," Mary mutters into her chest, her dark hair framing her face.

"Yes, you are. I thought you wanted to sing professionally?" says Barbara.

"We soon put a stop to that, didn't we?" Belinda laughs.

"I'd love to hear you sing sometime," says Kyle, bending down trying to make eye contact.

"I don't think that's likely," says Mary, forcing herself to look the handsome American in the eye. Her cheeks are pink with embarrassment, red blotches glare all over her neck, yet she still looks charming in her white broderie-anglaise top. "I'm very out of practice."

"Oh." His lips curl into a smile. "That's a shame. I'm a terrible singer." He laughs gently. "But I love to listen. What sort of stuff do you—"

"Anyway," says Belinda, clapping her hands together. "I'm starving. We should order."

"Of course." Lauren steps back. "And we should get to our table. Nice meeting you, guys."

"Yes, right," says Belinda, with her special stiff smile, before turning toward the kitchen. "Giovanna!" she shouts. "*Siamo pronti!* We *are* ready, aren't we, everyone? To order? It's not like we've never seen the menu before, now, is it?"

The group only manages to raise a couple of polite laughs as

Lauren and Kyle withdraw to their table and, with the main source of gossip and intrigue sitting all of three feet away, it is a while before the conversation picks up. In fact, they sit mostly in silence while Belinda talks loudly about the various meat options on the menu. Eventually, she rallies some sort of conversational banter between Derek and Howard about the merits of roast chicken versus the pork dish—no one is quite sure what it contains. Still, Belinda gets to speak a lot of loud Italian and share a couple of jokes with Roberto where she laughs heartily through the punch lines.

With the food ordered, and Giovanna and Roberto busy in the kitchen, silence descends on the restaurant. Lauren and Kyle enjoy the peace after the noise of their builders, and seem happy to sit not saying anything. The other table starts to stiffen. Mary keeps her head down and picks fluff off her skirt. Derek busies himself by reading the *"dolce"* section on the back of the menu for the fifth time while he chain-eats bread. Barbara smokes three St. Moritz Menthols, one after another, and Howard, not the most garrulous of conversationalists, chooses to ignore the mounting tension and drink as much white wine as he can. Belinda eats bread, drinks water, sips wine, and fights the terrible desire to turn and stare at Lauren behind her.

"Well, this is nice," says Barbara, flicking cigarette ash and picking at the filter-tip with a frosted-pink thumbnail.

"Mmm," says Belinda. "Isn't it?"

"So, I was thinking . . ." they both say at once.

"No, you . . ." says Belinda.

"No, you . . ." says Barbara.

"No, really, you," insists Belinda.

"Christ sake, one of you," says Howard, taking another sip of wine.

"Well, I was thinking . . . I wonder how your Belgians are getting on? Where are they today?" asks Barbara.

"They've gone on a trip to Siena," says Belinda.

"Siena? Really?" asks Barbara.

"Yes, Siena."

"I do like Siena," says Barbara.

"So do I," agrees Belinda.

"When did you last go to Siena?" asks Barbara.

"Just before Christmas," says Belinda. "When did you last go to Siena?"

"Oh, um, not sure," says Barbara. "Derek, when did we last go to Siena?"

"Jesus fucking Christ on a bicycle," says Howard suddenly, putting his glass down.

"You went to Siena at Easter, Belinda went to Siena at Christmas, I went to Siena last month, I'm sure Mary hasn't been for years. Now, can we all shut the fuck up about fucking Siena?"

"Howard!" hushes Belinda. Her face is horrified, her eyes are round as she gestures frantically with her head at Lauren, "Stop swearing!"

"What?" says Howard. "Like she fucking cares."

"Sssh," insists Belinda. "You're being embarrassing!"

"Embarrassing now, am I?" asks Howard.

Delayed somewhat by alcohol, he makes as if to stand up. But his little scene is drowned out by the arrival of the fabulously noisy Bianchi family—*la nonna,* Signor Bianchi, *la signora,* Marco, Gianfranco, Giorgio, Marco and Giorgio's wives, three children. A baby arrives in a Moses basket and is immediately placed under the long table. It is a whirlwind of jocularity. Roberto and Giovanna come out of the kitchen to be greeted by shouts, back-slapping hugs, cheers, and applause at the impending deliciousness of the lunch.

The three sons do the rounds of Belinda's table, shaking hands, kissing the backs of hands. The handsome Gianfranco winks at Mary. The enormity of their bonhomie is enough to reheat the frosty atmosphere in the restaurant, and the amount of noise the family makes together enables the other tables to relax and talk more freely. Perhaps most important of all, having taken Lauren and Kyle for tourists, the Bianchis ignore the Americans entirely.

Belinda can barely contain her triumph. *"Tutto bene?"* she shouts down the table at the family, raising her glass.

"Sì," they chorus. Marco and Gianfranco raise their glasses of water in return.

"Isn't this great?" says Belinda to her table, rubbing her hands together. "I think I might order some Prosecco."

"Ooh, good idea," agrees Barbara. "Do you know? I sometimes think I actually prefer it to champagne."

Sunday lunch appears to be going with a swing. Conscious of their audience and encouraged by Belinda's enthusiasm, everyone makes a concerted effort to demonstrate they are "such good friends" who thrive on one another's company and do this all the time. Belinda orders two bottles of Prosecco. Derek orders another carafe each of white and red wine.

Roberto and Giovanna can't believe their luck. Back and forth they go, generously serving the alcohol, accommodating smiles on their faces. The expat Sunday lunch party is rarely so jovial. Normally led by Howard's parsimony and poverty, they have a round of pizza, some salad, and a couple of bottles of wine. Two bottles of Prosecco and three carafes is a record.

Soon plates of salad make way for bowls of shiny pasta parcels, made that morning by Giovanna. Filled with spinach and ricotta and covered with parsley, garlic and olive oil, they are so firm and soft that they slip down the throat like oysters. Then, just as it seemed the expats are replete and can't consume any more, a great plate of roast chicken and fat pork cutlets arrives to quieten them down for a while.

But nothing can stifle the banter at the Bianchi table. In fact, they have only just got started. It's *la nonna*'s eighty-second birthday, and if the lunch is anything like it was last year, they'll sit around that table until the sun goes down with two bottles of red wine between ten of them.

*   *   *

Meanwhile, Lauren and Kyle don't seem to notice the display of expat exuberance that is being put on for their benefit. Instead, they sit opposite each other, enjoying their first hot food since they took possession of the keys to the Casa Padronale early on Saturday. While they savor every delicious mouthful of warming pasta, each crunchy forkful of hot peppery rocket and sweet tomato, they discuss their plans for the renovation of the house.

"I want to knock out as many of the walls downstairs as possible," says Lauren, sipping her mineral water, "to create the illusion of space. A feeling of light. I want to paint it white and open it up as much as possible. So people feel they're in a modern contemporary place but at the same time that they can relax and leave the city behind."

"That shouldn't take too long"—Kyle nods in agreement—"if we keep everyone motivated and focused."

"We haven't got long—we have to be open in three weeks," confirms Lauren, picking the Parmesan out of her salad. "That's what I've budgeted for in all my projections and forecasts."

"Don't worry, Mom." Kyle smiles warmly. "Whatever you've set your mind to doing, you'll do. You always have done."

"But this is dramatically different from Wall Street," she concludes. "You know, there it was more"—she pauses while a burst of hilarity emanates from Belinda's table—"there it was more dog eat dog. Here, it's more work like a dog." She raises her glass of water. "Anyway, cheers," she says. "To new ventures."

"To new ventures." Kyle grins. "You really shouldn't worry, Mom, I've never known you not be able to cope. Even after Dad died."

"Yeah, well," she says, raising her eyebrows. "That was over ten years ago." She smiles. "Anyway, I can't afford to fail at this project. I've invested most of my savings, and all my energy in it."

"That, and you've told everyone you're going to do it!" Kyle laughs. "Which, if I know the queen of hostile takeovers, is usually the biggest motivation of all."

"I'd quite forgotten how annoying you can be." Lauren laughs and gazes proudly at her handsome son.

"I'm a chip off the old block," says Kyle, with a broad grin and cheap wink.

"Are you accusing *me* of being annoying?"

"I wouldn't dare! Pick a fight with you? It's more than my life's worth. Anyway, we're here to celebrate. . . ."

"Quite right," says Lauren, flicking her smooth blonde hair and picking up her glass again. "To our success."

"To our success," he replies, gently tapping her glass with his.

"Now," says Lauren, "do you think we should paint over those pointless frescos, if you can call them that? I just can't bear the idea of those wretched art police, the *Bell' Arti,* coming down, declaring us a listed building and holding everything up."

❀ ❀ ❀

Over on the other table Barbara is decidedly giggly. She has definitely drunk too much and is starting to flirt with Howard. Although when Barbara drinks too much, she always flirts with Howard. Not that Derek seems to mind. Barbara and Derek have one of those surprisingly secure relationships: Barbara behaves quite badly in public and Derek enjoys it. He sits back and smiles, clasping his hands over his large waist, because he knows that, in her heart of hearts, Barbara is all mouth and overly tight trousers. After twenty-five years of happy marriage, it amuses him to watch her play the same old games. And they always are the same old games.

To start with, Barbara loses control of her breasts—not in a lap-dancing way: she simply becomes less aware of their expanse and tends to leave them behind on the table, allowing them to spill out over her scoop-neck T-shirt. Then she moves on to the touchy-feely octopus stage, when she normally turns on Howard, the only heterosexual male available who is not her husband. Finally just before she falls over and begins being violently sick, she releases her inner Liza Minnelli.

For Barbara has a theory that it is not only *in vino veritas* but also *in vino* that your true self comes out. It's just unfortunate, then, that the true personality that resides inside Barbara Hewitt is an all-singing, all-dancing Broadway starlet gagging to hit the boards.

Fortunately, Barbara is at the giggly, using-her-hands-quite-a-lot stage, and *Cabaret* seems a long way off. But she is not the only one who is slightly the worse for wear. Howard has long since released his inner Tolstoy, Derek his inner builder, and Belinda is well on the way to letting her Michelangelo come tumbling out. In fact, the only person whose inner personality is well under control is Mary. She sits quietly in the afternoon sun, the yellow rays dancing on her dark hair as she stares down the golden-green valley, sipping her water. Occasionally Franco catches her eye from the Bianchi table.

The afternoon wears on, and the expat table starts to make a noise about leaving.

"You're all welcome to come back to ours," mutters Derek, tripping slightly over his words. "I'd value Howard's opinion on the roof."

"Oh, there's nothing I'd like more to see than an honest roof, hewn from honest labor, as Levin once said," slurs Howard.

"And we could have a singsong," suggests Barbara, hopefully.

"We should probably get back, actually," replies Mary. "We've got the Belgians staying with us. Haven't we, Mum?"

Just as Belinda looks ready to leave, she suddenly picks up her chair, scrapes it along the stone floor, like a slowly moving crab, and parks herself at Lauren and Kyle's table. "Hello, there," she says, smiling, her face round, pink, and shiny like a beach ball.

"Hope you don't mind me joining you."

"No," says Lauren. "Please, pull up a pew."

"Oh, right." Belinda looks at her chair, confused. "I have."

"So you have," says Lauren.

"How's it all going?" asks Belinda, rubbing her puffy hands together. Now that she has arrived at the table, she is damned if she is going to leave it too quickly. "I'm very impressed that you have managed to get your builders to work on a Sunday. This being a Catholic country, it's usually more than their place in heaven is worth to turn up on the Lord's day." Belinda chortles.

"Yeah, you're right. But I'm afraid it has nothing to do with me. That efficiency is down to my architect."

"Good Lord!" shrieks Belinda, slapping both her thighs at once. "You've hired an architect?"

Mary's antennae are on full alert. Sensing her mother is about to hold forth, she comes up behind and places her hands on the back of the chair, just in case. Kyle smiles at her. Mary feels her cheeks blush, but manages a small smile back.

"Oh, yeah," confirms Lauren. "I find things are much easier when you use an architect."

"I don't think you'll need one of those out here!" continues Belinda, pleasantly pleased with herself. "The Italians are so artistic . . . so terribly, terribly artistic. They really don't need guidance or anything like that at all. I mean, I could understand if we were in England." She laughs. "Or America. But here . . . art is in their soul. It's in their blood, it's their landscape. They inhale it! They live it! I mean, this is the country of Michelangelo!"

"I'm well aware of that." Lauren smiles.

"But if you want to waste your money," Belinda leans back in her seat, her head to one side, "I suppose it's up to you. But take any carpenter, stonemason, or ironmonger and they'll be able to do just as good a job. Don't say I didn't warn you!" She taps the side of her short, shiny pink nose.

"Thank you for your kind words," says Lauren, getting up to leave. "Come along, Kyle," she says, and picks up some euros from the white saucer on the table. "It really is time we got back."

"Sure, Mom." Kyle glances at Mary. "See you around?" he says.

"Maybe," says Mary.

"But then again," continues Belinda, "I suppose for you it must be different."

"Sorry?" asks Lauren, looking down at her.

"It must be a bit different for you," repeats Belinda, looking up.

"Why?" asks Lauren.

"Well, what with you opening a hotel."

"A hotel?"

"Yes," says Belinda. "You know, your hotel. I imagine that must be complicated."

"I'm not opening a hotel," says Lauren, running her hands through her hair.

"You're not?"

"No." Lauren snorts. "Where on earth did you pick that up?"

"Oh," says Belinda, her cheeks blushing a darker shade of pink. "So you're not opening a hotel?"

"No, I'm opening a bed-and-breakfast."

"A bed-and-breakfast?" stutters Belinda.

"Yes," confirms Lauren. "Rather along the lines of yours," she adds, with one of her very special smiles. "Only quite a lot more glamorous."

Mercoledì ✽ Wednesday

Clima ✽ *fa caldo* (Hot! Hot! Hot!)

Good Lord, I see it is a whole two and half weeks since I last wrote anything in my diary but, then, given how busy Maria and I have been with the house, that should come as no surprise. Ever since my delightful Belgians left, with smiles on their faces and a relaxed spring in their stride, the villa has been more or less full. I've had some Austrians, some French, and two sets of Brits, who have filled me in on all the gossip back home. Apparently property prices are now so high no one can afford to buy homes anymore. All I can say is, it is always so pleasant to be reminded why one left!

Obviously, as a hostess, my first priority is my guests, so I haven't been able to help out our new *americana* visitor Lauren as much as I would have liked. But I gather from Barbara and Derek—who seem to have plenty of time to keep abreast of such things—she has had a few difficulties with that little house of hers. Apparently someone reported all her renovating activities to the *comune*, who sent some inspectors down to ascertain whether the frescos above the window in the small chapel on the side of the house should be saved for the nation—which I think, thankfully, they are going to be. Isn't it strange? Quite why someone would want to come to a beautiful country like this and actively go out of her way to destroy its culture is beyond me.

But, anyway, Lauren seems to have got over her little historical setback extremely quickly and is forging ahead with her refurbishment. Judging by the delivery of her new kitchen tiles yesterday, her copper piping the day before, and what looks like a large showerhead and new bath this morning, she is bulldozing along at breakneck speed.

On a more positive note, we have some returners arriving this afternoon. Major and Mrs. Chester are the most delightful couple and they have been coming to stay with me, as my guests, ever since last year. They found Casa Mia in an advert I placed in the *Sunday Telegraph* and have since been among some of our most loyal customers. They stay for a week, the same week each year. The major is a fellow artist and watercolorist so I am very much looking forward to taking him off on some long walks into the hills and spending whole afternoons in his company talking techniques, colors, and brushes. Sadly, his wife doesn't share our *passione,* but she always seems content to do some light reading (and I really do mean light!) by the swimming pool, whiling away her afternoons under the umbrella.

Maria seems to be getting along just fine. She has got the breakfast service and turning down of the rooms more or less down to a tee. I will have to watch her cooking, though. If I remember correctly, the major is very fond of his food. Or perhaps it was just my cooking he liked so much! Speaking of which . . .

INSALATA DI CASA MIA

This recipe is so delicious it makes me want to chuck away my U.K. citizenship and pretend that full-bodied red Italian blood courses through my passionate veins! And it's all to do with the ingredients that the wonderful peasants grow here. I don't know what it is about the Italian tomato, but when Maria and I buy them in the **mercato** we often can't control ourselves until we get home. We have to open the bag in the car and dive in. They are so luscious that eating one should be a private act! Fortunately in this fabulous recipe they have been tamed enough to save one's modesty!

* tomatoes
* avocados
* mozzarella (remember, **bufala** is best)
* olive oil
* your most expensive balsamic vinegar
  (take it from me, as a woman who has only ever made
  this mistake once, if you scrimp you will notice the
  difference!)

There is no need for weighing or measuring in this recipe. When it comes to quantities, just exhale and express yourself as you like. Slice up your tomatoes, avocados, and mozzarella, lay them on a plate, and drizzle over (isn't it funny how no one pours anymore?)

the oil and the vinegar. It's so simple. It's so Italian. It's salad with a spontaneous look.

Serve with an elegant smile and relaxed hair.

CHAPTER FIVE

* * *

"*Perfetto*," says Mary. She puts down the telephone and turns to face her mother.

"Well? What did they say?" asks Belinda, her head craning forward like a tortoise's, her blue eyes shining with excitement. "Did they agree? Are they going back for another look? Surely they're going back for another look. They must be. Did you tell them? What did they say?"

"Um . . ." Mary runs a hand through her long dark hair as she gathers her thoughts.

"What?" says Belinda, taking a step forward. "What? Come on, what did they say? Are they closing her down? They must be closing her down. Aren't they? Hurry up, Mary. Tell me."

Mary tries to retreat, shuffling away, but her mother advances and practically glues her daughter to the wall. Their faces are so close that Mary can feel the moist heat of her mother's breath against her cheek. She can see the pincushion of blackheads across her nose and the shiny patch of pink skin she missed when troweling on her foundation that morning.

Ever since her telephone call to the *comune* last week, reporting Lauren McMahon for breaking building regulations and threatening to paint over the frescos in the chapel attached to the side of the house, Belinda has exuded this heightened demonic air, like a woman on battle footing. Her actions have been swift, her decisions decisive, her mood somewhat manic. Obsessive in her surveillance of the comings and goings at the Casa Padronale, she has still found time for numerous forays to Giovanna's trattoria to share, commiserate, and dissect the most minute renovatory detail with anyone who would listen, namely Howard—who listens to anyone as long as they buy him a drink.

All this is in dramatic contrast to her behavior the week before. When, having discovered the full magnitude of Lauren's B-and-B plans during that Sunday lunch at Giovanna's, Belinda appeared to be thrown and went into a quiet and contemplative mood. Prone to hand-waving histrionics of *Towering Inferno* proportions when faced with the most banal inconvenience, her introspection was disturbing. Particularly for her daughter, who recalled that the last time Belinda was so monosyllabic was immediately after she'd encountered her husband's thrusting buttocks and been serenaded by the pleasured panting of her erstwhile next-door neighbor.

Yet now, pinned against the wall, confronted by her mother's enthusiasm for her cunning plan, Mary is not sure which mood is easier to contend with.

"Oh, for God sake, tell me what the half-witted little bastards said!" exclaims Belinda, throwing her short hands into the air and shaking her head as she walks away.

"Mum!" says Mary, peeling herself off the wall. "Calm down."

"Oh, shut up, darling. Don't be stupid," replies Belinda, with a shrug of her padded shoulder. "All's fair in love and war, and this is most definitely war."

"Well," says Mary, sitting on the arm of her father's favorite armchair, "they were quite pleasant. They thanked me for my third follow-up call on the matter of the Santa Caterina frescos and said they had been down to visit the site. They have stopped the conversion of the chapel into a bathroom suite, but as for stopping work on the whole building, they were not sure what grounds they had for such drastic measures."

"What grounds?" Belinda spins on the sole of her sunflower flip-flop and stares out of her french windows. "I'll give them 'what grounds.' Cultural rape! This is cultural rape. Cultural rape . . . and pillage of their national heritage. Italian heritage. Our heritage. European heritage." She turns. "Did you tell them she's American?"

"Um, yes. I said exactly what you told me to say. That it was 'cultural expansionism.' But they said that the frescos were only painted in the seventies by a member of the original family and they are of no real cultural significance."

"The thing about cultural significance is that it is all relative," replies Belinda, her hands now on her hips. "I mean, are there any other frescos in this valley? I think not. Therefore, although they may not be culturally significant when it comes to things like the Sistine Chapel, they are culturally significant to this area. Which, let's face it, can only boast one Etruscan tomb and a designer shoe outlet within a ten-mile radius. Which, when compared to the rest of Tuscany, is pretty fucking piss-poor, don't you think? For Christ sake even the Prada discount store is over an hour away!" Belinda's voice is raised, and the veins on her fat, crepey neck are standing out. "Did you tell them all that?"

"Um, no, not really," mutters Mary, unraveling the stitching along the hem of her white T-shirt.

"I don't suppose your Italian was up to the job, was it?" suggests Belinda. "Honestly, if a job's worth doing . . ."

She walks over to her desk and riffles through some papers. She bends down, exhaling like a slow puncture, and pulls out a heavy drawer. It is full of small glass and china animals in bubble wrap and old English newspaper, remnants of her past life in the U.K. Belinda has never quite gotten around to displaying them in her new house, and the longer they stay in the drawer, the less likely they are ever to see the light of day. She puts a large china spaniel with a baby blue collar and pleasingly pink tongue on the flagstone floor, then finds what she is looking for: a large yellow legal pad that still has a shopping list on it from her days in Tilling and regular trips to Asda.

"Right," she announces, and stands up straight. With a cursory glance at the list—tinned peach halves and a packet of mince—she rips off the top sheet and throws it into the bin. "I should have done this weeks ago," she says. "Honestly, I'm such a fool. I'm going to start a petition."

"A petition?" Mary looks up from her T-shirt.

"Yup." Belinda sorts through the collection of pens in a jar on her desk, and scribbles on the corner of her pad trying to find one that works.

"What are you petitioning for?"

"To save the Santa Caterina frescos, of course," says Belinda, frowning at her daughter's stupidity.

"Oh," says Mary. "Are you sure about this?"

"What do you mean, am I sure about this? All's fair in love and war," insists Belinda, still scribbling. "And this is war."

"So you say."

"Well, at least I'm doing something to safeguard our live-lihood," says Belinda, looking up. "If you're keen on a career in telesales, dear, then I suggest you carry on unpicking that grubby little T-shirt of yours. However, if you want to stay here, you could help me."

"Well, if you're sure it will do some good."

"All we really need is Derek, Barbara, and Howard on board, and we have most of the valley." She pauses. "We could even ask some of the Italians." She's talking to herself. "And then, per-haps, we could shame her into stopping."

"She doesn't look like a woman who shames easily."

"Do I look like a woman who loses easily?" says Belinda, with an efficient click of her Biro.

"No."

"No," confirms Belinda. "I'm going to call Derek."

Edging Mary to one side, Belinda dials Derek's number with the end of her ballpoint pen and waits. After a seemingly end-less litany of monotone rings, someone finally picks up the phone.

"*Finalmente,* Derek," declares Belinda down the receiver in one of her jolliest voices. "It's the Contessa here."

"Oh, hello, there, Belinda," says Barbara, breathing heavily. "I'm afraid it's me. Phew!" Belinda hears her patting her bosom down the telephone. "And I've run all the way from the terrace. I've no idea where Derek's put that wretched cordless phone."

"Oh, right." Belinda clicks her pen. "I do hope I'm not in-terrupting."

"Oh, no," giggles Belinda. "I was just sunbathing, and Derek's discussing some more work on the barn with Gianfranco."

"Oh, right. Franco . . ." Belinda clicks her pen again. "Well, I was just ringing up about Lauren McMahon."

"Ooh. Are you going as well?" enthuses Barbara.

"Going? Going where?" asks Belinda, standing to attention, gaining swift eye contact with Mary.

"To Lauren's," continues Barbara, making a clicking sound with her manicure as she cleans the suntan lotion out from under her nails. "I think it's going to be great. The whole valley's coming, it sounds like quite a night."

"Oh. Quite a night, you say."

"Mmm, yes. Lauren keeps pretending it's an informal drinks thing, just some people from the valley. She says Derek and I shouldn't expect too much . . ."

"She does, does she?"

"Yes, but I have a feeling it's some sort of housewarming thing. What do you think? What did she say to you?"

"What did Lauren say to me?" says Belinda, brusquely clicking her pen six times in succession. "Gosh!" She laughs. "She says so many things."

"I know," agrees Barbara, still cleaning her manicure. "She's ever so funny, isn't she? She's a bit like you, actually," she adds distractedly, "you know, funny. Only she's a bit more—"

"Yes, well, we do chat almost every day," interjects Belinda.

"I knew you would," agrees Barbara.

"Are you sure I'm not interrupting?" says Belinda, with a wave of irritation: she has not got Barbara's undivided attention.

"Oh, sorry," says Barbara. "I was miles away there, just watching Franco—oh, and Derek coming toward the house . . . Cooee!" she shouts. Belinda winces. "Derek! Derek! Darling! It's the Contessa on the phone! Hurry up! She wants to talk to you about Lauren's do!"

There is a clatter as Barbara puts down the receiver. Belinda strains to hear, hunching her shoulders as she pushes her ear tighter against the phone, but all she can make out is Barbara giggling and the low, rumbling Italian tones of Franco's voice echoing in the hall.

"Hello?" Derek's breath blasts down the line. After a momentary scrabble for the receiver, he brings it close to his ear. Belinda moves hers away. "So," he exhales, "are you coming along tomorrow, then?"

"Tomorrow?" says Belinda, like she has just sat on something sharp.

"Yes, Lauren's thing," he continues. "It should be quite a shindig."

"Oh, God, that!" exclaims Belinda. "Well, it depends on how busy we are. You know, high season and all that, Derek. And, as you well know, an upmarket establishment like mine hardly runs itself, now, does it?"

"No, indeed it does not," agrees Derek. "But it is a valley-wide event," he continues. "And as the Contessa, it wouldn't be a party if you didn't show your face, now would it?"

"Do you think so?" Belinda curls a stray strand of hair behind her ear.

"Oh, I know so," says Derek. "Now, what were you calling for, dear? I have Franco here, and he needs to get off."

"Oh, nothing pressing," says Belinda. "Just checking that you'd been invited to Lauren's event as well."

"Rest assured we have. That's ever so kind of you to worry about us, but I don't think the invitations are very restricted." He laughs. "I think the whole valley's going. We have no ideas above our station." He chuckles some more. "I'll see you tomorrow, then?"

"Absolutely," says Belinda, her shoulders shooting up to her ears. "Can't wait! *Arrivadeary!*"

"*Arrivadeary!*"

Belinda puts down the receiver and remains still, her hand resting on the telephone, her face crumpled in contemplation.

"She's having a party," she says quietly. "The *americana* is having a party."

"Oh, don't worry, Mum," says Mary, walking over and placing a hand on her mother's shoulder, giving it a concerned, padded squeeze. "I'm sure she meant to invite you."

"The whole valley's invited," whispers Belinda, still staring at the telephone. "She's invited the whole valley and not me—us," she corrects, turning to face Mary. "She has neglected to invite us."

Belinda's blue eyes are shining as she starts to pace up and down in her sitting room. Her red, white, and blue flowered skirt swishes as she moves, and her right shoulder pad slowly edges its way down her T-shirt sleeve and falls to the floor on her final turn. "I think we should go anyway," she announces, looking splendidly pleased with herself.

"Are you sure?" asks Mary. "I mean . . ."

"Well, you said it yourself—she's simply forgotten to invite us." Belinda is deaf to all contradiction. "It's easily done. I mean, I've done it myself before now and, as a fellow hostess, I understand these things happen. What's the little matter of an invitation between friends?"

"But we don't have an invitation," insists Mary. "What if she didn't want to invite us?"

"Oh, don't be silly, dear," says Belinda. "She's invited the whole valley—*my* valley, actually. You can't possibly have a party in my valley without inviting me. That's ridiculous! The poor woman has obviously made a mistake, and as a grown-up I'm prepared to overlook her error and attend her party. It's as simple as that."

"But Major Chester's arriving this afternoon. We can't leave him and his wife alone tomorrow—they expect supper every night."

"Oh, do be quiet, Mary. Major Chester is practically family; he won't mind if we go out to a party. Anyway, I have a life of my own. I can't possibly entertain all the guests all the time. They call themselves holidaymakers; they can go and make their own holiday without any help from me. And don't think you're staying behind to look after them either. You're coming with me."

"Do you really think it's a good idea?" asks Mary, in a tone that verges on pleading.

"Yes. I do. And no more arguing," replies Belinda, walking into the kitchen to signify that the discussion is over. "Have you made the major's bed?"

"Yes."

"Properly?"

"Yes, properly."

"Have you laid out the clean towels?"

"Yes."

"Good. Could you give the downstairs a once-over with the broom?"

While Mary sweeps, her mother stalks the terrace, binoculars around her neck. She walks her property like a territory-marking beast, pausing at various vantage points to take a closer and more studied look at the action on the other side of the hill. She watches the bright yellow construction vehicles churn up and down the driveway as they cover it with layers of gravel. She can also see a fleet of small white vans that dispatch busy-looking people into the house. As she watches, one white van gets stuck at the top of the drive and Belinda smiles. The more it strives to get out of the muddy rut, the better she feels.

"Do you know?" she says loudly. "Do you know, Maria, darling?"

"Mmm?" replies Mary, sweeping dust and hair off the balcony.

"I think the area around the pool needs tidying. I wonder if we shouldn't get Franco up here this afternoon?" She turns to face the french windows and the kitchen. "Mmm? What do you think? Maria?"

"Think about what?" mumbles Mary, leaning on her broom.

"About inviting Franco up here this afternoon to do some work."

"Oh, right, Franco," says Mary. "Um," she hesitates. "Well, if you think you need to."

"Indeed I do. He's so terribly useful." Belinda tweaks her one remaining pad as she wanders back toward the telephone.

While her mother's loud, giggly, and inaccurate Italian trills away in the background, Mary sets the table on the terrace for lunch. Back and forth, with a caterer's efficiency, she dextrously lays out hunks of white bread and cheese and plates of sliced tomatoes. Bronzed and toned since her arrival almost a month ago, Mary is physically different from the transparent, exhumed-looking specimen her mother collected from the station. Her numerous trips up and down the stairs, as she changes sheets and turns down beds in the guests' rooms, have made her fit and firm. Carting heavy trays loaded with half-eaten plates of macaroni and cheese has muscled up her arms. But this change has been subtle, gradual, and has happened without Mary noticing. She has remarked on her tan, all gold and even, but as for the rest of her metamorphosis, it has passed her by.

But, then, a lot of things have passed her by recently. Isolated from people of her own age and treated like a member of the domestic staff, Mary has spent most of the last month in her own world. She sits and watches conversations around her mother's supper table. She speaks only to answer questions posed directly to her and only if they have not already been seen off by her mother, who appears to be more *au fait* than her daughter on matters of the heart and career. On Tuesdays and Thursdays, light relief comes in the form of Giulia. A Bianchi cousin from the next-door valley, Giulia gossips with Mary in Italian while she cleans. Their banter irritates Belinda, who tends to find Mary other chores while Giulia is around. So, as Belinda sits down for lunch and announces Franco's arrival some time this afternoon, Mary is a little flustered.

"What time did he say exactly?" she asks, cutting a sliver of cheese.

"He was using the twenty-four-hour clock, so one can never be sure exactly when that is in English, let alone Italian," dismisses Belinda with a wave of her hand. She opens her mouth wide and advances it toward her cheese sandwich. "But"—she chomps, jaws grinding, mouth open, food swilling—"some time this afternoon," she concludes.

"Oh," says Mary, cutting her tomato slice in half. "I suppose I shall be inside doing the supper or something."

"There's no need for that," Belinda says with a little cough as she swallows. "We can defrost something for the major. Not that he'd notice anyway. But I want you to help Franco."

"You do?" says Mary, putting down her knife and fork, her cheeks pinking under her tan.

"Yes." Belinda sniffs. "A lot of old paving-stones need moving, and you can help him."

"Oh."

"I'll bring my lounger to the pool and conduct proceedings from there. I can't leave the two of you alone." She laughs. "There's no telling what would happen."

"Don't be silly, Mum," says Mary, looking down at her food. Come three thirty that afternoon, Franco is striding down the hillside toward Belinda's kidney-shaped swimming pool, dressed only in his jeans and a pair of sandals, with a heavy sun lounger hoisted high above his head. Belinda is ahead of him shouting, encouraging *"Bene"* noises, while Mary walks behind, staring at every strained, bronzed muscle in his beautiful back. Chiseled and sculpted, hewn from the shiniest and softest of materials, each sinew defined, each muscle distinct, Franco moves like a panther and looks like a god. Mary is transfixed, so transfixed that she forgets to look away when he puts down the lounger.

"Va bene così?" he asks Belinda.

"Oh, *bene, bene, bene,*" trills Belinda, tottering on the spot and clapping in her enthusiasm, her face stretched into a very wide smile.

"Bene," he agrees, stretching toward the sky. He exhales, runs his hands through his thick dark hair, and turns around to catch Mary staring at him. *"Bene."* He nods and smiles. "Okay?" he asks.

"Oh, yes, very . . . okay," says Mary, staring at her shoes, quickly tucking her hair behind her ears.

"Good," he says, shaking his arms. "That is *molto* heavy," he explains.

"Right." Mary nods.

The sweet smell of his sweat is making her feel light-headed. His masculinity is intoxicating. Actually, all of Gianfranco Bianchi is intoxicating. The big, swinging Adonis of the valley, his good looks, grand physique, and charming smile have beguiled everyone around. His arrival at anyone's house, villa, and, indeed, Giovanna's trattoria is always heralded with much excitement and applause. The only unmarried son left in the Bianchi household, he has driven his mother mad with frustration at his refusal to settle down. Happy to spend his days working on his father's farm and helping out the expat community with their DIY problems, Franco has never been interested in the lure of the city or university—too interested in girls to study, he spent his teens flirting on the bus to Serrana and failed to get into technical college in Poggibonsi. He hibernates during the winter, working hard for his father, but come the summer, there are enough tourists and DIY problems to keep him entertained.

"So," claps Belinda, mindful that, no matter how delightful the view, it is still costing her over ten euros an hour. "Right, Franco." She squeezes out another smile. "*A laboro*. To work."

"*Sì*, yes, right, Signora Smith. Where are these stones?" he asks.

"Maria, darling, will you take him to the stones and tell him what to do?" says Belinda, exhaustion pouring out of her voice. "I think I might just have a lie-down and point a few things out."

* * *

Belinda relaxes into the lounger, and Mary and Franco set about shifting the large pile of flagstones left over from paving around the pool. They have sat stacked up against the side of the hill for the past three years and Mary doesn't understand the need to move them in the heat of the afternoon on this particular day, but her mother is insistent. And she doesn't really mind how hot it is or how heavy the stones are: she is working with the valley's most handsome assistant, if only she could look him in the eye.

For the first ten minutes, neither of them speaks. The stones are heavy and Belinda keeps making demands, pointing her short pink fingers in the direction of the pile. But then she relaxes and reclines on her cushions. After another five minutes or so, Franco and Mary can hear the snuffles, crackles, and pops of phlegmy snoring. With their sentinel off duty, they relax. Franco catches Mary's eye, as they walk back and forth carrying their heavy loads. His dark eyes, with their thick, curly lashes, glint at her. The next time they cross, his handsome mouth breaks into a wide, white smile. At the third meeting he winks, and Mary manages a brief smile back. The fourth time, he pretends that the stone is too heavy and drags it along like an old man. Mary grins. Then, finally, he lays down a stone and mops his brow with his strong brown forearm.

"Fa caldo," he sighs. "Let's rest."

Mary puts down her flagstone next to his and straightens her back. "You're right," she says, shaking her hair off her shining shoulders. "It's very hot."

"So," he says, taking a small golden tin of tobacco out of his back trouser pocket. "Are you having a good holiday?" He lays a slim tissue of cigarette paper on his wide palm and seasons it with tobacco. Used to chatting up tourists and expat women *d'un certain âge,* Franco's English is good, if a little limited to holidays and the weather.

"It isn't really a holiday," says Mary, giggling for no reason other than the embarrassment of conversing with Franco for the first time. "I'm out here working for my mother." She laughs again.

"Oh, right, yes." Franco's dark brows furrow at the apparent missed joke. "Signora Smith."

"Yes," says Mary.

Franco leans forward, his eyes study her face as he licks the length of his rolled cigarette with the tip of his tongue. Mary's mouth goes dry and her stomach tightens as she stares back. "Signora Smith," she says slowly.

"She is like a wild pig," he laughs, imitating her snore. "You know, *cinghiale*."

"Oh, yes, wild boar," agrees Mary, her body collapses in a quiet, breathless enthusiastic laugh. She touches his forearm and breathes in the high, sweet smell of his skin.

"But, you know, she is nice person." He lights his roll-up, and inhales a curl of smoke deep into his lungs, then exhales it out of the side of his mouth. "Do you want?" he asks, handing over the damp, licked, and sucked cigarette.

"Mmm, thanks," says Mary, taking the moist end and placing it between her lips. She takes a drag, half closing her eyes. The damp paper burns her skin. Her cheeks flush. Her eyes shine. Her breath quickens. She coughs just once as the smoke hits her lungs, and lets out a thin ribbon of smoke from between her parted lips.

Franco stares at her intently. His dark eyes move slowly down her face. They are drawn to her mouth. His eyelids are lowered. He does not take his eyes off her lips. He takes a step closer. His hands move toward her hips. Mary doesn't move. She can't. She is standing there, cigarette in one hand, the other hanging limply by her side. She waits, her chin turned upward, her lips parted.

"Are you smoking?" comes a squawk from the lounger. "Mary!"

Franco and Mary jump apart. She drops the cigarette on the ground. He treads on it, turns, and smiles. "*Buongiorno*, Signora Smith," he says, ambling toward her with his arms outstretched like he is greeting a long-lost cousin. "Good sleeping?"

"Franco, Franco," flutters Belinda, smoothing down her T-shirt, "have I woken up and caught you on a break?"

"Just a little rest," he says, his finger and thumb coming together to make the smallest of gaps. "A very little rest."

"Good," says Belinda brusquely, swinging her small feet on to the grass. "Because you know how much I hate slack workmanship."

"Yes, yes," laughs Franco, as if he understands what she means.

"So, Maria," says Belinda, still smiling at Franco, "I hope I didn't see you with a cigarette."

"No."

"Good, right. How far have you got with the flagstones?"

"We're nearly there," says Mary. "About halfway, I suppose."

"Super," says Belinda. "You carry on with that, dear, and I shall take Franco down the garden. I'm having a little problem with my fig, and I need him to help me out. Come with me, Franco," she says, beckoning with a pink forefinger.

"Okay, signora," he says, smiling broadly. "Whatever you want."

"Whatever I want." Belinda giggles and flicks her brown hair. "You'll regret saying that, Franco, you really will."

Franco and Belinda walk off down the hillside, leaving Mary on flagstone duty. But she doesn't mind. She walks back and forth carrying the heavy pieces of stone with renewed vigor. She has a smile on her face and strength in her stride. The stones aren't that heavy, after all. Could it be that the handsome Franco was just about to kiss her? Does he *like* her? The man who could have any woman in the valley had noticed her, and she couldn't believe it. No one had looked at her like that for some time. Actually, no one had ever looked at her like that before. The last man to make any advances on her had been Jeremy in Accounting at the Christmas party, and that was over six months ago. Even then, he had only groped her in the back of the cab after he'd drunk six Snowballs. He'd rubbed his bendy erection up and down her thigh for a while, then fallen asleep with his mouth open—and all before she dropped him off at Victoria station for the last train home. But Franco is different from English boys. For a start, he's a real man. He's the hunter-gatherer type, who can do things with his hands. He can make things, mend things. He's strong. He's gentle. He's what all men used to be before they discovered computer keyboards and Clinique. Mary doesn't mind how many stones she has to move. In fact, she could do it all day and not feel a thing.

She finishes at just after five. Franco has already gone, winking at her as he walked up the hill. Belinda was apparently more than satisfied with his diagnosis on her fig: all it needed was a bit more care and attention and then it would bear fruit like the others in the valley. She is almost as elated as her daughter. In fact, the Franco effect on the Casa Mia household is enough to put both women in an excellent humor. Belinda marks her light mood by putting Russell Watson on her CD player and turning "Nessun Dorma!" to full volume as she conducts the orchestra from the arm of her ex-husband's favorite chair.

Mary decides to take a long hot bath, which is not a pleasure she usually affords herself since she has to clean the whole bathroom afterward and leave it in a state fit for any guest.

At seven thirty Mary and Belinda are sitting on the terrace. A chili con carne is defrosting in the kitchen, and they each have a drink in their hand as they watch the full red sun attempting to slide behind the hillside.

"What time is the major coming?" asks Mary.

"Who knows?" says Belinda, looking at her watch. "But if he's not here in the next ten minutes, then I think we can start thinking about supper. I'm not waiting for him."

"Do you think so?"

"Well, I'm not running a hotel," says Belinda. "This is an upmarket bed-and-breakfast, and guests are here at my convenience, not their own."

"I know, but—"

"When I say check-in time is seven fifteen at the latest, I mean it. It's on all the new literature."

"You haven't sent it out yet." Mary sips her wine.

"Yes," Belinda sniffs, "but technically it's on all the literature. And what is the point of making rules if I end up breaking them myself? It appears a little foolish, don't you think?"

Fortunately for the major he arrives within the next ten minutes and spares Belinda the inconvenience of breaking her rules and himself the same inconvenience of driving all the way to Poggibonsi, which is where Belinda sends anyone who displeases her or who doesn't fit into her important schedule.

She is in the kitchen, fixing herself a third gin and tonic, when she hears a car door slam. "They're here!" she announces to Mary, indicating her head toward the door. "You can go and meet and greet them. Returnees don't get the official greeting party—they get a ten percent discount instead."

By the time Mary gets to the front door and out into the drive, the major is already efficiently taking suitcases off the roof rack. "Good evening, Mary, my dear," he says, abandoning his suitcase and walking over to greet her. Sporting a pair of khaki shorts, beige knee socks, sandals, and a cream Aertex shirt, Major Chester looks as if he has just come off an exercise in the Gulf. Were it not for the amount of extra weight he is carrying around the middle, the short, thick whiteness of his legs, and the dimples at either side of his knees, he could have passed for a man in regular service. With a fringe of sandy hair around his skull, he stands erect and carries himself with the bullish determination of a short man.

His wife, Mrs. Patricia Chester, is at least four inches taller than her husband and of slim, neat build. She has the sort of steel gray, *bouclé* perm that bedecks every woman of her age, and an immensely thick pair of glasses that magnify her eyes to opossum proportions. In a pale pistachio flowered blouse and matching trousers, creased in a fan formation at the crotch, she looks a little tired from traveling.

"Did you have a good journey?" asks Mary, as she walks toward one of the major's smaller suitcases. She bends over, taking care that her buttocks face in the opposite direction from the major's jabbing fingers. Just in case the man still can't resist a good old-fashioned goose, like last year.

"It was all fine and dandy after the Mont Blanc tunnel," says the major, licking his rather fat wet lips.

"Oh, good," says Mary, straightening quickly.

"Yes. Right," says the major. "Come along, Pat, let's secure our quarters while there's some daylight left."

"Major! Dear! Mrs. Chester!" Belinda comes outside, after a suitably discounted time, a pleasant guest-greeting smile on her face. "How lovely to see you! How lovely of you to return to Casa Mia! I feel I should kiss you! So I will!" Belinda gives her guests warm gin kisses on both cheeks. "Welcome! Welcome! Welcome to you both!"

"Thank you, Belinda. It's nice to be back." Patricia blinks behind her specs.

"Oh, it's a pleasure to have you both back, Patricia. You're practically family," enthuses Belinda.

"Well, Pat and I can certainly orient ourselves around here," chuckles the major, picking up the suitcases in the swift maneuver of a man used to carrying kit bags. "Our usual room, Belinda?"

"Of course, your usual room, Major dear." Belinda smiles, her hands clasped as if in prayer. "Down the stairs and um . . ."

"Left," supplies the major.

"That's right, left," says Belinda. "Just like last year."

"Do you need help with that bag, Mrs. Chester?" asks Mary.

"Oh, no, love," replies Pat, with an owl-like stare. "This bag is for you and your mum. Some little presents from the mother country. You know, little things you just won't be able to live without."

"Presents?" says Belinda, with a generous gift-receiving smile. "How lovely! But, really, there's no need."

"Don't be silly," says Pat. "As you said, we're practically family, and I wouldn't dream of going to see any of my relations without taking them a little something."

"Oh, but you shouldn't have," says Belinda, wagging a finger with one hand while making a grab for the bag with the other. She walks off quickly, like a dog with a bone. She takes it into the kitchen and empties the contents onto the counter: out pours a box of English Breakfast tea, some fudge, a tin of evaporated milk, Ovaltine, a packet of Angel Delight, some digestive biscuits, a Battenberg cake, a pot of Marmite, Branston pickle, a slab of mild Cheddar and some Cadbury Dairy Milk.

"Oh, God," mutters Belinda, snapping off a line of chocolate and placing it all in her mouth at once. "What a load of English rubbish." She eats at such speed her eyes water. "Honestly," she crunches away, picking up the Battenberg cake and sniffing it through the wrapper. "I can't even remember what this stuff tastes like." She cuts herself a large slice through the plastic, breaks off a pink-marzipan-coated square, and pops it into her mouth. "Mmm, mmm." She adds two white squares. "Mmmm. Mmmm."

"All the comforts of home, eh?" says a voice, so loud and so close to Belinda that she jumps and snorts with shock.

"Pat!" she says, opening her mouth to display its contents. "I didn't see you there!" She swallows. Her head and shoulders force the large indigestible sponge bolus down her throat. "You sneaked up on me!"

"I did say hello, but I presumed you were so busy looking at all those memories of home that you didn't hear me," Pat explains, with blinking accompaniment.

"Yes, well, it's very kind of you. . . . Did you find your room all right?" inquires Belinda, smoothing down her skirt and slowly trying to edge the woman out of her kitchen.

"It's in the same place as last year," confirms the major, as he strides through the french windows and out onto Belinda's terrace and stands with his hands clasped behind his buttocks, looking at the view.

"Oh, there you are, Major!" Belinda smiles through the kitchen door and wipes the crumbs off her lips with the back of her hand. "Everything all right?"

"It looks shipshape to me," says the major, turning around. "Tell me, what's that new place being done up on the other side of the valley? I don't remember it from last year."

"Oh, that," says Belinda. "It's owned by an American woman."

"How awful," says the major. "Poor you."

"I know." Belinda nods. "I'm worried she'll lower the tone of the whole valley. I mean, she's already destroying the frescos in her chapel."

"Really?" says the major. "Dreadful people, the Americans. I know they were our allies in the war, but I really do think they shouldn't travel. They have no appreciation of culture." He shakes his head as if to rid himself of unpleasant thoughts. "So, did you enjoy the hamper?"

"Hamper? Oh, yes, of course, the food," says Belinda. "Very kind."

"An army marches on its stomach," insists the major, cradling his own. "And I honestly find, these days, I can't move without my PG, Branston, and, more increasingly, a small box of Angel Delight."

"Angel Delight?" says Mary, walking into the kitchen. "How, um, interesting."

"I just don't think any Johnny Foreigner can make a mousse properly," he declares.

"Well, I could make you some tonight," says Mary. "I couldn't think of anyone else who would want—who I'd rather make it for."

* * *

An hour later, the four of them are sitting down on the terrace under the sweet-smelling jasmine and honeysuckle to a late supper of chili con carne and strawberry Angel Delight. The major cannot stop talking. Belinda pretends to listen as he fills her and Mary in on all their family news from the past year, from the shiny new conservatory extension to their next-door neighbor's new hip, the death of his anemones, and the possibility of his running in the parish elections. The major debriefs in tremendous detail. Bolt upright in his chair, his forearms just touching the table, his hands tense and poised, he occasionally pauses for breath and to congratulate himself on entertaining the ladies. Meanwhile, his wife looks on quietly, blinking behind her double glazing.

"So," says the major, polishing off a glass of rather robust red wine that Belinda had picked up on special offer in the supermarket, "what do you intend to do about the American?"

"I don't know. What do you mean, Major?" asks Belinda, resting her chin in the palm of her hand.

"Well, what do you intend to do about her destruction of

the wall paintings?" he says, running his spoon around the edge of his bowl, scooping up the last pink snake of Angel Delight.

"Oh, right. Well, I've started a petition."

"Excellent," he replies, pointing with his spoon. "How many signatures?"

"Well, I've only just started," says Belinda.

"Good," says the major. "How many so far?"

"Um, none—well, one, if I include Mary, who will be signing, won't you, dear?"

"What? Yes, of course," says Mary, whose mind is back at the pool and moving slabs of stone with the handsome Franco. "Whatever you want," she says, running her hand down her hot neck and over her shoulder. "I don't mind."

"So, one," says Belinda optimistically. "Two, including myself, and perhaps you two will sign?"

"Mrs. Smith!" says the major, looking pompous and put out all at the same time. "It would be an honor and a pleasure. In fact, I consider it my duty to sign! And so does my wife."

"Oh, yes," agrees Pat.

"Well, there we go, Major," says Belinda. "Four!"

"I'm afraid that's not going to win the war, though, is it?" he says.

"Well, I should imagine not," says Belinda, with a knowing laugh. "But it's a start."

"So, it *is* a war?" asks the major.

"Oh," says Belinda.

"I thought as much." The major knowledgeably taps the side of his red nose. "When you've witnessed as many battles and stood on as many front lines as I have, you get a sixth sense for conflict. You can smell the tension in the air. And I knew it as soon as I mentioned the new house. There was tension."

"Well, she's opening a rival B-and-B, and when one's liveli-hood is under attack . . ." says Belinda, by way of explanation.

"And, as your regulars, it's our duty to help you in this bat-tle," rallies the major. "I need to school you in tactics. We need to try and work out what are their weaknesses, what would be the best plan of attack. Find out all there is to know about them, then beat them at their own game. Do you know the property? Have you been behind enemy lines?"

"Not totally," admits Belinda.

"Well, that's no good," says the major, shaking his head. "That's no good at all. We can't operate without a good recce."

"But she's having a party tomorrow," announces Belinda.

"Excellent," he says. He leans back in his chair and gives Mary a gentle goosing as she bends over to pick up his bowl. "Patri-cia, my darling! It looks like we arrived in the nick of time."

His wife smiles and blinks back.

Giovedì ❉ Thursday

Ciima ❉ *fa brutto* (Not very hot)

Oh dear, what a shame! I woke up this morning expecting the usual shiny bright sun and cobalt blue sky, dotted with diving swallows, but sadly it seems a few clouds are gathering on the horizon. I say "sadly" because although the valley needs the rain (we've had nothing substantial for weeks), my American neighbor, Lauren, is having a party tonight, and it looks as though the weather may ruin it. Wouldn't that be too, too awful? She's throwing open the doors of her tiny house and inviting the whole valley apparently. How terrible it would be if a downpour were to ruin such an indiscriminate gathering. If only her guest list had been smaller, more intimate, perhaps the climate would not be such an issue. But as it is her exuberance and, some uncharitable people might say, her arrogance have brought the whole evening into jeopardy.

It sounds silly, I know, but if she had spoken to me, or asked my advice on such things, as a hostess who has been living and entertaining in the valley for some time, I would have advised her to keep it small. Small is always successful. Or, at least, my soirées are. But, I have been so terribly busy with my guests that I would have been unable to spare her housewarming hooley a second thought.

Our returnees are settling in nicely. I put them in the same room as they had last year, which I think they appreciated! It is these little touches that make an upmarket bed-and-breakfast like mine so successful. I also served some of the major's favorite food, and both he and Mrs. Chester sent the chef (i.e., me!) their compliments!

That's another thing I must do when I have time. I must invite Lauren up to the house to show her the ropes and teach her a thing or two about service and being a proper *italiana* hostess. It is, after all, what neighbors do, isn't it? Help each other out? Oh, and invite each other to parties, of course. Truth be known, I am not looking forward to her do tonight. People always say that I am the life and soul of the party, but, oddly, I feel rather shy. I admit I have plenty to say, but often I find it more effectual to say it to a smaller group of people. It isn't in my nature to show off in front of a large crowd. Perhaps it's the artist in me! I'm really so much more at home with a brush in my hand, and a view in front of me, and perhaps some pleasant company by my side. To say I'm looking forward to my watercolor session with the major today is something of an understatement! You see, we artists must stick together at all costs!

TACCHINO DI CASA MIA

When you have spent as much time in Tuscany as I have, you will start to notice details that make all the difference. They single you out from a tourist, or a traveler who is merely passing through, and identify you as someone who is here to stay, and could even be mistaken for an Italian. I can't tell you how often that happens to me! Especially when I'm in Serrana market sourcing my food.

Anyway, here's a little detail that will impress your friends. The Italians eat quite a lot of turkey, and when they do it is mainly the breast. So, when cooking turkey Toscana-style, remember breast is best. Like this dish, for example, which I often find myself whipping up when I have some of my many, many friends over for supper.

* 8 turkey breasts
  (or however many friends
  you are entertaining)
* parsley

* garlic
* onions
* wine

Take the breasts and panfry them. Halfway through cooking add the garlic, onions, and wine, and sizzle away in a relaxed fashion till ready. Put the breasts on the plates and scatter over a luxuriant amount of chopped parsley, freshly picked by hand from the garden. I tend not to use the tense English parsley when its freer Mediterranean cousin is available. But living where you probably do, sadly, you have no choice.

Serve with some warming mashed potato and plenty of friends. This is a sociable dish, and it needs to be entertained.

❄ ❄ ❄

CHAPTER SIX

"Do you think it will rain later?" demands Belinda, standing on her terrace in her blue artist's smock, her brown hair scraped back into her red-spotted handkerchief. The response to her question is so muted she turns the corner and stands next to her guests, who are eating their breakfast. With her mouth open and one eye closed, she proceeds to squint down the valley, her arm out, measuring the heights of trees with her paintbrush. "Do you think so, Major?" she asks again, measuring up his wife the other side of the table. "Do you think it will rain?"

"Well . . ." says the major, putting down his Andy McNab novel and his piece of toast and marmalade. He looks down the valley. Two sharp arrowheads of snot-soaked hair peek out of his flared nostrils as he contemplates his weather forecast. "Mmm." He ponders. "Well, I can't smell rain."

"What does rain smell like, dear?" asks his wife, her jaw muscles flexing hard as she tries to make short shrift of the slightly stale bread roll that has been in her mouth for the last minute.

"Metal," replies the major definitively. "It smells like damp metal."

"Oh." His wife blinks, taking a sip of milky English Breakfast. "I never knew that."

"It's all part of my army training," asserts the major, picking up his toast and taking a man-size bite. "Weather and orienteering are absolutely essential for an officer in the field."

"I knew you'd know, Major, I just knew it," says Belinda, pulling up a chair. "So we'll be okay for watercoloring this morning. But it'll pour with rain later, won't it?"

The major raises his buttocks off the chair and scans the horizon. "Quite possibly."

"Quite possibly," repeats Belinda, with a smile. She shifts Pat's plate to one side as she leans her elbows across the table. "You seem to know so much, Major," she enthuses, "surely you can't put it all down to army training?

"Most of it is," says Pat, standing up and pulling her turquoise shorts out of her backside. "I'd rather thought, as the weather is not so special today, that we'd go shopping in Serrana, dear. Isn't that what we discussed earlier?"

"Shopping?" says Belinda, sounding a bit surprised.

"Yes." Pat nods. "Shopping."

"Yes, well, that *is* what we discussed just before breakfast, actually, Belinda," says the major.

"Oh," says Belinda. "There's no reason why you couldn't do both. If Pat is so keen to shop, then perhaps Mary could take her into town. I was going to send her in anyway. Then you and I could do our watercolors while the weather holds. That way"—she shrugs—"everyone is happy. Mary!" she shouts, before anyone can answer, interrupt, or express an opinion other than her own.

"Yes?" comes a call from the kitchen.

"Will you take Mrs. Chester into town with you this morning when you go shopping for me?"

"Oh? Right, yes, of course. If you want me to go shopping, then of course Mrs. Chester may come with me, if she wants to," Mary replies as she comes out onto the terrace, drying her hands on a tea towel.

"Of course she does," says Belinda, standing up and handing to Mary Pat's breakfast plate. "She's desperate for you to point out all the bargains. She's mad keen to get out of all her dull old English clothes, aren't you, Pat? While I make sure that her husband is well looked after and entertained, shan't I, Major?"

"Well, if you insist," chuckles the major.

"Oh, but I do." Belinda turns on her flip-flop. "How fortunate that I was on hand to help sort things out."

It is rare that Belinda doesn't get what she wants, and her watercolor morning with the major has been in the cards ever since the short man and his opossum-eyed wife booked three and a half months ago. Belinda has planned it in her mind's eye right down to the head scarf she's wearing and the conversation she intends to have. And, sadly, there is little or nothing that Pat or, indeed, the major can do about it. So, while Mary tidies away, studiously keeping her backside away from the major's foxed-up forefingers, Pat resigns herself to a morning's shopping without her husband.

Belinda can barely keep the triumphant trill of victory out of her voice. "Come along, Major," she says. "If we're to get any light at all we should move now."

"I'll be as quick as I can, Belinda," he replies, trotting off in the direction of his bedroom. "Just let me ablute, and I'll be with you in ten minutes."

Within seconds of Pat closing the front door, and Mary turning the car in the drive, Belinda is on the major's terrace, rattling his shutters.

"Are you ready yet, Major?" she asks, eyeing a large pair of white Y-fronts, drying on the back of a deck chair.

"I'm coming as quick as I can," he says, appearing at the french windows. His threads of sandy hair are wet, his face is newborn pink, and he is accompanied by the smell of drains and toothpaste. "Just let me gather my equipment."

"Gather away, Major, gather away." Belinda smiles, with a wave of her hand. "I just don't want you to miss out on anything now that we have this all-too-brief opportunity for Art."

"Quite right, Belinda," says the major, carefully packing his black tin of watercolors into a brown leather satchel. "Lead on!"

"Wherever the muse takes us!" says Belinda with a spin, and she takes the major off down the valley past the swimming pool to a discreet copse she has had in mind for some time.

After a convenient stroll down the hillside (Belinda never likes to walk very far for Art), she directs him to a group of wind-battered and somewhat gnarled-looking cypress trees with a perfectly adequate view over the back of the Bianchis' farm: fields of sunflowers just breaking into bloom, paddocks of bright green tobacco plus some crumbling outbuildings that Signor Bianchi neither uses nor has any intention of renovating—they house a couple of long-legged sheep and some fairly rampant goats.

The major, having spent most of his life painting gift-shop fronts in Chipping Campden, seems delighted and brings out what looks like a small canvas fishing chair from his leather satchel. He stands and stares along the length of his right arm, framing imaginary tableaux with the end of his paintbrush, before finally choosing his spot. Pulling up his knee socks and khaki shorts, he eases himself slowly onto his precarious-looking seat. Belinda plonks her well-padded backside on a stone next to him.

"Don't you just love the way the sun warms the buildings when it breaks through the cloud?" muses Belinda, her head cocked to one side. "The textures are amazing."

"Mmm," says the major, his nose in his satchel. "I thought I might try to get my sky right first."

"Oh, of course, of course," agrees Belinda, taking her paint box out of a patchwork bag. "I was merely remarking on the beauty of it all."

"You are so fortunate to live here," pronounces the major, "surrounded by so much beauty."

"Yes," says Belinda, taking the lid off her water jar. "Sometimes I find it hard to control my reaction to it."

"I can imagine," says the major, lining up his paper.

"There are times when I just have to release my inner artist," says Belinda, untying the top of her smock.

"Yes," says the major, shifting in his seat.

"There are times when it's healthy just to let it all go," enthuses Belinda, her large bosom heaving as she exhales. "To release."

"Yes, right," agrees the major, selecting a blue for his sky.

"I knew you'd understand, Major," she continues, hitching up her skirt to display a rather heavy, veiny white thigh, covered with short, thick, dark hairs, "being an artist."

"Yes," says the major. "But I am, first and foremost, an army officer. The artist in me unfortunately has to come second."

"Oh, but a close second, Major. Surely, a close second? A passionate man like you can't keep his desires suppressed all the time. You must let yourself go sometimes." Belinda's thighs are apart, her loose cleavage seeping over the top of her open smock. "You must have to erupt . . . Major! Erupt like a—a vicious, violent volcano."

"I often think one can't overestimate the value of self-control," says the major, his eyes firmly on the view.

"Oh, indeed, Major?" Belinda leans forward on her stone, trying to penetrate his eye line. "I quite like the idea of someone forcing me . . . forcing me to take control."

"Yes . . . well," says the major, brusquely rattling all the color out of his brush into the water jar. "Is that the American's house I can see tucked away behind the hill?"

"What?" asks Belinda.

"The American, is that the house down there?" asks the major.

"Um, yes," dismisses Belinda. "Where were we?"

"Have you come up with a plan for tonight?" he asks.

"What? Sorry? No," says Belinda, with her first strategy for the day already not working out, she is reluctant to launch into another.

"Oh, well, here's what I would do," says the major, selecting a nice gray for the clouds. "I would make a detailed journey around the house. If she's in direct competition with you, you need to know exactly what she'll be doing. Forewarned is forearmed."

Belinda leans on her elbow as she begins halfheartedly to paint the green hill she sees before her. The major carries on talking, regaling her with the various methods and means open to her. He describes battles he has been involved in and ends up talking for nearly an hour about his experiences in the Falklands and the first Gulf War. By the time his conversation has dried up, so has Belinda's passion for the major, the view, and, indeed, Art. Sadly, she also has the painting to prove it. Two green stripes, a blue and gray panel, and a brown square do not really do justice to the vista. Feeling sour, unsated, and deeply bored, with a numb backside, she announces that she must return to Casa Mia: Mary never has any idea where to put the shopping. The Major says he needs another ten minutes to finish his oeuvre and will join her in a while.

Back at the villa, Belinda can hear laughter as she approaches.

"What's so funny?" she demands, climbing the stairs to her terrace and discovering Pat and Mary drinking coffee together.

"Nothing, really." Mary smiles.

"No, come on," demands Belinda. "Tell me."

"Oh, it's just that we ran into that handsome boy who lives in the village," giggles Pat, "and he couldn't keep his eyes off Mary."

"Which boy?"

"Oh, it was nothing," says Mary.

"Don't be silly," insists Pat. "I may be shortsighted, but I'm certainly not blind, and he couldn't keep his eyes off you. I almost felt like making myself scarce. Honestly, Belinda, I tell you. He carried our bags and opened the car door for us. He kissed the backs of our hands." She sighs. "I swear he's in love with her—he's in love with you." She laughs, wagging her finger at Mary.

"*Who?*" says Belinda, stamping her right foot and raising her voice a bit too much. "Who? Who's in love with her?" she asks, again, more politely.

"That handsome boy, Franco—Gianfranco." Pat grins, her huge eyes blink rapidly with excitement.

"Oh," says Belinda, rearranging her artist's smock. She is rigid with annoyance. "The local handyman-peasant—how terribly exciting."

No one says anything. Mary looks at her shoes, and Belinda stares down the valley.

"Ye-e-es," mumbles Pat into the silence as she stands up. "Well," she says, looking at the clearing sky, "it's turned out nice again, the weather. No chance of rain for your party later."

"Yes," hisses Belinda, walking toward the french windows. "I am well aware of that."

Belinda swans upstairs and spends the rest of the day locked in her bedroom riffling through her wardrobe. Having her advances thwarted, and her painting trip more or less ruined, it has made her even more determined that her arrival at tonight's party is to go without a hitch.

The role of uninvited guest is a difficult one to dress for, and she is determined to get it right. A little overdressed and there'll be the whiff of desperation—you look as if you've tried too hard. A little underdressed and you look as if you've caught yourself, as well as your hostess, unawares. So, something along the lines of smart, casual, and terribly relaxed is what she's after. Relaxed, of course, being the most important. She is, after all, arriving with an air of forgiveness. She is forgiving Lauren for leaving her off the list.

So, Belinda spends the majority of the afternoon trying to work out which is the more forgiving color: green or purple? Green is too associated with that grubby emotion, jealousy, she thinks, and eventually plumps for purple. It's imperial, as well as relaxed, which, in Belinda's eyes, is such a winning combination. So, in the purple kaftan costume, she whistles with delight as she admires, in the hall mirror, the genius way in which she has wrapped the purple-and-gold-trimmed belt around her hair. It makes her head look like a boiled sweet.

"Do you think this is a little too much?" she asks Mary, her large, beaded, chatty earrings swinging wildly.

"Well . . ."

"I don't want to dominate the proceedings."

"Right."

"I don't want to overshadow the *americana*'s party in the slightest," she continues, "but occasionally one does have to look the part. And as far as I can remember Derek couldn't keep his hands off me when I last wore this."

"That was mainly because he'd drunk so much grappa after Barbara had gone home when she'd split her Aladdin hot pants up the back," says Mary.

"Lord! That was so embarrassing." Belinda chortles at Barbara's humiliation. "I always said she was too overweight and middle-aged to play Aladdin." She shakes her purple and gold head. "Honestly, the vanity of some people."

"Yes."

"Ooh, *bella donna! Bella donna!*" says the major, on walking into the hall. "Two *bella donna!*"

"Two *belle donne*," corrects Belinda. "Honestly, Major, have you made no progress at all in your Italian since last year?" she asks with a small laugh. "But I have to agree with you that Maria has scrubbed up rather well."

"Sorry?" says Mary, rather taken aback by her mother's compliment.

"But you do, darling, you do," says Belinda, craning forward with a tight smile. She takes her daughter's hand. "You and me together tonight, darling, allies, partners in crime!"

In a ruby-red top with a low drawstring neck and a tiered black skirt, Mary has scrubbed up extremely well and looks like some exotic Spanish dancer. Her long, dark hair is smoothed off her face and clasped at the back of her neck with a red flower. It is a simple and beguiling combination. The major can't resist giving her backside a squeeze as he walks by.

"So," continues Belinda, "I think we deserve a couple of drinks before we go, don't you, Maria, to get the show on the road, so to speak?"

Three gin and tonics and a short drive later, they arrive at the Casa Padronale to find the party in full swing. Mary pulls up on the smooth stone drive, alongside a line of cars already tucked on the verge. The sound of a jazzy trumpet calls them toward the house.

"I've never seen so many cars in the valley," says Belinda, teetering along in a pair of gold sandals.

"It's amazing, isn't it?" agrees Mary, as she breathes in the warm evening air and gazes up at the young stars shining in the clear dark blue sky. "Look! Howard's here—there's his car. And so are Derek and Barbara and . . ." She pauses. "Is that the Bianchis' Panda?"

"I don't know, darling," says Belinda, looking down her short nose at the dusty, rusty car. "She can't have invited them, surely."

The jazz grows louder as they approach the house. Despite the large tracts of torn-up earth where the construction vehicles have been driving back and forth, the house and the land surrounding it look amazingly presentable for having just undergone such a dramatic refurbishment.

"I see she's bought the garden center," says Belinda, remarking on the line of ten terra-cotta pots full of red geraniums outside the house and the new row of cypresses along the drive. "She's even shipped in a few olives. Has she got money to burn?"

"The front looks lovely," says Mary, staring at the new shutters, the clever use of old tiles on the new roof, and the shiny copper gutters.

The front door is open, so they walk in. The hall is white. In the middle there is a long plain wooden table with a large stone bowl on it containing water, rose petals, and floating scented candles. Through another large open door to the right they can see an expansive four-poster bed of unvarnished oak, made up with crisp white linen and covered with a couple of pashmina shawls. Belinda and Mary carry on through in silence. Mary is on tiptoe, as if she's about to burgle the place, and even Belinda is feeling a touch reticent. The music grows louder as they go through the next door. They both stop.

"Oh, my God," says Belinda, eventually. "She's knocked out nearly the entire ground floor."

Mary can only stare at the stunning open-plan kitchen, sitting room, and dining room area. "It's enormous," she says, eyes shining.

"It's very un-Italian," says Belinda.

The white space is huge. The kitchen is made up of wooden free-standing units, including a butcher's block, shelves, and cupboards that flank a catering-size steel cooker with eight rings. Pots, pans, and strings of garlic hang from hooks in the ceiling. Opposite stands a long wooden table, capable of seating twenty with an eclectic collection of chairs, all made from the same wood, around it. There are three large bowls on the table filled with a similar water, rose petals, and candles combination as they saw in the hall. The whole room is lit by small candles— they grace nearly every flat surface. They cover the wooden tables at either side of the fat cream sofas. They run the length of the bookshelves, and they are also along the edge of the terrace outside.

Inside, the jazz competes with the noise of the guests, who are sitting on the chairs and sofas. Mary recognizes the majority of the Bianchi family at the long table. The parents, the brothers, and their wives are sitting down talking animatedly, but Gianfranco is nowhere to be seen.

"Good God! The Bianchis are here," sighs Belinda, walking over to the line of Prosecco bottles on the side in the kitchen. "I think I need a drink." She picks up a flute and takes the dregs from three empty bottles to fill her glass. There is a blue bowl of small eggs on the side. "Good Lord," says Belinda, curling her nose. "What are they?"

"Quails' eggs," says Mary. "Don't you think we should find our hostess?"

"Quite right," says Belinda, taking a large sip of her flat fizz.

Outside, blue fairy lights are glinting in the trees, and bamboo flares light the garden paths. A four-piece band is playing to the left of a collection of small tables covered with candles and white cloths. About fifty people are talking, laughing, drinking, and dancing.

Standing on the terrace in her purple ensemble, Belinda is nothing if not conspicuous.

"Contessa!" shouts Derek from his table, where Barbara and Howard are sitting. He stands up to give her a large wave. "Over here!"

Belinda raises her glass an inch and gives a small wave back. As she surveys the party, offering little smiles and waves to Giovanna and Roberto's table, which also contains her hairdresser from Serrana, Belinda notices a tall blonde figure in a white cotton dress approaching her. It is Lauren, and she is coming at speed.

"Betina!" she says.

"Lauren! Dear!" says Belinda. "How lovely to see you. What an amazing party!"

"How amazing to see you here," replies Lauren, putting her hands on her hips, her toned arm blocking the way.

"It is so lovely of you to invite me," says Belinda, taking a sip

of her drink and smiling over her hostess's shoulder. "You remember my daughter?" she adds, pushing forward a reluctant
Mary.

"Yes . . . I remember your daughter," replies Lauren, looking
at Mary with a warm, sympathetic smile.

"Anyway, we're thrilled to be here," continues Belinda, still
looking over Lauren's shoulder.

"But you weren't invited," says Lauren, in a low but perfectly
audible voice.

"Oh, I know," agrees Belinda, giving Lauren's white shoulder a little shove with her hand. "I've made the same mistake
myself." She nods, her eyes rolling. "Anyway, just in case you're
worried," she leans forward to whisper in Lauren's ear, "I forgive you. I mean, what's a little invitation between friends?"

"There you are!" blusters Derek, edging between them.
"We've been wondering where you were, Belinda. The invitation said six!" he chortles. "Trust you to be fashionably late.
You'll learn this, Lauren," he says, turning to his hostess, "about
Belinda, when you get to know our little gang properly. She's
always fashionably late, but, then, she's such a fashionable person." He places a hand on each of her shoulders. "You look fantastic, dear. Fantastic. Don't you think so, Lauren?"

"Yes," says Lauren, eyeing Belinda up like a prize heifer in an
agricultural show. "I'd say you look truly fantastic." She smiles.
It doesn't reach her eyes. She leans forward and whispers, in
Belinda's ear, "Very brave." Before she sashays away, she adds,
"Have a nice evening, Betina."

"Oh, Betina! That's a good nickname." Derek chuckles.
"Haven't heard that before. Come along, Betina—"

"Belinda," hisses Belinda.

"Oh, right." He stands corrected. "Come along! Barbara and

Howard are keen to see you." Putting his arm around Belinda, Derek weaves her through the party, while Mary follows behind, eyes scanning the crowd, looking out for Gianfranco.

"Sit down, sit down," says Barbara, her large blue eyes round with excitement, a heavy golden bangle shining in the candlelight. "Honestly, Belinda," she enthuses, "can you believe such a party? Can you believe the house? It's so stunning, so beautiful. We've never seen anything like it in Val di Santa Caterina! Oh, have you seen the food? She's got these little yummy things.... Have you seen the band? Have you seen the decorations? Have you seen *all* the champagne?"

"It's Prosecco," says Belinda.

"I know but, really," Barbara draws breath, "this is the best party I've ever seen in this valley. Ever. Howard agrees with me. Don't you, Howard?"

"Absolutely," says Howard, his eyes almost closed with intoxication.

"You've got to admit, Belinda," Derek leans back in his chair, "this . . . this is better than any party any of us has ever given."

"Well, technically, I've never actually given a party," says Howard.

"Well, neither of us, then," continues Derek. "I mean, you haven't done anything like this, have you, Belinda?"

"I have also never painted over frescos like her either," pronounces Belinda, pouring herself some more Prosecco from the bottle on the table.

"Has she?" says Barbara, popping an anchovy toast into her mouth. "Mmm, oh, my God, that's delicious. Belinda, have one."

"Yes. She's actually painted over the whole thing. Even though those *Bell' Arti* art police had to come and stop her."

Belinda goes on to explain Lauren's cultural vandalism to a distracted and disinclined audience.

✻ ✻ ✻

Mary is bored. The evening is young, the stars are shining, and the jazz is so beguiling that she is almost tempted to go and dance on her own. But instead she sits, taps her feet, sips her Prosecco, and stares at those on the dance floor. Giovanna and Roberto are trotting around the floor together looking like an old couple still very much in love. Belinda's hairdresser looks as if she can really move, as can Kyle. In a white shirt and jeans with bare feet, he is twirling one of the Bianchi daughters-in-law around as if her life depended on it. Mary watches him. He is laughing and smiling, making giant gesticulating gestures with his hands as he talks in Italian. The girl is smiling back at him. Mary smiles, too. She scans the crowd again for any sign of Franco. They hadn't talked of the party earlier when they met in Serrana, but now, having seen his whole family here, she is sure he must be, too.

Suddenly there's a rustling in the bushes behind them. Derek turns around. "What the heck?" he says.

"Bloody hell," says Howard, trying to focus.

There's more noise and, from the darkness, a tall dark figure appears. It's Franco. His open-necked black shirt is unbuttoned, his smooth, toned stomach shines in the candlelight, his dark hair is ruffled. He looks so handsome that Mary has to dig her nails into her palm to stop herself from making a noise.

"*Signore*," he says, his lips curling into a smile as he bows and clicks his heels together.

"Hello, Franco," say Belinda, Barbara, and Mary in unison, as they all smile and stare.

"It is a very nice evening," he states.

"Yes." All three women nod.

There is some more rustling, and out pops a pretty girl with long, dark, curly hair. Her head is down as she stands posting her round bosoms back into her white, front-loading bra.

"Oh, Dio!" she says as she looks up, shocked to find she has an audience. "Um. *Buona sera,"* she adds.

All three women at the table deflate like punctured party balloons.

"Buona sera." Franco nods as he takes her hand and they giggle off into the darkness.

"The Italians are incorrigible," says Belinda, draining her glass. "The things we've done for that boy and look how he behaves."

"I know," says Barbara.

"We have him in our houses."

"I know," nods Barbara. "I mean, we employed him only the other day. Yesterday—"

"Excuse me." Someone taps Mary's shoulder.

She turns around. "Kyle," she says, startled.

"Would you like to dance?"

"Who? Me?"

"No, your mother." He laughs. "Of course you."

"Oh, um . . ." Mary hesitates.

"Please," he smiles. "I don't often beg."

"Oh, okay, then," says Mary, standing up. "I'm not very good."

"Neither am I," he lies, putting his hand into the small of her back, directing her toward the dance floor. He weaves her expertly through the tables and the crowd, taking her hand as they reach the dance floor. As they stand opposite each other, the music moves up tempo. "I love this one." He nods in time to the music. "Are you ready?" Mary smiles. "Just follow me."

For a man who is really rather good at everything, Kyle is particularly good at dancing. He steps forward, takes hold of her waist in one hand, then turns and twirls her in time to the music. Mary is nervous at first, hesitant and unsure, but Kyle is so certain of his moves that all she needs to do is relax and feel the music flow through her. Within a couple of minutes they have created quite a space on the dance floor, as people move back and out of their way. Others stand at the edge tapping their feet or clapping along as they watch. Kyle's dark hair and wide smile catch the light as he spins Mary around the floor. At the end of the song, just as the trumpet reaches its crescendo, he holds her up in the air, catching her back in his arms on the final beat. As they stand cheek to cheek, breathing heavily, Mary can feel the heat of his body and his heart beating against her own chest.

"Thank you," says Kyle, pulling her away from him. "That was great." He bends down to kiss her cheek. "You dance quite well."

"No." Mary laughs. "You dance extremely well. I was putty in your hands."

"Well, you make mighty fine putty," he says. "Do you fancy a drink?"

"That would be lovely," says Mary, following him to a table.

"Stay here," he says. "What would you like?"

"A glass of Prosecco would be nice."

"Some bubbles it is, then." He points a finger at her. "And don't you dare move!"

He runs off up the stairs into the kitchen. Mary smooths her hair and gazes into the crowd. Suddenly she sees Franco, sitting with his brothers at another table. He is full of sexual swagger, his arm draped around the dark, round-breasted girl. They are laughing and talking loudly, his right hand wanders lazily down her top and plays with her bosom. She doesn't say anything, but every so often he pulls her toward him and puts his tongue into her mouth. Mary rests her chin in her hands and stares. *Did* Franco like her? Or was he just leading her on? Playing with her like a cat with a mouse? Had the whole flirtation been in her head?

"Here you go—one glass of bubbles," says Kyle, sitting down opposite her and blocking her view of Franco. "Are you okay?"

"Thank you, I'm fine," says Mary, sitting up straight.

"Oh, you looked deep in thought."

"No, I'm fine," she insists. "Thank you. To your new house," she says, changing the subject.

"To our meeting," says Kyle, clinking glasses.

"To our meeting *and* your new house." Mary smiles, taking a small sip of Prosecco.

✳ ✳ ✳

Meanwhile, on the other side of the party, Belinda has finished off a whole bottle of Prosecco and, with the resultant conversation, her three friends.

"What the rest of the *comune* thinks about her painting over the frescos I dread to think," she says, her chin up as she tries to look out from underneath her head wrapping. "It is part of our heritage, you know. I did tell them she was American. . . ."

"Well, most of the *comune* is here." Barbara points with a square-tipped index finger. "And none of them seem to mind."

"She's winning over their hearts and minds with champagne," says Howard, helping himself to another glass. "She's given them a shock-and-awe party with some hearts-and-minds canapés. The woman's a genius." He laughs. "And a rather attractive genius as well."

"Oh, shut up, Howard," says Belinda. "She's not that clever."

"Yes," agrees Barbara. "Or that pretty."

"Well, I'm having a lovely time," says Derek, running his thumbs along his sweaty waistband. "Would you like to dance, Barbara?"

"Ooh, Mr. Hewitt," she giggles, her shoulders rounding in delight, "I thought you'd never ask."

"Come along, my little munchkin," he says, slapping her backside as she trots along ahead of him. "Let's show those youngsters what us oldies can do."

"Aaah," says Howard, waving his glass at them. "Ain't that sweet?"

"Oh, stop it, Howard," snaps Belinda. "You're drunk."

"And in the words of Sir Winston Churchill, 'My lady, you're ugly, but I shall be sober in the morning,'" slurs Howard, as his elbow slides slowly down the length of the table.

"Urgh," says Belinda, getting up and brushing down her kaftan. "I'm leaving," she says, then sets off a little unsteadily in the direction of the house.

"*Arrivadeary*," says Howard, as his head hits the table.

With the major's reconnoitering advice ringing in her ears, Belinda begins to snoop around the house. A small pad and pencil in her handbag, she plans to walk around the villa taking notes. The ground floor is relatively easy to recce, open plan and full of other guests. It is simple enough for Belinda to jot down her small and not entirely sober *aperçus*—the great collection of kitchen gadgets for juicing, slicing, and steaming, the small stack of yoga books, the pile of English newspapers and magazines, with the classified sections marked, the attractive pile of white china.

However, upstairs it is slightly more difficult to pass unnoticed. Belinda tiptoes from room to room, noting the smooth white decor, the natural wooden furniture, and the stunning limestone *en-suite* bathrooms. There are five spare rooms, plus a beautifully decorated master bedroom with white muslin trailing from the ceiling and a large cream silk chaise longue, a mirrored dressing table, and a couple of large wall mirrors from India. But stalking around dressed as a giant purple Quality Street is perhaps not the best for undercover work. Also, Belinda is rather tight, and she thinks she is more subtle—and, indeed, more invisible—than she actually is. This means that it is not long before someone tells Lauren that a "purple woman" is poking her nose around the place.

Belinda is in the chapel, scratching at the paintwork, trying to pick her way down to the frescos when Lauren walks in. She stands and watches Belinda for a second, then clears her throat. "What are you doing?" she asks. Her voice is more quizzical than accusatory.

"Oh!" Belinda jumps around. Her turban, like a candy wrapper around her head, slides down her face, and the front of her dress is covered in telltale flakes of white paint. "Nothing!" she says, like a child whose face is covered with chocolate and still denies eating sweets. "Absolutely nothing."

"Well, you're patently doing something," says Lauren, walking languidly toward Belinda as she pins herself against the wall.

"I was looking for the loo," says Belinda.

"Oh, really?" says Lauren. "Well, ever since we had a call from the *Bell'Arti,* I'm afraid we've had to change the layout of the place, and what was supposed to have been the most magnificent bathroom and plunge pool is now the yoga room. So I'm afraid you'll find no facilities in here."

"A yoga room?" says Belinda. "You're having a yoga room?"

"Yes," says Lauren, with a little nod. "But, then, you'd know all about that now, wouldn't you?"

"No, I'm afraid you've got me there." Belinda smiles, walking away from the wall and making as if to pass Lauren. "I know absolutely nothing about yoga. Nothing at all."

"I suppose that's to be expected from a provincial woman like you, isn't it?" says Lauren. "You know nothing about yoga and everything about furtive phone calls to local bureaucrats."

"I have no idea what you're talking about," declares Belinda. "Your domestic DIY problems are of no interest to me."

"Oh, but they are," says Lauren. "You seem to be fascinated by what's going on in my house. In fact, you can't leave the goings-on in my house alone. I only have to pop into Giovanna's to hear how much you're gossiping about me."

"Me? Gossiping about you? Don't make me laugh. Ha, ha, ha," laughs Belinda.

"Well, that's not what I hear," says Lauren. Her voice is pleasantly controlled. "I hear you're quite upset about my presence in the valley."

"My valley," snaps Belinda, her face quite pink with alcohol and anger.

"Your valley," laughs Lauren, her smooth blonde hair swinging about her face.

"Yes, my bloody valley," insists Belinda. "I was here first!"

"Oh dear," says Lauren, raising a finely plucked eyebrow as she turns to leave the chapel.

"I was *fucking* here first," hisses Belinda, her fists clenched. Every vein in her neck pumped with blood.

"I think I'd really like you to leave my party," says Lauren. "You're lowering the tone."

"I am already leaving your ghastly party," shouts Belinda as she marches past her out of the chapel and onto the side of the terrace. She turns back and shouts, "In fact, it's so bloody ghastly I can't work out why I've stayed so long in the first place."

"Neither can anyone else, Betina dear," says Lauren, walking slowly onto the terrace, shaking her head. "Neither can anyone else."

"My name's bloody Belinda!" screams Belinda at the top of her voice. There's a dramatic pause in the party as everyone falls silent, turns, and stares.

"I know," says Lauren, with a special smile.

"Mary! Mary! Mary!" Belinda looks frantically around for her daughter. "Maaa-ry!" she yells, her short retroussé nose in the air as she tries to see through the turban, which is now covering her face. "Mary! Hurry up! We're leaving! We're leaving—right now!"

"Arrivadeary," says Lauren, with a little English wave.

Venerdì ❧ Friday

Clima ❧ *fa caldo* (hot)

What a night! What a dreadful night! What an absolutely ghastly
evening. In fact, last night has to have been one of the worst nights
of my life. Honestly, dear readers, I don't mean to crow, but it was
truly awful. For as many of you must know by now, there is an art to
entertaining. A real art. To be a proper hostess requires flair. It
requires panache, dedication, an ability to put the needs of others
ahead of one's own. It also requires a little smattering of magic party
dust plus a pinch of je ne sais quoi. And, sadly, my poor dear
americana neighbor has none of the above. In short, her soirée last
night was a disaster.

I mean, where to start? The music was too loud. There was not
enough alcohol. The food was very poor. There were too many
people, and, actually, if I'm being honest, there were so many Italians
one couldn't even hear oneself speak English! Normally we expats
out here enjoy tucking up together on a sofa for a sticky and a chat.
But because our new resident *americana* had insisted on inviting the

whole valley, there was no room in the house, so we had to spend the evening milling around outside!

Not that we would have wanted to spend much time inside that small house of hers. From what little I saw, she seems to have painted the whole thing white. Quite apart from it being a devil to clean, I can't understand why anyone would want a white house in the middle of the Tuscan countryside. It's so un-Italian. Also, it seems she's planning to make that beautiful fresco-filled chapel next door into some sort of New Age yoga room full of chanting hippies and tantric sex! Really! For the sake of the taste and decency of the valley, I'm beginning to think I shall have to take it upon myself to make sure that her B-and-B closes down as soon as possible! Forgive me if I sound a little upset, but when one's way of life and livelihood is threatened, the British bulldog spirit comes barking out of everyone!

But apart from last night's disaster, everything else is going well. My returnees are settling in. Mrs. Chester went shopping yesterday and came back with the usual leather goods and some suitable outfits for a sojourn in Toscana. It always amazes me what the English wear to go on holiday. Their poor-quality fabrics and unstylishly cut clothes stick out a mile in Tuscany. No Italian would ever mix pale green with cream. Even their skin tone doesn't fit with the color of the stone. As an artist, I find the clashing colors often offend my eye.

Speaking of which, I have so far spent one wonderful morning painting with the major. It is in troubled times like these that one turns to nature to feel its beauty reoxygenate the blood in one's veins. From my window this morning as I am writing, I can feel the height of summer tighten its grip on the valley. The air is warm, the tobacco is high, the Bianchis' sunflowers are in full bloom, as are most of my flowers. Only a couple of stubborn vines resist my little green fingers!

One piece of news that I did hear at last night's party (if one can call it that) is that the sporty girls who all share the Santa Caterina monastery are coming soon. Perhaps I should invite them over for a simple Toscana soirée? In fact, in the light of last night's dreadful evening, perhaps I should invite a few more people over for a simple Toscana soirée? If only to show everyone how it should really be done!

PIZZA DI CASA MIA

In my years of entertaining out here, I have found that nothing gives a simple Toscana soirée a sense of occasion like bits of pizza. The ultimate in finger food, small sections of pizza can be eaten midconversation and will hardly ever interrupt the flow. They are easily picked up between thumb and forefinger and not at all messy. I swear by them. Although I do, rather shamefully, remember reheating prebought, prefabricated pizza when I lived in the U.K. Those were the days! But now I like to spoil my guests. I love to treat them to the myriad topping choices we get over here! But a word of warning: anyone who likes their pizza thick and filled with piped cheese should really stick to the U.K. because over here **pizze** are as thin as paper, twice as crunchy, and four times more devilish and delicious!

- ❋ pizza base
  (available at any good local
  family-run bakery)
- ❋ tomato paste
- ❋ mozzarella
- ❋ anchovies
- ❋ olives
- ❋ pineapple
- ❋ ham
- ❋ and anything else that
  tickles your fancy!

Roll out your base, cover it with tomato paste and mozzarella, then lay each topping ingredient on the dough in an attractive pattern. There are some people who think that toppings should be thrown on, to make it appear that the food has not been touched too much, but, sadly, I feel that that looks as though the cook has not made any effort. So release your inner artist, and make patterns or pictures with your anchovies—flowers, starbursts, little sunsets, pastoral scenes. Your guests will appreciate that little extra detail.

Serve at a simple soirée or any other festive occasion with a discreet beverage.

✷ ✷ ✷

CHAPTER SEVEN

Having spent the greater part of the morning locked in her bedroom, writing in her journal and brooding over the events of last night, Belinda suddenly appears on the terrace. She exudes all the faux-efficiency of someone resolved to wreak vengeance but is not sure quite which direction the wreaking will take. She announces her arrival to Mary, who is, rather slowly, clearing away Mrs. Chester's breakfast things, and gives the major a passing wave, before deciding to telephone Derek for the full lowdown on last night.

"*Pronto,* Derek! *Pronto!*" she trills when he picks up. "It's the Contessa here."

"Oh," says Derek, sounding uncharacteristically flat. "Hello, Belinda."

"How are you, Derek dear?"

"A little the worse for wear, Belinda, I have to admit."

"Worse for wear?" she queries. "I wasn't aware it was that sort of party. It seemed a little dull to me."

"Dull?" coughs Derek. "Do you think so? I thought it was ever such a laugh."

"Do you really think so?" says Belinda, eyebrows raised in

disdain. "Honestly, Derek, if you'd been to as many parties—or, indeed, given as many parties—as I have, you would understand that Lauren doesn't know the first thing about entertaining."

"Oh," says Derek.

"I mean, there were far too many Italians there for a start. You couldn't hear yourself speak English." Derek does not reply. "So," continues Belinda, talking through the pause and corkscrewing her backside into the arm of her ex-husband's favorite chair, "tell me what happened after I left."

"We-e-ll," replies Derek, hesitantly, "after your, um, your . . . departure, gosh, um, let me see . . ."

"Don't tell me it's *that* difficult to think of something! Surely Howard was badly behaved? He normally is."

"No, no," corrects Derek. "I was just wondering what I should say first."

"Oh."

"Yes, well," continues Derek, and clears his throat, "Howard was quite badly behaved in the end as he did dance on a table. But, then, quite a few people were dancing on tables."

"Oh dear," says Belinda. "I knew something uncouth like that would happen."

"Lauren was encouraging them."

"She was?"

"Oh, yes!" Derek starts to laugh. "She really knows how to throw a party, that woman. You should have been there." He is still chuckling. "What I mean is, I wish you hadn't had to go. Kyle got his saxophone out and started to play with the band, and everyone was dancing. It was amazing, just your scene, actually. Your daughter was the belle of the ball."

"What Mary? Dancing?" Belinda's head recoils from the telephone.

"Yes," says Derek. "Ever so well, dear, as it happens."

"How bizarre—are you sure?"

"Oh, yes," confirms Derek. "After she'd got back from her tour of the grounds with Kyle and found you'd driven off, she was going to come after you, but Kyle persuaded her to stay and dance with him some more, and she eventually ended up dancing in front of everyone at the party."

"But Mary can't dance," persists Belinda.

"Well, she can now."

"So, what else happened?" asks Belinda, trying to hide her irritation with a singsong cadence.

"Were you there for the fireworks?"

"Fireworks?" Belinda sits bolt upright.

"I forget what time you left exactly," says Derek.

"You escorted me to my car," informs Belinda.

"It was early, wasn't it?"

"Not that early," says Belinda. "Around ten thirty."

"Well, that was early for this party," laughs Derek. "Barb and I didn't get home till gone four!"

"Four!" Belinda cannot control her surprise. "What did you do there till four?"

"We had fun. I can't believe you missed the fireworks. Did you not see them from your side of the valley?"

"No," says Belinda. "I did hear some rather annoying banging, but fortunately my bedroom window faces the road."

"Oh," says Derek. "They spelt 'Welcome' right at the end."

"Welcome? Welcome to whom? Welcome to what? Welcome to where?" quizzes Belinda, firing one question after the other.

"Her house? The valley, I suppose," says Derek. "I didn't ask."

"God! How *nouveau riche!*" spits Belinda.

"*Nouveau riche?*"

"First-generation rich, Derek. Ghastly."

"I know what *nouveau riche* is, Belinda," says Derek, sounding put out, "but I thought that this was just a bit of fun."

"Oh, Derek, now you're being silly," says Belinda placatingly. "There are ways of spending money that is not flash or *nouveau riche* . . . um, your cypresses, for example. I know you told me a few times they cost ten thousand euros to plant, but they aren't *nouveau riche* at all."

"Right," says Derek, sounding confused. "How about my mosaic swimming pool?"

"No-o-o," insists Belinda.

"My barn conversion?"

"No-o-o."

"My chandelier from Harrods?" asks Derek, going through the list of his largest financial outlays.

"Derek, seriously now, I don't know what you're talking about," bluffs Belinda.

"Anyway, I was only calling to invite you and Barbara around to mine for a party. I sort of think that I should reply for the valley, as it were, and welcome Lauren to the area, after her little do, don't you think?"

"Oh, that would be ever so nice of you," says Derek.

"I know," says Belinda, running her hands through her hair.

"You're right," says Derek. "I mean, the only person I know who could possibly entertain like Lauren is you."

"I know," says Belinda again.

"Absolutely," agrees Derek.

"You're right," says Belinda, agreeing with herself and Derek. "There really is no one else." She turns around to try to catch an admiring glimpse of herself in the mirror and instead comes face-to-face with Giulia, who is waiting patiently for Belinda to finish her conversation. "Jesus Christ!" she says in surprise, shooting off the arm of her ex-husband's chair.

"What?" says Derek.

"No! Not you," says Belinda. "Listen, Derek, I'm afraid I have to go. I have staff standing next to me awaiting instruction."

"Righty-ho!" says Derek.

"*Arrivadeary,*" says Belinda.

"*Arrivadeary,*" replies Derek.

"Giulia," says Belinda, fanning herself, "I had no idea you were there. You gave me a terrible fright." She pats her bosom dramatically. "You nearly killed me."

"*Buongiorno, signora,*" says Giulia, smiling through Belinda's admonishment.

"Yes, yes," says Belinda, taking hold of Giulia's shoulders. "Hurry up now, come along . . ."

Belinda ushers Giulia toward the cupboard under the sink where she keeps her yellow bucket of cleaning sprays and polishes, plus her extra-small candy-pink pair of rubber gloves.

"Right, today we have *molto, molto laboro,*" says Belinda, handing over the bucket and adding a couple more canisters of Pledge. "*Molto laboro.*"

"*Molto laboro.*" Giulia nods. The mother of two little boys, Giulia is in her early thirties but looks younger. Neat and thin, with large dark eyes, her long dark hair is always scraped back into a ponytail. She is a good worker with a sunny disposition. Belinda much prefers her to her last domestic, Marta, the surly Slav she had in Tilling who used to breathe tragedy wherever she went and always wore black as if she were in mourning for her life. But despite all of Giulia's charm and diligence, Belinda still feels compelled to follow her throughout the house, just in case she misses anything. Somehow, and Belinda has been known to share this, no one quite has her eye for dust, detail, and detritus. Perhaps it is the artist in her. Or even the hostess. Either way whenever Giulia comes to clean the house, so does Belinda. Although it should be pointed out that Belinda doesn't actually touch anything when she cleans, so much as stand right next to Giulia while she scrubs and points out when she misses something. At first Giulia found her hygiene stalker unusual and a little irritating, but she has since got used to Belinda breathing down her neck.

"Guests' bathrooms *primo.*" Belinda leads the way downstairs and into the guests' quarters. "Hello." She coughs as she comes downstairs. "Only me!" she announces. "Anyone there?" She knocks loudly on the door. "I don't want to catch anyone out," she says, laughing lightly before opening the bathroom door. "Anyone there?"

The room is empty. White and slightly airless, designed with function and practicality entirely in mind, it is small and smells of damp towels and toothpaste. Belinda directs Giulia to go in, and suggests in sign language where she might start and where she might finish, indicating areas, like the basin and the bath, that may need special attention. Giulia gets to work. She hitches up her black skirt and fills her yellow bucket with warm water. Spilling some over her feet, she bends down to dry off her brown plastic flip-flops and maroon-painted toenails. She covers the white tiles with Cif and scrubs. All the while Belinda leans in the doorway, her arms folded, watching to see if Giulia makes a mistake.

"*Un po' di più,*" says Belinda, shaking a pink finger toward the back of the taps. "*Qui, qui,* and over *qui.*" She makes a vigorous scrubbing gesture with her fist. "*Molto, molto.*"

While Giulia scrubs away, Belinda grows gradually and painfully bored. She glances over her shoulder. The wantonly half-open door of the Chesters' bedroom is just too tempting.

Belinda sees riffling through her guests' possessions as one of the few perks of her job. Entertaining and useful, it goes a long way to help her when it comes to making snap judgments about people. How else is she going to know who to be pleasant to, who to keep at arm's length, and who to invite back next year?

For instance, what had really swung it for Major and Mrs. Chester last year—quite apart from the watercolor art and Belinda's frisson for the major—was the fact that Pat Chester had some rather nice face cream that Belinda had liked the look of, or, indeed, the smell of—and actually, after three days, she noticed it had reduced her crow's-feet. So far this year, she has not managed to get inside their room. What with her watercoloring trip with the major and all the trauma caused by the arrival of the *americana,* the delights of drawer riffling and Pat Chester's face cream had quite slipped her mind.

"Molto, molto," she repeats, in the vague direction of Giulia and the bathroom, as she pushes open the door.

Her heart is beating hard and fast as she walks into the room. She has to be quick. She saw Pat walk down to the pool earlier that morning, but as to the exact whereabouts of the major, she cannot be sure. The french windows are open. The white curtains are billowing in the breeze, and the room smells of some sort of man spray mixed with the sweet smell of geranium wafting in off the terrace. The bed is made and the room looks neat. On one bedside table there is a pile of army-inspired paperback novels, covered in insignia and gold writing, their butch titles shout *Last Man Standing, Ultimate Force, Collateral Damage.* Over on the other side there is a large, plump Barbara Taylor Bradford lying facedown on the glass.

Belinda casts an expert eye around the room and heads straight for the chest of drawers. She opens the top right. It has nail clippers, a hairbrush, some Kouros aftershave, and a collection of ironed white handkerchiefs. There's nothing of particular interest so she moves on to the top left: a large roll of cotton wool, a pink plastic hairbrush and a pale-pink-and-white-spotted makeup bag. She takes it out of the drawer.

"Aha," says Belinda. The bag is ringing bells. She takes out lipstick and recoils at the bright pink color. She pulls out a very used compact with most of the Lancôme lettering scratched off. There is a collection of cotton buds, mascaras, blushers, tweezers, and powder. Finally, right at the bottom, she finds the cream.

"Bingo," she says, taking it out and holding it up to the light. "Mm," she says, unscrewing the white-and-gold lid. She lowers her nose and sniffs. "Oh, that's nice." She nods. "Very nice indeed." Then, for fear that this may be her one and only cream-stealing opportunity, she proceeds to cover her face in an excessively generous layer. Down the nose, across the chin, she pats it around the eyes and smooths it across her forehead. Her face is white with unction. She looks like a Pierrot.

"Belinda!" comes a male voice from the terrace.

"Major!" replies Belinda, hiding the pot behind her back and turning around.

"What are you doing in here?" he asks, taking a proprietorial step toward her.

"Major, Major, Major," says Belinda, screwing the lid onto the pot behind her back. "Major, Major," she repeats. "I'm so glad to have caught you. Where have you been?"

"What?" says the major, his face contracted with confusion, eyes shifting. "Where have I been? Um, reading by the pool. What are you doing in here?"

"What am I doing in here?" Belinda smiles. "Why, looking for you, Major! I was wondering if you wanted to go water-coloring or, indeed, if I could suggest a few little trips that you might want to do while you're here."

"Oh," says the major. "Right."

"Obviously San Jimmy is a must," says Belinda, ushering him ahead of her out of his room, placing the pot of cream on the side as she goes. "I can't remember, did you go there last year?"

While Belinda escorts the bemused-looking major up the stairs and into the sitting room on the pretext of lending him a book, the telephone rings.

"Mum! Phone!" shouts Mary from the kitchen.

"Coming!" says Belinda, only too thrilled to be able to leave the major's side.

"*Pronto,*" she says, arriving at a trot. "Casa Mia!"

"Oh, hello," comes an American voice.

"*Sì, pronto,*" continues Belinda, looking at her reflection in the french windows as she tries to rub the cream into her face.

"Mrs. Smith?"

"*Sì,*" says Belinda.

"Hello, Mrs. Smith, this is Kyle."

"Kyle?"

"Yes, Kyle—you know, from across the valley?"

"Oh," says Belinda. "That Kyle."

"How are you doing, ma'am?" asks Kyle.

"I'm doing fine," says Belinda, her mouth narrowing.

"It was very nice to meet you again at the party last night," says Kyle.

"Y-e-s," says Belinda. "What exactly do you want, Kyle?"

"Oh," says Kyle. "Um, actually, I wanted to speak to Mary."

"Mary?"

"Yes, Mary—you know, your daughter," explains Kyle.

"I'm well aware of who Mary is," says Belinda. "I'm just surprised that you want to speak to her."

"Oh," says Kyle. "Um, well, I do, if that's okay with you? Is she there?"

"Yes, well," says Belinda, trying to make up her mind. Perhaps it's the shock of being discovered slathered in a guest's face cream that puts her off guard, or maybe she's just too tired to lie. "Mary!" she shouts. "It's for you!"

"Me?" says Mary, coming out of the kitchen, rubbing her wet hands on her denim-clad backside.

"Yes, you," says Belinda. "It's Kyle."

"Kyle?" Mary stops in her tracks, and her cheeks flush pink. "What? American Kyle?"

"Well, I only know one man with such an unfortunate name," says Belinda, dangling the telephone receiver in the air. "Come on, hurry up. I need to get online and do some e-mails."

* * *

Mary hurries toward the telephone, tucking her hair behind her ears and smoothing her skirt. "Hello? Kyle?" she says tentatively into the telephone, not sure that her mother is telling the truth.

"Mary," says his warm American voice. "How are you?"

"Fine," says Mary, curling the telephone cord around her finger. "How about you?"

"Great," says Kyle. "Just great . . . Great. I really enjoyed last night. I really enjoyed our dancing."

"Oh, God, me, too," says Mary, probably a little too enthusiastically. "It was, um, nice," she says, trying belatedly to sound nonchalant.

"Oh, good," says Kyle. "Good. That's great. Um, I was just wondering . . ."

"Yes?"

"If you wanted to go out to dinner tonight?" he asks.

"Dinner?" says Mary, her voice rising an octave. "Tonight?"

"Oh—my—God!" screams Belinda, from her armchair. "I don't believe it. I don't believe it. I don't bloody believe it!" She stands up and throws her *Spectator* magazine against the wall. "Above us. Above us! How did she get above us?"

"I'm sorry, Kyle," says Mary. "Something's just happened here, can you hold on a second?"

"Sure."

"What?" says Mary, her hand over the phone. "He's only asked me out for dinner tonight. That's all."

"I'm not talking about that," hisses Belinda. "The world does not revolve around you and your sad little friends. I am talking about this!" Belinda says, picking up the *Spectator* and jabbing it repeatedly with her finger. "Look! The silly cow has advertised in the same magazine as us and—and—they've put her higher than us! She started her advert with an *A*—'A Tuscan retreat'— so she's at the top of the list! Typical! The American *shit*!" She collapses back into her chair.

"Mary?" Kyle's voice is in the earpiece. "Are you still there?"

"Hang on a second, Kyle," says Mary, taking her hand off the mouthpiece, then replacing it. "Mum?"

"What?" Belinda turns round, her greasy face looks stunned and slack, her eyes are glazed.

"Kyle's asked me out for dinner tonight. Can I go?"

"What? Dinner? Oh, right, um, I suppose . . ." Belinda seems dreadfully confused. "Well, I don't think . . ." Then, slowly but surely, her expression changes. "Actually, yes! Of course you must go," she says, getting out of her chair. "Go!" she says, shooing her daughter along. "And I want you to find out everything that's going on. What bookings they have, what sort of inquiries they're getting, the lot. Hurry up," she adds. "I've got things to do."

Mary accepts her dinner invitation. They decide to keep it simple and informal and meet at Giovanna's.

Belinda sends her daughter off into the garden to sunbathe or do something useful. She wants complete privacy at the telephone and computer.

The first thing she does, when Mary's back is turned, is put in a call to the *Spectator* to cancel Lauren's advertisement. "I know," she says, "it's terribly sad, but the fire has made it impossible for us to stay open. I'll call again when I know more."

Then after a suitable five minutes she calls back again to make a few alterations to her own advertisement. "So, have you got that?" she asks. " 'Aah, it's Tuscany!' With two *A*'s at the beginning? Good. That's great." She smiles, so pleased with herself. "Very kind of you indeed."

So, with Lauren's advertisement canceled and her own placed at the top of the list, Belinda goes on to initiate phase two of her plan. She turns on the computer, clicks into the secret "Rejects" pile of e-mails that she has placed in a folder marked "Extra Personal." They are full of inquiries from people who, for some reason or other, have been refused entry to Casa Mia. The Longworths from Cornwall were rejected because the husband was a vegetarian, and the Parkers because they had posed the odd golfing question. Mr. and Mrs. Davies were turned down simply because she was called Sandra, and Belinda thought she might lower the tone. The Salaverts from France had wanted to bring their child, some Americans had asked about air-conditioning, two Londoners had required collection from the airport by taxi, and an Irish couple requested that, as asthmatics, they didn't want too many stairs. Now, smiling, her finger hovering over the Reply to All button, Belinda is going to pass them on to Lauren.

"Dear Potential Guests," Belinda's group e-mail begins. "I don't know if this might be of any use to you, but since, sadly, I could not accommodate you, I was wondering if you might consider a charming little place that has opened up in the same valley as the ever popular Casa Mia. It is a small place, run by an American woman, who is only too keen to cater to your every need. Feel free to contact her at . . ." Belinda copies out the details from the *Spectator* advertisement and presses Send. As her telephone line crackles, she wriggles with joy at her own genius and decides to pour herself a rather large sherry to celebrate.

* * *

While her mother plots and drinks not-so-fine sherry downstairs, upstairs Mary is sitting on her single bed, in her small white room, staring at her reflection in the wardrobe mirror. Her right leg bounces as she twists a cheap silver and turquoise ring on and off her left hand, running over in her mind exactly what happened last night.

Kyle came over and asked her to dance. Dressed in his loose white shirt and jeans, he had bravely approached her in front of her mother and the whole of the valley. And, God, could the man dance! She had never danced like that before. She'd shuffled from one foot to the other at discos and nightclubs, or swayed with her feet stuck rigidly to the floor, but this was proper dancing. His hand in hers. His arm around her waist. It was contact. It was romantic. It had made her heart so tight in her chest that she could hardly breathe.

Then he'd asked her if she wanted a drink, and they'd drunk

Prosecco and talked, and he'd made her laugh a couple of times, and then he'd suggested a walk in the garden. He'd taken her hand and led her past Derek and Barbara's table, and Howard had given her a wink, although perhaps he hadn't been in complete charge of his facial muscles—it might simply have been a case of wind. But then, as the noise of the chatter and the laughing and the jazz faded, and the heady smell of jasmine increased, Mary cared less and less who had seen them and what would be said tomorrow. Kyle pointed out a soft patch of grass, surrounded by old lavender and jasmine planted by the previous owner. He lay down, she joined him, careful not to sit too close to him, and he suggested they stare up at the stars.

The moon was high, the crickets were chirping, the sky was dark blue, and the stars were so numerous it looked as though someone had emptied a can of white paint across the heavens.

"This is one of my favorite places I've found so far," he said, propping himself up on his elbow, the light from the party flares dancing on his dark hair. "Not that I've been here long," he smiled, "but this is really quite fine."

"I think it's beautiful," said Mary, giddy on Prosecco, the smell of the jasmine and the proximity of such a handsome man.

Kyle leaned forward and fumbled in his back pocket. Eventually he brought out what looked like a very fine, very thin-rolled cigarette. "Do you want some?" he asked, holding it up so that Mary could see.

"It's a remarkably small cigarette." Mary smiled.

"It's remarkably strong pot," replied Kyle, with a gentle laugh.

"Oh," said Mary.

"Do you want some?"

He lit the joint, inhaled it, and held his breath. Unable to speak, he handed it to Mary, nodding encouragingly, as his eyes watered. She took it between her fingers. The end wasn't wet and sodden like Franco's roll-up, it was merely damp with just the impression of where his lips had been.

"Phew," said Kyle, with a cough, releasing a plume of smoke. "Unlike Bill Clinton, I do inhale. Go on," he urged. "Just smoke it like a cigarette."

"Why not?" said Mary, suddenly sounding very English. "You've got to try things in life."

"Absolutely." Kyle grinned.

Mary inhaled a huge amount, coughed a huge amount, and flapped her hands in front of her face. "Oh, my God," she managed eventually. "That's gone straight to my head."

"It can't have!" Kyle grinned.

"It has," confirmed Mary. "I feel a little bit strange."

"How strange?" asked Kyle, his dark eyes looking up at hers. "Tell me exactly."

"What exactly?" asked Mary, suddenly finding the word *exactly* rather amusing. "Well, 'exactly,' I feel floppy, giggly, slightly naughty, and the world around me seems a whole lot brighter."

"You're stoned," nodded Kyle, seemingly pleased with her description. "You're definitely stoned."

"Am I?" Mary started to laugh.

"Yup." He took a drag.

"Well, I'm a cheap date." She laughed.

"Very cheap," confirmed Kyle.

"Maa-ry! Maa-ry!" She sat up straight as soon as she heard her name screamed. "Maa-ry! We're leaving—*right now.*"

"Oh, my God," said Mary, attempting to get to her feet. "I'd better go."

"Why?" asked Kyle.

"That's my mother calling."

"Let her," said Kyle, shrugging his shoulders. "Let's just say you didn't hear her. What's the worst that could happen?"

"Um," said Mary, trying to think.

"She'll go home and leave you here and all that means is that I'll take you home later."

"Mary! Mary!" came the scream.

"Ssssh," said Kyle, hunching his shoulders.

"Sssh," said Mary, doing the same.

"Anyway," asked Kyle, "what is it with your mother?"

"What do you mean?" whispered Mary.

"She's driving my mother mad."

"Really?" asked Mary.

"Oh, yeah," said Kyle, taking another drag of the joint. "She knows your mother reported us to the art police guys and does nothing but slander us in town."

"Oh," said Mary.

"Yeah," said Kyle. "I personally don't give a shit. But my mom is a Wall Street witch, who used to specialize in hostile takeovers. She's cool, she's calculating, she takes no prisoners, and she has your mom right between her sights. I just thought I'd warn you."

"Really?" said Mary again.

"Yeah," said Kyle. "Why do you think you weren't invited tonight? I'm really pleased you're here," he grinned, "but my mom's not!" He started to laugh. "Fuck them," he grinned. "Hey? Shall we dance?"

Kyle and Mary wandered back to the party. The jazz had picked up a beat by the time they reached the floor, and Kyle's shoulders were moving back and forth as he turned Mary around.

"This is great." She smiled.

"I know. It's even better now that we're stoned, don't you think?"

Mary felt great. The music was great. The party was great and Kyle was even greater. She was dancing and everyone was watching, and for the first time in her life she didn't mind. She didn't want to fade into the background—she was having far too much fun for that. Kyle left her briefly and still she carried on dancing. He came running back with a not-so-shiny, obviously well-loved saxophone.

"Watch this," he said, with a wink, then walked over to join the band.

His first few notes brought the whole party to the dance floor, hands in the air, clapping their approval. No one more so than Lauren who, with batlike hearing, could have distinguished her own son's playing if he'd been in the next valley. Breaking off from a conversation, she appeared on the terrace, clapping above her head, yelping like a southern rancher. "Go, honey, go!" she shouted, cupping her hands around her mouth, her blonde bob framing her face. "You show them!" She strode toward the dance floor but, finding it too crowded, stood on one of the tables to dance to her son's tune. It wasn't long before Howard and one of the Bianchi boys did the same. Derek, flushed with fun and alcohol, merrily tapped his toes on the sidelines, while Mary swirled and danced right in front of Kyle and the band.

What a night! What a party. What a finale. Just as Kyle was taking Mary home, the fireworks started. Green and red starbursts lit up the night sky. The "ohs" and "ahs" of the crowd were audible along the gravel track. The bangs and crackles and technicolor accompanied them to the other side of the valley, where Kyle promptly dropped Mary at her door, as he had said he would, and he did not even attempt to kiss her. She'd stood with her eyes half closed and her mouth puckered, awaiting his approach. It wasn't until she'd heard the car door slam that she realized he'd gone.

She'd spent a sleepless night, excited yet confused, serenaded by her mother's deep snoring, which penetrated the back wall. And now he'd called. When she had given up all hope. When she had thought that perhaps he was just trying to be nice and friendly and didn't see her in *that* light at all. He'd called and asked her out to dinner. And her mother, who can't have been concentrating, had said she could go.

By the time Mary comes downstairs in the early evening, dressed in her calf-length tiered black skirt and a tight white T-shirt that shows off her slim tanned arms, her mother is asleep on the sofa. Too many sherries and too much planning have made her pass out like a soft pudding, and she is seeping over the side of the cushions. Her body is relaxed, her legs are slightly parted; her crackling snore disturbs her loose cheeks. Mary closes the french windows onto the terrace, securing the house. The doors bang in the wind.

"What?" says Belinda, sitting up with a start. "What are you doing?"

"I'm closing the windows."

"Right. Oh," says Belinda, her dry tongue getting in the way of her speech. "Why? What are you doing dressed like that?"

"I'm going out to dinner."

"Dinner?"

"Yes, dinner, with Kyle from across the valley," says Mary anxiously. "You said I could go earlier today."

"Did I?"

"Yes, yes," confirms Mary. "It's all part of your grander plan to find out what sort of guests and bookings and goings-on there are at the Casa Padronale."

"Ah, yes," says Belinda, stretching and swinging her stiff legs off the sofa. "Has the major gone out?"

"I don't know," says Mary. "I think so. I've been in my room most of the afternoon."

"Oh," says Belinda, with a small yawn. "I hope so, I suggested he and his wife make alternative arrangements tonight as we weren't cooking."

"Good," says Mary.

"Yep . . . He wasn't too pleased. He did remind me that he'd booked supper tonight and paid up front for it." Belinda shrugs. "I said I'd go some way to reimburse him. But quite frankly," she smiles, "I don't really care. I haven't enjoyed the Art with him very much this year. He used to be so much jollier." She sighs. "I don't think I'll bother to have them back again next year. Do you?"

"Whatever you want," says Mary. "I should go. I don't want to be late."

"No, absolutely." Belinda taps the side of her nose. "Use what few worldly charms you have, and remember I want details, details, details."

"Okay."

"Didn't you wear that skirt last night?"

"Um, yes."

"Oh, dear," says Belinda with a little shrug. "Let's hope he doesn't notice! Have a nice evening. Don't be late."

Mary walks down the hill, leaving Belinda to her bottle of wine, a packet of crisps, and her *Pride and Prejudice* video, in which the Darcy-wet-breeches moment has lost its sound and color.

By the time she reaches Giovanna's, the scattering of *riservato* signs on most of the tables means that it promises to be a busy night. Kyle is not there when she walks in to be greeted by the rotund Roberto.

"*Buona sera!*" he says, embracing her, slotting her nose into his armpit. "*Come va?*"

"*Va bene, grazie, Roberto, e lei?*"

"*Tutto bene.*" He leads her to a small table for two, next to a group of four very pink blonde tourists, who seem already to be on their pudding. "*Va bene così?*"

"*Sì, sì,*" says Mary, sitting down.

"Hello there, Mary!" someone calls across the terrace.

"Oh, hello, Howard," says Mary. "Did you have fun last night?"

"Excellent evening," he replies, raising his denim-clad arm and taking a slug from his birdbath of red wine. "Not with your mother?"

"No," says Mary.

"Good."

"Um, how's your book going?" asks Mary. "Got your hero out of bed yet?"

"Oh, Lord," he replies. "Yes, I've done that. . . . Only problem now is that I have no idea what to do with him next."

"Oh dear," laughs Mary.

"You could say that," says Howard. "Is that your date?" He asks, indicating the entrance, where Kyle is standing, dressed in a dark blue shirt and jeans.

"Um, thank you," says Mary, blushing, as she watches Kyle approach, accompanied by his mother. "Hello, Kyle," she says. "Hello, Lauren."

"Hey," he says. "Don't you look beautiful!" He kisses her cheek. "Don't worry about my mother, she will *not* be joining us. Will you, Mother dear?"

"I'd rather pluck my own eyes out." Lauren smiles. "Hello, Mary. How are you?"

"Fine thank you," says Mary. "Thank you for a lovely party. It was a great evening."

"Good," says Lauren, looking her up and down. "Didn't you wear that skirt last night?"

"Go away, Mother," says Kyle, pushing her in the direction of Howard. "I'm sorry about her. She just can't help herself. Any girl I'm interested in, and she's off." He laughs. "And your mother's no help either."

"Let's not talk about mothers."

"I agree," says Kyle, leaning over to tuck a stray strand of Mary's hair behind her ear. "And you do look stunning tonight."

"Thank you," says Mary, plucking at her napkin as her cheeks glow a darker pink.

"Let's order some wine!" he says ebulliently. "I think you and I are going to have a wonderful evening."

❋ ❋ ❋

On the other side of the terrace, next to a table of four women, Howard and Lauren are joined by Derek and Barbara. The atmosphere is jovial. Howard is sharing his creative problems with the table. Barbara is letting Lauren know how much she envies her figure and how Americans always look after themselves so much better than the English. Derek is enthusiastically recounting anecdotes from Lauren's party, as if none of the guests had been there. And Lauren is smiling, listening, and saying very little. No one could tell that she's bored at all. A woman used to working in a man's world, Lauren hides her feelings well and always thinks of the long term. The evening is pleasant enough for her, no more dull than the numerous Wall Street dinners and client drinks she used to have to attend.

But as the evening wears on and pasta is followed by meat, and wine by wine, Lauren finally brings the conversation to her own agenda. "So, Derek," she says, "tell me about the *Festa di Formaggio*. It sounds like great fun. How does one get involved?"

"Oh, the *Festa di Formaggio*," says Derek, rubbing his hands together. "It's the best night of the year, bar the panto—or maybe it's better than the panto, but it's certainly a day and a night to remember." He chuckles. "Well, we all gather together—you know, the Brits, the expats, the Italians, and a couple of Germans—and we have an enormous party. Each group does their own food on tables on the green. Then we start the cheese-rolling competition."

"Cheese rolling?" laughs Lauren.

"Oh, yes." Derek nods. "It's very serious, with trophies and everything. These great big *pecorinos,* which we roll down the hill."

"It's a devil to organize," Barbara chips in.

"Oh, right," says Lauren. "Maybe I could help?"

"Oh, Derek, that's a good idea," says Barbara. "Lauren could use all those people skills she's been telling us about. All that time in New York has got to be useful."

"Oh, that's right, Barb. What an excellent idea. I know," Derek sits back as though he has experienced a revelation, rather than the result of slow, subliminal campaign, "why don't you run it this year? Why don't we make her Big Cheese?"

"Oh, Derek," exclaims Barbara. "Do you think so?"

"Honestly, I couldn't," says Lauren, the epitome of modesty.

"No, no, go on with you," says Derek, giving Lauren's elegant shoulder a little shove.

"Belinda's been Big Cheese for years. She won't mind."

"What do you think, Howard?" asks Barbara.

"Leave me out of this," says Howard, hands in the air. "I only came out for a quiet drink."

"Well, I think it's a great idea," says Barbara.

"You guys are too kind," says Lauren. "But do you know what? I think rather than rock the boat too much with Belinda, as we all know how difficult she can be"—she gives a light laugh, which Barbara reciprocates—"I'd rather offer my services to the community, such skills as I have, rather than do anything so presumptuous as take over."

"Oh, Lauren, you're so clever," gushes Barbara. "What a great compromise. Isn't she clever, Derek?"

"Absolutely," confirms Derek. "Cheers."

"Cheers," says Lauren right back.

"What are we all cheersing?"

"Oh, Belinda!" says Derek, leaping out of his chair with shock and guilt. "I thought you were at home."

"Oh, I was, Derek," she says. "But after I telephoned your house and Howard's and received no reply, I presumed you'd all be here. Although," she stares at Lauren, "I wasn't expecting you, Lauren . . . dear. What a surprise!"

"We're celebrating Lauren's addition to the *Festa di Formaggio* fold," babbles Barbara. "You're going to find all her Wall Street skills invaluable."

"Right," says Belinda. "Whatever they may be!"

"You're still in charge, though," adds Lauren. "I couldn't take that away from you."

"Is your B-and-B open yet?" asks Belinda, changing the subject.

"Any day now." Lauren nods.

"Bookings?" Belinda smiles, her hands clasping the back of Derek's chair for support.

"Fine," says Lauren. "I had a little problem with the *Spectator* today, though."

"Really?" says Barbara.

"Very bizarrely they thought I'd had a fire and was canceling my advert. It's lucky they telephoned to check, isn't it?" says Lauren, staring at Belinda, her blonde hair swinging. "But apart from that, it's going great. I have some L.A. studio exec arriving. He's booked in to finish his film script for a couple of weeks."

"Oh, how glamorous," enthuses Barbara. "You must introduce us to him."

"A writer in residence," adds Howard. "Every smart establishment should have one."

"Have you ever had a writer, Belinda?" asks Derek.

"Apart from myself, and I'm permanently in residence," says Belinda, with a little light laugh, "I simply can't recall."

"Oh," says Derek.

"Well, anyway," says Barbara. "Oh, Lauren, Belinda was thinking of organizing a party for you."

"She was?" asks Lauren, seemingly pleased.

"Yes, well," says Belinda, her eyelids batting one thousand to the dozen, "it had crossed my mind. But you know—"

"How sweet of you!" exclaims Lauren.

"Yes, well . . ." says Belinda again.

"Only I have a feeling . . ." Lauren goes on, topping up everyone's glasses, but leaving Belinda high and decidedly dry.

"Yes?" says Belinda, leaning in.

". . . that, what with all these Hollywood people, I might well be very . . . very . . . busy."

Mercoledì ✳ Wednesday

Clima ✳ *fa nuvoloso* (cloudy)

It is an oddly cloudy day today at Casa Mia. Here, in the land of the blazing sun, it is unusual for such a day to happen in the middle of the summer. The thing about Toscana is that, unlike other less glamorous holiday-home destinations, like Provence in France or even vulgar places like Spain, the sunshine is not totally guaranteed. But that's what makes us a bit different here, doesn't it? We're not golfing sun worshippers; we're a cultured group of expats who like art and food just as much as we do a good climate. Anyway, perhaps it will burn off later. Who knows?

Last night I had a little light supper with the famous writer Howard Oxford. We talked and talked about interesting and clever things till way past ten thirty. It was a good intellectual evening. Derek and Barbara were unable to attend, due to some bridge game at the *americana*'s. I always thought we *all* left the U.K. to escape such suburban pursuits, but apparently not.

Anyway, before I lose myself in a discussion about bourgeois hobbies, I have to say that, sadly, my returnees are leaving me today. The delightful Major and Mrs. Chester are moving on. It has been a joy to have them to stay again, it really has. I feel tinged with sadness. We have laughed, we have painted, we have discussed so many cultural things. The thing about running a beautiful home, as I do, is that it is so lovely to have what can only really be termed friends to stay. You see, unlike other, pushier guests, the Chesters know how to entertain themselves, and don't constantly ask my advice on things. It is sometimes exhausting to be the fount of all knowledge all the time. I have some Scots arriving today whom I suspect will not be so easy. Normally I wouldn't have taken them in, but they are staying only two nights, and they seemed so terribly keen. In the end, who am I to come between a man and the joys of the Tuscan countryside?

Maria, I am glad to say, has taken up strolling. It is so nice for her to find a hobby. After all, it can't be good for a girl to hang around her mother like a lame puppy all the time, now, can it? And she always appears so jolly, refreshed, and conversational after her strolls, which also comes as something of a relief. When I suggested she curtail her friendship with that *americana*'s awful son, I was worried she might not find other things to do.

Talking of the *americana,* I have a meeting at her small house this afternoon. When I say meeting, I mean I am chairing a meeting. As head of the *Festa di Formaggio* I chair, I don't attend. We normally have the meetings at Giovanna's or, indeed, at Casa Mia, but this year, for some reason, the *americana* has muscled in. Oh, well, poor woman, I expect she doesn't know any better, and I suppose as a woman in my position, I must try to be a little forgiving.

INSALATA DI PASTA DA CASA MIA

There is nothing that nourishes like a pasta salad. Hearty, substantial, yet still a salad. After a hard day shoe shopping in the market, or tending your garden, there is something about a cold plate of deliciously garnished pasta that hits the spot! It is also one of those terribly handy preprepared dishes that, as a hostess, I am constantly searching for. Preparation time is minimal, and it can sit in the cool confines of the fridge for a couple of days until you are ready to indulge.

Oddly, the Italians are not quite as fond of pasta salad as we Brits, but I'm sure if we ask for it constantly in their restaurants, it is only a matter of time until they get to grips with this truly international delicacy—after all, a hundred or so airlines and Bella Pasta chains can't be wrong! Serves six, or a hungry post**mercato** four!

- ❋ 1 box of fusilli pasta (by far the best salad pasta—I'm amazed anyone could use anything else!)
- ❋ dressing—olive oil and red wine vinegar with a spoonful of peppercorn mustard
- ❋ capers
- ❋ 1 finely chopped red pepper
- ❋ 1 tin of tuna (do make sure it's dolphin friendly—let's save the planet and eat well at the same time!)
- ❋ 1 tin of sweet corn

Although spontaneously simple and effortlessly enticing, the real art of this recipe is to prepare the ingredients in the right order. Cook the pasta first; drizzle over the dressing, and let it cool. Cover with the chopped pepper and capers, then open the tins in order, first the tuna, and then the sweet corn. In the past I have let the sweet corn dry out before I put it on the pasta. Make sure you don't do the same! Dress, toss, and then bring to the table. Toss, and toss again.

Serve on sophisticated plates.

❀ ❀ ❀

CHAPTER EIGHT

Foolishly, the Major and Mrs. Chester have left their swimming costumes laid out to dry on Belinda's lawn. Quite apart from the fact that this indicates that they have been swimming before ten o'clock, which is against pool rules, they may also be causing the grass to yellow, patch, and stain. There is, as Belinda pointed out a week ago, a short washing line, out of sight on the other side of the house, provided specifically for the hanging of guests' underwear and swimming things.

"Ma-jor! Ma-jor!" shouts Belinda from her terrace, one hand shading her eyes as she surveys the route down the garden and toward the pool. "Ma-jor!"

"Yes, Belinda," says the major, trotting toward her up the path in a pair of beige shorts and nothing else, his man breasts bouncing with kinetic energy. "Yes, Belinda, you called," he states. He is, after all, a man who responds well to shouts, commands, and orders.

"Major, dear," says Belinda, looking down her short nose at the short man on the grass below her. "Maybe you didn't quite hear me when I gave you the tour on arrival," she suggests, "or perhaps you've forgotten since last year, but not only have you been swimming outside pool hours, you have left your swimming things on my lawn to dry. Now, I would hate us to fall out, especially as this is your last day and you've been doing so terribly well up until this point. But, as I have pointed out to you in the past, there is a perfectly good plastic line."

"Belinda," says the major, clasping his hands with suitable deference. She nods. "I'm so terribly sorry, but Pat was keen for a swim before we packed this morning, and as the guests' washing line doesn't get any sun until the last half hour of the day, we thought you wouldn't mind if we dried our things on the lawn."

"Well, you thought wrong," says Belinda. Her face softens into her generous service-industry smile. "Major," she adds, "between you and me, it is exhausting throwing one's house open to the general public, no matter how accomplished a hostess one is. And although one does try to be accommodating and cope with everyone's little whims, one does just like to be consulted about things in one's own home."

"Right," says the major. "I would have consulted you this morning, Belinda, but you were still asleep."

"Major, really." She smiles. "We both know that is beside the point. Rules are rules, Major, and rules are there for a reason. You, of all people, should understand that. Now," she adds, as she turns to walk back on to the terrace, "clear up those offensive items, and we won't refer to the matter again."

"Righty-ho, Belinda," he says, and bends down to pick up his damp shorts. "Thank you very much indeed, Belinda, thank you."

"Think nothing of it, Major," she says with a little wave. "Think nothing of it."

Fortified by her battle and ultimate victory over the compliant major, Belinda wanders back into the house and contemplates a good strong cup of Nescafé with a touch of Russell Watson before she sits down at her computer to go through her bookings and e-mails.

"Here we go," she says, her shoulders bracing slightly as she prepares to meet her public. She takes the large gray mouse in her pink-tipped hand and manages to make the e-mail icon work after a couple of attempts. "Go on," she mutters, "work, you bastard." The old machine whirls into action and dials. While she waits, Belinda notices that her Uffizi souvenir calendar is on the wrong month. She stands, changes it, and by the time she sits down at her desk again she has three new messages. She clicks on the first.

"Dear Mrs. Smith," it goes. Belinda does like a formal beginning to an e-mail. "My partner and I . . ."

"No!" says Belinda, with a dismissive click of the mouse. "Partner," she mutters at the screen. "What does that mean? Business or sexual? Partner . . . Honestly, whatever happened to the word *boyfriend*?"

She opens the next.

Dear Mrs. Smith,

We have long been planning a trip through Italy and are truly delighted to have stumbled upon your advertisement in the *Spectator*. Your house looks like just the perfect place for me and my friend Edith to pass a couple of idyllic days. We are both in our eighties and as Edith has just had her hip replaced we were wondering if stairs and access would be a problem. Edith can negotiate most things. It's just that a handrail goes a long way to alleviate her mobility problem. . . .

" 'Dear Veronica and Edith,'" sighs Belinda, " 'I'm afraid we have no facilities for the disabled, Yours Belinda Smith.' Honestly," she presses Send, "this is just too depressing. Do they seriously want me to turn my house upside down adding handrails so that Peg-leg Edith can jog up and down my stairs? Really!" She sighs as she clicks on to the third and final e-mail.

Dear Ms. Smith

[Belinda is not a fan of the "Ms." form of address but she decides to overlook it just this once],

We r 4 kids frm California on a grand tour of Europe. We r doin' France, Spaine and Italy and we were hopin 2 come 2 u're place some time in August. As we r students on a budget we r wondering if we cld get a discount for 4 of us. Yours fingers crossed:

—Burt, Jenny, Adam, and JoJo.

It takes Belinda a while to understand this message. The shorthand and spelling mistakes confuse her and their request for a discount astounds her. "Dear Burt, Jenny, Adam, and Jojo, Piss off, Yours Belinda Smith," she writes, and is about to press Send when she thinks better of it.

Dear Burt, Jenny, Adam, and Jojo,

Sadly, due to the exclusive nature of my establishment, I cannot take tour parties. However, there is a place in the same valley— the Casa Padronale—that is also run by an American who I'm sure would be happy to accommodate you. Please find her details below.

Yours, Mrs. Smith

Belinda sits back, smiles, sends, and gets up from her chair. She turns on her Russell Watson CD and walks onto the terrace, stretching out her arms. Just as she is about to launch into the chorus of "Bridge over Troubled Water," the telephone rings. Two short monotone blasts, and then it stops. Very odd, thinks Belinda. It keeps doing that. But Russell distracts her. The thought of his 'laying himself down' is enough to entertain any woman *d'un certain âge,* particularly since no one has done that for Belinda in a while. Well, more like three years. Or is it four? And does that time when she pinned the rather nice farmer from Cirencester up against the hall wall after too much grappa actually count? He did feel her breasts, after all?

The telephone rings again.

"I'll get it," shouts Mary, sprinting down the stairs from her bedroom. "You carry on," she says, sounding remarkably civil. *"Pronto,"* she sings. *"Sì . . . Sì . . . certo."* She replaces the receiver.

"Who was it?" calls Belinda, from the terrace.

"Wrong number," says Mary.

"Really?" says Belinda, turning to look at her daughter.

Mary seems different these days. It's not something she can put her finger on. But she definitely looks different. She looks shiny and glossy. Maybe it's just the tan.

"It seems to be happening a lot recently."

"What does?" asks Mary, sounding distracted.

"Wrong numbers."

"Oh," says Mary, "no more than normal."

"I bet it's got something to do with the *americana,*" says Belinda, her finger in the air.

"Why do you say that?" asks Mary, looking at the floor.

"Oh, all my problems stem from that cow," says Belinda. "The whole *festa* committee has to meet at her house this

afternoon. Quite what's wrong with Giovanna's or here, I have
no idea. We've all got to troop down to her monstrosity of
a place. Anyway"—Belinda smiles—"I got my own back this
morning. I've sent on some more requests to her."

"Mum!"

"What? I'm only helping her out, darling. We're full, and I
was merely being a generous neighbor. The fact that they're
Californian students on a budget is not my fault. I just thought
she might like some fellow Americans."

"Honestly, Mum," says Mary, shaking her head. "I'm going
for a walk."

"Now?" says Belinda. "Is that a new top?"

"It has to be worn some time."

"If you insist." Belinda shrugs. "But you will say good-bye to
the major? He and his wife are leaving in a while."

"I'm sure they won't notice if I'm not here," she says, walking toward the door.

"Don't be silly, Mary, the major's very fond of you."

"Yes, but I really must go."

"Have it your way," says Belinda, with a wave of her hand. "I
have more important things to think about." She exhales. "I'm
just glad you've found yourself a nice cheap hobby."

As Mary sets off on her walk with surprising enthusiasm,
Belinda, faced with the departure of the major and the arrival
of the Scottish couple later that afternoon, decides she needs to
do something about her dearth of interesting guests. She telephones Howard. "Hello," comes a hungover voice down the
telephone.

"*Pronto,* Howard. It's the Contessa here."

"Oh, hello, Belinda."

"I haven't woken you up, have I?" she asks. "It is eleven
o'clock," she justifies herself.

"No," says Howard. "I got up at six."

"You don't sound as though you've been up since six."

"Well, I tried to write some of my book, I drank a bottle of red wine, and I went back to bed. But I did get up at six, which was the main thing," insists Howard, with all the logic of a seriously blocked author.

"Good," says Belinda. "So I did wake you?"

"Technically, yes." Howard yawns. "I was asleep. But I was awake earlier."

"Right," says Belinda. "Anyway, I'm glad I've got you. I just wanted to pick your brains, ask *un po d'adviso.*"

"Okay," says Howard. "I'm not sure how useful I'll be."

"Well, you see, I am looking to expand my client base," she begins. "I do have most of my avenues covered, and, indeed, I'm booked up for the whole summer. In fact, I'm turning people away. . . . I'm busy, busy, busy."

"Ri–ight," says Howard, thinking about opening another bottle of red wine just to get through this conversation.

"The short of it is, Howard," continues Belinda, sensing his waning attention, "I want to know what sort of magazines you read?"

"Oh," says Howard, evidently susprised by the question. "What magazines I read?"

"Yes, Howard," confirms Belinda. "I'm after the intellectual pound, Howard. Where do I find it?"

"Interesting," says Howard. "The intellectual pound, you say? One problem with intellectuals, Belinda, is that they tend not to have many pounds."

"Oh," says Belinda, sounding terribly disappointed. "What, none?"

"Not many, and certainly not many spare ones."

"Oh."

" 'Fraid so."

"But they must holiday somewhere?"

"At home."

"All of them?"

"Or with one another."

"Howard, you're being no help whatsoever."

"I'm sorry, Belinda, but I'm not sure what I'm supposed to say."

"Give me the titles of the magazines you take, that's all."

"Well, that is also just it. Magazines are expensive, so I don't take many of those either."

"Oh."

"But I do subscribe to the *TLS*," he adds optimistically.

"The *TLS*," repeats Belinda, jotting it down.

"The *Times Literary Supplement*," says Howard.

"I knew that," she says.

"Of course."

"Anything else?"

"The *New Humanist*."

"Oh?" says Belinda, not sounding terribly sure. "The *New Humanist* . . . What are humanists? Do I want humanists in my house?"

"Ooh, I don't know," says Howard. "They're terribly anti-establishment."

"Are they?" says Belinda. "Would that mean they'd be anti my establishment?"

"Possibly."

"Well, in that case," says Belinda, "any other magazines?"

"Not really," says Howard. *"Razzle?"*

"Razzle?" repeats Belinda, jotting it down. "What sort of magazine is that?"

"It's a gentlemen's magazine," says Howard, trying to stifle his laughter.

"Really?" asks Belinda, approving and intrigued. "That sounds perfect. What sort of gentlemen?"

"Well . . ." Howard starts to laugh.

"Howard Oxford!" trills Belinda. "Are you teasing me?"

"I might be." Howard giggles.

"Well, in that case," she says, "I'm hanging up."

"Oh, I'm sorry, Belinda," he says. "I was just brightening an otherwise dull and frustrating morning."

"You creative types," laughs Belinda. "Honestly!"

"Yes, well . . ."

"Am I seeing you later?"

"What for?"

"The *festa* meeting."

"Oh, Lord, that. I was thinking I might give it a miss. Deadlines and all."

"Oh, Howard, you can't," remonstrates Belinda. "I need an ally."

"An ally?"

"I mean a friend."

"But I am your friend. Derek and Barbara are your friends. We're all your friends."

"I would just like you particularly to come," she says, childishly.

"Whatever for?"

"Just in case . . ."

"In case of what?"

"Oh, God," she snaps. "Arguments, Howard, arguments. I'd like to be able to count on your support and loyalty. I'd like to know that you'll back me up."

"Right," says Howard. "Um . . ."

"So, will I see you later?" she asks.

"I'll think about it."

"I'm counting on you, Howard," she says. "I'll expect to see you there. *Arrivadeary.*"

"*Arrivadeary,*" replies Howard, his voice flat and resigned.

❄ ❄ ❄

The loud scraping sound of the major's suitcase being dragged up the stone stairs and into the hall announces the Chesters' departure.

"Do, please, try to lift your suitcase, Major," suggests Belinda, walking toward him with a pleasant smile and clutching her flowered visitors' book and matching pen. "It creates terrible wear and tear."

"Sorry, Belinda," huffs the major, his face pink and sweaty. "It's all the pottery that Pat bought in Serrana market—it weighs a ton."

"Oh, really?" says Belinda. "Did she buy a lot of that blue-and-white stuff?"

"Judging by the weight of this thing, she bought the whole stall."

"Right," says Belinda, with a tight little smile. "It's very popular with tourists."

"She showed you some of it the other day," says the major.

"Did she?" says Belinda, sounding suitably vague. "One tries to forget these things."

Pat appears behind the major, wearing her pistachio traveling slacks and matching floral blouse.

"Careful with all the china, dear," she says, blinking down at the suitcase.

"Yes, all right, dear," replies the major. "I've no idea why you had to buy so much."

"Anyway," breezes Belinda, "do please sign the visitors' book."

"Oh, don't mind if I do," says the major, putting down his suitcase. "It will be interesting to see what we wrote last year."

"Yes," agrees Pat, following him to the small table in front of the mirror in the hall that Belinda keeps especially for signings.

"Look," says the major, leafing back through the collection of names, addresses, and little bons mots left by other guests. "Here we are. 'Lovely house, lovely food, lovely swimming pool, lovely hostess—thank you, love Major and Mrs. Chester. P.S. Don't forget to buy some lovely pottery in Serrana Market!'"

"Well, you haven't forgotten this year," says Belinda.

"No!" says Pat, letting off a clap of laughter. "I think we've made up for last time!"

"Ye-es," replies Belinda. "You certainly have."

"Oh, here's a good one," says the major, still reading the book. "'Roses are red, violets are blue, this place is great, and so are you! Love Dave and Angela from Southampton. P.S. Go to the English-speaking restaurant in Poggibonsi.' And further on down someone went there," continues the major. "'Thanks for the tip, English-speaking restaurant great—good chips!' That's great," says the major, looking up at Belinda. "You should keep this book out all the time so people can look through it for little bits of information."

"Well, it's not really for the comfort and convenience of the guests," says Belinda. "It's just a little record for me of who has been here and what they thought. I tend not to leave it out to be leafed through."

"Oh," says the major, "but it would be good to know about things like the English-speaking restaurant."

"Oh," says Belinda, sounding deeply disappointed. "I wouldn't have thought it was your sort of place, Major. A cultured man like you. Had I only known—"

"No, no, perhaps you're right," he says, and clears his throat. "Now, where would you like Pat and me to sign?"

"Wherever you want, Major, but chop-chop," she says, looking at her watch. "Ticktock, ticktock, it's almost twelve, and you really should be checked out and gone by now."

"Oh, gosh, is that the time? I think I'd better load up the car while Pat does the signing. Come along, Pat, here you go," he says, handing over the flowered pen.

The major marches back and forth, loading up the suitcases and various plastic bags, straining under the weight of retail.

Pat bends down and, blinking rapidly behind her large spectacles, strains to think of something interesting or witty to say. "Oh dear," she says, hunched over the desk, atrophied by her own creative indecision. "Hum . . ."

"Just say something along the lines of 'Thank you, I had a lovely time,'" says Belinda, arms folded as she leans against the wall, waiting, staring.

"I'm sure I can come up with something a bit better than that."

"Yes, well, you'd better hurry up about it," says Belinda. "If you'll excuse me, I really must get on. I have a meeting to attend this afternoon and more guests to welcome, and I have to organize Mary to sort out your room."

"Of course, you go ahead, dear, I won't be another minute here."

After a few more of Belinda's chivvying remarks and ticktock comments, the Major and Mrs. Chester leave. Their overloaded car crawls out of the drive, back up through the Mont Blanc tunnel, and on to the U.K. As Belinda stands on the steps, giving her special departing-returnee-with-a-ten-percent-discount wave (a gentle window-polishing movement she'd perfected that morning in the mirror) she wonders again whether she will bother to accept their reservation next year. After all, the Chesters had been something of a disappointment. The major had been a lot less keen on Art than before. They had managed only two watercoloring sessions in total, and he had agreed to the second sortie only after much insisting on Belinda's part. Also, last year he had certainly been a lot more racy and jovial. Belinda had quite fantasized about spontaneous clinches in various attractive and fecund spots around the house and its grounds, but the major had rather annoyingly proved to be all over his wife. Last year Mary had complained about the odd goosing, and he was still up to his old tricks, so his sex drive wasn't on the wane. It was most odd, Belinda thinks, and even a little irritating. What is the point of having the major to stay if he isn't going to flirt and paint with her? Surely she can't have imagined that he'd taken a shine to her the year before? No, those little looks, those little glances, they were definitely real. She walks back into the house and picks up the visitors' book, keen to see Pat's long list of platitudes. "Thank you, we had a lovely time," it says. "Major and Mrs. Chester."

"I definitely need some more upmarket guests," mutters Belinda, putting the book away in its special drawer. "That is the only way forward."

Walking back into the sitting room to scroll through some e-mails and work out a new plan, she hears the unmistakable crunch of fat tires on gravel as a car pulls up in the drive. Belinda sighs and tweaks her hair in the mirror. Then she rearranges her red, white, and blue skirt and white T-shirt as she steels herself to go outside. Her new guests are very early. How is she going to convey her irritation at their arrival, as well as maintain some sort of hostess meet-and-greet charm? She walks outside with a tight smile. *"Buongiorno."*

A wide grin suddenly cracks across her entire face, lighting it all the way up to her irises as she comes face-to-face with a large black Mercedes with smoked windows. The back right window lowers and a dark-haired, middle-aged man with a close haircut and sharp black spectacles pokes out his head. "Hello, *buongiorno,*" he says, in a distinctly American accent. "I'm looking for Lauren McMahon's place. Do you know it? The new B-and-B place that's opened up around here?"

"Come?" says Belinda, in her best Italian.

"Lauren McMahon?" he says again. Belinda does her best to look puzzled. "Casa Padronale? *Americano?"*

"Ooh, sì," she replies. *"Americana!"* She nods and smiles and makes a suitably Italian gesture of surprise and recognition.

"Where?" asks the man. Belinda looks puzzled again. He brings out a small new phrase book. *"Dove?"*

"Dove americana?" suggests Belinda.

"Sì, sì." The man nods, smiling enthusiastically. *"Dove americana?"*

"Qui, qui!" Belinda walks down the steps to the end of the drive, indicates for the car to turn around and go back down into the next-door valley. *"Qui, qui, qui!"* she repeats, nodding, gesturing, being terribly Italian.

"Okay, then," says the man, somewhat hesitantly, "I could have sworn it was down here. She told me to pass the small modern villa at the top of the hill—which is you, right?—and carry on down—"

"Non è qui," says Belinda, indicating the way to the Casa Padronale. *"Sì, qui,* ye-es, 'ere," she adds, in very broken English just to make her point, and indicates left.

"Great, thank you, *grazie*," he replies. He sits back in the cool, air-conditioned leather interior. "Turn around, driver," he says. *"Grazie,"* he says again, out of the smoked-glass window.

"Prego," replies Belinda. *"Prego, prego."* She gives him a little wave on his way. Belinda trips back to her sitting room with a grin on her face and a spring in her stride. Lauren's first guest has been seen off at the pass. Things are looking up, she thinks, her fat foot swinging as she sits, legs crossed, at the computer. Her position, as first house in the valley as you arrive on the main road, is ideally suited to misdirection, misinformation, and general sabotage. It is all too perfect. All she has to do is deny the existence of the *americana* and her annoying business will disappear. Forever. They'll drive around and around, and eventually they'll come back to Belinda wanting somewhere to stay. Perhaps she could poach them. Her house is a perfect combination of *rustica*-meets-a-little-bit-of-England—Americans will love it. Maybe she should hang a sign outside her house, saying B&B, so when they call they'll know to come back to her afterward.

"Hi, Mum!" Mary's cheery voice announces her arrival back from her walk.

"In here," says Belinda. "Now, what do you think?" she continues, looking up from her piece of paper. "Good Lord." She sits up. "What's happened to you?"

"What do you mean?" asks Mary, glancing at her reflection in the french windows.

"You look all glowing and pink and—I don't know—well," she says. "You look well."

"I've just been for a walk," explains Mary, doing up the top button of her shirt.

"That all?" asks Belinda, looking at her daughter suspiciously. "Are you sure you haven't been drinking or something?"

"No, of course not!" Mary's laugh sounds relieved. "Do you want to smell my breath?"

"Yuk," says Belinda, wrinkling up her short nose. "No, thank you. I'd sooner smell a dead dog on a hot day than go anywhere near your rancid mouth. Where did you go?"

"I went down toward Howard's and on past Derek and Barbara, past the, um, Casa Padronale—"

"Oh, did you see anything?"

"Like what?"

"You know, comings, goings, things, anything?"

"No, not really. But I do know that they're expecting the Hollywood scriptwriter today."

"Oh, really. How?" asks Belinda.

"You told me," says Mary, not looking her mother in the eye.

"Did I?" says Belinda. "Oh dear, well, I think they might be waiting for him for rather a long time—like forever," she says, collapsing into a fit of childish giggles.

"What?" asks Mary, looking down at her mother, who is still sitting in her chair.

"I sent him packing," announces Belinda, with a satisfied smile and a wobble of her head.

"You did what?"

"I sent him packing," she repeats, with relish.

"How?"

"I told him that the Casa Padronale was in another valley. Oh, the joy of seeing that swanky Mercedes turn around was just too, too much."

"Mum, you didn't!"

"I did." She grins. "Isn't it great?"

"Lauren will find out," says Mary.

"Oh, who cares what the *americana* thinks?" says Belinda. "She's not long for this valley, anyway."

"I think she's much more of a force to be reckoned with than you realize," says Mary. "She was a Wall Street ball breaker who specialized in hostile takeovers."

"Oooh . . . Very scary, darling," says Belinda, with a little fake shiver. "One thing is certain, she doesn't know this valley like I do. She doesn't know the people like I do, and she will not be staying around to find out. My advantage is cultural, you see. She's the invading force, and I'm a stealthy local. I shall fight a guerrilla war. You'll see."

"But, Mum," says Mary, "she knows all about what you've been doing."

"She does?" says Belinda, sitting rigid in her seat.

"Yes. She knows you called the *Bell' Arti* to try to shut her down."

"That's old news," Belinda assures her. "And, anyway, she can't prove anything. It's not like I actually went ahead with the petition or anything."

"She knows that you canceled her advert in the *Spectator* and tried to put yours above hers, and she knows you keep sending on dud guests, so she'll also know you turned away her Hollywood scriptwriter."

Belinda looks stunned and a little terrified. Her pink hand clasps the arms of the chair. The knuckles turn white. "She knows all this for certain?" she asks.

"Yes." Mary nods slowly.

"How do you know?" asks Belinda, her small blue eyes staring at her daughter.

"Um," says Mary, taking a step back and turning toward the open french windows. "Well, I've . . . um, heard something and um, well . . . Kyle told me a bit when you allowed me to have dinner with him, before you said that I wasn't to see him, so that's . . . how I know all that stuff . . ." she mutters, tugging her right earlobe.

"Oh," says Belinda. "But some of it was after your dinner."

"I know," answers Mary, with stiff jocularity as she moves from one foot to the other. "But you know I hear things . . ."

"And you've only just decided to tell me?" says Belinda, standing up.

"Would it have made any difference if I'd said anything earlier?" asks Mary, her hands on her hips.

"Um," says Belinda, trying to think. Lauren knows. But how does Mary know that Lauren knows? Who told her? Who has she been talking to? Who knew that Lauren had known all along? It's all so confusing.

"Coo-ee!" comes a broad Celtic brogue from in the hall. "It's only us! Sorry we're so early, but there was some sort of problem at Glasgow airport and we touched down earlier, and driving on the right was much easier than we thought so . . . here we are."

Belinda turns the corner into her hall to be greeted by two large white Scots in matching black T-shirts and black cut-off denim shorts that stop just around the crotch. They are both wearing black sandals and matching, impenetrably black sunglasses that suggest their guide dogs are still in the car.

"Morag," pronounces the one with hair the color of an orange highlighter pen, as she steps forward to shake Belinda's hand.

"Maureen," nods the dark-haired one, whose shorts ride so high and tight around her backside it looks as though she was poured into them and someone forgot to say "when."

"We're not lesbians, but we're sharing a room," declares Morag, scraping her bright purple holdall along the floor. "Just in case you're a little confused."

"It never crossed my mind," Belinda tells them. "Anyway," she laughs, "some of my best friends are lesbians."

"It's a great place you've got here," says Maureen, dropping her pink bag from waist height and walking out onto Belinda's terrace. She performs a yawn and stretch with such gusto that Belinda half expects a wind-breaking finale. "The views are good and I like the look of the pool down there." She comes back into the sitting room. "Och," she says. "I've got one of these old computers at home," she adds, coming over to double-click on Belinda's e-mail icon. "Yes, it's exactly the same. They're okay, aren't they?"

"Yes, very nice," mumbles Belinda, her back pinned to her hall wall. The invading Scottish hordes have wrong-footed her, and she isn't sure what to do. The normal hostess meet-and-greet scenario has gone right out of the window.

"Let me take your bags," says Mary, as she's supposed to. Well done, Mary. Thank God for Mary. Belinda stirs into action.

"Yes, well." Belinda recovers. "Welcome to Casa Mia, *buongiorno.*" That came out in the wrong order, but so far, so good. "Let me give you a little tour and explain a few house rules." She feels life ebbing back. "Maureen's little visit to my terrace is her last," she continues pleasantly, "as it is a private area."

"Oh, right." Morag nods vigorously. "I'm sorry."

"That's okay," says Belinda, her head on one side, "but don't do it again." She lets go a little laugh; the two Scottish women join in halfheartedly. "As Morag noticed there is, of course, a swimming pool."

"Maureen," says Maureen.

"What?" says Belinda.

"As Maureen noticed," she says. "As Maureen noticed the pool. I'm Maureen."

"Are you?" says Belinda. "Good. Anyway," she says, drawing

an exaggerated breath to continue, "there are pool rules. No swimming before ten o'clock and after six . . ." She lists them off on her fingers.

"Why?" asks Morag.

"Why?" repeats Belinda. "Health and safety."

"Oh," says Morag, seemingly satisfied, if a little confused.

"Good," reprises Belinda. "Anyway, there is a washing line for your wet things out of sight around the back." Belinda points like an air hostess indicating emergency exits.

"Now, washing," interrupts Morag.

"Yes?" sighs Belinda turning to face her.

"It says here in your stuff that you can do washing."

"Only very, very occasionally," says Belinda, flaring her nostrils.

"Well, how much for this lot?" says Morag, unzipping the bright purple holdall, releasing the dank smell of dirty clothes into the air.

"Thirty euros," says Belinda, without looking.

"That's about twenty pounds," says Morag. "That's more expensive than the Laundromat."

"Yes, well," snaps Belinda, "this is an upmarket bed-and-breakfast and we only do laundry in exceptional circumstances."

"Right, well, thirty euros is fine," agrees Morag, leaving her open purple holdall in the hall. "What other rules are there?"

"No smoking in the rooms, only in the areas where an ashtray is provided," snaps Belinda.

"Where are they?" asks Maureen.

"Oh, they're around," Belinda lies, with a small smile. "So," she continues, "no personal stereo things by the swimming pool as they're so unattractive. Mobile telephones don't work here," another lie, "so don't bother switching them on. Breakfast is served between eight and eight twenty-five and, of course, if you want supper you must inform us before midday. So, I presume you're eating out tonight?"

"Oh," says Morag. "We'd planned on eating here."

"So sorry," says Belinda, with a little shrug. "Had we known in advance . . . but may I suggest the charming little town of Poggibonsi where there is an English-speaking restaurant with lovely chips?"

"Right," says Morag.

"Do feel free to go down to your rooms," Belinda continues, "where you will find you own personal terraces, which get quite a lot of sun. Although," she laughs, "with skin as pale as yours, I shouldn't think you'll be spending much time in it! Sometimes it does amaze me that you Scots travel at all! It must be such a chore covering up all the time."

"Right," says Morag, making to go downstairs.

"I'm afraid I'm chairing a committee meeting all afternoon," adds Belinda, "so any little questions, you'll have to ask my daughter, Mary."

"Oh, all right," says Maureen. "Just a quick one. We were thinking about going in to Ser-anna, some time, possibly for dinner tonight?"

"Where?" asks Belinda.

"Ser-anna?"

"I'm not sure where that is," she says.

"You know, the big Etruscan town down the road," explains Maureen.

"Oh! Serraaana. Serraaaaana . . . What—instead of Poggibonsi?"

"Possibly."

"If you insist. There are plenty of places there. Just keep your eyes open. You're bound to come across something. There really isn't a dud meal to be had in Tuscany. But then again," she pauses, looking her guests up and down, taking in their soft pastiness, "if you don't like fresh fruit and vegetables, you might be a little stuck."

Inspired by her little victory over her guests, Belinda feels upbeat as she wafts upstairs to change and reaccessorize herself for her *festa* meeting. Her previously anxious mood has been replaced by something more optimistic. Lauren may specialize in hostile takeovers, but Belinda is among friends, good friends, loyal, close friends, whom she has known for nearly five years. Quite why she is worrying about her position as chair of the *festa* meeting she has no idea. She is being silly. She is the Contessa of the Valley after all. She chooses a dark red shirt and a long navy skirt that stops just above the ankles, and adds a cacophony of silver bangles on her right arm for a more relaxed Bohemian effect. Just as she is about to walk out of the door, she remembers the yellow legal notepad. She rushes back to the sitting room to collect it, picks up a pen, and attaches it to the top of the pad. She checks the final effect in the hall mirror and is pleased. Efficient, businesslike, relaxed, and very Italian, it is the perfect ensemble to chair a *Festa di Formaggio* meeting in Tuscany.

❀ ❀ ❀

As she walks through Lauren's open front door, Belinda is greeted by banter and light laughter from the open-plan kitchen area. There is a beguiling smell of coffee and warm cakes. She stands stock-still in the hall. She is late. But she can't be late. She's on time. It's everyone else who is early.

"Oh," she declares, as she enters the elegant white room and sees the long wooden table lined with people. "I can't be late?" she asks, with a rattle of her bangles as she checks her wrist for a watch. The table falls silent and turns to stare. "How strange.

I thought you said four, and it's four. Well, anyway, here I am! I'm *sooo* sorry to have kept you all waiting." She weaves her way toward them. "I had guests arriving and guests leaving . . . guests, guests, guests. But I'm here now." She lifts her chin in the air as she tries to see through her very large, very round, very dark glasses. "You may start," she adds, wincing as she knocks her shin on a chair, and sits down. She brings out her pad and clicks her pen. "So . . ." she starts, looking through her glasses. "Who've we got? It's very dark in here."

"You've got your sunglasses on," drawls Lauren, from the other end of the long table.

"Oh, God, of course I have," laughs Belinda whipping them off. Two dark circles of sweat are already growing under her arms. "Would anyone like some of my paper to take notes on?" she asks hopefully, tearing off a leaf of the yellow paper.

"Actually," says Barbara, from halfway up on the left, "Lauren has done these." She waves a little pad, attractively ring-bound with a transparent plastic cover and a little cheese motif in the top left-hand corner of every page. "Aren't they gorgeous?" She adds, with a little shrug of her shoulders. "There's even one left over for you."

"How kind," says Belinda, pushing her fancy pad to one side. "So," she says, with another click of her pen, "I was thinking—"

"Actually," interrupts Lauren, "we were in the middle of discussing how to improve on what happened last year."

"Oh," says Belinda.

✳ ✳ ✳

In a white silk shirt and slim denim jeans, Lauren's sleek frame is backlit by the sun as it pours through the glass doors behind her. Her outline is silhouetted and her expression is impossible to read. Belinda squints. Lauren smiles. It's one of the oldest tricks in her negotiating book, but it always works. That, and starting a meeting fifteen minutes early.

❊ ❊ ❊

"Okay then," says Lauren. "What I was thinking was—" She stops. "Oh, Belinda," she says slowly, "do you know everyone here?"

"Of course I do." Belinda's head wobbles at the suggestion. "I've lived here for years. This is my valley." She smiles looking down the table at Barbara, Derek, Howard . . .

"We haven't actually met," says a rather attractive-looking woman with copper hair and russet skin. "I'm Jaqui," she says, standing up and offering her hand. "Spelled J-a-q-u-i, just so you know."

"Oh, how lovely to meet you," replies Belinda, with a limp shake.

"I'm one of the founding members of the monastery commune."

"How lovely." Belinda coughs, searching for her P.C. face. "The Australian women's commune," she adds, finally finding her liberal smile. "Lovely."

"Yeah." Jaqui nods. "We're really rapt about being involved in the cheese fest this year; we've never been invited before. Oh, and this is my partner," she says, indicating the slim Eurasian-looking girl opposite with long black hair to her waist.

"G'day." She nods. "I'm Paloma."

"Paloma." Belinda exudes tolerance. "That's very unusual."

"I know, isn't it?" she enthuses. "I chose it myself! It's after a song I heard on the radio. My real name's Kylie but I got so bored of it—everyone's called Kylie in Sydney, and I mean everyone. You hear it all the time. Kylie! Kylie! So I changed it a couple of years back, and now everyone calls me Paloma."

"Good," says Belinda. She smiles. "Excellent."

"Right," says Lauren. "Now that Belinda has been introduced, shall we get on?"

"Oh," says Belinda.

"Sorry?" says Lauren, her long silhouette leaning down the table. "Did you have something to say?"

"Um," says Belinda.

"Good," says Lauren. "So what else do we think was wrong with last year?"

"Well . . ." says Barbara. Belinda shoots her a look. "Not an awful lot . . ."

"The food on the expat table," says Derek.

"The food?" asks Belinda, a little shocked. "What was wrong with it?"

"Well, it wasn't exactly gourmet, was it?" says Howard.

"Howard!" hisses Belinda.

"What?"

"You don't really mean that. The food last year was wonderful. I made the pasta salad myself."

"Yes, well," says Howard, looking down at his cheese-motif pad, "I was only making a suggestion."

"Might I suggest that as someone who clearly knows terribly little about cuisine, you keep your suggestions to yourself?" says Belinda. "Honestly . . . Where were we?"

"Improvements," says Lauren.

Belinda begins, "Well, I'd thought I could—"

"We could do a barbie," interrupts Jaqui.

"Sorry?" says Belinda, looking down her short nose. "I—"

"Yeah, great idea," agrees Paloma. "We Aussies are practically born with tongs in our hands."

"I'm sure you're jolly good at barbecues," says Belinda, "but they're not very Italian."

"Neither is pasta salad," says Lauren.

"What?" says Belinda, turning to look down the table.

"Neither is pasta salad," repeats Lauren's silhouette. "I think a barbecue is an excellent idea," she continues. "All those in favor raise their hands."

"Actually, hang on a second," says Belinda, half getting out of her seat. "I thought I was chair of this meeting."

"Oh, I'm so sorry," says Lauren, sitting down. "I'm just so used to chairing things. Of course, you are indeed in charge of the cheese-festival committee." She smiles. "Please go ahead."

"Good, right," Belinda taps the sides of her yellow pad and double-clicks her pen. "So, who wants pasta salad? Like we had last year. And every year before that?" She looks up and down the table. No one moves. "What?" she asks. "No one? Howard?" He shakes his head. "Barbara?" She does the same. "Oh," says Belinda, tweaking her damp red shirt out of one of her armpits. "No one for pasta." She tries to write it down on her pad, but the pen doesn't work. "Gosh," she says, clicking quickly again. "So no . . . nice . . . Italian pasta," she mutters, as she writes. "And who wants an Australian barbecue?" she asks, her top lip curling. The whole table raises their arms. "Oh," she says. "All of you."

"I think that's what's known as unanimous," laughs Jaqui, leaning back in her seat.

"Yes." Belinda makes a small note.

"Okay," says Derek suddenly with a little cough, and he stands up. "Now who's going to be the Big Cheese this year? Who's rolling the expat cheese?"

"Well, I'm the Big Chee—" says Belinda, cheeks pinking.

"Belinda has done it every year for the past five years since she arrived in the valley," continues Derek. "Haven't you, Belinda?"

"Indeed I have." She allows happy memories of past races to flicker across her face.

"But it would be nice to win for once," declares Derek.

"It's the taking part—" Belinda starts, hovering over her seat.

"So," says Derek, with his hand in the air to stop her, "I was thinking that perhaps someone else should have a go."

"But—"

"It's only fair," continues Derek. "You've had a good run for your money, Belinda."

"Or roll," giggles Barbara.

"And I think . . . Lauren should be the Big Cheese and represent us this year," he announces, looking down the table for Lauren's approval.

Lauren smiles and slowly gets out of her chair. Howard looks down at the table and plays with his pad. Barbara laughs with embarrassment. Derek stands stiffly, looking at Lauren. The Australian lesbians stare at each other, bemused, while Belinda inhales sharply and stands up. The two women stand at opposite ends of the table facing each other.

"No," says Lauren, with a relaxed flick of her hair. "Big Cheese? I couldn't."

"She couldn't," says Belinda quietly, her hands gripping the table.

"It's Belinda's little thing," says Lauren.

"It's my little thing," echoes Belinda, her eyes scanning the table for some sort of support or reaction. "It's my little thing," she repeats, imploring someone to come to her rescue. "My little thing . . ."

No one says anything. No one moves.

"That," Belinda continues, desperately trying to save face, "that . . . I am prepared to let you do."

"What?" says Howard.

"Oh, yes! You don't think I care about representing the expat community in the cheese-rolling competition, do you? Honestly!" She chuckles on valiantly. "Big Cheese! That little thing! Really! What do you take me for?"

"You see? I said you wouldn't mind," agrees Barbara. "Didn't I, Derek? When we discussed it."

"You discussed it!" Belinda laughs as if she has just heard the best joke ever.

"Yes!" says Barbara.

"When?"

"Oh, over dinner the other day."

"Ha, ha, ha!" is all Belinda can manage.

"So, you agree?" Derek asks Lauren.

"Well, only if Belinda insists," says Lauren.

"She insists, don't you, Belinda?" says Derek.

"Yes," says Belinda, in a very high, very tight voice.

"Oh! But she's got to insist it," says Lauren, flapping her hand like a coy teenager. "Only if she *says* she insists."

"Go on, Belinda," says Derek. "Insist!"

"Yes, go on," giggles Barbara. "Say it."

"Lauren, I insist that you become Big Cheese and take my place in the cheese-rolling competition representing the expat community instead of me," says Belinda, a rictus smile on her face, as if she has been electrocuted.

"Oh, now I feel awful," says Lauren, clutching her white silk–clad bosom, her knees bending as she smiles. "Just terrible. I feel like I've stolen your crown!"

Sabato ❀ Saturday

Clima ❀ *fa caldo* (hot)

It is so hot today, I can hardly write. In fact, I notice I haven't been fulfilling my authorial duties terribly well of late. Whole days seem to be drifting by without my comments or *aperçus*. But I shall battle on, if only to tell you a funny little thing that happened the other day. It is terribly amusing, but I suppose, quite simply put, there has been a coup d'état in the valley!

For the past five years I have been what is affectionately known as the "Big Cheese"—in charge of the *Festa di Formaggio* committee and, indeed, responsible for the rolling of the cheese on behalf of our small, intimate, friendly expat community that we have built here in Val di Santa Caterina. And I have looked upon this duty as an honor. I have enjoyed organizing the food, the table decorations, telling the others what they should be doing. I have also enjoyed the burden of the cheese rolling. It is a complicated skill that requires timing, application, talent, savoir faire, dedication, total support from others, and a deep understanding of all things Italian.

And for the past five years I have served our expat group well. But now, it seems, my services and dedication are no longer required. They have decided to let the *americana* have a go. Actually, when I say "they," I mean "we." It was a group decision, a sort of generous way of trying to include her in our little community. Otherwise, what a horrid group of Judases they would be!

Anyway, I really do wish the *americana* well. She will find that it is a lot harder being "Big Cheese" than she can possibly imagine. There are always people rolling up the rear, trying to knock you over onto your side. Arms, legs, necks have been broken in the past. The game is a lot more dangerous than it looks.

Apart from that minor, insignificant change, life in Casa Mia is looking *rosa*. My delightful Scottish girls left the day before yesterday. I can't think why I had any reservations about them, they proved to be very law-abiding in the end, and they took direction well. I only had to point out and explain things to them a couple of times before they understood. It was a shame they had to leave early. I normally have a two-night minimum stay, which I think is standard in most B-and-Bs in the U.K. and also *gîtes* in France. But, sadly, they announced that one of their mothers had been taken ill and they needed to return to Scotland as soon as they could. They were happy to pay for the extra night, and I was very sorry to see them go. As a hostess, you do want people to relax and enjoy their holiday, and it is very inconvenient when something like family illness interferes.

However sad I am at the departure of the Scots, it does come as a bit of relief to have no guests in the house as I am entertaining tonight. I am throwing open my doors to all my many friends, plus some Australians. What a cosmopolitan bunch we are! The confirmed spinsters who own the monastery are coming, as are Barbara and Derek, plus the *americana* and her rather unattractive son, as well as the famous writer Howard Oxford. I am planning a spontaneous evening that will be exciting, fun, and terribly, terribly relaxed.

SPAGHETTI BOLOGNESE DI CASA MIA

When one is entertaining in a relaxed way, there is nothing better than spaghetti Bolognese (or spaghetti with a meat and tomato sauce). It's hearty, it's warming, it's like a great big blanket on a cold winter's night. Spaghetti Bolognese is the mother of all comfort food. There are some houses where a version of Spag Bol—as it is sometimes known—has been passed down through the generations, and could be described as its signature dish! But this one is all mine! And when I say all mine, I really do mean all mine, and not my mother's as she was a beef-and-suet woman, who didn't have much truck with foreign food.

This serves a welcome and relaxed six.

✵ onions	✵ Worcestershire sauce
✵ garlic	✵ spaghetti (out of a packet is fine)
✵ oil	✵ parsley (optional)
✵ mince	✵ cheese (optional)
✵ tinned tomatoes	

This is a quick dish that can be whipped up at a moment's notice, provided you have the ingredients **a mano,** of course! Chop the onions and garlic together and throw into a pan of oil. You can use vegetable oil, but with the rivers of olive oil we have in Tuscany, I feel it would be criminal not to indulge in one's local natural bounty. Add enough mince for six, plus a tin of tomatoes and their juice, then stir. Splash in the Worcestershire sauce. Cook the pasta. When the meat has been bubbling away for a while, pour it over the pasta. Just before you serve, sprinkle with some hand-picked, hand-chopped parsley for that **rustico** homey effect. Oh, and on naughty days when I'm not watching my figure, I like to cover it liberally with grated cheese.

Serve with popular friends and a garrulous wine.

CHAPTER NINE

Belinda's demotion from Big Cheese to not-so-large cheese in charge of tables and chairs hit her hard. At the time she tried to take it well. Sitting in the bright sunshine, under the spotlight at the end of Lauren's table, she took her defeat on the chin. She smiled with a tense graciousness, went on to declare herself a "terribly good sport," and then, as if to demonstrate exactly how *sportif* she was, she became positively, hysterically good-humored for the rest of the afternoon.

She complimented Lauren on the strength of her delicious coffee, said how much she loved her homemade muffins, and interrupted everyone when they tried to speak. Rather like an overexcited Labrador, her conversation careered around, desperate to please. She insisted on talking Lauren through her cheese-rolling technique, she repeatedly told Derek and Barbara how clever they were for suggesting Lauren in the first place, and then, just as everyone thought she might spontaneously combust with joviality, she invited the entire lesbian community to her little soirée on Saturday night.

Powered on by her own magnanimous marvelousness, she drove home, drank a whole bottle of corked white wine, sang loudly to Russell Watson, and picked a fight with her Scottish guests. They then rose early the next morning, announced that one of their mothers had been taken seriously ill, and left. Mary, in the meantime, was left desperately trying to think of some sort of positive spin to place on the whole wretched incident.

But there really is nothing to be done. The next day Belinda is inconsolable, and no amount of forwarding e-mails from downmarket guests to Lauren's bed-and-breakfast or misdirecting others is going to make her feel any better. And, to cap it all, she is bored.

Coming as it does at the end of July and the beginning of the school holidays, the *Festa di Formaggio* is one of the highlights in Belinda's calendar at what is usually a quiet time at Casa Mia. While beachside resorts are teeming with families of tetchy parents and screaming offspring in diminutive clothing, Casa Mia, due to its child-free policy, has plenty of vacancies. It is not until August, when the family bandwagon has moved on, that the executive couples and the migrating European masses start to fill up the rooms again. In the meantime, Belinda usually organizes the expat end of the *festa* and spends hours talking about cheese and rolling large pecorinos around the grounds of Casa Mia. But this year's task of organizing chairs and tables for the group will hardly detain her at all. All it will take is one telephone call to each of the cheese-festival guests to ensure that they bring their own seating, a little note to Giovanna about her trestle table, and her duty will have been done.

So with little or, perhaps more honestly, nothing and no one to occupy her time, Belinda throws herself into the preparations for her party and, indeed, gives it a theme. She has concluded that if she can't roll cheese down a hill, she is going to throw a much better party with more panache than Lauren, and prove that, if nothing else, she is the best hostess in the valley.

"It's *rustica,*" she enthuses to Derek.

"Oh," he says, apparently not quite understanding exactly what *rustica* means. "Barbara was rather hoping she could wear those Aladdin hot pants. She's had them repaired at great expense."

"Oh, that'll be a treat," replies Belinda. "Let's hope the seams are a bit stronger than they were last time." She laughs a little too enthusiastically.

"Yes, well," says Derek, sounding a little quiet. "*Rustica,* you say?"

"*Rustica,*" she repeats.

"Is that a theme?"

"Of course it's a theme, Derek."

"Mmm," he muses. "So, have you organized your task for the cheese festival?"

"My task?" asks Belinda.

"Yes," says Derek. "Tables and chairs—that's what you got in the end, wasn't it?"

"Honestly, Derek," exhales Belinda. "When one is used to organizing, as well as competing in, the *Festa di Formaggio,* something as little as chairs and tables can hardly be considered a task."

"I know, Belinda," he says, "but they're still important, you know. We've got to have somewhere to sit, and the monastery girls have got to have somewhere to put their food."

"Really, Derek, what do you take me for?" laughs Belinda. "As former representative of the expat community, I'm sure I can manage a few chairs. Anyway," she says optimistically, "I'm much more interested in my soirée tonight . . . Mark my words, Derek, it's going to be the party of the year!"

"Well, you've got a bit of competition." He chuckles.

"What?" says Belinda, checking her reflection in the french windows.

"You've a bit of competition after Lauren's do the other week."

"Call yourself a friend, Derek!" snaps Belinda. "You know perfectly well that my soirée will not only be more elegant, and more fun than the American's, but it will also be a whole lot more *relaxed*!"

"Forgive me, Belinda," says Derek, "but you're sounding a little tense."

"Tense!" she replies, her voice rising three octaves in one word. "I'm not tense, Derek," she comes down the scale. "It is you that I might suggest who is being a little disloyal!"

"Oh," says Derek quietly. "I'm sorry you feel that way but—"

"Don't interrupt, Derek," she says. "Anyway, I'm afraid I can't talk to you now. I have things to do and finger food to prepare. So I will see you later," she states, "with your wife hopefully not in her industrially stitched hot pants, and we will have a great party. All right?"

"All right," says Derek.

"Good," says Belinda. "At about seven thirty?"

"Seven thirty," repeats Derek.

"Don't be late."

"No."

"*Arrivadeary*," says Belinda.

"*Arrivadeary*," mutters Derek.

Derek is not the only one desperately seeking enthusiasm for Belinda's party: Mary is also finding it difficult. But, then, Mary is finding it difficult to do a lot of things at the moment. Eating and sleeping are right up there with trying to whip up some sort of soirée interest, coupled with trying not to smile too much. Ever since Lauren's valley warming, Mary has been on cloud Kyle. What had started off as a mere marijuana meeting on a Tuscan hillside has now graduated into a full-blown love affair, and all of it behind her mother's back. And although Kyle is still technically not her lover, Mary is very much in love with him.

Fortunately, her mother is too busy hating his mother for either of them to notice that their offspring disappear most afternoons for hours at a time. During those lazy postprandial moments, when the sun is high and hot and Belinda is normally flat on her back, snoring in sharp rapid bursts like a roadside drill, Mary makes her escape. She runs across the dusty fields of yellowed grass and butterflies toward the ancient gnarled olive tree that Kyle chose as their rendezvous point three weeks ago. And while his mother presumes him reading Yale texts in his bedroom, and chants away her stresses in the fresco-free yoga room, he lies in the long grass, his arms around Mary, running his hands through her hair, as they whisper how happy they are that they've found each other.

"You're nothing like any . . . other . . . girl . . . I . . . have . . . ever . . . met," he says to her as they lie together in the grass, him kissing her hot lips between every word. "You . . . are . . . amazing."

"Do you think so?" she whispers, sitting up on one hip, her long dark hair falling over her shoulders.

"Hell, yes," he whispers right back.

They spend at least an hour together and possibly, sometimes, almost two, horizontal in the long grass, trading thoughts, secrets, and dreams, while kissing and touching hair, skin, and hands. The rest of the day is spent in expectation of their hour together, or replaying the hour just past over and over again.

And all day they each contend with derogatory comments from their parents. Lauren simply feels sorry for Mary: that the poor girl should have such a difficult mother inspires pity, plus a small amount of annoyance for what she regards as Mary's rather aggravating lack of spine. Belinda, on the other hand, views Kyle as a simple subset of all things *americana* and can't stand the sight of him. His straight white teeth, his intelligent, handsome face, his dark hair and eyes all get on her nerves. She is terribly glad to have nipped that relationship in the bud.

"Is the *americana* bringing that ghastly son of hers, Kevin, along tonight?" asks Belinda, chopping up small squares of cheese on the sideboard in the kitchen. Mary does not bother to reply. Even the deliberate misnomer makes her heart race and her face blush. "I can't remember what I said when I got back after the *festa* meeting, whether he's coming or not. I do hope not," Belinda continues, popping a cheese square into her mouth. "I can really do without his white smile in my house. What do you think, darling? Don't you agree?"

"I don't know," says Mary, concentrating on chopping her pineapple.

"Don't know what?" quizzes Belinda, turning to face her, a knife in her hand. "Whether he's coming? Or whether his smile is too big and white and American?"

"Either," says Mary, keeping her head firmly down. "Um, are these the right size?" she asks, offering her mother a small square of pineapple.

"Let's see," says her mother, picking up a cocktail stick and sliding on a cube of cheese followed by another cube of pineapple. "Not bad," she says, holding the ensemble up to the light for inspection. "It is usually so much easier with tinned. Just as well you're here to do the chopping, darling."

"I hope people find the seventies retro food amusing," says Mary, still searching for her soirée interest. The possibility of Kyle's arrival in her mother's home fills her with both dread and delicious hope. The joy of seeing him will be muted by her inability to betray her true feelings.

"What retro food?" asks Belinda, threading another cocktail stick.

"The cheese and pineapple," says Mary.

"Don't be silly, dear," says Belinda. "We used to have these all the time in Tilling. Or at least right up until I left."

"Oh," says Mary.

"My finger food was always highly appreciated. Anyway, the olive," she adds, taking a green one out of a preserving jar and forcing it on to the stick, "the olive on the end makes the whole thing terribly Italian and *rustica*. Look!" She smiles. "Delicious."

Even with the little that she can remember from her term spent at Swindon catering college, Mary knows that a combination of cheese, olive, and pineapple is not a winner on any canapé circuit.

"How about we do pineapple and cheese and serve the olives on the side?" she suggests, trying to be helpful.

"Really?" says Belinda, looking surprised. "D'you know, darling? Catering is very much your little thing. I think I'll just go and concentrate on what I'm good at." She smiles and takes off her apron. "Being a hostess."

"Right," says Mary, putting down her knife and blowing fronds of hair off her face.

"Yes," she smiles. "I think I might leave you to get on with it, you know, fill those vol-au-vents I bought with some prawns, that sort of thing, and I think I might pop up to Giovanna's for a light lunch." She smiles again, squeezing her hands together, raising her shoulders at the same time. "I'll get out of your rather sweaty hair."

* * *

Belinda decides to walk down the hill to the trattoria, thinking the exercise might do her some good. After all, Mary's walks have proved to be extraordinarily restorative: the girl has undergone a makeover of Richard and Judy proportions. Sporting her wide-brimmed *mercato* hat and long yellow and blue flowered dress, which she picked up at a boutique sale in Serrana, Belinda fancies she looks rather fabulous as she strolls along. She plucks a long grass out of the hedgerow and pops it into her mouth Tom Sawyer–style. She swings her hips and admires her ankles in the red strappy sandals as she walks along. She gazes down at the valley that falls gently away to her right.

The cypress trees that line the road stand still, exhausted by the heat. The fields of maize rise tall as men and the sunflowers are in their final flourish. Their bright yellow petals curl in the strong sun. The whole valley is enveloped in a shivering, shimmering haze. The crickets are humming. "When the animals sing, you know you're in trouble," Belinda says to herself. It is hot, possibly the hottest day of the year so far.

Derek and Barbara are at home, she notes, and from the way the light dances on the water, it looks as though someone is in their swimming pool. The Bianchis' farm is unusually quiet. They must all be inside having lunch or asleep escaping the sun. There are also no cars parked outside the Casa Padronale. The *americana* is reassuringly low on guests. Belinda smiles. She too must be affected by the late July rush for the beach. Not that she is turning away guests: since the dawn departure of the Scots, Casa Mia has been empty, and will remain so till the middle of next week. But at least the *americana* isn't doing well either.

Turning the corner, Belinda walks into Giovanna's car park, through the now grape-heavy arches, and out onto the terrace. The place looks relatively full for a lunchtime. A couple of cars are parked, and a tandem is propped against the stone wall. At one end of the terrace a family of four are perusing their menus. Next to them is a young couple, with a small baby between them, drinking glasses of iced water and snapping breadsticks. An elderly couple in his-and-hers plus fours sit in the far corner, away from the entrance, and are already tucking into what looks like a long and languid lunch. They both have wind-worn faces and wild white hair that stands to dusty attention. They are either English or German, Belinda can't tell which, but they have obviously spent many a summer cycling through Italy and are totally at home in their environment. They are eating the sort of food Belinda can never bring herself to order. The woman is lunching on a plate of raw shelled broad beans and a hunk of cheese, while the man has a plate of cold pork cuts, including different kinds of blood-rich salami. As Belinda walks past, her nose in the air, trying to see out from under her hat, they both nod and in accentless Italian say: *"Buongiorno."* Belinda nods back.

The elegance of the elderly couple makes her sit straighter, and stare more meaningfully at the view. She smooths down her yellow flowered dress, flares her nostrils, puts her head gently to one side, and arranges her smile to appear to be thinking about beauty, watercolors, and art in general. Roberto arrives to take her order and is ebulliently enthusiastic enough to make Belinda look nice and local. She smiles across at the elderly couple. They nod back.

She settles back in her chair, looking like a regular and thinking about her party, flicking her *insalata mista* around her plate. Just as she is about to let off another smile in the direction of the smart couple in the corner, she sees two plump white women dressed in black shorts and black T-shirts walk through the grape-heavy arch.

"How about sitting here, Maureen?" asks the first, with bright orange hair scraped tightly into a face-lifting ponytail.

"But, Morag," says the other, her black hair top-knotted in a pink scrunchie, "the view is better from here."

Belinda recognizes her ex-clientele immediately—her antennae are working overtime. She has had walkouts before: the young Californians who couldn't stand her cooking, the middle-aged couple from London who couldn't stand her conversation, the brace of smart Parisians who couldn't stand her cooking or her conversation. But none of them had ever had the audacity to stay around in the valley to rub her retroussé nose in it. They spin their yarn about sudden illness, or bereavement, then usually have the decency to disappear, never to be seen or thought of again. Yet these two are still here and, judging by the conversation Belinda is overhearing, they appear to have booked in at the *americana*'s.

"Och," says Morag, "I'm so glad I listened to you, babe, and made the switch. That shower I had this morning was amazing."

"I know," agrees Maureen. "And that Lauren is such a terribly nice woman. I really like her setup. You know, cool house, cool yoga room, and the food . . ."

"Yeah," nods Morag. "Figs and peaches at breakfast. So Italian. It's just what you want."

"That other place," laughs Maureen. "I mean, please!"

"What was the old cow's name?"

Belinda sits stiff with irritation, listening to their eulogy of Lauren and ultimate dismissal of herself. They have so little regard for her and the delights of Casa Mia that they can't even remember her name. Safe behind the large brim of her *mercato* hat, she listens to a diatribe on the awfulness of her cooking, the unattractiveness of her decoration, the dullness of her conversation, and, inevitably, the width of her behind.

"And the place smelled," adds Maureen.

"Yeah," agrees Morag. "I'm not sure of what, though."

"Old woman," says Maureen.

"God, yes! You're right, old woman. That's exactly the smell. Fusty old woman."

"Miserable old woman, more like. Miserable old woman who's going to die on her own and only be found weeks later by cats." Maureen laughs, her plump pink legs launching into the air.

Belinda is on the verge of confronting them, and berating them for their bad taste and general impertinence, but she hesitates and loses her nerve. The idea that her house smells of "miserable old woman" cuts her to the quick. She grabs hold of the table to steady herself. She stares at the view and inhales. What are they talking about? She isn't old. She's actually rather glamorous, sitting here in her yellow flowered dress. Lauren is the same age as her, for Christ sake. Belinda isn't miserable either. She has plenty of friends. Lots of them. In fact, if they really looked into things they would realize she is actually very popular indeed. And the idea that she might die on her own, only to be found by cats, is patently risible. Belinda hates cats. In fact, Belinda hates cats almost as much as she hates smokers and children. But instead of facing the two harpies, she decides an elegant exit is required. She stands up, pulls her hat low over her eyes, leaves Roberto a ten-euro note, and shuffles toward the archway. Just as she passes the Scottish girls' table, her nose in the air, she walks slap-bang into a short middle-aged man with dark hair and sharp black-rimmed spectacles.

"Jesus Christ!" he yells, his hands up like he's surrendering in a shoot-out. "Look where you're going, lady!"

"I'm terribly sorry," says Belinda, all flustered and bothered as her hat falls off. She bends down to pick it up, and as she straightens she comes face-to-face with Lauren's Hollywood screenwriter.

"You!" he says, wagging his finger, his pigeon chest poncing about with anger. "I know you. I never forget a face. You're the woman who fucking sent me on a wild-goose chase all over the fucking Tuscan countryside." His voice increases in nasal tone. "It's definitely fucking you!"

"Oh, my God, it's her!" squeal the two Scottish women, as if they've been caught bitching out of class—which, of course, they have. They cover their mouths with their hands and re-tract their legs for good measure.

"Good afternoon." Belinda threads the brim of her hat through her hands as she nods to each of them in turn. "I trust you're all having a pleasant stay on the other side of the valley."

"Yeah," says the screenwriter, with plenty of "what of it?" at-titude.

"Ladies?" asks Belinda.

"Yes." Morag and Maureen nod, their pink cheeks blending with their sunburn.

"Good." She smiles and makes her way toward the arch. "A nice sterile place with all the charm and atmosphere of a labo-ratory." She pauses. "No wonder you three lab rats feel so at home there." She turns and nods a departing smile to the el-derly couple in the corner, and before any of Lauren's guests can recover themselves, she trots out on to the road as quickly as her strappy red sandals will take her.

✻ ✻ ✻

Back at Casa Mia, Mary has been working hard. The plates of cheese and pineapple, bowls of olives, peanuts, crisps, and trays of prawn vol-au-vents and cocktail sausages are all laid out on the side, ready for the guests. She has put out the plastic beakers for drinks, and is sitting cross-legged, sifting through her mother's CD collection, thinking about music, when Belinda walks in.

"Maria, darling," she announces, with a swish of her *mercato* hat as she wafts around the house opening the windows, "I simply don't think all that finger food on the side is Italian enough."

"Oh?" says Mary, looking up, a *Nothing but Country* CD in her lap.

"Yes," says Belinda, opening a window, flapping her arms, marshaling air into the house. "I want prosciutto, *melone,* prosciutto *e melone,* salami, mozzarella and—and—broad beans."

"Broad beans?" asks Mary, finding a Paul Simon CD at the back of the shelf.

"Yes," confirms Belinda. "The *americana*'s party was very American—"

"It was?"

"Yes, of course it was," insists Belinda frowning at Mary's interruption. "And this party is going to be *rustica* and Italian, *rustica italiana*—in fact, *molto* Italian. Spontaneously Italian. With little bits of Italy everywhere. Full of culture and atmosphere. Italian culture and atmosphere." She pauses. "Do you think this house smells?"

"No," says Mary, getting up off the floor. "Of what?"

"Old woman?" asks Belinda.

"No," shrugs Mary, looking at her mother. "What do old women smell like anyway?"

"I've simply got no idea," laughs Belinda, flinging open another set of windows, letting in blasts of warm air. "Anyway, darling, you set about doing some *molto* Italian food. I'm off into town to buy lots of Italian things."

Come seven o'clock, all is ready. Belinda is wearing what she describes as her very Italian Gina Lollobrigida outfit—a long black skirt with a long-sleeved, loose-necked gypsy top also in black, which should be held in at the waist with a shiny black-patent buckled belt, but no amount of heaving and hoeing or lying on the bed and breathing in could bring the buckles together. So Belinda concentrates on her accessories. A red plastic comb pulls back one side of her hair, and a pair of silver high-heeled sandals, with slave straps that crisscross up her calves, give her legs a surgically laced salami effect. Even though she finds it hard to walk, Belinda is insistent on striding around, with her backside out and her breasts pointing toward the ground, to adjust her Italian decorations.

And in terms of buying Italian things, Belinda has done herself proud. So proud, in fact, that Casa Mia looks like the Italian section of a European Union home-produce fair. The sitting room is lined with red, green, and white bunting. The terrace is swathed in little red, green, and white flags and all around are melons, peaches and figs, slices of *salame,* whole *salame,* slivers of prosciutto, bowls of broad beans, and on one table a whole pecorino of the sort that Belinda would normally practice rolling about this time of year. Even the cheese and pineapple have been upgraded. Loath to throw away perfectly adequate finger food, Belinda made Mary put little Italian flags on top of every cocktail stick, changing it from Essence-of-Surbiton to Siena in one swift move.

"A relaxed evening . . . a relaxed evening," mutters Belinda, as she totters around tweaking flags. "A relaxed . . . elegant *rustica italiana* evening."

"I'm sure it will all be fine," says Mary, as she stands in the doorway in her simple white sundress, which flares below the bosom and stops at the knee. Its thin straps show off her brown shoulders; her long dark hair is clipped at the back with a single white flower.

"You look, um, suitably *rustica,*" says Belinda, looking Mary up and down. "Well done."

"Thanks." Mary chooses to take her mother's comment as a compliment. "You look very glamorous."

"You don't think it's too much?" asks Belinda, walking to the hall mirror and snaking her hips and skirt into shape. She pulls out a red lipstick from her black clutch bag and draws a scarlet bow shape on her mouth. Her design has nothing to do with what nature intended, but Belinda admires her handiwork all the same. "I do hope it will be a good evening," she says, leaning toward her own reflection and placing her finger in the corner of her open mouth to rearrange the bow. "It is quite important that tonight works."

There is a knock at the door.

"Quick," hisses Belinda. "Put some music on."

"What?" says Mary.

"Something Italian."

"Like what?"

"The Three Tenors, they're Italian," says Belinda, checking herself once more in the mirror. "Whoever this person is, they're early," she adds.

"I bet it's Howard," says Mary.

Belinda opens the door. It is, indeed, Howard, and he looks ready for a party. He has on his usual festive wardrobe of open-necked denim shirt, jeans, brown sandals, and a jaunty red-and-white-spotted scarf tied around his neck. His wiry blond hair has been flattened into a side part with water and a comb.

"Belinda!" he says, giving her wide hips a small, drunken squeeze as he walks in, heading straight for the kitchen. "This looks very nice indeed."

"*Bene . . . bene.* Do you think so, Howard?" asks Belinda trotting along behind. "As a fellow artist I'm interested in your opinion. Do you think it looks *rustica italiana*?"

"Rustic Italian?" asks Howard, looking up and down the sideboard. "Um . . . Do you have any gin?"

"Gin?" asks Belinda, looking up at her flags. "Oh, sorry, gin." She giggles, tweaking her Lollobrigida skirt. "I was thinking of just serving Italian wine tonight. But for you, Howard"—she smiles, bending down to open a cupboard—"there is gin."

Ignoring the rows of plastic cups, Howard finds himself a half-pint glass on a shelf and adds a cube of ice.

"Say when," smiles Belinda, pouring the gin. Howard looks the other way and appears to lose himself in deep thought. "When!" says Belinda. The glass is half full.

"Oh, sorry, when," says Howard.

She adds a burst of tonic and a slice of lemon and hands it over. "There you go."

"Cheers," says Howard. He clears his throat, then opens it and pours down half his drink. "That's better," he announces as he comes up for air. "Now, the decoration," he says, looking around. "I see what you mean now, Belinda. I see what you mean. Yes." He nods. "Very rustic. Very Italian. Good use of flags. Excellent use of produce. No, the whole thing has come together very well."

"Do you think?" says Belinda, playing with her red comb. "Really?"

"Oh, no," nods Howard again. "Certainly. Excellent. Rustic Italian. Well done."

"If you think I've done well," she smiles, ever so satisfied, "then I can rest easy."

"Good," says Howard, taking another large sip.

"So, how is your work going?" questions Belinda intelligently, her index finger curled around her chin. "Because, as I shared with you the other night, I've been having a bit of difficulty with mine. I mean, there are days, such is the block, when I simply can't put pen to paper. And then . . . then there are days when, quite simply, not even an e-mail inquiry could stop me!"

"Well, I've got my character out of bed." Howard drains his glass.

"That's good," says Belinda optimistically. "I thought you did that a while ago."

"Yes," agrees Howard, "but at least he hasn't crawled back in again."

"Oh," says Belinda, nodding slowly. "And that's good?"

"Very good," says Howard, rattling his ice cube. There is a loud knock at the door. "I'll just get myself another," he says, "while you go and get that."

"Yes, right you are." Belinda smiles, tottering back toward the door. "Mary!" she hisses, as she walks past her daughter, who is sitting in a chair, "go and mingle."

Belinda opens the door, her hostess smile in place.

"G'day!" announce four smiley female faces, all crowded into the door-frame.

"Hello," says Belinda, taking a quick step back.

"Oh, this looks great," announces the copper-haired woman

with freckled skin as she walks in. "Jaqui," she says to Belinda, shaking her hand firmly. "We met at Lauren's the other day?"

"Oh, yes, of course," says Belinda. "From the commune."

"That's right."

"And your partner, Paloma," says Belinda, shaking her hand.

"Er . . . no," declares Jaqui. "My girlfriend is Janet here." She indicates a neat pretty woman with a dark urchin crop, in cream linen trousers and a white shirt. "Paloma is my business partner."

"Yuk," says Paloma, with a flick of her long dark hair and a tinkle of her Indian-belled skirt. "I can't believe you presumed we were girlfriend and girlfriend. I can't stand redheads."

"My hair's not red," says Jaqui.

"Well, not naturally, anyway," says a slim blonde, with bright blue eyes. "Duran," she says, offering Belinda her hand, "and I'm very pleased to meet you."

"I suppose you chose that name yourself?" observes Belinda.

"I'm sorry?" says Duran.

"You know, like Paloma?"

"No," she replies. "My parents were ahead of their time. I was christened way before the pop group."

"Good," says Belinda, not understanding what the girl means. "Well, come in."

"Oh," says Jaqui, rummaging around in her large beaded handbag. "We've brought you a nice Australian Riesling. Not too sweet."

"Thank you," smiles Belinda as she accepts the bottle of wine. "It looks lovely."

"Oh, it is," confirms Paloma. "We have the best wines in Australia. Have you ever been?"

"No," says Belinda.

"Well, you should," continues Paloma. "We have the best

food in Australia. We have the best climate in Australia. We've got the best beaches as well as the best wines."

"It sounds wonderful," says Belinda.

"Oh, it is," she confirms with a smile. "It's great."

As the four stunning young lesbians walk into the sitting room and out onto the terrace, Howard perks up no end. He follows on after them, gin in tow, and tries to engage them in conversation. "So what are you four beautiful women doing in a place like this?" he jokes.

"Sorry?" says Jaqui.

"We were invited," replies Duran.

"Excellent," says Howard. "I'm Howard Oxford," he says, offering his hand to Duran.

"We met the other day," says Jaqui.

"Yes, I know, but I haven't met your two friends," he says.

"Girlfriends," corrects Jaqui.

"Oh, yes indeed ... girlfriends," purrs Howard, a pleasant sexual fantasy of a grin on his face. "So where are you all from?"

"Sydney," they reply.

"Well, actually," adds Duran, "I'm from Perth, the most isolated city on the planet, so as soon as I got the chance I went to Sydney."

"The gay capital of the world," shares Paloma. "It's a really great place," she smiles. "Sydney's really great. Have you been there?"

"Um, no," agrees Howard. "But it sounds like I might enjoy it very much."

"Oh, you would," she continues. "It's got the best food, the best restaurants. The lifestyle's really good. Sydney's great."

"Good," says Howard. "That's marvelous." He pauses. "Would anyone care for some nibbles? Ah, Mary," he says, turning around to greet Mary, who is holding up a tray of cups filled with red or white wine. "Alcohol, ladies?" he suggests. "And some cheese on a stick?"

The women gather around and help themselves.

"Pineapple and cheese," says Paloma, her pretty lips curling. "That's a very odd combination. It doesn't even sound edible."

"Not at all," insists Janet. "My rellos serve it all the time in Tassie."

"But that's Tassie," laughs Paloma.

"Would anyone like an olive?" asks Belinda, balancing on the back of her heels. "They're produced locally."

"Are they?" asks Jaqui, plucking a shiny black one out of Belinda's bowl. "How clever of you to source them."

"It was nothing," she says. Her olives are locally purchased from a local supermarket, which is local enough for anyone. "I always find it so much more rewarding to go to the local market and talk to the local people selling their own produce, rather than the supermarket. Don't you?"

"We try and do the same," Jaqui tells her, "but it's difficult for us because we're back and forth all the time. We find it quite a lot easier to go to the supermarket since my Italian is nonexistent."

"Right . . . oh dear," sympathizes Belinda. *"Che peccato."*

"I suppose you must speak like a native," says Jaqui.

"Well, I *am* a native." Belinda smiles. "You know, I've lived here for nearly five years now. These things just rub off on you."

"Yeah." Jaqui smiles. "I suppose they do."

"Will you excuse me?" says Belinda. "I'd better go and answer the door."

Opening her front door Belinda is greeted with a sight that makes her inhale sharply and clutch the doorframe.

"Ta-daah," says Barbara, twirling in her hot pants and smock top. *"Rustica* enough for you?"

"Barbara! Derek! Lauren! Kyle!" she says, just managing a smile. "You've come together!"

"I know! Wasn't it a good idea?" chirps Barbara. "Lauren suggested it, and it made sense to come as a gang. Anyway, how are you? This looks great. What do you think of the outfit?"

"A gang?" says Belinda.

"I know," says Derek. "With Lauren at the wheel, I shan't have to drink and drive ever again. This looks great, Belinda, with the little flags. You've made an enormous effort."

"Effort?" she says. "No, no effort Derek. This is a relaxed soirée. Terribly, terribly relaxed."

"Well, it certainly looks very Italian to me," says Lauren. "Good evening, Belinda. Thank you for welcoming us into your home." She ducks her head unnecessarily as she comes through the doorway. "It's very cute. Where do you put all your guests?"

"Oh, it's a terribly deceptive house," replies Belinda. "There are rooms off rooms and floors above floors. It's a Tardis. Sometimes I can lose myself in it."

"Right. I'm sure you can."

"Anyway, Kyle," says Belinda, "do come in. Oh," she adds, spotting a rather slim, soignée-looking woman standing behind him. "I'm sorry I didn't see you there."

"I'm so sorry," drawls Lauren, clutching her tight-fitting white T-shirt, "I've brought a guest with me."

"Oh," says Belinda.

"I'm sorry," says the girl, her French-polished fingernails thrust forth. "I'm Selina, a journalist with *Bride's* magazine. We're doing a honeymoon-retreats special, and I'm doing a whole double page on Lauren's place."

"Oh," says Belinda again.

"Isn't it just the most romantic place you've ever seen?" she enthuses. "It's almost worth getting married just to honey-moon there."

"Yes, right," says Belinda, shaking hands, gathering her across the threshold. "*Buongiorno, buongiorno.* Do come in. Have an *aperitivo.* I must show you around Casa Mia." She puts an arm around Selina's well-worked-out waist, and leads her away from Lauren and toward the alcohol. "What's interesting about this area is that you'll find some places have been sympatheti-cally restored and some places, quite simply, have not. Did you know the McMahons had a problem with the art police peo-ple?"

"I heard about that!" Selina laughs. "Apparently some old bat in the valley rang up and complained. I thought it was very magnanimous of Lauren to do nothing about it. I personally would have had her hounded out of the place."

"Yes," agrees Belinda, pouring Selina a large gin and tonic in the kitchen.

"I mean, it's not as if the frescos were any good," continues Selina. "They're the sort of thing you'd get in some DIY make-over show, or a pizza restaurant in Fulham."

"Yes, right," says Belinda, steadying herself on the sideboard. "Grab a little nibble and I'll give you a quick tour so you can see something terribly Italian for your pages."

As Selina follows Belinda down the stairs to the guests' *can-tinas,* the rest of the guests start to mix. The commune girls tire of Howard's lascivious enthusiasm and move out onto the ter-race to admire the view. Barbara picks up Howard and pins him into a corner to discuss the merits of her outfit. Derek talks Lauren through the subtleties of cheese rolling.

Mary and Kyle find a quiet corner, near the french windows.

"How are you?" he whispers, his lips brushing her earlobe as his hand takes hers. Avoiding eye contact, they stand side by side and look out toward the terrace, pretending to take in the view.

"I've missed you," she says, her eyes shining, color mounting in her cheeks, "I thought you weren't coming tonight."

"I know," he replies, his grip tightening around her hand, his breath shortening. "I didn't think she'd let me."

"Really?" She turns to him and immediately looks away.

"Yeah," he says. "Don't look at me like that," he whispers. "You make me want to kiss you. It's hard enough just standing here pretending to be normal."

"Sorry."

"Yeah, well, Mom almost made me stay behind to look after the screenwriting guy."

"Oh?"

"But fortunately he's doing the Atkins diet, so he was more than happy to cook his own steak."

"Thank God for Atkins," she smiles, squeezing his hand.

"Yeah," laughs Kyle. "That's got to be a first."

They stand for a while, holding hands, their hips brushing together. An electrical heat pulsing between them, they don't need to talk. They are lost in their own forbidden company. The tension between them is so strong, so powerful, it takes all their will to keep control of themselves.

"What are we going to do?" asks Kyle, squeezing her hand more tightly.

"I don't know."

"Well, one thing I do know," he says, and turns toward her. He stares down at her mouth and unconsciously licks his lips. "I don't think I can stand this much longer."

"Stand what?" says a voice.

"Mother," says Kyle, moving swiftly away from Mary and dropping her hand. "I didn't see you there."

"Stand what?" Lauren repeats, maintaining eye contact.

"Nothing," he says.

"Good," smiles Lauren. "I'm not interrupting, am I?"

"No," say Kyle and Mary together.

"Good," repeats Lauren. "If that's the case you can escort me out onto the terrace to take some air. Good evening, Mary."

"Good evening," says Mary, looking at the floor. "I think I'll hand around the prawn vol-au-vents. Would you like one?" she asks, picking up the tray.

"Um," says Lauren, leaning in for a closer inspection and recoiling at speed, "I think I'll pass."

"Kyle?" she asks, trying to contain the flutter in her voice.

"Lovely," he says, taking one.

"Those Australians seem keen," says Lauren, indicating with her head that Mary should move on. "They've had a whole plate already."

Mary walks off, tray in hand, to the girls on the terrace. Kyle unconsciously watches her go, smiling as the fading sunlight pours through her white dress.

"Come along, Kyle," says Lauren, linking arms with her son. "Put that disgusting prawn thing down and let's go outside."

They go to stand on the edge of the terrace, sipping their wine and looking down over the valley.

"I had no idea you can see everything from up here," says Lauren, taking in the view of her house, the Bianchis' farm, Derek and Barbara's swimming pool and cypress complex. "Do you think she sits and spies on us all day?"

"Well, that's what I've heard," confirms Kyle, swilling the wine in his cup.

"Amazing," says Lauren, shaking her head. "I left New York to get away from the boredom of petty boardroom squabbles only to arrive in this little hornet's nest." She gives a little wry laugh. "The sad thing is that she's picked a fight with someone who's used to fighting for a living."

"Anyway, Selina, *siamo arrivati.*" Belinda's trill hostess voice floats up to them from the terrace below. "You see what I mean about it being a traditional Tuscan country house? I took extra care when renovating to keep all the features in the house. In my quite substantial experience, when people travel here for a holiday, they do like to see traditional features in their Tuscan house. There are some people who think that it is fine to take all the features out of a house and paint it white. They think that's good taste. Like the McMahons' place," she whispers loudly. "What was she thinking?" She laughs. "Between you and me, that might be all right in one of those New Loft things. But in the Tuscan countryside? Honestly! I think it looks terribly cheap. And I do hate cheap. Don't you, Selina?" Belinda succumbs to a little shiver just to prove her point. "Ghastly. To be honest with you, I'm amazed that the readers of *Bride's* would be interested in such a place—Aaaarrrgh!" Belinda screams. Her hands shoot into the air and her eyes widen in shock as warm alcohol pours over her hair and her face and down the back of her neck.

"Oh, my God, I'm *sooo* sorry!" shouts Lauren, from the terrace above. "I didn't see you down there. I was just throwing away this plonk. Very acidic," she adds, with a sucking-lemons face. "I had no idea you were down there. I'm sorry. Did I get you?"

"Jesus!" says Belinda, shaking her arms as rivers of wine course down her back, between her breasts, and under her armpits. Her mascara spreads out from her eyes like a spider's web. Her hair hangs limply, stuck to her scalp, yet the red comb valiantly holds on to the side of her head. "What the hell . . ." She catches Selina's eye. "What the hell does it matter?" She recovers. "I'm rather partial to a glass of wine, but I've never quite had it served like that," she says, firing off a burst of hysterical laughter. "I'll just go and change."

"I'm so sorry," says Lauren again.

"I can't believe you just did that," mutters Kyle out of the corner of his mouth.

"Shut up," hisses Lauren, through a smile. "You heard what she was saying—I'm so sorry," she shouts again.

"These things happen," Belinda trills.

"Mum!" comes a shout from the other side of the terrace. "You'd better come quick!"

"Mary!" Belinda calls back from the terrace. "I'm slightly indisposed at the moment."

"Mum!" Mary shouts again. "This is serious."

Mary is not lying. Kyle and Lauren turn around to find two of the Australian girls, Paloma and Janet, doubled up in pain.

* * *

"I really don't feel very well," mutters Paloma, one hand on her stomach, the other holding a terra-cotta geranium pot for support. "I'm all hot and sweaty and I'm dizzy, too."

"Yeah, right," says Janet. "So am I."

"To be honest," announces Jaqui, "I don't feel that great myself."

"Mum!" calls Mary.

"Coming," says Belinda, jogging into her party in her silver heels with her streaked makeup, wine-soaked hair, and a Gina Lollobrigida outfit that is now clinging in all the wrong places. "Ladies, what seems to be the problem? Paloma?"

"I think I'm going to be—" Paloma looks up and vomits all over Belinda's silver sandals.

Belinda stands rigid with shock. She doesn't dare to look

down. She can feel the warm prawn vol-au-vent and wine mixture seeping between her toes.

"Oh, my God, so am I!" Janet sprints through the party, her hand covering her mouth as she tries and fails to make it to the bathroom.

"Derek," Barbara grabs Howard's arm as she sways on her platforms in her hot pants, "I'm feeling a little off color myself."

"Do you think it's the prawns?" asks Derek, putting down his half-eaten canapé. "Belinda?"

"What?" says Belinda, still stuck to the spot, incapable of moving or looking. Her hands are in rigid fists and her eyes are half closed as she tries not to inhale the sweet smell of vomit that engulfs her.

"The prawns?" asks Derek. "Do you think they might be off?"

"Mary?" asks Belinda, her voice tight and strained.

"You did the vol-au-vent mixture, Mum." Mary replies quietly. "I just stuffed them."

"Right," says Belinda, her shoulders beginning to hunch.

The Three Tenors CD grinds to a halt, and the party is silent as everyone stares at their wine-soaked hostess, standing in a pool of pale pink vomit, waiting for some sort of explanation.

"They were a couple of days past their sell-by date," says Belinda, almost as if she is speaking to herself. "I really didn't think it would matter. Only a couple of days, that's all," she mumbles. "They always mark these things down early anyway. Health and safety—"

"Jesus." Jaqui grabs her stomach and runs down the terrace steps into the garden, retching as she goes.

"Derek, I've got to go home while I can," announces Barbara, fanning her face with a brown hand. "I can feel it coming on."

"Yes, love," he says. "I don't feel too special myself."

"Right," says Lauren, stepping into the breach. "Who hasn't eaten the prawns, apart from myself and Kyle?" She scans the terrace. No one has their hands up. "Howard?"

"I'm afraid I can't remember," he says, taking another swig of his gin. "I don't tend to snack at parties, so possibly not."

"Anyone else?" she asks.

"I've had only one," says Selina, walking up the terrace steps. "But I have to say I don't feel great."

"Okay," nods Lauren. "Kyle and I will split up and drive everyone home."

"Hurrrr," comes a gut-wrenching noise from behind the rosemary bush.

"We need plenty of plastic bags," continues Lauren. "Belinda?"

"Hum?"

"Mary," says Lauren, "can you deal with this?"

"Yes, of course," says Mary, rushing into the kitchen to riffle through the cupboards for bags.

"Okay, everyone." Lauren claps. "Follow me. Divide yourselves into groups. Derek, Barbara, you're coming with me. Jaqui!" she yells into the garden.

"Hurrrrrrrr."

"Kyle's taking you home, if you can make it to the car."

"Okay," Jaqui manages to shout back. "I'll come around the side."

"Good," says Lauren. "Off we go, then. Thank you, Mary," she adds, taking the bunch of plastic bags. "Are we all ready?"

"Yes," says Howard, moving slowly toward Lauren, holding his stomach. "Looks as though I might have had a vol-au-vent after all."

"Right, that's it, we're off before you start throwing up,

Howard. Come along, everyone. Selina come along," she ushers. "Oh, good evening, Belinda," she says, as she walks out of the door taking Belinda's poisoned guests in various stages of contortion with her. "Thank you for your party. What a great evening," she says. "We must do it again some time."

"Mm?" says Belinda looking up. "Oh." She smiles. *"Arrivadeary,"* she adds, in a quiet little voice.

Domenica ✳ Sunday

Clima ✳ *fa caldo* (Hot)

Forgive me, dear reader, if I ask you a question. I know the whole
point of my jottings is to share my thoughts, ideas and observations,
but sometimes even I don't know everything. Tell me, at what point
in a failing relationship does one decide to withdraw the charming
hand of friendship?

Is it when someone arrives in your valley in her flashy four-wheel-
drive car and buys up the house you vaguely had your eye on? Is it
when, having torn up the valley with her heavy-goods vehicles, and
painted over some world-heritage frescos, she decides to open a
business to rival yours? Is it when her hormonally challenged son
can't leave your lovely daughter alone? Is it when she manages to
usurp your position on the committee that you've put your life and
soul into for nearly five years? Or, finally, is it when she abuses you
with alcohol at your own party, then leaves, taking all your guests
with her? At which point is it, dear reader, that one should consider

withdrawing one's hand? For I now consider my appendage well and truly retracted.

And it's not as if I haven't made an effort to welcome her into my valley. I was in the first wave of the welcoming committee; I introduced her to everyone important in the valley. I even went to her party. I sent guests to her when, as so often happens, I was full. I have also helped direct her guests to her house. I then, pleasantly, invited her back to mine and entertained some grubby journalist type whom she insisted on bringing to my soirée, lowering the tone and everything. I can't for the life of me think that I could have been any more delightful or *simpatico*. All I can say is that she really will feel how cold and miserable life can be here without my support. I am Contessa of this valley. It is my valley and she and her white-toothed son really aren't welcome anymore.

I'm sorry. I don't know why I'm being so negative today. Today is a day for great celebration. It is the *Festa di Formaggio,* at which every year the whole expat community, including some of the waifs and strays from the neighboring valleys, come together to celebrate the rolling of the pecorino cheese down the hill. Lots of Italians come as well. Each group sets up its own trestle table and has a giant picnic that lasts all afternoon. There are various races—the children's race, the OAP race, and the open race where each table chooses its champion. I have, of course, rolled for the expats every year for the past five years. Until now.

And actually now, between us, I don't think I shall mind terribly that I'm not doing so this year. It comes to all ancient festivals eventually, and I'm afraid I suspect this one, too, might have had its day. I'm sure it won't be as good as last year when, if I remember correctly, I cooked up a storm, rolled like a dervish, and everyone said it was the best day of the year.

BRUSCHETTE DI CASA MIA DA
FESTA DI FORMAGGIO

These little bits of toasted deliciousness are so good for entertaining at a **festa.** They are handy, easily eaten and, last year, even my Italian neighbors came back for seconds! A trick with **festa** food is that it should be eye-catching. When it has to compete with the noise, the flags, and the fun of the party, your food should be nice and loud. I, therefore, tend to favor bright, jolly, luscious peppers and buxom tomatoes to make my table look enticing and vibrant. I also like to try to keep the theme of the **festa** going, so I serve cheese at the cheese **festa,** mushrooms at the mushroom **festa,** and so on. It is, after all, a celebration of local produce, so one should be as celebratory and as local as possible.

Serves a trestle table.

* plenty of hunks of **rustica** bread, toasted and dipped in olive oil, then rubbed with garlic
* grilled peppers
* slices of tomato
* anchovies (from your local fishmonger—although tinned are passable)
* pecorino cheese (there is plenty going at my local **festa**)
* a jar of pesto (I have heard that some people make this tasty, tangy sauce, although I have yet to find a recipe!)

Put your toppings on the toasted bread and flash grill, taking care not to burn either the bread or the toppings, as nothing detracts from the color of the peppers more than a whole load of black.

Serve on a jolly tablecloth with jaunty **festa** folk.

❀ ❀ ❀

CHAPTER TEN

Belinda wakes up in a determined mood. Not quashed by last night's debacle, she appears to have dug deep, regrouped, and is ready to do battle with Lauren McMahon all over again. In fact, as she walks downstairs in her cream nylon floor-length nightie, which she saves for guest-free days, Belinda seems remarkably buoyant, despite the bottle of *limoncello* she finished off while watching reruns of *Changing Rooms* on satellite television. A fan of the makeover-show format, Belinda spent most of the evening, somewhat uncharacteristically, shouting and spitting at Laurence Llewelyn-Bowen and his team while they restyled a sitting room in Solihull into Moroccan boudoir. But perhaps the yelling and the releasing of bile helped because when she finds Mary at the breakfast table, nibbling tentatively on a piece of buttered toast, Belinda is initially pleasant.

✢ ✢ ✢

"Looking forward to today?" she asks, flopping down on the hard chair usually reserved for breakfasting guests.

"Um, yes," says Mary, looking up, and hoping it to be the correct response.

"Good," says Belinda, picking a sugar lump out of the white china bowl, a habit for which she has often scolded Mary. "I don't think I'll go."

"Oh, Mum!" says Mary, with a warm, encouraging smile. "Don't be silly. You can't not go. It wouldn't be a party without you. You're the Contessa of the Valley; you've got to go. You'll be missed."

"Good," Belinda pops the sugar lump into her mouth. "That's exactly the answer I was after. I have a plan." She crunches. "I think I'm going to turn up late today," she adds, smiling at her reflection in the window, trying to smooth down her Einstein hair. "You know, late enough that everyone thinks I might not be coming so they miss me and get worried and then—then when they're all bored, waiting for some fun and excitement to begin, I shall arrive." She gets out of her chair and starts to paint in her arriving marvelousness. "I shall waft in, looking fabulous, with a fabulous picnic and . . . and save the day."

"You won't need a picnic, Mum." Mary smiles. "The Aussie girls are bringing that, remember?"

"The lesbians?" huffs Belinda, tiring of her picture, putting her hands on her hips. "Don't you know anything, Maria?"

"What?" asks Mary.

"Homosexual men can cook like a dream; homosexual women cannot," she pronounces. "It's famous."

"Is it?" asks Mary.

"Of course it is. Anyway, I've always done the picnic. And I don't see why I shouldn't do it again this year."

"There might not be many takers after last night." Mary is trying to jolly her mother along.

"That was absolutely ridiculous," disagrees Belinda, leaning on the back of the chair. "I have never heard such a load of fuss and nonsense about a few off prawns in my life. Honestly, you'd have thought that World War III had broken out, the way the *americana* was carrying on. God! And that smug son of hers—" Mary looks away. "Did you flinch then?" asks Belinda.

"No," says Mary.

"Are you sure?" Belinda peers down at her daughter. "Because we know where we stand on Kevin."

"His name is Kyle," says Mary, her voice almost snapping.

"Kyle, Kevin, it's all the same to me," says Belinda. "He's dreadful, and you're having nothing to do with him. In fact, I don't want to see you so much as look at him at the *festa* today, do you hear me?"

"What? Not even a quick glance?"

"Don't get pert with me," says Belinda. "You know exactly what I mean. I don't want you to have anything to do with him."

"I don't know what you have against him," Mary continues. "I really don't. He's intelligent, he's handsome, he's studying music at Yale. Most mothers would be proud to have their daughter associate with a man like that."

"Yes, well," Belinda moves closer to her, "there's only one problem with that. I've met the mother!" She raises her eyebrows and turns away. "So, unless you want to be thrown out on to the street with no money, no job, and nowhere to live, I suggest you play by my rules." She adds, with a shrug, "Or you could go home to your father's."

Mary doesn't bother to reply. Instead, she slips lower into the hard guest's chair and carries on trying to eat her toast. The situation between Kyle and her is becoming unbearable. Last night as she cleared up after the party, listening to her mother shouting at the television, all she could think of was Kyle: the touch of his skin as he held her hand; the softness of his breath on her cheek as he spoke; the smell of his body as he stood so close to her, yet so out of reach. She knows he feels the same way about her. The illicit hours they've spent lying in the grass side by side, or sitting and talking under an olive tree, or very occasionally when they've dared to walk along the stream on the valley floor. All of the warm and private moments they've spent together tell her he likes her, too—the yearning in his voice, and the way he looks at her when he thinks she isn't paying attention. She knows he feels the same. She takes a small bite of her toast. The idea of going to the *Festa di Formaggio* and sitting next to her mother watching him, not being able to talk to him, touch him, or be with him—it's too much for her to endure.

"Mum?" she says quietly.

"Yes?"

"I don't think I want to come to the *festa*."

"What?" says Belinda, turning around to pay attention. "Of course you're coming."

"I really don't feel like it, Mum. Please don't make me come," says Mary, the full horror of the idea unfolding in front of her. She shivers. "I just don't want to go."

"Are you seriously suggesting I go on my own?" queries Belinda. "After all that has happened? After the terrible mess you made catering for my party. You think you can leave me to face the music on my own? Covering for your mistakes?" Mary tries to speak. Belinda raises her hand and shakes her head. "I don't think so, young lady. You're coming with me, even if I have to drag you by the hair. And I'll hear no more about it. Now, go and telephone Giovanna and order a picnic in your very best Italian, will you, dear? I don't want any mistakes, so I'm going to get her to do it just this once. Tell her I want it as *rustica* and *Tuscano* as possible, all right?"

"*Rustico* and *Toscano*?" checks Mary, wearily getting out of her chair and walking to the telephone. When her mother is as belligerent and insistent as this, there really is no point in trying to argue back. Mary is going to the *Festa di Formaggio,* she is going to have to sit next to the love of her life and not speak to, or look at, or communicate with him, and she's going to have to pretend she's enjoying herself.

Belinda rubs her hands together, congratulating herself on a job well delegated. She walks out onto her terrace and stretches in the morning sun. The valley below basks in soft, warm, yellow light. The Bianchis have harvested the tobacco field directly opposite Casa Mia. A few of their sunflowers are still in full bloom, their garish faces all pointing in the same direction, like a pool of secretaries on a lunch break, soaking up the sun. Belinda surveys her estate. The grass is dry and crisp from lack of water. Her lavender bushes need to be deadheaded, as do the geraniums. The fig tree sports three green fruit that have yet to ripen. She smiles; perhaps she should get Franco over for a little light labor next week. Her terrace could also do with a sweep. Giulia really should pull her weight a bit more. There are still a couple of half-drunk cups of last night's wine propped up in flower pots, such was the swift flight of her guests. Standing at the top of the steps, she spots a half-eaten prawn vol-au-vent sitting under a rosemary bush that not even the ants have seen fit to finish off.

"An awful lot of fuss about nothing," mutters Belinda, walking over to kick the vol-au-vent out of sight. "Why that woman had to take everyone home with her I'll never know."

"Mum?" says Mary, from the steps.

"What?" says Belinda.

"The picnic will be ready to pick up in about an hour."

"Okay. Did you tell her *rustica* and *tuscano?*"

"I said *rustico* and *toscano,*" confirms Mary, "about three times. She checked, and I confirmed it."

"Good," says Belinda, rubbing her hands together. "That should show the others up, then, shouldn't it?"

"Anyway, I think I might have a shower, before we go?" says Mary.

"Off you go," says Belinda, deep in thought.

"What time does the *festa* start?"

"Twelve," says Belinda

"What time are we going?"

"Two."

✳ ✳ ✳

At one fifteen Belinda is putting two chairs into the back of the car. It is a complicated maneuver that seems to require her to push, shove, and swear a lot while her large backside, encased in a pair of rather tight and not overly *sportif* jeans, moons out of the car to not very elegant effect. She emerges with every pore on her pink face open and producing sweat. Her pale blue T-shirt is striped in damp, and the effect of someone who spends most of her time mucking around on boats, attending Tuscan picnics at weekends, is almost certainly ruined.

"Mary!" yells Belinda, sticking out her bottom lip and blowing up her face. "Where are you?"

"Here," says Mary, coming out of the front door at a jog. "I'm sorry. I thought we weren't going till two." She is wearing a white T-shirt and denim skirt with a pair of white sneakers. It's the sort of fresh look that Belinda is after, which looks annoyingly good on her daughter.

"Yes, well, it's too late now, isn't it?" huffs Belinda. "And I'm so hot and sweaty in this I'm going to have to change. Do you have any idea how difficult it is to find an outfit that says, 'Tuscan picnic'?"

"Well, I'm sorry," says Mary, "but I thought we weren't leaving till two."

"Yes, well," says Belinda again, on her way into the house, "I couldn't see any point in hanging around any longer."

"You just couldn't wait, could you?" mutters Mary.

"What?" says Belinda, turning swiftly.

"Nothing," says Mary. "I'll wait for you here."

Such is her desire to see if she has been missed that Belinda changes in two minutes flat, into the yellow and navy flowered dress, which she wore the day before. She pauses only to don a pair of fun flip-flops covered in plastic fruit and find her wide-brimmed *mercato* hat in case she needs a couple of concealed conversations at Lauren's expense. She comes out of the house at a swift pace and meets Mary sitting on the steps outside the front door.

"Hurry up, hurry up," she chivvies. "We've got a *festa* to get to."

"I'm the one who's been waiting," Mary points out.

"Oh, don't start being difficult, dear," says Belinda over the car roof. "Not today of all days. I really don't need it."

"I was merely stating a fact."

"Get into the car," says Belinda, placing her hat between the chairs on the backseat.

"Right." Mary slams the door.

"Happy smiles when we arrive, and last night's prawns are a conversational no-no. Our response is something along the lines of 'How very odd, I had five or six vol-au-vents and nothing happened to me.'"

"But we didn't."

"Mary!" Belinda rolls her eyes. "Whose side are you on?"

"Yours."

"Good." Belinda smiles tightly. "Now . . . Barb and I were very ill last night," she says, in a deep northern voice, flattening her vowels in an attempt to sound like Derek.

"Oh, I know, Derek," responds Mary, in a mock-innocent high voice. " 'How very odd. I had five or six vol-au-vents and nothing happened to me.' "

"Good," says Belinda, and starts the car. "That's about right. Run into Giovanna's on the way and pick up the picnic."

By the time Belinda pulls up outside the Santa Caterina church and the small patch of grass that constitutes the village green, everything is exactly as she'd planned. She is looking elegant in her hat, she has Giovanna's tasteful basket, covered in a white tea towel, containing her *rustico toscano* picnic, and everyone else is there, she presumes, awaiting her arrival.

The small green is packed with people, shouting, talking, laughing, gesticulating, drinking wine, smoking cigarettes. At the top to the side of the church, there is a sun-bleached sideless tent that contains a table loaded with three enormous silver cups. Mounted on wooden stands, they have silver plaques of winners' names shining all over them. They glint in the sun, and consistently pull quite a crowd of observers. All around the edges of the green, which has a square for dancing in the middle, there are long trestle tables loaded with wine and grapes, large round cheeses, and green-glass bottles of water. There are smaller round tables with families of six or eight squeezed around them. There are a few rugs, and a few canvas chairs. There is also a table, chaired by the ironmonger who made Belinda's gates, that is a plank balanced on giant logs with all the festive guests sitting on smaller logs.

The air is hot and dry, full of smoke and the sweet smell of cooking meat. Like some medieval fair, there are small fires with skewered steaks and chicken, and more professional barbecues with root vegetables and aubergines. The young man who runs the *porchetta* van, selling cold roast pork in Serrana market, is roasting a whole pig. Having lit his coals at six thirty this morning, he is hoping to make a return on his investment when the aroma becomes too intoxicating to resist, come three or four in the afternoon.

Belinda adjusts her hat and directs her nose into the air, then places Giovanna's basket on her hip and walks toward the expat table, jauntily covered with Barbara's red-and-white gingham tablecloth. A proud owner of a bottle of Heinz tomato ketchup and three rolls of kitchen towels, the expat table loudly announces itself among the Italians. On close inspection it also has a greater wine-to-water ratio than on the Italian tables. Belinda strolls through the curling smoke toward it, leaving Mary to struggle with the two chairs. Deaf to the world, in elegant slow motion, Belinda's smile is fixed on her face as she feels the apparent gaze of all assembled.

"Here I am!" she announces triumphantly to the table, as if they had been waiting anxiously all along. "I am *sooo* sorry to be *sooo* late. You must have been wondering where I'd got to!" She exhales, as she puts her apparently heavy basket on the table. "It's good to be here," she says, implying a struggle and a journey, rather than a two-minute drive down the hill.

"Oh, there you are," says Derek, with a large glass of white wine in his hand. "Do you fancy a drink?"

"Oh, Derek, I'd love one," she says, and collapses into the chair Mary has just arranged at the table. "I'm exhausted!"

"I bet you are, clearing up after all those prawns," says Derek, rubbing his expansive stomach. "I tell you, I still feel a bit raw this morning," he announces. "I don't think I've ever shat like that in my life. I didn't know which end to point where!"

"How very odd." Belinda smiles. "I had five or six vol-au-vents and nothing happened to me."

"Call yourself lucky!" says Derek. "The only person who's pleased is Barbara. She says she must have lost a couple of pounds overnight. Barb, my love," he calls down the table, "look who's here."

Barbara turns. Clearly she believes she's lost weight because she has dressed accordingly. She is wearing a lemon-yellow scoop-neck top, which demonstrates to the group exactly where her bra and rolls of fat are, and she is zipped into a tight, red knee-length skirt with yellow hearts stitched onto the buttock pockets. She has a long gold chain in her crepey cleavage and matching wedge mules.

"There you are," she says.

"I'm so sorry," Belinda smiles. "You must have been so worried that I'm so late."

"Are you?" asks Barbara.

"Yes," nods Belinda. "Very."

"Actually, we were more worried about Lauren," says Barbara. "We've been wondering where *she* is."

"Yeah," says Howard, resting his denim-shirt-clad elbow on the table. "Have you seen her? We're beginning to get a little worried."

"Yeah, actually," asks Jaqui, from the other side of an extremely professional-looking round black barbecue, "do you have any idea where she might be? We've rung the house a couple of times on our mobiles and there's been no reply."

"And we've made all this delicious Australian food for her to try," puts in Paloma. "We were talking about it last night in the car, and she seemed really excited."

"Right." Janet nods. "And she's our representative.",

"Yes," agrees Derek, scanning the horizon. "We're all relying on her."

"Well, I suppose." Belinda smiles generously and tweaks her dark hair. "If she doesn't turn up, I'm sure I could—"

"There she is!" shouts Duran through the barbecue smoke.

"Where?" asks Derek, searching the crowd.

"There!" says Jaqui. "The tall, blonde, slim woman coming toward us in white, carrying a tray."

"Oh, good," says Derek, taking a sip of his wine. "Thank God for that." He stands and faces the length of the table. "Lauren's here, everyone!"

"Hurrah!" A cheer and a ripple of applause starts around the barbecue and travels down the table with Barbara, Howard, and Derek all joining in.

"Well, thank God," says Belinda, with heavy sarcasm, sitting back in her seat.

"I know," enthuses Barbara. "To be honest," she says, her lemon-yellow cleavage relaxing on the table, "we were a bit worried that she might not come, you know, after last night. We thought maybe she might be too ill or perhaps we'd put her off."

"How very odd," says Belinda. "I had five or six vol-au-vents and nothing happened to me."

"Lauren!" shouts Derek, waving frantically like a drowning sailor. "Coo-ee! Lauren! Over here! Lauren! Here! Hi! Oh, good," he says. "She's spotted me, she's on her way over." He sits back down. "Now the *festa* can begin. Cheers!" He goes to clink glasses with Belinda.

"Cheers," she replies limply.

Even in the smoky heat of the afternoon, Lauren looks cool and fresh as she walks through the crowd. Head held high, blonde hair swinging about her shoulders, she doesn't weave or dodge her way to the table, so much as glide in a straight line, fellow *festa*-goers parting before her. Dressed in a short-sleeved white shirt and white jeans, a pair of Gucci sunglasses perched on top of her head, she looks like a woman who travels with her own air-conditioning. She is carrying a large silver platter laden with delicacies.

Behind her, also in sunglasses, is Kyle. He has on a loose white linen shirt that is half undone and a pair of beige shorts that show off his long strong brown legs. He is also carrying a silver tray, and he searches the table for Mary. He grins as he spots her. She smiles back and indicates her mother with wide-open, urgent eyes. Evidently he takes the hint that perhaps he should not sit next to her, so he stands behind his mother with his tray and two canvas chairs.

"Hi," says Lauren, as she puts the tray on the table.

"Thank God you're here!" exclaims Derek, getting to his feet. "It's the cheese-rolling registration in about twenty minutes, and I was beginning to think you weren't going to represent us after all."

"Don't tell me you were looking for a replacement." Lauren gives Derek's shoulder a little pat. "O ye of little faith."

"Oh, no, I didn't mean we were planning to replace you," insists Derek, flushing with pleasure at Lauren's attention. "I was merely hoping you'd get here sooner."

"Well, I'm here now, so you can all relax," she announces to the table.

"Hey, Lauren." Jaqui waves from the barbecue.

"Hey, girls!" She waves back. "Are you all feeling better after last night?"

"Yeah." Paloma nods. "Thanks for all those herbal teas you gave us last night. You're a savior."

"No problem," says Lauren, taking the tinfoil off her plate. "Just so long as I was helpful."

"You were amazing," says Paloma. "Quite how I survived—"

"Oh, hello, Belinda." Lauren smiles, looking down to her left. "I didn't see you all the way down there."

"Hello," says Belinda, looking straight up Lauren's nose. "Nice of you to turn up."

"Well, after last night," says Lauren quietly, with a wide smile, "I thought you might do us all a favor and fail to do the same. Belinda," she adds, with a light laugh and a whole lot more volume, "do tell us the story behind those prawns."

"How very odd," stammers Belinda, with an overcompensating smile that she shoots up and down the table as she looks for allies, "I had five or six vol-au-vents and nothing happened to me."

"What sort of explanation is—" starts Lauren.

"Um, Lauren," says Mary, standing up next to her mother, "what have you brought? It does look lovely."

"They're salmon and ginger kebabs to put on the barbecue," she says. "I've marinated them a bit, but not quite as long as I would have liked. And Kyle's got a tray of orange and almond Florentine biscuits I made last night."

"You made those last night?" asks Barbara, leaning over to smell them. "Mmm," she continues, jabbing her red-tipped finger to make her point. "They look amazing. But you didn't leave our place until past eleven," she says. "I'm amazed you found the time."

"Well," says Lauren, "I used to fit a lot more into my day than I do now." She laughs. "A bit of baking is easy compared to what I did before."

"Oh, great," says Jaqui, coming toward the table for some

water. "Are those the ginger salmon sticks we discussed last night?"

"Yes." Lauren nods.

"You genius." Jaqui slaps her on the back. "I can't believe you got salmon around here."

"I didn't," Lauren tells her. "I got it in Florence this morning. That's why I'm a bit late—I had to drive the Hollywood screenwriter into Florence early this morning. He had a breakfast meeting with some celebrity who is holidaying here, and there were no appropriate trains."

"Couldn't he use his chauffeur-driven Mercedes with the blacked-out windows?" laughs Belinda, taking a sip of red wine.

"No," says Lauren, looking puzzled. "How do you know about that car? He only arrived in it. The day he got terribly . . . lost?"

"Yes, well . . ." says Belinda, looking swiftly at the ground.

"You drove him to Florence?" asks Mary, amazement writ large across her face.

"How else was he going to get there?" asks Lauren, with a shrug. "He's an important client. And I do work in the service industry. I'm sure Belinda would do the same, wouldn't you?"

"Oh, absolutely," says Belinda, after another sip of wine. "I'm back and forth to Florence all the time."

"You see?" smiles Lauren, her slim finger whipping between her and Belinda. "Exactly the same."

"I could have sworn I heard you say you hadn't been to Florence in years," Howard pipes up at the other end of the table. "You said that it was too hot and too full of tourists, and that there's nothing much to see."

"Did I, Howard?" asks Belinda. "Are you sure it was me? I

know things get a little confusing for you at times, what with all the wine."

"Belinda!" says Derek, looking shocked. Howard's fondness for drink is never a subject for conversation, particularly in front of Howard.

"Well, whoever said it was wrong," says Lauren, taking a canvas chair and unfolding it next to Derek. "There's plenty to see in Florence, isn't there, Belinda?"

"Oh, I agree," says Belinda, suddenly feeling on firmer ground. "There's so much art. Art everywhere you look. You breathe it in. As an artist, it really is one of the places I love most. There's *David*."

"David," repeats Lauren, starting a list. "Go on."

"Um, *David,*" says Belinda. "And, um . . . *David* . . . and the lovely things that they've got in the Uffizi that are just too numerous to name."

"Like?" asks Lauren.

"Oh, God!" says Belinda, flapping a hand in front of her face. "Where to start?"

The table stares, waiting for her to hold forth. "Where to start?" she says again. "There are so many—"

"Giotto, Titian, Raphael, Michel—" begins Lauren.

"Angelo." Belinda nods.

"Leonardo—"

"Da Vinci," adds Belinda.

"Anyone else?" asks Lauren, pausing to look at Belinda.

"Phew," she says, puffing out her cheeks. "Can't think."

"Caravaggio, Rubens, Van Dyck, Rembrandt . . ."

"Yup, that's right, all of them," agrees Belinda.

"Correct," says Lauren. "All of them. Who else?"

"Isn't it time you went to register for the cheese rolling?" asks Belinda.

"Oh, absolutely," says Derek, getting up. "Come along, Lauren, we need to go to the cup tent over there."

As Lauren leaves the table, accompanied by Derek, Belinda is left with Mary, while Kyle hovers in the background. Since Howard is ignoring her, and Barbara is chatting with Duran, Belinda decides to join the other Australians at the barbecue.

Gathered around the fire, Paloma, Jaqui, and Janet prod with various types of tongs, drinking their glasses of wine. They are all charmingly forgiving of Belinda for poisoning them, and go on to explain the delights of the marinated lamb they are cooking and the all-encompassing deliciousness of Donna Hay cuisine.

"She's Australian, you know," says Paloma, poking a lamb kebab.

"Really?" says Belinda, in an effort to be jolly.

"Yeah." Paloma nods. "All the best chefs are Australian."

"Right," says Belinda.

"It's because we've got the best ingredients in Australia, isn't that right, Jaqui?"

"Oh, yeah," says Jaqui, wielding her tongs with life learned dexterity. "Really fresh."

"That's right, ever so fresh," says Paloma, tossing her waist-length dark hair. "It's the lifestyle. The lifestyle's really great in Australia. Have you ever been?"

"No," says Belinda.

"Oh you should," continues Paloma. "It's great."

❁ ❁ ❁

Back at the table Kyle spots his chance. Without saying a word, he takes Mary by the hand and leads her silently through the crowd and a haze of heat and smoke. Guiding her behind the cup tent, he finds a small oak tree and pushes her up against it.

He starts to kiss her. Like a starved man, he runs his lips all over her face as he consumes her mouth, her cheeks, and her eyes, covering them in hungry kisses. His hands are around her waist, and he starts to glide his soft fingers up under her T-shirt, lifting it over her breasts toward her shoulders. He puts his hands under her bra and cups her bosom, burying his head in her cleavage and running his tongue between her breasts as he tries to taste every inch of her. Mary can hardly breathe. Her head leans against the tree. Her eyes are closed, her mouth open in ecstasy, the tip of her tongue touching her top lip.

"Kyle," she whispers.

"Mary." He comes up to kiss her plump lips. "I can't cope with not seeing you anymore." He leans his forehead against hers, tracing the outline of her mouth with his thumb. "Come away with me," he says, both hands cupping her chin now as he stares into her eyes.

"I'd do anything for you," she says.

"Let's leave, then," he says, his dark eyes flashing with arousal and defiant energy.

"Let's leave the two of them to their petty fights, and stupid social one-upmanship, and you and I run off together."

"I can't," says Mary, pushing him back.

"You can." He kisses her again. "You can do anything with me. Anything." He kisses her yet again. "Anything."

"God, Kyle," she runs her hands through his ruffled hair, "you almost make me believe you."

"You should believe me," he declares with youthful certainty. "I love you. It's as simple as that. I love you. And I'll do everything in my power to make you happy."

"What did you . . ." asks Mary, her mouth dry, her lips parted.

"I love you," he says again, a large smile on his handsome

face. She smiles. Her face flushes. "Of course, I love you," he says again.

"No one has ever said that to me before." Her eyes water.

"Come on," he says, kissing her eyelids. "Don't be sad."

"I'm not," she says. "You make me the happiest person in the world."

"Then run away with me." He seizes her hand.

"I can't."

"You can," he insists.

"We can't," she says. "Let's get back before we are missed." She smooths down her T-shirt, and tucks her hair behind her ears.

"I'm never letting you go, you know that?" says Kyle. "We're meant to be together. I knew that the first time I saw you standing outside your house, waving, dressed only in your underwear. I thought you were the most gorgeous thing I'd ever seen."

"A large T-shirt and my underwear," she corrects.

"Oh, I know." He grins. "Nice butt." Taking her in his arms and kissing her again, he says, "I do really love you, Mary, you know, never forget that." Mary smiles and kisses him back.

They wander back to the table through the crowd. Neither of them is in a hurry, their footsteps slow, their hold on each other tight. Just as they come in sight of the red-and-white checked cloth, they split up and approach from different angles, Kyle waiting a couple of minutes before making his arrival.

"Ah, there she is, Belinda," says Barbara as Mary approaches. "We were going to send out a search party for you, Mary!"

"Sorry." Mary sits down next to her mother. "I went to the loo and there was a terrible queue."

"Really?" asks Paloma. "It was all right when I went a couple of minutes ago. No one there at all."

"Well, you must have just missed the rush." Mary can smell the tang of Kyle's citrus aftershave on her skin.

"I do hope you haven't been talking to Kyle," Belinda hisses out of the corner of her mouth. "You know how angry that makes me and how much you hate to see me like that."

"No," says Mary, playing with her knife and fork.

"Ah! Kyle," says Lauren. "I don't suppose you've been to the bathroom as well?"

"What?" says Kyle, doing a very good impression of being puzzled. "No, I went to check the place out. The Bianchis have a table over there." He gestures to it. "Those guys who run the supermarket are on another. The whole village, plus a hundred or so other people I've never seen before, is here."

"Sounds rather like your party," laughs Belinda from across the table.

"I understand you've brought your own picnic," says Lauren. "Afraid someone might poison you after last night?"

"No actually." Belinda smiles. "I wanted something real and *rustica* and *tuscano* for the *festa,* but having seen all those Aussie delicacies . . ." She chortles, trying to endear herself to the other end of the table.

"Tucker's on the table!" declares Paloma, dropping two large white serving dishes from quite a height onto the table. "Rosemary and garlic lamb marinated overnight and cooked in *son jus* in that one," she points, "and grilled veggies in that. We've got some lemon and chili chicken still to come. Tuck in while your tucker's hot."

"Yeah," agrees Jaqui, now looking distinctly sweaty at the barbecue. "Go for it!"

"Well, I suppose I'd better get my *rustica* picnic out." Belinda is trying to contain a sudden rush of saliva in her mouth. She bends down, picks up her basket and takes off the white tea towel. Everything has been individually packed in silver foil. "Mmm," says Belinda as she unpacks six peaches. "Lovely." Next she comes across a large silver sachet. "Ooh," she says enthusiastically. "Broad beans." She lays a fistful on her plate. Next up is a small packet. She opens it. It's white, solid, and square. "Interesting."

"Oh, Lord," says Kyle across the table. "That looks like *lardo* to me."

"Lardo?" repeats Belinda.

"Yeah, you know, smoked pig fat. I can't believe you eat that stuff. Did you make that picnic yourself?"

"Of course I did!" Belinda lies, opening up another sandwich-shaped packet. "Sandwiches," she says, "of "—she puts her nose between the crusts of ciabatta—"Um . . ."

"Lampredotto," says Kyle, peering over. "Tripe," he translates.

"Mm, very *rustico,*" smiles Lauren, cutting into a tender piece of lamb and popping it into her mouth. "Enjoy!"

"I will." Belinda takes a bite of her tripe sandwich, mixing it with a huge swig of wine. She chews and just manages to swallow. "Oh, look," she adds, her eyes watering as she forgets not to be surprised by her own picnic, "a small piece of cheese."

"Yummy," says Lauren.

"Do you want some of Mummy's picnic?" Belinda asks Mary, a pleading look in her eyes.

"I'll mix and match between the two," says Mary. "But I think I'll pass on the tripe."

"Did someone say tripe?" asks Derek, raising his head from his plate, his mouth moist with meat.

"Belinda's eating tripe sandwiches," Lauren tells him as she slices into a grilled aubergine.

"Oh, delicious. I haven't had one in ages. Can I have a bite?"

"Derek, don't be silly," says Belinda, handing over the tripe sandwiches. "I made it especially with you in mind."

"Oh, fantastic," he says, pushing his lamb to one side. "This brings it all back. My childhood in Manchester. Oh, thank you." He takes a large bite. "Mm, mm, mm," he says, eyeing Belinda's plate again. "Is that pork fat?"

"Yes," says Belinda.

"Oh, may I?"

"Have it, Derek dear, do."

"Oh, Contessa," he grins, "with all this offal you are really spoiling me."

"You've won him over," declares Barbara. "He loves a bit of fat, that man, reminds him of those beef-dripping sandwiches his ma used to make."

"Mm." Derek beams.

While Derek's taste buds tap-dance down memory lane, everyone else gorges themselves on the antipodean feast served by the commune girls. Everyone, that is, except Mary, who can't eat, and Lauren, who is hardly eating. Mary is too tense and too excited even to think about lamb or salmon and ginger sticks. Kyle is sitting opposite her. He has just told her he loves her. And he has asked her to run away with him. She can barely stop herself from screaming with happiness. Never has a picnic proved to be so long, so dull, and so protracted.

Lauren, having asked around, has learned that one of the main reasons why Belinda always came in last in the cheese-rolling competition was because she drank too much wine and ate too much food before the race. To keep her chance of victory high, Lauren is abstaining from both.

Meanwhile, the others are not holding back. Derek's on his second tripe sandwich. Howard, having gotten over Belinda's smarting alcohol comment, is working his way speedily through a bottle of wine. Paloma is on her fourth glass; Duran and Janet are on their third each. Jaqui is trying to pace herself but not succeeding, due to dehydration at the coal face of cooking. And Kyle is so excited that he has finally admitted to Mary he loves her that he can hardly stop smiling and sipping his wine.

Just as everyone is about to sit back to let their food digest, the announcement comes over the loud-speaker that the cheese rolling is about to commence. Lauren stands up and starts to loosen her shoulders and relax her legs by shaking them out. Derek is impressed. "Bravo!"

"Go, Lauren! Go, Lauren!" chant the Aussies.

Everyone gets up to walk toward the finish line just before the church. The roadsides are already packed with Italians who stand two or three deep in places, waiting for the races to begin.

First up is the children. Six young boys stand in a row at the top of the hill, each with a round cheese the size of their own heads at their feet. The elderly man who runs the café on the Serrana road walks the length of the line checking each cheese. Dressed in a black jacket and trousers with a white shirt and the Italian flag worn as a sash, he takes his job very seriously. As, it seems, do the boys. Aged between eight and eleven, their faces are determined, and their dark eyes are trained on the road. Their parents are already shouting encouragement. The elderly man mutters something. The children pick up their cheeses. Then, suddenly, without any ceremony, they're off.

One rolls his cheese immediately over the side of the road and is disqualified. His face goes pink as he tries not to cry. Another child falls over and grazes his knee on the white stone road. The other four cheeses keep careering down the hill. Another boy goes over the edge. A cheese falls flat on its side.

Finally, there are only two boys left in the running. The technique is hard—to keep patting the cheese along while keeping it upright and not slowing it down. Then it's all over—the taller, older, and more experienced of the two boys crosses the line first. A corner of the crowd erupts. The Bianchi family joins in—he's a cousin from a nearby valley. There is much cheering, clapping, and celebration. The boy is held aloft and bounced from shoulder to shoulder.

Next up are three old men whose cheeses are twice the size of the children's. Each is dressed in black trousers with gnarled bowlegs like olive trees, only their shirts are different: one is white, another is maroon, and the last is a pale pistachio green. They start off at a more dignified pace. Their cheeses are well controlled as they trot behind them, keeping them perpendicular. The crowd is loud and boisterous. They cheer them on. It is neck and neck. There is nothing to choose between them. Then, suddenly, the man in the pistachio shirt loses control of his cheese. It careers off in the direction of the maroon-shirted man. The pistachio man's cheese collides with the maroon man's cheese and takes them both off the edge of the road and into instant disqualification. While the man in the white shirt graciously crosses the line to claim his victory, the other two are farther up the hill, shouting and slapping each other aggressively on the arms.

Finally, it is Lauren's turn in the open race. Here, the lineup is packed and clearly more competitive. Gianfranco and Marco Bianchi are standing near her, rubbing their large cheeses for a smoother, more even roll. Other groups of men appear to have arrived from outside the village. They are professional cheese rollers with different-colored sashes around their waists and silverware stacked up at home.

"Go on, Lauren!" shouts Howard, raising a glass of red wine

in her direction. She salutes back like a gymnast about to mount her apparatus.

"Go, Lauren! Go, Lauren! Go, Lauren!" chant the Aussie girls, stirring the air like a *Jerry Springer* audience.

"Go, Lauren, go!" shouts Barbara, shaking a sweaty pink fist.

"Go on, Mom, stick it to them!" shouts Kyle, his hands cupped around his mouth.

The atmosphere is tense. The thirty or so competitors jostle for position. Elbows are out, cheeses are ready, some of the more determined are pawing the ground like bulls about to charge. Her head above the herd, Lauren looks cool and serene.

"Uno, due, tre!" shouts the elderly man in the sashed Italian flag.

They're off, flying down the hillside at full pelt. The tactics are dirty, people are being thumped, tripped, their cheeses kicked over and out of the way. Others forge forth. Lauren is in the running.

"Go on!" shouts Derek.

The noise is deafening.

"Come on, Mom!" yells Kyle.

They round the corner into the home stretch. Franco Bianchi is out in front. He's being pursued by a burly man in a red sash. Lauren is third, running along, patting furiously, keeping up with the men.

"Go, Lauren! Go, Lauren! Go, Lauren!" The Aussie girls stir.

"Come on, Franco, come on, you bastard, come on," mutters Belinda, her face puce with wine and worry. Her hands are sweaty and tense.

The finish line is only a few rolls away. Franco and Red Sash are head to head. Lauren is in third. The rest of the field is not far behind. Franco makes his move. He goes to knock Red Sash out of the way. They hit each other, their cheeses collide, they both fall flat on their sides, and Lauren frantically pats her way to the first expat victory in the history of the *Festa di Formaggio.*

The Aussies go crazy, Kyle jumps for joy, Barbara cries with emotion, and Belinda is nearly sick. Fortunately her groan of despair is drowned in the roars of applause from everyone else. As Lauren is held aloft, her elegant limbs bounced from handsome Italian shoulder to handsome Italian shoulder, Belinda leans against a tree for support. Weak with fury, she almost passes out as the *americana* and her large silver cup bob past on their victory parade.

As Belinda's *festa* goes from bad to worse, she takes solace from the nice Riesling wine brought along by the Australian girls. She sits at the opposite end of the table from the victorious Lauren, telling long-winded stories about the joy of taking part.

Night falls and the dancing begins, and while Lauren enjoys entertaining the very attentive Derek, Barbara, and Howard, and Belinda continues to repeat herself in the company of Paloma and Duran; Kyle and Mary spot their opportunity for a discreet dance.

The air is warm and the stars are just beginning to show in the night sky. The members of the village band, with rotund Roberto on the fiddle and the two brothers who work in the supermarket near Serrana on piano and trumpet, are striking all the right notes. Hidden in the middle of the crowd, Kyle's arms are wrapped around Mary as they sway in time to the music.

"This is wonderful," he whispers.

"Mm," she agrees, inhaling his warm, sweet smell as she leans against his chest.

"You're wonderful," he says, brushing his cheek against her hair.

"What a magical evening," she says. "I don't think I've ever been so happy."

Suddenly Kyle feels a tap on his shoulder. He turns swiftly around. Gianfranco Bianchi is standing behind him, his hair dank with sweat, his shirt transparent. His eyes are glazed with drink. "My go," he announces, pointing to Mary.

"Oh, no, mate," says Kyle, smiling, putting a protective arm around her. "She's with me."

"I want dance," slurs Franco, as he lunges forward and shoves Kyle, stumbling, to the ground.

"Honestly, Franco," says Mary, taking a step back.

"Hey," says Kyle, standing up and brushing himself off, "what are you doing?"

"I want dance," explains Franco, walking toward Mary and making swinging, dancing moves with his hips.

The crowd, sensing that something is going on, starts to move away and clear a space around the three of them.

"Dance, dance," says Franco.

"No, thank you," replies Mary.

"Dance, dance," he repeats.

"Oy, Franco," shouts Kyle, tapping him on the shoulder making him turn around, "the lady's said no."

"Fuck off," says Franco, taking a swing at Kyle and missing.

"Fuck you," says Kyle, hitting him full on the jaw.

The music stops, the crowd moves farther away, and the three of them are left on their own. Franco stoops in the middle, holding his jaw, working up the energy to make another strike.

"Just leave her alone, man," says Kyle, his palms out in front of him.

"What's going on?" asks Lauren, making her way toward the circle in the crowd.

Franco makes another lunge. The crowd draws breath as he fails to make contact.

"Oh, Gawd, Mary," says Belinda, zigzagging through the crowd. "Is that ghastly American boy pestering you again?"

"Pestering her? Puh-lease!" yells Lauren, swinging around, her hands on her hips. "As if my grade-A-student son would want to have anything to do with your deadbeat daughter!"

"Your grade-A-student son? Honestly, if you could hear yourself. Mary has no interest in your ghastly son, no matter how many stupid bloody grades he has. Mary, come here," demands Belinda.

"Mary, stand your ground," says Kyle, taking a step toward her, his eyes fixed on hers.

"Mary, come here," demands Belinda again. "I won't ask a third time."

"Mary," says Kyle, his voice urgent, his eyes pleading. "Anything," he says. "Remember, we can do anything together."

"What the hell are you talking about?" asks Lauren.

"Come here, Mary," snaps Belinda. "I'm not joking."

"Mary?" says Kyle.

Mary looks from one face to another, then slowly but surely, almost imperceptibly at first, she starts to move. Her eyes fixed on his, her footsteps uncertain, she walks toward Kyle.

"Come on," he urges, his arms outstretched. "Come on, you can do it." He smiles.

"Come on. Mary, anything," he says, as she falls into his arms.

Someone claps. Belinda scans the crowd. "You traitor!" she shouts at her daughter. She takes an unsteady step forward. "I never want to see you again!"

"Mum!" pleads Mary, trying to move forward. Kyle holds her back.

"I mean it, you ungrateful little tart!" roars Belinda. "I never want to see you again. In fact, if you so much as darken my door . . . Never again, you understand. Never!"

CHAPTER ELEVEN

Walking around her house in her cream nylon nightie, Belinda looks as if she has been exhumed. The lack of sleep, the bottle of red wine she consumed last night on her return from the *festa,* coupled with that morning's strong, milky coffee, have all curdled in her stomach, making her grumpy, disoriented, and on the verge of throwing up. She is also in shock. After all it is not every day that one loses a daughter.

Last night, when she returned to Casa Mia, furiously red-faced and humiliated, she sat up for a while knocking back medicinal red wine while awaiting Mary's humble arrival. The silence in the house was overwhelming. A hot wind whistled. Even the crickets were muted. At the faintest sound of a door rattling or a shutter banging, Belinda called out her daughter's name, expecting to see Mary's sheepish face in the doorway and hear an abject apology following swiftly in its wake. But she never came. And the longer Belinda waited up, the more she realized that Mary's departure was not some adolescent joke or teenage tantrum, but something rather more real.

Yet even this morning, when Belinda flung open the door to Mary's bedroom, she half expected her daughter to be there.

Actually, she was completely expecting her daughter to be there, sitting up in bed, with an embarrassed will-you-ever-forgive-me look on her face. But no. When Belinda opened the door to Mary's small white priest's hole of a room, all she found was a well-made bed, some neatly piled clothes, and a few sprigs of lavender in a water glass by the bed. All her inexpensive beauty products were balanced along the window ledge and her laundry bag was still beside the shower in the corner of the room.

Well, at least she hadn't actually planned to run away with the ghastly Kevin, Belinda thought. That, and the fact the *americana* seemed equally horrified that her son had run off, was Belinda's only consolation. But, sadly, Lauren had not made quite such a scene in front of the whole village and people from the surrounding valleys. Lauren hadn't raised her voice. Belinda had walked off screaming like a professional wailer, her hands waving in the air, and swearing until her own face almost turned blue. The whole thing was too humiliating to think about. Belinda hadn't felt quite so demeaned, debased, and degraded since she'd found her husband at it like a terrier with her friend-and-next-door-neighbor.

How could it have come to this? she wonders, as she sits on her terrace, all alone, staring at the Casa Padronale below. What had she done to deserve this? She'd come to Tuscany nearly five years ago to try to make a new life for herself, to escape the shame of her husband's infidelity. She'd come with new resolutions, new hopes and dreams, new ideas. She'd reinvented herself. She'd changed her clothes. She'd cut her hair. She'd opened herself up to new things. She'd grown to like garlic. She'd discovered Michelangelo. She might even, one day, learn how to paint a watercolor foreground. She had planned to live the

Frances Mayes dream, a fecund life in the fecund hills of the Tuscan countryside. And now it all lies in tatters around her.

Belinda starts to cry. Not the usual crocodile tears she uses on Derek and Howard when she wants their attention and support. But real tears. Silent tears of despair. They roll slowly and quietly down her face. She doesn't even have the energy to wipe them away. Belinda hasn't cried with grief rather than histrionics for more than five years. Even during the divorce, and the breakup of her marriage, she'd managed only a couple of very public blubs, but they were when her husband most deserved them.

However, this hot Monday morning is different. Mary is gone, and Belinda has no one to turn to for help and support. In her battle to keep control of the valley, she has managed to alienate every ally and friend she ever had. A tear crawls the length of her nose, hangs for a while, clinging to the end, before it slowly drops off, landing on the table. No one has telephoned this morning. No one has called around. In a time of crisis the expat community normally sticks together. Like the time when Howard's roof blew off in a storm: she and Derek had taken turns in having him to stay until he had found enough money to get it fixed. The expat community always sticks together—except, of course, when it's fighting among itself.

Belinda stares down the valley and strains to see the goings-on at the Casa Padronale. Lauren's car is there. The *americana* is in. God, how she wishes that woman had never chosen to make this particular corner of Tuscany "work for her." Why couldn't she have gone north toward Lucca, where the rich Brits hang out, or east toward Cortona, where the Bohemians live? Why did she have to arrive slap-bang in the middle of Tuscany, in the heart of Chianti, and make it her tasteful home? Nearby Poggibonsi is famously the ugliest town in Tuscany: hadn't that been enough to put her off?

The woman has been nothing but trouble since she arrived, pushing her long nose into things that shouldn't concern her, taking over the valley, usurping Belinda's well-defined position, turning her friends against her. Of course she had to become Big Cheese, and of course she had to win the cheese-rolling competition. The woman is so vulgar, so pushy, and so American. All this mess is her awful fault. It has absolutely nothing to do with Belinda. She is not responsible for it in any shape or form.

She pushes away a tear with a short finger and swallows the fleshy lump in her throat. She cranes forward for a better view of Lauren's house. Her heart stops. She slowly covers her mouth with her hand. Is that Kevin she can see moving about the grounds? In a white shirt and jeans? He's certainly tall enough to be the *americana*'s son. Belinda stares. She frantically scans the hillside for anyone who resembles her daughter. What was she wearing yesterday? A white top and a denim skirt? Is someone moving behind the boy? She strains forward, her bloodshot eyes squinting into the sun. Where are her wretched binoculars when she needs them? She stands up. Belinda is prepared to wager the nylon nightie off her back that Mary is shacked up at the Casa Padronale. Her own daughter, sleeping with the enemy. It's almost more than she can bear.

She rushes toward the telephone, dialing finger at the ready. The number! The number? What is the American bitch's number? She should remember it by heart now, the amount of times she has half dialed it. She finds the piece of paper it is written on and dials. She waits. The long tones ring out.

"Answer. Answer, you bitch," mutters Belinda. "Hurry up."

"Hello?" It's Lauren's familiar voice. It is less cool, slightly more frantic than usual.

"I want to speak to her," barks Belinda down the telephone.

"Who is this?" quizzes Lauren.

"You know who it is," replies Belinda, her voice twisted with sarcasm. "I want to speak to Mary."

"She's not here," snaps Lauren.

"I don't believe you."

"Are you calling me a liar?" asks Lauren, sounding increasingly annoyed.

"Gee," says Belinda, imitating Lauren's voice to the extent that the woman now hails from Ireland, "I think I might be."

"She's not here," says Lauren slowly, as if communicating with the hard of hearing.

"Liar!"

"She's not."

"Liar!"

"Oh, for God sake," snaps Lauren. "Talking to you is like dealing with a child. No wonder your daughter left you. She's not here, and has not been here in the last twenty-four hours. Neither, for that matter, has my son. I have no idea where they are, or what they're doing, or what they plan to do." Lauren is beginning to sound a little nervous and tense herself. "Neither of them has contacted me, and I presume neither of them has contacted you. I have no idea where they could have gone. Do you?"

"No," says Belinda quietly.

"You see, Kyle doesn't really know Italy. I mean, he knows the language and his way around, but he doesn't have any friends here. Does Mary?"

"What?" asks Belinda.

"Does Mary have any friends in Italy?"

"I don't know."

"You don't know if your daughter has friends or not?" asks Lauren, sounding shocked.

"No."

"Really! Sometimes—"

"Sometimes you sound like a mother who didn't know her son was having an affair with a girl in the same valley!" declares Belinda.

"This is not helping."

"Why should I help you?"

"Because our children are lost together," snaps Lauren.

"They're not lost," says Belinda. "They just don't want to be found."

"Anyway," says Lauren.

"Anyway," repeats Belinda, "I blame you."

"Me?" yells Lauren.

"Yes, you!"

"Now *you're* being unreasonable."

"Now *you're* sounding insane," replies Belinda.

"You're the one who's insane." Lauren laughs. "I don't think I've ever met anyone more fucking crazy than you."

"Your son kidnapped my daughter."

"Bullshit!" shouts Lauren. "Your daughter ran away from you!"

"Your son ran away from you!" shouts Belinda. *"Touché!"*

"This is not fucking helping!" shouts Lauren again, and slams down the phone.

Belinda stares at the receiver. Lauren hung up on her! The bitch! That woman is just too rude and too impossible. Well, at least her son isn't there either, thinks Belinda, walking slowly to her ex-husband's favorite chair and sitting down. And Mary, thankfully, is not sleeping with the enemy. That really would have been too much to bear. But where can they be? Mary doesn't have any money. She doesn't have any clothes. She has got only the denim skirt and white T-shirt she went to the *festa* in. Belinda stares out of the french windows, repeatedly scratching the back of her hand. Should she go to the police? What would she say? My daughter has run off with her lover. They'd laugh in her face. They'd think it was some beautiful romantic story. This is the country of love affairs, after all. "And I can't speak the language," mutters Belinda, slapping the arm of her chair. "God! Where could they be?"

The telephone rings. Belinda starts in her chair, leaps up, and runs toward it as if her life depended on it. "Mary?" she says, asks and demands all at once.

"Er, no," says Howard. "It's Howard."

"Oh, Howard," says Belinda, expectation ebbing out of her shoulders.

"I'm sorry to disappoint," he says. "I was just a little worried about you."

"Oh," says Belinda, somewhat taken aback.

"Well," he says, sounding embarrassed by his own concern. "You know, yesterday . . ."

"Yes," says Belinda, trying to work out which part of yesterday Howard is concerned about. The part when she declared him to be a shambling alcoholic in front of the group? The part when she sniped nonstop about Lauren's unsporting desire to win the cheese rolling? The part when she made a hysterical scene in front of the whole *comune,* demanding her daughter choose between her mother and her boyfriend? The part when Mary chose the boyfriend? Or the mad hand-waving moment at the very end?

"But you're okay, are you?" he asks.

"Um, yes," says Belinda. "Well, you know, I'm a little upset."

"Clearly," agrees Howard. "I once made someone do that."

"Do what?" asks Belinda.

"Choose," says Howard.

"Oh," says Belinda.

"Yeah. Between me and her long-haired dachshund called Heathcliff. It used to bring me out in a rash."

"Right," says Belinda.

"And she chose Heathcliff," continues Howard. "That's the thing about asking people to choose. You have to live with the consequences of their choice."

"Yes." Belinda's voice is heavy with sadness.

"So count yourself lucky," he says, allowing an element of breeziness to come into his voice. "At least you weren't rejected for a sausage dog."

Belinda smiles. "Are you trying to cheer me up?"

"A little," says Howard. "Has it worked?"

"A little," says Belinda.

"What are you going to do?"

"I don't know."

"Have you heard from her?"

"No."

"I'm sure she'll be in touch," he says. "Anyway, it's not as if she's gone off with anyone too horrendous, is it?"

"Well, I'm afraid that's where you and I have to differ," says Belinda, stiffness returning to her voice.

"Oh," says Howard, retreating at the first whiff of confrontation. "Right."

"As far as I'm concerned, she couldn't have run off with a worse person."

"Oh," says Howard.

"Yes," says Belinda. "Of all the people to choose."

"Right," says Howard. "If that's how you feel—"

"It is."

"Okay, then."

There is a loud, important knock on Belinda's front door. "Howard?" says Belinda.

"Mm?"

"I've got to go; there's someone at the door. It could be Mary."

"Go," says Howard.

"Arrivadeary," says Belinda.

"Bye."

Belinda puts down the receiver and runs to the front door, a broad, forgiving smile gracing her face. Her heart is racing, her palms are clammy with excitement. She throws open the door, she stands back, her arms open, awaiting her daughter's embrace.

"Oh," she says, taking an unsteady step back. "It's you."

"It's me," says Lauren with a tight smile. "You and I need to talk."

She is dressed in a pair of crisp jeans, a white T-shirt, and a pair of JP Tod's loafers; her hair is washed, her face moisturized, her teeth are clean, and her eyelashes have been Vaselined.

Belinda is barefoot, still in the cream nylon nightie, devoid of underwear. Her hair has not seen a brush since yesterday morning, and she hasn't quite got around to washing. "I'm not even dressed," she informs her visitor.

"I can see that," says Lauren, looking Belinda up and down.

"You can't come here unannounced."

"I just did," she says with a little shrug. "Are you going to let me in?"

"I don't see why I should," says Belinda as defiantly as one can when not wearing underwear.

"Well, I'm not leaving," says Lauren.

The two women stare at each other, one showered and

dressed, the other not, yet both tired, feeling the same anguish at the loss of her child. Belinda's hand is on the door. Her short pink fingers gently apply pressure for it to close. Lauren's leather-clad toes are wedged against the bottom of the door, bent backward on themselves to ensure that it does not. They are locked in stalemate. Neither is prepared to give any ground. Belinda's knuckles grow white with strain, Lauren's toes crunch under the pressure.

Then, suddenly, Belinda loses concentration and Lauren seizes her chance. With one swift, elegant move, she crosses the threshold into the hall.

"I think we should try to work together on this," says Lauren, leading the way to the sitting room, her well-practiced negotiating skills kicking in.

"Together," repeats Belinda, injecting disdain into her voice, yet trotting along behind her uninvited guest.

"Yeah," asserts Lauren. "That way we can cover all the avenues more quickly and not waste time doubling up on things."

"And why on earth should I help you?" asks Belinda.

"Because not helping me would fly in the face of logic," announces Lauren, trying to keep her voice as restrained as possible. "By helping me, you're helping yourself. It's a simple statement of fact."

"Of course it is," says Belinda sarcastically.

"Oh, God," says Lauren, succumbing to a wave of irritation. "You are an unbelievable nightmare of a woman."

"Well, the words 'pot' and 'kettle' come to mind." Belinda shakes her head in witty triumph.

"What?" asks Lauren, not understanding the bluntness of Belinda's supposedly razor-sharp response.

"Pot calling the kettle black," says Belinda, with an evident jadedness.

"Oh, God," says Lauren as she makes to walk back to the front door. "You really are some sort of—" She stops in her tracks. "What the hell is—" She looks at the floor, and then above her, as the ceiling begins to shake.

"It's only a passing lorry," says Belinda nervously as her feet vibrate under her.

"No, it's not," says Lauren, her eyes wide.

The shelves behind Belinda start to wobble—they appear to bounce up and down while still attached to the wall. Belinda's cheap collection of glass objects jump along in great leaps, career off, and smash on the floor. A great crash of broken glass comes from the kitchen, followed by a series of lesser ones as plates frisbee out of cupboards as individuals, and then whole piles come falling to the floor.

"Earthquake!" shouts Lauren.

"Earthquake!" shouts Belinda.

For a second, they both remain rooted to the spot. Then, as books fly off the shelves with supernatural force, and the computer dives to the floor next to them, adrenaline kicks in.

"Terrace!" shouts Belinda.

"We won't make it!" yells Lauren.

"Table!" they scream, launching themselves headfirst under the small, solid, oak computer table.

As they do so, the full force of the 'quake hits Casa Mia. The shelves crash off the wall, the kitchen units explode, every pane of glass in the windows bursts free of its frame and shatters. The porch falls off the front of the house, the ceiling above one of the *cantinas* collapses, sending dust and terra-cotta tiles pouring into the rooms below. The outside wall of Belinda's terrace cracks and then, due to the poor finish and substandard cement used to point it by the rip-off British developer from whom Belinda had bought the house, it collapses, bringing the roof and two other walls with it. In fact, within twenty-five seconds Casa Mia has imploded as if made from a deck of playing cards and the two women are buried within it.

The noise is deafening. The screams of twisting metals, the cries of ancient beams breaking, the piercing shattering of glass. It is as if the very mouth of hell opens and allows Belinda and Lauren to hear what goes on inside. After the noise, there is a momentary reprieve, before the loud whoosh of all-encompassing, cloaking, choking dust. And then total silence.

Belinda is the first to make a sound. She coughs to clear her throat, and makes the mistake of inhaling deeply, filling her lungs with dust again. It sets off a coughing fit as she chokes and wheezes, emptying and filling her body with the pulverized contents of her house. Eventually, she pulls up the hem of her nightie and covers her nose and mouth. The aerated perforations allow her to breathe, and the fabric filters the air. Lauren does not make a sound. Her heavy body is flopped over Belinda's feet at the other end of the table.

"Lauren?" says Belinda. "Lauren? Are you alive?" Nothing. Panic sets in. Belinda's heart races and her hands shake. Her insides are shivering. "Lauren? Lauren?" She gives the limp body at her feet a little kick. "Lauren?"

"Mm?"

"Are you alive?" asks Belinda.

"What?"

"Are you alive?" asks Belinda. "Are you hurt?"

"Um . . . yeah . . . sure, yeah . . . It'll take more than a god-damn 'quake to kill me," drawls Lauren as she brings herself up to a sitting position in the rubble. "I'm 'quake-proof. Or didn't I tell you?" She starts to cough. She hacks and hacks, struggling for air.

"Cover your mouth," instructs Belinda. Lauren tugs at her

now filthy gray T-shirt and pulls it over her mouth. "Breathe slowly."

The two women stare at each other. Both are gray with dust, their faces thick with it, like some deep-pore face mask. Only the whites of their eyes shine brightly in the filth and darkness. Their hair is thick with dust. Belinda's is decorated with a smattering of rubble and sticks out at various angles, while Lauren's hangs thick and straight and gray, as if someone has covered her with wallpaper paste. They both sit with their legs stuck out in front of them, their mouths covered with their makeshift masks. Belinda's bare feet are covered in little cuts that slowly ooze blood into the dust. Lauren's shoulder is broken. Although the endorphins that course through her do something to dull the agony, a red-hot poker of pain shoots through her whenever she moves. She tries to keep as still as possible.

"How are we going to get out of here?" Belinda asks, shifting around under the small table.

"I've no idea," says Lauren.

"Stay there," orders Belinda. "Let's just see if I can move at all."

She gets onto her hands and knees and makes as if to crawl out from under the table.

"Careful!" says Lauren.

"I am," says Belinda as she pokes out her head. "Oh, my God! My whole house has collapsed! There's nothing left." Her ex-husband's chair is pushed up against the table, and she tries to move it out of the way.

"Careful!" repeats Lauren.

"Will you bloody shut up?" hisses Belinda. "I know what I'm doing." She gives the chair another push. It moves, as does the rubble balanced on top of it. There is a loud crash as it falls.

Just in time, Belinda manages to get her head back under the table before they are buried all over again.

"Shit!" says Belinda, as she coughs and flaps the dust away from her face.

"That was a really crap idea," says Lauren.

"I don't hear you coming up with anything else," snaps Belinda. "It appears business brains aren't terribly useful in the Tuscan countryside."

The two women sit in silence as the full hideousness of their predicament hits them. Not only are they stuck here together until they are rescued, there is no guarantee of when, or indeed if, that will happen. As Jean-Paul Sartre said, *"L'enfer, c'est les autres"*—Hell is other people—and they are beginning to understand exactly what that means. Lauren sighs and hugs her shoulder, leaning her dusty head against the table leg.

"I blame you," says Belinda.

"What?" Lauren coughs.

"I blame you for it all," says Belinda.

"Jesus Christ, Belinda," she says, shifting slightly. "I may be a powerful person, but not even I can pull off an act of God."

"I know that. But if you hadn't come to this valley, then I wouldn't have had all the problems I have had, and I wouldn't be sitting here, buried alive, with you right now."

"No, you'd be buried alive on your own," says Lauren.

"Exactly!" she says triumphantly.

"So you're saying you'd rather be buried alive on your own than with me?"

"Yes."

"Boy!" says Lauren. "Well, I can't say I'm exactly thrilled by the company either. In fact, if it helps, on a scale of one to ten then I'd rather be buried alive with George fucking W. Bush than go through this with you."

"There's no need to swear," says Belinda.

"Oh, fuck off," says Lauren. She pauses. "So, do you really dislike me?"

"I do," says Belinda.

"Oh," says Lauren.

"You ruined my life," says Belinda.

"I ruined your life? I ruined your life!" says Lauren. "Don't make me laugh." She laughs. "From all accounts your life was pretty ruined before I came here."

"Who told you about my husband being unfaithful?"

"Puh-lease!" says Lauren, flapping her hand and immediately regretting it as the pain shoots through her. She grabs her shoulder a little tighter. "It's hardly the best-kept secret in the valley."

"I wouldn't expect you to understand."

"Why not?" asks Lauren. "My husband was unfaithful as well."

"I thought your husband was dead?"

"That doesn't stop him from being unfaithful."

"Well, technically, it does," says Belinda.

"You know what I mean," replies Lauren, sounding a little tired.

"Does your shoulder hurt?"

"It fucking kills," says Lauren.

"Oh."

"How about your feet?"

"They just sting, really," says Belinda, looking down at the ever-increasing pool of blood.

"Do you think we'll ever get out of here?"

"I don't know," says Belinda, looking at the small dusty hole they are sitting in.

"They're bound to come," asserts Lauren.

"Yeah." Belinda nods. She looks up. *"Help!"* she shouts at the top of her voice. The noise disturbs the pile of dust above them and sends another filthy cloud crashing down. "Shit!" Belinda coughs.

"Fuck!" Lauren coughs, holding her shoulder. "Don't fucking do that again."

"No," agrees Belinda, hacking until her eyes water. "I won't shout another word."

They sit in silence, Belinda's cut feet slowly seeping blood into the surrounding dust, Lauren's broken shoulder freezing and locking all the muscles down her back and side. They both sigh. They have enough oxygen to breathe. They have enough light to see each other. But both women are in pain and cannot move. They sigh again.

"So," says Lauren.

"What?" says Belinda.

"Nothing."

"Nothing what?"

"Nothing."

"Oh, don't do that," huffs Belinda. "You can't start something and not finish it. So—what?"

"Okay. What did I do to ruin your life?"

"Oh, you know . . ."

"No."

"Well, for a start, you moved here."

"So my mere presence ruined your life?"

"Well, for a start, you bought the house I had my eye on," says Belinda.

"For how long?"

"Five years."

"Ooh." Lauren laughs and coughs again. "You're a fast mover!"

"Oh, shut up," says Belinda, screwing up her face. "Anyway, you moved here and you opened up a rival B-and-B."

"My house is nothing like yours. How can it possibly be a rival to it?" asks Lauren. "Seriously, we're not even after the same clients. I'm looking for people who want to stay for a month, writing and doing yoga, having massages. You want quick in-and-out tourists."

"You're still a rival," mutters Belinda, "whichever way you look at it."

"I'm your social rival."

"No, you're not!" snaps Belinda.

"Yes, I am."

"No, you're not!"

"Well, explain to me, why don't you, exactly why you were so unpleasant to me when I arrived in the valley?"

"I wasn't."

"If that was pleasant, then it's a wonder you have any friends at all."

"I don't now, thanks to you."

"Of course you do," says Lauren.

"You took them over and got them to vote you Big Cheese," Belinda accuses her, exuding indignation.

"Only because you reported me to the *Bell' Arti,* canceled my adverts, misdirected my guests, sent me rubbish replacements."

"The Scottish girls weren't bad," says Belinda.

"They were a fucking nightmare and you know it. That's why you were so rude to them and got rid of them," says Lauren. "Pushing their noses in where they're not wanted."

"Well . . ."

"Exactly," confirms Lauren. "So I decided that enough was enough and the cheese rolling was the only way to get you off my back."

"So you went for it?"

"Oh, yeah." Lauren nods. "Getting everyone to vote for me was the easy part," she says. "You just plant the idea in some-one's head, talk around and about it, then let them come up with you as their own suggestion. It's an easy technique. I've used it in business for years. The winning was the hard bit. I spent ages looking up cheese rolling on the Internet, and then I found this video online. I bought it and studied. If I was going to take over, I had to win. There was a bit of luck involved, too. But, then, there's always a bit of luck involved when you're planning a hostile takeover."

"What?" says Belinda, looking incredulous. "That's amazing. All I ever did when I was Big Cheese was—"

"Talk about it a lot. Make a great show of being Big Cheese, and then getting drunk on the day, throwing the cheese down the hill, and hoping for the best. Yes." Lauren smiles. "I know—or, at least, that's what I've gathered from the people I spoke to."

"Oh," says Belinda.

"Oh," imitates Lauren.

"Well, if you'd only been more pleasant when I came around to say hello right at the beginning, things might have been a lit-tle easier," says Belinda, trying to shift around under the table.

"I was tired. We'd just arrived and you turned up drunk, knocking on our door, welcoming us to your valley when it wasn't yours to welcome us to in the first place."

"I wasn't drunk," insists Belinda.

"You were," says Lauren. "You fell at my feet."

"I tripped."

"You were drunk," says Lauren. "Anyway, I don't mind drunk. In fact, I like drunk. But not on my doorstep last thing at night."

"It wasn't that late," says Belinda.

"Whatever," says Lauren.

They both sit in silence. Lauren leans hard on the table leg. Her shoulder is in agony. There is no comfortable position. Her legs are numb and so is her backside. She is shaking and sweating with pain, all color has drained from her lips. Belinda is beginning to feel faint. She is losing quite a lot of blood. Her mouth is dry and she feels cold. Where are the people coming to rescue them? Surely someone has noticed that Casa Mia has collapsed. Help has to be on its way.

"Where are they?" asks Belinda.

"They'll come," says Lauren.

"They're taking their time."

"Perhaps they're a little busy."

"I wish they'd hurry up," mumbles Belinda, closing her eyes.

"Don't worry, they will. I'm not going to end up dying here with you."

"I have no desire to die with you either," mutters Belinda. "Particularly . . . particularly . . . after you've just admitted politicizing the *Festa di Formaggio*. My *Festa di Formaggio*." She is mumbling, slurring, getting increasingly weak. "I've always been a firm believer in keeping politics out of sport. A firm believer. I bet you're the sort of person who supported the U.S. boycott of the Moscow Olympics?"

"What?"

"The Moscow Olympics, with Misha the bear?" continues Belinda.

"Please be quiet," mutters Lauren out of the corner of her

mouth. "I really don't want my dying thoughts to be of a thirty-year-old cartoon bear."

"Twenty-four-year-old," says Belinda.

"Thirty, twenty, who cares?"

"Yeah, well," says Belinda, sounding oddly contrite, "that's what comes of a rush of blood to the feet."

"Are you displaying a British stiff upper lip?" asks Lauren, slowly.

"Possibly," says Belinda. "I'm feeling a little odd."

"How odd?" Lauren moves and winces. Her eyes shine with pain.

"Like I want to go to sleep," says Belinda, eyes rolling as her head falls back.

"Don't do that."

"It would be nice," mutters Belinda.

"Don't! Stay awake."

"Just a quick snooze," suggests Belinda.

"No!" shouts Lauren.

"Sssh," says Belinda. "Don't disturb the dust."

"If you fall asleep now, Mary will have no one to turn to when she leaves Kyle," says Lauren.

"Is she leaving Kyle?" asks Belinda.

"Well, he's not marrying her, that's for certain."

"At least we agree on one thing." Belinda smiles.

"I haven't struggled on my own to raise a son and put him through college for him to end up with a girl who cooks badly in the local B-and-B," says Lauren. "So you can rest assured he will not be marrying Mary."

"Hurrah!" cheers Belinda weakly, shaking her fat pale fist briefly in the air. "I can't stand your smug uptight Kevin either."

"Kyle," corrects Lauren.

"Kyle, Kevin, it's all the same to me," says Belinda. "He's a ghastly man with a ghastly name. And, anyway, Mary's not a bad cook. She's a failed receptionist."

"A failed receptionist?"

"Yup." Belinda coughs. She rests her head on the opposite table leg. "She had a job as a receptionist and she lost it. That's why she is out here all summer."

"Well, he's definitely not marrying her," says Lauren.

"Good!" Belinda coughs again. "That's settled, then."

"Yeah."

"Yeah."

"You see, you and I can have a fairly reasonable discussion when we put our minds to it," murmurs Lauren.

"That's only because there's no one else to talk to," says Belinda. "I bet you could have a reasonable conversation with George W. Bush if he were in here now."

"No, I couldn't," says Lauren.

"I'm sure you could."

"No." Lauren smiles weakly. "I was lying when I said I'd prefer him in here to you."

"Oh," sniffs Belinda, opening one eye to look at her. "Are you paying me a compliment?"

"Do you know?" says Lauren. "I think I might be."

"Thank you," mumbles Belinda, and slides down the table leg.

"It's my pleasure," says Lauren.

They both sit in silence. Lauren closes her eyes. Her face is covered in a heavy sweat that runs down her cheeks, causing the thick layer of dust to streak. The pain in her left shoulder makes her retch. She has now lost all feeling in her body except for the burning agony of her broken shoulder. Belinda is listless with dehydration and loss of blood. The corners of her mouth are dry. It is slightly open and her tongue hangs out. All she wants to do is lie down and sleep.

"Hang on in there," says Lauren.

"Mm."

"They *will* come, I promise."

"Just a little sleep won't hurt."

Suddenly, through the heavy silence, there is a gentle tapping noise. It sounds like a teaspoon hitting a drainpipe. It's faint, but audible.

"Did you hear that?" asks Lauren, eyes wide with excitement. She tries to sit up. "That! There! Can you hear it?"

"Mm?" says Belinda.

Lauren sits rigid, straining to hear through the silence, her heart pounding in her ears. The tapping is renewed. "There it is. Can you hear it?" she asks again.

"Mm? What?" asks Belinda, opening her glazed eyes.

"The noise?" says Lauren. "Can you hear that noise?"

The tapping gets louder.

"Oh, yes," says Belinda, hauling herself out of her stupor. "I can hear that."

"Hello! Helloooo!" shouts Lauren at the top of her voice. A small cloud of dust falls under the table. "Helloooo!" She coughs, then shouts some more. "In here! We're in here! Hello! Hello . . . in here!" Each time she shouts her shoulder burns. "Hello!"

"Hello!" Belinda coughs, as she tries to slide up the table leg, holding on with her soft white hand. "Hello! Hello!"

The noise stops, as if everyone is standing still, listening.

"Hello!" shouts Belinda.

"She *is* in there!" yells a voice that sounds like Howard. "In there! Belinda!" he calls. "It's Howard. Can you hear me? Belinda? Are you in there?"

"Howard?" Belinda's feeble voice drifts out through the rubble. "I'm here . . ."

"She's in there! *Qui! Qui! La Signora è qui!*" shouts Howard, directing his voice over the top of the rubble. "*Qui! Sbrigati! Quickly! Sbrigati!*"

His calls release an army of footsteps that scramble all over the rubble, causing the house to shift, releasing more dust over the two women buried beneath it.

"Watch out," yells Lauren. "You're burying us!"

"Lauren?" says Howard's voice, sounding surprised. "What are you doing in there?"

"Having lunch," she shouts back. "What do you think?"

"Oh," says Howard. "There are two of them in there!" he shouts. *"Due signore! Due!"*

* * *

The response is rapid. A group of about twenty firemen spreads out all over the collapsed building. Orders are yelled back and forth as they form lines from the top of the mound and start picking off the rubble, stone by stone, and passing it from hand to hand down to the grass below. Howard is right in there among them, his wild hair catching the sun as he picks up stones, hurling them to the ground. For a man who is normally atrophied by indecision and rendered intellectually and physically inert by alcohol, he is rising, phoenixlike, to the occasion. The crisis releases his inner man of action, who must have been there all along.

"Derek!" he shouts at Derek, who is pacing the ground, mincing his hands. "Make yourself useful and get some water from Giovanna's. These people will need liquid. Barbara," he adds—she is standing, open-mouthed, staring at what remains of Casa Mia, "you can help him." Barbara walks on after her husband, pleased to be given something to do. "Lauren! Belinda!" he shouts. "Hang on. We won't be long."

"Hurry up," yells Lauren's voice from underneath him. "Belinda's in a bad way. She's lost a fair amount of blood."

"Sbrigati! Sbrigati!" He urges the firemen on. *"C'è qualcuno che si è ferito!"*

They work with more urgency. The stones start coming off the pile more quickly. Their tight navy blue T-shirts stick to their backs with sweat, and their brown, muscled arms glow. If only Belinda could see the army of handsome men rescuing her, she would enjoy the process a whole lot more. But as it is, she is feeling queasy, her mouth is parched, and she can barely feel her body anymore.

"I can see daylight," shouts Lauren. "I can feel a breeze."

"Oh, my God," shouts Howard. "We need more help. They're here! *Qui! Qui!*" Howard jumps up and down, indicating the place where Lauren's voice came from.

They focus their effort on the spot, crawling over the debris. The mound moves, the stone shifts.

"Attenzione!" shouts the lead fireman, his strong arm in the air. *"Attenzione!* Stop!"

Everyone stands still again, as they try not to disturb the shifting rubble. The whole process grinds to a halt as, one after another, the firemen look at what is underneath.

"What?" asks Howard, his hands bleeding, his fingernails snapped and cracked from his efforts. "Why are we stopping?"

"Guarda," says the fireman. "Look."

Howard looks down at the fireman's feet. A huge, ancient

beam is leaning right over where Lauren and Belinda are sitting. Although undoubtedly it saved their lives in the earthquake, it is now stopping the firemen and rescue workers from
reaching them. The firemen look at one another. The fire engine parked outside what remains of the house will not be able
to pull out the beam on such a slope. They scratch their heads,
the sweat pours off their faces. No one knows what to do.

"Hurry up," yells Lauren, from inside the rubble. "It's unbearable in here."

"We're coming," yells Howard.

"Why have you stopped?"

"We haven't," says Howard.

"We can't hear you anymore," says Lauren.

"We're coming," yells Howard again.

Then as they all stand and stare, feeling defeated, Howard
spots rotund Roberto running down the hill toward them. His
body ripples as he moves. His round face is puce with effort.
His eyes shine an alarming red.

"Bianchi!" he huffs. "Bianchi!" he puffs, jabbing the air with
his fat fingers, indicating behind him.

The firemen on the rubble all look down the valley. Crawling up the hill on a tractor with a trailer in tow is the whole
Bianchi family. The father at the wheel, the mother on the back
with her three sons, their children and two others, one in a
white top and a blue denim skirt, the other in a white shirt and
shorts.

"Kyle and Mary?" says Howard, squinting into the sun.
"What the hell—"

"Bianchi." Roberto smiles, resting his fat hands on his fat
knees, catching his breath. *"Ho telefonato . . ."*

The firemen applaud as the old man directs his tractor around the rubble and parks it next to what used to be the french windows with the view down the valley. The firemen scrabble off the pile and start attaching ropes to the beam.

"Mum!" says Mary, standing next to Kyle and the remains of what used to be her house. "Mum, it's me. Are you okay?"

"Mary," comes Belinda's feeble voice. "I'm fine. Where have you been?"

"Don't worry about me," says Mary. "I'm here now, and that's all that matters."

"Mom!" calls Kyle. "Are you okay in there?"

"Kyle!" calls Lauren right back. "Where the hell have you been?"

"We spent the night at the Bianchis'," he says. "They were decent enough to offer us a place to stay in one of their barns. To make up for what happened."

"You slept with my daughter?" asks Belinda's indignant voice.

"Mrs. Smith, I love your daughter," yells Kyle.

"Oh, God," says Belinda, and slides back down the table leg, defeated by exhaustion.

"Keep quiet," yells Lauren. "All this talking isn't doing Belinda any good. She's lost a lot of blood."

"Oh, my God, Mum!" says Mary, covering her mouth with her hands. "Come on, Mum. Please."

"Don't worry," says Kyle, putting his arms around her. "If anyone's a fighter, she is."

They all stand and watch as the firemen add the finishing touches to their ropes. Kyle hugs Mary. Barbara holds Derek's hand. Howard mops the sweat from his brow.

"*Uno, due, tre!*" shouts the foreman, gesturing to Signor Bianchi that he should start the engine.

Signor Bianchi fires it up and slowly heads down the hill toward what is left of Belinda's jerry-built swimming pool. The ropes tense. Franco and Bruno Bianchi guide them over the rubble. There is a squeaking and a moaning as the ropes tauten.

"*Attenzione,*" shouts the foreman as the beam begins slowly to lift. "*Attenzione.*" Two ropes snap under the strain. The stone and mortar shift. "*Attenzione!*"

Signor Bianchi's face is covered in sweat, and the veins on his neck stand out as he tries to control his tractor, keeping its advance steady and straight. Finally, there is an almighty crack as the beam shifts free, the rubble pours down the hillside, Signor Bianchi spins forward, the beam drags along the ground, and a huge cloud of dust is sent into the air.

Howard is the first through the dust. "Belinda! Lauren! Are you okay?" he asks, swiping the clouds out of his way.

As the dust settles, a small, sturdy table emerges. Howard is the first to approach it. He bends down and looks in. "Are you okay?" he asks, looking from Lauren's sweat- and dust-stained face to Belinda's glassy eyes. They both nod. "They're okay!" he shouts, and waves to the crowd.

"Thank God," says Mary, collapsing into Kyle's armpit. "Thank God for that."

"Thank you," says Kyle, glancing heavenward, before kissing Mary on the forehead.

Barbara applauds, Derek and Franco join in, and soon the whole rescue team is clapping. Franco congratulates his father on a job well done, and two stretchers appear around the remains of the house. Four firemen arrive and remove the table. Belinda and Lauren blink in the unfamiliar sunlight, their condition drawing gasps from the crowd. Kyle and Mary run forward. A fireman holds them back.

"Mom!" shouts Kyle. "Thank God you're alive."

Lauren is first out. Her dusty face contorts with pain as she is helped onto a stretcher and transported over the rubble to the emergency first-aid area set up on the grass. Belinda is unable to walk, so she is lifted out of the rubble by two strong, handsome firemen. Unfortunately, her legs are lifted first, and her cream nylon nightie falls over her head, revealing her pantlessness for all to see. The fireman quickly tries to cover her up, but not before the whole valley has glimpsed a rather sparse triangle of pubic hair.

"Mum!" cries Mary. "Are you okay?"

Her body is heavy, her head hangs loosely to one side, her cut and bloodied feet flop with each step that the stretcher bearers take over the stones. Belinda is placed on the ground, and a paramedic gets to work, pumping her full of fluid and plasma, covering her nose and mouth with an oxygen mask. Mary runs to take her mother's limp hand. Everyone stands and holds their breath. The color returns to Belinda's dusty cheeks as another paramedic concentrates on stemming the flow of blood from her feet.

"Thank God you're safe," says Mary, stroking her mother's face. "I'm so relieved."

"My home," wails Belinda, as she sees what is left of it. "What has happened to my beautiful house?"

"Casa Mia was the only house to collapse in the *whole* valley," explains Barbara helpfully. "Amazing."

"That's what comes of having Ital—" Belinda stops herself and catches the eye of Signor Bianchi, who is still being congratulated, standing by his tractor. "That's what comes of having cheap builders," she says.

"So, where are you going to stay?" asks Barbara, more out of curiosity than concern. "When you come out of hospital, I mean."

"With me," says Lauren, sitting up on her stretcher, feeling all the better for painkillers. "She'll stay with me."

"Oh, Lauren, I couldn't," mutters Belinda.

"I insist," says Lauren. "How else are we going to keep an eye on these two?" she says, pointing to Kyle and Mary.

"But, really—" says Belinda.

"No, no, I really do insist."

"Well, it doesn't look as though I have much choice," says Belinda, glancing back at what was once her home.

"You have no choice at all." Lauren laughs. "You have nothing left."

"Right," says Belinda. "That's very kind."

"Yes," says Lauren. "I do like it when a plan unexpectedly works out so well."

She smiles a special tight smile. The one she always employs after a particularly satisfying hostile takeover. Unfortunately, Belinda is looking the other way.

*T*USCANY *for* *B*EGINNERS

A READER'S GUIDE

Imogen Edwards-Jones

A Conversation with Imogen Edwards-Jones

Q: *Tuscany for Beginners* is told from two vantage points—we hear Belinda's version of the events that unfold in Val di Santa Caterina, and then we get the "real" story. How did you decide to tell the story with these alternating narratives?

A: I like the idea of artifice, of lying, not only to everyone else, but also to one's self. A certain type of Brit is very good at putting a gloss or a brave face on things. And Belinda typifies this. She is a woman who is obsessed with the idea of not losing face. She has been humiliated once before and she is determined that it will not happen again. I thought it would be more interesting, and hopefully amusing, for the reader to be able to see this right from the start. Belinda tells lies all the time, and she is kidding no one, least of all her audience.

Q: You're an Englishwoman who spends a fair amount of time in Tuscany, right? Is that how you were able to capture the details of the Italian people and the towns in Tuscany so authentically? How much of what you write about comes from your own experience in Italy?

A: My mother has lived in Italy for nearly twenty years, and I spent most of my late teens and early twenties traveling back and forth, so I have experienced first hand quite a lot of what Tuscany has to offer. Hopefully all this stood me in good stead when it came to writing the book, as most of the characters, festivals, and fantastic food mentioned are inspired by the people and places I have come across. Particularly the handsome Gianfranco Bianchi—there is someone rather like him near my mother's place!

Q: Was the character of Belinda inspired by an experience of a less-than-pleasant B-and-B owner? I've been told that Italian B-and-Bs are wonderful. Are there any you can recommend in Tuscany? Any Italian wine recommendations?

A: Fortunately I have never met anyone running a B-and-B as unpleasantly as Belinda. The inspiration for her was the idea of a misanthrope who is forced to work in the service industry. Italian B-and-Bs are indeed wonderful, and I could heartily recommend my mother's (www.stoppiacce.com), which is in the hills outside Cortona. As for wine, Tignanello is delicious, if rather expensive, or you could try a Montepuliciano.

Q: Is Val di Santa Caterina a real town in Italy? If not, is it based on a real town?

A: Thankfully, it is not a real valley, nor is it based on any place.

Q: *Tuscany for Beginners* is almost a parody of the stereotypes that exist of people from other countries. Belinda is a bit cold, unwilling (or unable) to express her inner feelings and very aware of the image she conveys; Lauren makes a big, brash, very American-like entrance and wants to fight her way to the top. Were you conscious of these common stereotypes as you wrote, or did the characters come to you fully formed, warts and all? Do you think there's anything to the stereotypes of Americans, the Brits, and the Italians?

A: We all conform to certain stereotypes. The English are usually polite and love to form a queue; the Americans tend to not speak terribly quietly; the Italians, more often than not, produce a nice dinner; and the Japanese photograph everything. Obviously there are many exceptions to these rules, but when it comes to writing comedy, stereotypes are essential. Grotesques are usually much more amusing than well-rounded, reasonable people.

Q: Let's project into the future a bit. Is Belinda still running the B-and-B? And has her Italian improved?

A: Belinda's Italian will never improve, as she is convinced that she speaks it fluently already. She will most certainly be running her B-and-B but she will have updated it a bit, having stolen as many ideas as she could from Lauren.

Q: How about Mary and Kyle? Have you thought at all about what happens to these characters in the years to come? What about a sequel?

A: I would love to do a sequel, as I did rather fall in love with the characters when I was writing the book, particularly Belinda, whose company I enjoyed hugely. As for Kyle and Mary,

I am not sure. Kyle is Mary's first true love, but I have a feeling that Kyle is a little more worldly. I would love to write a sequel if only to see exactly what happened to the two of them.

Q: There's a great comic flair throughout *Tuscany for Beginners*—many tongue-in-cheek, laugh-out-loud moments. Have you always written comic novels? Are there any comic novelists that you admire or were influenced by? Who are your favorite authors?

A: You are very kind! *Tuscany for Beginners* is my fourth book in a line of, hopefully, comic novels. I have always favored comedy over any other genre, as I like to be entertained when I read. I loved Jay McInerney's *Story of My Life* when I read it a long while back, I think it is hilarious. But the greatest influence for this novel was E. F. Benson's Mapp and Lucia books. They are little works of genius not too dissimilar to Evelyn Waugh's. I have even set the initial opening scene in Tilling, which is the small town Benson writes about.

Q: What are you working on now?

A: I am working on a nonfiction book at the moment that, as an ex-journalist, I tend to do from time to time. But I have another novel up my sleeve that I am planning to start toward the middle of this year. I also have a baby to deliver at the end of May!

READING GROUP QUESTIONS AND
TOPICS FOR DISCUSSION

1. The opening scene of the novel paints a very sympathetic picture of Belinda—a woman who sets out on an adventure in Tuscany after she has been humiliated by her cheating husband and so-called friend. Do you understand this scene differently after getting to know Belinda a little better?

2. After reading the novel, what do you think of the title *Tuscany for Beginners*? What advice would you give a friend looking to stay at a bed-and-breakfast in Tuscany?

3. Inspired by Frances Mayes's *Under the Tuscan Sun,* Belinda flees England in order to pursue her dream of opening a bed-and-breakfast in Tuscany. She insists upon creating the ideal Italian retreat for herself and her guests. How well do you think she achieves this? What are some of the ways she creates this experience for them? How is her experience of Italy more about being English in Italy than about how Italians live? In what ways is Belinda more English than she might want to admit?

4. Even when her business was not doing well, Belinda still insisted on turning away guests that were not up to her high standards. What do you think about her method of guest selection? Why do you think she was so discriminating?

5. Upon first appraisal, many things are not what they appear to be in this novel. Explore how your initial impression of Belinda, Mary, Lauren, and Kyle evolved as the novel unfolded. How do you think each of the characters would describe themselves and one another? Do these descriptions differ from how you would characterize them?

6. Explore the relationship between Belinda and Mary and between Kyle and Lauren. In what ways are they different, and in what ways are they alike? Why do you think Mary and Kyle fell in love so easily? Were you surprised that Lauren and Belinda were not aware of the love affair occurring right under their noses?

7. There is no shortage of food in the novel, and it reveals a lot about the characters. What do Belinda's recipes reveal about her cooking skills and knowledge of Italian cuisine?

8. On the surface, Belinda and Lauren are almost polar opposites, but they also have much in common. Explore the ways in which the two women are similar. Why do you think they felt so much hostility toward each other? Do you feel that one is more to blame? Why or why not?

9. How is Belinda's life in the Tuscan countryside portrayed before Lauren's arrival? How does this event change the way in which you think of Belinda?

10. What do you think of Belinda's nickname, "the Contessa"? Is it well deserved?

11. What do you think of Belinda's diary entries, her *aperçus*? As the story progresses, how do they add to your understanding of her character? Compare Belinda's portrait of her life with the way she is described by the narrator.

12. Belinda and her friends in the valley have a lot of stereotypes about Americans. What are some of these? How does Lauren compare to these stereotypes? What are some of the stereotypes about the Italians, the Australians, and any other nationality that come to Belinda's valley?

13. Next time you're in Tuscany, where are you going to stay?

PHOTO: JOTH SHAKERLY

IMOGEN EDWARDS-JONES is an award-winning journalist, columnist, and broadcaster who writes for many national newspapers and magazines. She is the author of three previous novels, the highly acclaimed *My Canapé Hell*, *Shagpile*, and *The Wendy House*. She co-edited the War Child anthology, *Big Night Out*, and lives in London.

ABOUT THE TYPE

This book was set in Bembo, a typeface based
on an oldstyle Roman face that was used for
Cardinal Bembo's tract *De Aetna* in 1495.
Bembo was cut by Francisco Griffo in the
early sixteenth century. The Lanston Mono-
type Company of Philadelphia brought the
well-proportioned letterforms of Bembo to
the United States in the 1930s.